CONTENTS

Also available from Silhouette Books
and Harlequin Books by

NORA ROBERTS

CAPTIVATED & ENTRANCED
The first two books featuring the magical Donovans

LOVE BY DESIGN
Two beautiful romances

CHANCES
Two lovely stories about
the endless possibilities of love

CHARMED & ENCHANTED
The last two books featuring the magical Donovans

THE MacKADE BROTHERS:
RAFE AND JARED
The tales of two brothers–
their rebellions, passions and loves

WHERE THE HEART IS
Two remarkable stories of finding love
where you least expect it

And coming soon
THE MacKADE BROTHERS:
DEVIN AND SHANE
Two brothers–two unforgettable romances

Be sure to look for more Nora Roberts titles
in your local stores, or contact our
Silhouette Reader Service Center,
U.S.A.: 3010 Walden Avenue
P.O. Box 1325, Buffalo, NY 14269
Canada: P.O. Box 609, Fort Erie, Ontario L2A 5X3
Visit Silhouette Books at www.eHarlequin.com

LAWLESS

To Ruth, Marianne and Jan,
For taking me to Silverado

Chapter 1

He wanted a drink. Whiskey, cheap and warm. After six weeks on the trail, he wanted the same kind of woman. Some men usually managed to get what they wanted. He was one of them. Still, the woman could wait, Jake decided as he leaned against the bar. The whiskey couldn't.

He had another ninety long, dusty miles to go before he got home. If anybody could call a frying pan like Lone Bluff home. Some did, Jake thought as he signaled for a bottle and took his first gut-clenching gulp. Some had to.

For himself, home was usually the six feet of space where his shadow fell. But for the past few months Lone Bluff had been as good a place as any. He could get a room there, a bath and a willing woman, all at a reasonable price. It was a town where a man could avoid trouble—or find it, depending on his mood.

For now, with the dust of the trail still scratchy in his throat and his stomach empty except for a shot of whiskey, Jake was just too tired for trouble. He'd have another drink, and whatever passed for a meal in this two-bit town blown up from the desert, then he'd be on his way.

The afternoon sunlight poured in over the swinging doors at the saloon's entrance. Someone had tacked a picture of a woman in red feathers to the wall, but that was the extent of the female company. Places like this didn't run to providing women for their clientele. Just to liquor and cards.

Even towns like this one had a saloon or two. A man could depend upon it, the way he could depend on little else. It wasn't yet noon, and half the tables were occupied. The air was thick with the smoke from the cigars the bartender sold, two for a penny. The whiskey went for a couple of bits and burned a line of fire straight from the throat to the gut. If the owner had added a real woman in red feathers, he could have charged double that and not heard a single complaint.

The place stank of whiskey, sweat and smoke. But Jake figured he didn't smell too pretty himself. He'd ridden hard from New Mexico, and he would have ridden straight through to Lone Bluff except he'd wanted to rest his horse and fill his own stomach with something other than the jerky in his saddlebags.

Saloons always looked better at night, and this one was no exception. Its bar was grimy from hundreds of hands and elbows, dulled by spilled drinks, scarred by matchtips. The floor was nothing but hard-packed dirt that had absorbed its share of whiskey and blood. He'd been in worse, Jake reflected, wondering if he should allow himself the luxury of rolling a cigarette now or wait until after a meal.

He could buy more tobacco if he had a yearning for another. There was a month's pay in his pocket. And he'd be damned if he'd ever ride cattle again. That was a life for the young and stupid—or maybe just the stupid.

When his money ran low he could always take a job riding shotgun on the stage through Indian country. The line was always looking for a man who was handy with a gun, and it was better than riding at the back end of a steer. It was the middle of 1875 and the easterners were still coming—looking for gold and land, following dreams. Some of them stopped in the Arizona Territory on their way to California because they ran out of money or energy or time.

Their hard luck, Jake thought as he downed his second whiskey. He'd been born here, and he still didn't figure it was the most hospitable place on the map. It was hot and hard and stingy. It suited him just fine.

"Redman?"

Jake lifted his eyes to the dingy glass behind the bar. He saw the man behind him. Young, wiry and edgy. His brown hat was tipped down low over his eyes, and sweat glistened on his neck. Jake nearly sighed. He knew the type too well. The kind that went out of his way looking for trouble. The kind that didn't know that if you hung around long enough it found you, anyway.

"Yeah?"

"Jake Redman?"

"So?"

"I'm Barlow, Tom Barlow." He wiped his palms on his thighs. "They call me Slim."

The way he said it, Jake was sure the kid expected the name to be recognized…shuddered over. He decided the whiskey wasn't good enough for a third drink. He dropped some money on the bar, making sure his hands were well clear of his guns.

"There a place where a man can get a steak in this town?" Jake asked the bartender.

"Down to Grody's." The man moved cautiously out of range. "We don't want any trouble in here."

Jake gave him a long, cool look. "I'm not giving you any."

"I'm talking to you, Redman." Barlow spread his legs and let his hand hover over the butt of his gun. A mean-looking scar ran across the back of his hand from his index finger to his wrist. He wore his holster high, a single rig with the leather worn smooth at the buckle. It paid to notice details.

Easy, moving no more than was necessary, Jake met his eyes. "Something you want to say?"

"You got a reputation for being fast. Heard you took out Freemont in Tombstone."

Jake turned fully. As he moved, the swinging door flew back. At least one of the saloon's customers had decided to move to safer ground. The kid was packing a .44 Colt, its black rubber grip well tended. Jake didn't doubt there were notches in it. Barlow looked like the type who would take pride in killing.

"You heard right."

Barlow's fingers curled and uncurled. Two men playing poker in the corner let their hands lie to watch and made a companionable bet on the higher-stakes game in front of them. "I'm faster. Faster than Freemont. Faster than you. I run this town."

Jake glanced around the saloon, then back into Barlow's dark, edgy eyes. "Congratulations." He would have walked away, but Barlow shifted to block him. The move had Jake narrowing his eyes. The look came into them, the hard, flat look that made a smart man give way. "Cut your teeth on somebody else. I want a steak and a bed."

"Not in my town."

Patience wasn't Jake's long suit, but he wasn't in the mood to waste time on a gunman looking to sharpen his reputation. "You want to die over a piece of meat?"

Jake watched the grin spread over Barlow's face. He didn't think he was going to die, Jake thought wearily. His kind never did.

"Why don't you come find me in about five years?" Jake told him. "I'll be happy to put a bullet in you."

"I found you now. After I kill you, there won't be a man west of the Mississippi who won't know Slim Barlow."

For some—for many—no other reason was needed to draw and fire. "Make it easy on both of us." Jake started for the doors again. "Just tell them you killed me."

"I hear your mother was a squaw." Barlow grinned when Jake stopped and turned again. "Guess that's where you got that streak of yellow."

Jake was used to rage. It could fill a man from stomach to brain and take over. When he felt it rising up, he clamped down on it. If he was going to fight—and it seemed inevitable—he preferred to fight cold.

"My grandmother was Apache."

Barlow grinned again, then wiped his mouth with the back of his left hand. "That makes you a stinking breed, don't it? A stinking yellow breed. We don't want no Indians around here. Guess I'll have to clean up the town a little."

He went for his gun. Jake saw the move, not in Barlow's hands but in his eyes. Cold and fast and without regret, Jake drew his own. There were those who saw him who said it was like lightning and thunder. There was a flash of steel, then the roar of the bullet. He hardly moved from where he stood, shooting from the hip, trusting instinct and experience. In a smooth, almost careless movement, he replaced his gun. Tom they-call-me-Slim Barlow was sprawled on the barroom floor.

Jake passed through the swinging doors and walked to his horse. He didn't know whether he'd killed his man or not, and he didn't care. The whole damn mess had ruined his appetite.

Sarah was mortally afraid she was going to lose the miserable lunch she'd managed to bolt down at the last stop. How anyone—*anyone*—survived under these appalling conditions, she'd never know. The West, as far as she could see, was only fit for snakes and outlaws.

She closed her eyes, patted the sweat from her neck with her handkerchief, and prayed that she'd make it through the next few hours. At least she could thank God she wouldn't have to spend another night in one of those horrible stage depots. She'd been afraid she would be murdered in her bed. If one could call that miserable sheetless rope cot a bed. And privacy? Well, there simply hadn't been any.

It didn't matter now, she told herself. She was nearly there. After twelve long years, she was going to see her father again and take care of him in the beautiful house he'd built outside Lone Bluff.

When she'd been six, he'd left her in the care of the good sisters and gone off to make his fortune. There had been nights, many nights, when Sarah had cried herself to sleep from missing him. Then, as the years had passed, she'd had to take out the faded daguerreotype to remember his face. But he'd always written to her. His penmanship had been strained and childish, but there had been so much love in his letters. And so much hope.

Once a month she'd received word from her father from whatever point he'd stopped at on his journey west. After eighteen months, and eighteen letters, he'd written from the Arizona Territory, where he'd settled, and where he would build his fortune.

He'd convinced her that he'd been right to leave her in Philadelphia, in the convent school, where she could be raised and educated as a proper young lady should. Until, Sarah remembered, she was old enough to travel across the country to live with him. Now she was nearly eighteen, and she was going to join him. Undoubtedly the house he'd built, however grand, required a woman's touch.

Since he'd never married again, Sarah imagined her father a crusty bachelor, never quite certain where his clean collars were or what the cook was serving for dinner. She'd soon fix all that.

A man in his position needed to entertain, and to entertain he needed a hostess. Sarah Conway knew exactly how to give an elegant dinner party and a formal ball.

True, what she'd read of the Arizona Territory was distressing, to say the least. Stories of ruthless gunmen and wild Indians. But, after all, this was 1875. Sarah had no doubt that even so distant a place as Arizona was under control by this time. The reports she'd read had obviously been exaggerated to sell newspapers and penny dreadfuls.

They hadn't exaggerated about the climate.

She shifted for a better position. The bulk of the woman beside her, and her own corset, gave her little room for relief. And the smell. No matter how often Sarah sprinkled lavender water on her handkerchief, there was no escaping it. There were seven passengers, crammed all but elbow-to-knee inside the rattling stagecoach. It was airless, and that accentuated the stench of sweat and foul breath and whatever liquor it was that the man across from her continued to drink. Right from the bottle. At first, his pockmarked face and grimy neckcloth had fascinated her. But when he'd offered her a drink, she had fallen back on a woman's best defense. Her dignity.

It was difficult to look dignified when her clothes were sticking to her and her hair was drooping beneath her bonnet. It was all but impossible to maintain her decorum when the plump woman beside her began to gnaw on what appeared to be a chicken leg. But when Sarah was determined, she invariably prevailed.

The good sisters had never been able to pray or punish or lecture her stubbornness out of her. Now, with her chin slightly lifted and her body braced against the bouncing sway of the coach, she kept her eyes firmly shut and ignored her fellow passengers.

She'd seen enough of the Arizona landscape, if one could call it that. As far as she could see, the entire territory was nothing but miles of sunbaked desert. True, the first cacti she'd seen had been fascinating. She'd even considered sketching a few of them. Some were as big as a man, with arms that stretched up to the sky. Others were short and squat and covered with hundreds of dangerous-looking needles. Still, after she'd seen several dozen of them, and little else, they'd lost their novelty.

The rocks were interesting, she supposed. The buttes and flat-topped mesas growing out of the sand had a certain rugged charm, particularly when they rose up into the deep, endless blue of the sky. But she preferred the tidy streets of Philadelphia, with their shops and tearooms.

Being with her father would make all the difference. She could live anywhere, as long as she was with him again. He'd be proud of her. She needed him to be proud of her. All these years she'd worked and learned and practiced so that she could become the proper, well-educated young lady he wanted his daughter to be.

She wondered if he'd recognize her. She'd sent him a small, framed self-portrait just last Christmas, but she wasn't certain it had been a truly good likeness. She'd always thought it was too bad she wasn't pretty, in the soft, round way of her dear friend Lucilla. Still, her complexion was good, and Sarah comforted herself with that. Unlike Lucilla, she never required any help from the little pots of rouge the sisters so disapproved of. In fact, there were times she thought her complexion just a bit too healthy. Her mouth was full and wide when she would have preferred a delicate Cupid's bow, and her eyes were an unremarkable brown rather than the blue that would have suited her blond hair so much better. Still, she was trim and neat—or she had been neat before she'd begun this miserable journey.

It would all be worthwhile soon. When she greeted her father and they settled into the lovely house he'd built. Four bedrooms. Imagine. And a parlor with windows facing west. Delightful. Undoubtedly, she'd have to do some redecorating. Men never thought about such niceties as curtains and throw rugs. She'd enjoy it. Once she had the glass shining and fresh flowers in the vases he would see how much he needed her. Then all the years in between would have been worthwhile.

Sarah felt a line of sweat trickle down her back. The first thing she wanted was a bath—a nice, cool bath laced with the fragrant lilac salts Lucilla had given her as a parting gift. She sighed. She could almost feel it, her body free of the tight corset and hot clothes, the water sliding over her skin. Scented. Delicious. Almost sinful.

When the coach jolted, Sarah was thrown against the fat woman to her left. Before she could right herself, a spray of rotgut whiskey soaked her skirts.

"Sir!" But before she could lecture him she heard the shot, and the screams.

"Indians!" The chicken leg went flying, and the fat

woman clutched Sarah to her bosom like a shield. "We're all going to be murdered."

"Don't be absurd." Sarah struggled to free herself, not certain if she was more annoyed by the sudden dangerous speed of the coach or the spot of chicken grease on her new skirt. She leaned toward the window to call to the driver. As she did, the face of the shotgun rider slid into view, inches from hers. He hung there, upside down, for seconds only. But that was long enough for Sarah to see the blood trickling from his mouth, and the arrow in his heart. Even as the woman beside her screamed again, his body thudded to the ground.

"Indians!" she shouted again. "God have mercy. We'll be scalped. Every one of us."

"Apaches," the man with the whiskey said as he finished off the bottle. "Must've got the driver, too. We're on a runaway." So saying, he drew his gun, made his way to the opposite window and began firing methodically.

Dazed, Sarah continued to stare out the window. She could hear screams and whoops and the thunder of horses' hooves. Like devils, she thought dully. They sounded like devils. That was impossible. Ridiculous. The United States was nearly a century old. Ulysses S. Grant was president. Steamships crossed the Atlantic in less than two weeks. Devils simply didn't exist in this day and age.

Then she saw one, bare chested, hair flying, on a tough paint pony. Sarah looked straight into his eyes. She could see the fever in them, just as she could see the bright streaks of paint on his face and the layer of dust that covered his gleaming skin. He raised his bow.

She could have counted the feathers in the arrow. Then, suddenly, he flew off the back of his horse.

It was like a play, she thought, and she had to pinch herself viciously to keep from swooning.

Another horseman came into view, riding low, with pistols in both hands. He wasn't an Indian, though in Sarah's confusion he seemed just as wild. He wore a gray hat over dark hair, and his skin was nearly as dark as that of the Apache she'd seen. In his eyes, as they met hers, she saw not fever, but ice.

He didn't shoot her, as she'd been almost certain he would, but fired over his shoulder, using his right hand, then his left, even as an arrow whizzed by his head.

Amazing, she thought as a thudding excitement began to race with her terror. He was magnificent— sweat and grime on his face, ice in his eyes, his lean, tense body glued to the racing horse. Then the fat lady grabbed her again and began to wail.

Jake fired behind him, clinging to the horse with his knees as easily as any Apache brave. He'd caught a glimpse of the passengers, in particular a pale, dark-eyed girl in a dark blue bonnet. His Apache cousins would've enjoyed that one, he thought dispassionately as he holstered his guns.

He could see the driver, an arrow piercing one shoulder, struggling to regain control of the horses. He was doing his best, despite the pain, but he wasn't strong enough to shove the brake down. Swearing, Jake pushed his horse on until he was close enough to the racing coach to gain a handhold.

For one endless second he hung by his fingers alone.

Sarah caught a glimpse of a dusty shirt and one powerful forearm, a long, leather-clad leg and a scarred boot. Then he was up, scrambling over the top of the coach. The woman beside her screamed again, then fainted dead away when they stopped. Too terrified to sit, Sarah pushed open the door of the coach and climbed out.

The man in the gray hat was already getting down. "Ma'am," he said as he moved past her.

She pressed a hand to her drumming heart. No hero had ever been so heroic. "You saved our lives," she managed, but he didn't even glance her way.

"Redman." The passenger who'd drunk the whiskey stepped out. "Glad you stopped by."

"Lucius." Jake picked up the reins of his horse and proceeded to calm him. "There were only six of them."

"They're getting away," Sarah blurted out. "Are you just going to let them get away?"

Jake looked at the cloud of dust from the retreating horses, then back at Sarah. He had time now for a longer, more interested study. She was tiny, with *East* stamped all over her pretty face. Her hair, the color of honeycombs, was tumbling down from her bonnet. She looked as if she'd just stepped out of the schoolroom, and she smelled like a cheap saloon. He had to grin.

"Yep."

"But you can't." Her idea of a hero was rapidly crumbling. "They killed a man."

"He knew the chance he was taking. Riding the line pays good."

"They murdered him," Sarah said again, as if she were speaking to a very dull pupil. "He's lying back there with an arrow through his heart." When Jake said nothing, just walked his horse to the back of the coach, Sarah followed him. "At least you can go back and pick up that poor man's body. We can't just leave him there."

"Dead's dead."

"That's a hideous thing to say." Because she felt ill, Sarah dragged off her bonnet and used it to fan hot air around her face. "The man deserves a decent burial. I couldn't possibly— What are you doing?"

Jake spared her a glance. Mighty pretty, he decided. Even prettier without the bonnet hiding her hair. "Hitching my horse."

She dropped her arm to her side. She no longer felt ill. She was certainly no longer impressed. She was furious. "Sir, you appear to care more about that horse than you do about the man."

He stooped under the reins. For a moment they stood face-to-face, with the sun beating down and the smell of blood and dust all around them. "That's right, seeing as the man's dead and my horse isn't. I'd get back inside, ma'am. It'd be a shame if you were still standing here when the Apaches decide to come back."

That made her stop and look around uneasily. The desert was still, but for the cry of a bird she didn't recognize as a vulture. "I'll go back and get him myself," she said between her teeth.

"Suit yourself." Jake walked to the front of the coach. "Get that stupid woman inside," he told Lucius. "And don't give her any more to drink."

Sarah's mouth fell open. Before she could retaliate, Lucius had her by the arm. "Now, don't mind Jake, miss. He just says whatever he damn pleases. He's right, though. Those Apaches might turn back this way. We sure don't want to be sitting here if they do."

With what little dignity she had left, Sarah stepped back into the coach. The fat woman was still sobbing, leaning heavily against a tight-lipped man in a bowler. Sarah wedged herself into her corner as the stage jumped forward again. Securing her bonnet, she frowned at Lucius.

"Who is that horrible man?"

"Jake?" Lucius settled back. There was nothing he liked better than a good fight, particularly when he stayed alive to enjoy it. "That's Jake Redman, miss. I don't mind saying we was lucky he passed this way. Jake hits what he aims at."

"Indeed." She wanted to be aloof, but she remembered the murderous look in the Apache's eyes when he'd ridden beside the window. "I suppose we do owe him our gratitude, but he seemed cold-blooded about it."

"More'n one says he's got ice in his veins. Along with some Apache blood."

"You mean he's…Indian?"

"On his grandmother's side, I hear." Because his bottle was empty, Lucius settled for a plug of tobacco. He tucked it comfortably in his cheek. "Wouldn't want to cross him. No, ma'am, I sure wouldn't. Mighty comforting to know he's on your side when things heat up."

What kind of man killed his own kind? With a shiver, Sarah fell silent again. She didn't want to think about it.

On top of the stage, Jake kept the team to a steady pace. He preferred the freedom and mobility of having a single horse under him. The driver held a hand to his wounded shoulder and refused the dubious comfort of the coach.

"We could use you back on the line," he told Jake.

"Thinking about it." But he was really thinking about the little lady with the big brown eyes and the honey-colored hair. "Who's the girl? The young one in blue?"

"Conway. From Philadelphia." The driver breathed slow and easy against the pain. "Says she's Matt Conway's daughter."

"That so?" Miss Philadelphia Conway sure as hell didn't take after her old man. But Jake remembered that Matt bragged about his daughter back east from time to time. Especially after he started a bottle. "Come to visit her father?"

"Says she's come to stay."

Jake gave a quick, mirthless laugh. "Won't last a week. Women like that don't."

"She's planning on it." With a jerk of his thumb, the driver indicated the trunks strapped to the coach. "Most of that's hers."

With a snort, Jake adjusted his hat. "Figures."

Sarah caught her first glimpse of Lone Bluff from the stagecoach window. It spread like a jumble of rock at the base of the mountains. Hard, cold-looking mountains, she thought with a shudder, fooled—as the inexperienced always were—into thinking they were much closer than they actually were.

She'd forgotten herself enough to crane her head out. But she couldn't get another look at Jake Redman unless she pushed half her body through the opening. She really wasn't interested anyway, she assured herself. Unless it was purely for entertainment purposes. When she wrote back to Lucilla and the sisters, she wanted to be able to describe all the local oddities.

The man was certainly odd. He'd ridden like a warrior one moment, undoubtedly risking his life for a coachful of strangers. Then, the next minute, he'd dismissed his Christian duty and left a poor soul beside a lonely desert road. And he'd called her stupid.

Never in her life had anyone ever accused Sarah Conway of being stupid. In fact, both her intelligence and her breeding were widely admired. She was well-read, fluent in French and more than passably accomplished on the pianoforte.

Taking the time to retie her bonnet, Sarah reminded herself that she hardly needed approval from a man like Jake Redman. After she was reunited with her father and took her place in the local society, it was doubtful she'd ever see him again.

She'd thank him properly, of course. Sarah drew a fresh handkerchief from her reticule and blotted her temples. Just because he had no manners was no excuse to forget her own. She supposed she might even ask her father to offer him some monetary reward.

Pleased with the idea, Sarah looked out the window again. And blinked. Surely this wasn't Lone Bluff. Her father would never have settled in this grimy excuse for a town. It was no more than a huddle of buildings and a wide patch of dust that served as a road. They passed two saloons side by side, a dry goods store and what appeared to be a rooming house. Slack-legged horses were hitched to posts, their tails switching lazily at huge black flies. A handful of young boys with dirty faces began to race alongside the coach, shouting and firing wooden pistols. Sarah saw two women in faded gingham walking arm in arm on some wooden planks that served as a sidewalk.

When the coach stopped, she heard Jake call out for a doctor. Passengers were already streaming out through the doors on both sides. Resigned, Sarah stepped out and shook out her skirts.

"Mr. Redman." The brim of her bonnet provided inadequate shade. She was forced to lift her hand over her eyes. "Why have we stopped here?"

"End of the line, ma'am." A couple of men were already lifting the driver down, so he swung himself around to unstrap the cases on top of the coach.

"End of the line? But where are we?"

He paused long enough to glance down at her. She saw then that his eyes were darker than she'd imagined. A smoky slate gray. "Welcome to Lone Bluff."

Letting out a long, slow breath, she turned. Sunlight treated the town cruelly. It showed all the dirt, all the wear, and it heightened the pungent smell of horses.

Dear God, so this was it. The end of the line. The end of her line. It didn't matter, she told herself. She wouldn't be living in town. And surely before long the gold in her father's mine would bring more people and progress. No, it didn't matter at all. Sarah squared her shoulders. The only thing that mattered was seeing her father again.

She turned around in time to see Jake toss one of her trunks down to Lucius.

"Mr. Redman, please take care of my belongings."

Jake hefted the next case and tossed it to a grinning Lucius. "Yes, ma'am."

Biting down on her temper, she waited until he jumped down beside her. "Notwithstanding my earlier sentiments, I'm very grateful to you, Mr. Redman, for coming to our aid. You proved yourself to be quite valiant. I'm sure my father will want to repay you for seeing that I arrived safely."

Jake didn't think he'd ever heard anyone talk quite so fine since he'd spent a week in St. Louis. Tipping back his hat, he looked at her, long enough to make Sarah flush. "Forget it."

Forget it? Sarah thought as he turned his back and walked away. If that was the way the man accepted gratitude, she certainly would. With a sweep of her skirts she moved to the side of the road to wait for her father.

Jake strode into the rooming house with his saddle-bag slung over his shoulder. It was never particularly clean, and it always smelled of onions and strong coffee. There were a couple of bullet holes in the wall. He'd put one of them there personally. Since the door was propped open, flies buzzed merrily in and out of the cramped entrance.

"Maggie." Jake tipped his hat to the woman who stood at the base of the stairs. "Got a room?"

Maggie O'Rourke was as tough as one of her fried steaks. She had iron-gray hair pinned back from a face that should have been too skinny for wrinkles. But wrinkles there were, a maze of them. Her tiny blue eyes seemed to peek out of the folds of a worn blanket. She ran her business with an iron fist, a Winchester repeater and an eye for a dollar.

She took one look at Jake and successfully hid her pleasure at seeing him. "Well, look what the cat dragged in," she said, the musical brogue of her native country still evident in her thin voice. "Got the law on your tail, Jake, or a woman?"

"Neither." He kicked the door shut with his boot, wondering why he always came back here. The old woman never gave him a moment's peace, and her cooking could kill a man. "You got a room, Maggie? And some hot water?"

"You got a dollar?" She held out her thin hand. When Jake dropped a coin into it, she tested it with the few good teeth she had left. It wasn't that she didn't trust Jake. She did. She just didn't trust the United States government. "Might as well take the one you had before. No one's in it."

"Fine." He started up the steps.

"Ain't had too much excitement since you left. Couple drifters shot each other over at the Bird Cage. Worthless pair, the both of them. Only one dead, though. Sheriff sent the other on his way after the doc patched him up. Young Mary Sue Brody got herself in trouble with that Mitchell boy. Always said she was a fast thing, that Mary Sue. Had a right proper wedding, though. Just last month."

Jake kept walking, but that didn't stop Maggie. One of the privileges in running a rooming house was giving and receiving gossip.

"What a shame about old Matt Conway."

That stopped him. He turned. Maggie was still at the base of the steps, using the edge of her apron to swipe halfheartedly at the dust on the banister. "What about Matt Conway?"

"Got himself killed in that worthless mine of his. A cave-in. Buried him the day before yesterday."

Chapter 2

The heat was murderous. A plume of thin yellow dust rose each time a rider passed, then hung there to clog the still air. Sarah longed for a long, cool drink and a seat in the shade. From the looks of things, there wasn't a place in town where a lady could go to find such amenities. Even if there were, she was afraid to leave her trunks on the side of the road and risk missing her father.

She'd been so sure he would be waiting for her. But then, a man in his position could have been held up by a million things. Work at the mine, a problem with an employee, perhaps last-minute preparations for her arrival.

She'd waited twelve years, she reminded herself, resisting the urge to loosen her collar. She could wait a little longer.

A buckboard passed, spewing up more dust, so that

she was forced to lift a handkerchief to her mouth. Her dark blue traveling skirt and her neat matching jacket with its fancy black braid were covered with dust. With a sigh, she glanced down at her blouse, which was drooping hopelessly and now seemed more yellow than white. It wasn't really vanity. The sisters had never given her a chance to develop any. She was concerned that her father would see her for the first time when she was travel-stained and close to exhaustion. She'd wanted to look her best for him at this first meeting. All she could do now was retie the bow at her chin, then brush hopelessly at her skirts.

She looked a fright. But she'd make it up to him. She would wear her brand-new white muslin gown for dinner tonight, the one with the charming rosebuds embroidered all over the skirt. Her kid slippers were dyed pink to match. He'd be proud of her.

If only he'd come, she thought, and take her away from here.

Jake crossed the street after losing the battle he'd waged with himself. It wasn't his business, and it wasn't his place to tell her. But for the past ten minutes he'd been watching her standing at the side of the road, waiting. He'd been able to see, too clearly, the look of hope that sprang into her eyes each time a horse or wagon approached. Somebody had to tell the woman that her father wasn't going to meet her.

Sarah saw him coming. He walked easily, despite the guns at his sides. As if they had always been there. As if they always would be. They rode low on his hips, shifting with his movements. And he kept his eyes on her in a way that she was certain a man shouldn't keep his eyes on a woman—unless she was his own. When she felt her heart flutter, she automatically stiffened her backbone.

It was Lucilla who was always talking about fluttering hearts. It was Lucilla who painted romantic pictures of lawless men and lawless places. Sarah preferred a bit more reality in her dreams.

"Ma'am." He was surprised that she hadn't already swooned under the power of the afternoon sun. Maybe she was tougher than she looked, but he doubted it.

"Mr. Redman." Determined to be gracious, she allowed her lips to curve ever so slightly at the corners.

He tucked his thumbs into the pockets of his pants. "I got some news about your father."

She smiled fully, beautifully, so that her whole face lit up with it. Her eyes turned to gold in the sunlight. Jake felt the punch, like a bullet in the chest.

"Oh, did he leave word for me? Thank you for letting me know. I might have waited here for hours."

"Ma'am—"

"Is there a note?"

"No." He wanted to get this done, and done quickly. "Matt's dead. There was an accident at his mine." He was braced for weeping, for wild wailing, but her eyes filled with fury, not tears.

"How dare you? How dare you lie to me about something like that?" She would have brushed past him, but Jake clamped a hand over her arm. Sarah's first reaction was simple indignation at being manhandled. Then she looked up at him, really looked, and said nothing.

"He was buried two days ago." He felt her recoil, then

go still. The fury drained from her eyes, even as the color drained from her cheeks. "Don't go fainting on me."

It was true. She could see the truth on his face as clearly as she could see his distaste at being the one to tell her. "An accident?" she managed.

"A cave-in." He was relieved that she wasn't going to faint, but he didn't care for the glassy look in her eyes. "You'll want to talk to the sheriff."

"The sheriff?" she repeated dully.

"His office is across the street."

She just shook her head and stared at him. Her eyes *were* gold, Jake decided. The color of the brandy he sometimes drank at the Silver Star. Right now they were huge and full of hurt. He watched her bite down on her bottom lip in a gesture he knew meant she was fighting not to let go of the emotions he saw so clearly in her eyes.

If she'd fainted, he'd happily have left her on the road in the care of whatever woman happened to pass by. But she was hanging on, and it moved something in him.

Swearing, Jake shifted his grip from her arm to her elbow and guided her across the street. He was damned if he could figure out how he'd elected himself responsible.

Sheriff Barker was at his desk, bent over some paperwork and a cup of sweetened coffee. He was balding rapidly. Every morning he took the time to comb what hair he had left over the spreading bare spot on top of his head. He had the beginnings of a paunch brought on by his love of his wife's baking. He kept the law in Lone Bluff, but he didn't worry overmuch about the order. It wasn't that he was corrupt, just lazy.

He glanced up as Jake entered. Then he sighed and

sent tobacco juice streaming into the spittoon in the corner. When Jake Redman was around, there was usually work to be done.

"So you're back." The wad of tobacco gave Barker a permanently swollen jaw. "Thought you might take a fancy to New Mexico." His brows lifted when Jake ushered Sarah inside. There was enough gentleman left in him to bring him to his feet. "Ma'am."

"This is Matt Conway's daughter."

"Well, I'll be damned. Begging your pardon, ma'am. I was just fixing to send you a letter."

"Sheriff." She had to pause a moment to find her balance. She would not fall apart, not here, in front of strangers.

"Barker, ma'am." He came around the desk to offer her a chair.

"Sheriff Barker." Sarah sat, praying she'd be able to stand again. "Mr. Redman has just told me that my father…" She couldn't say it. No matter how weak or cowardly it might be, she just couldn't say the words.

"Yes, ma'am. I'm mighty sorry. Couple of kids wandered on up by the mine playing games and found him. Appears he was working the mine when some of the beams gave way." When she said nothing, Barker cleared his throat and opened the top drawer of his desk. "He had this watch on him, and his tobacco." He'd had his pipe, as well, but since it had been broken—like most of Conway's bones—Barker hadn't thought anyone would want it. "We figured he'd want to be buried with his wedding ring on."

"Thank you." As if in a trance, she took the watch and

the tobacco pouch from him. She remembered the watch. The tears almost won when she remembered how he'd taken it out to check the time before he'd left her in Mother Superior's lemony-smelling office. "I want to see where he's buried. My trunks will need to be taken out to his house."

"Miss Conway, if you don't mind me offering some advice, you don't want to stay way out there. It's no place for a young lady like you, all alone and all. My wife'll be happy to have you stay with us for a few days. Until the stage heads east again."

"It's kind of you to offer." She braced a hand on the chair and managed to stand again. "But I'd prefer to spend the night in my father's house." She swallowed and discovered that her throat was hurtfully dry. "Is there... Do I owe you anything for the burial?"

"No, ma'am. We take care of our own around here."

"Thank you." She needed air. With the watch clutched in her hand, she pushed through the door. Leaning against a post, she tried to catch her breath.

"You ought to take the sheriff up on his offer."

She turned her head to give Jake an even look. She could only be grateful that he made her angry enough to help her hold off her grief. He hadn't offered a word of sympathy. Not one. Well, she was glad of it.

"I'm going to stay in my father's house. Will you take me?"

He rubbed a hand over his chin. He hadn't shaved in a week. "I've got things to do."

"I'll pay you," she said quickly when he started to walk away.

He stopped and looked back at her. She was determined, all right. He wanted to see how determined. "How much?"

"Two dollars." When he only continued to look at her, she said between her teeth, "Five."

"You got five?"

Disgusted, Sarah dug in her reticule. "There."

Jake looked at the bill in her hand. "What's that?"

"It's five dollars."

"Not around here it ain't. Around here it's paper."

Sarah pushed the bill back into her reticule and pulled out a coin. "Will this do?"

Jake took the coin and turned it over in his hand, then stuck it in his pocket. "That'll do fine. I'll get a wagon."

Miserable man, she thought as he strode away. She hated him. And hated even more the fact that she needed him.

During the long, hot ride in the open wagon, she said nothing. She no longer cared about the desolation of the landscape, the heat or the cold-bloodedness of the man beside her. Her emotions seemed to have shriveled up inside her. Every mile they'd gone was just another mile behind her.

Jake Redman didn't seem to need conversation. He drove in silence, armed with a rifle across his lap, as well as the pistols he carried. There hadn't been trouble out here in quite some time, but the Indian attack had warned him that that could change.

He'd recognized Strong Wolf in the party that had attacked the stage. If the Apache brave had decided to raid in the area, he would hit the Conway place sooner or later.

They passed no one. They saw only sand and rock and a hawk out hunting.

When he reined the horses in, Sarah saw nothing but a small adobe house and a few battered sheds on a patch of thirsty land.

"Why are we stopping here?"

Jake jumped down from the wagon. "This is Matt Conway's place."

"Don't be ridiculous." Because it didn't appear that he was going to come around and assist her, Sarah struggled down herself. "Mr. Redman, I paid you to take me to my father's home and I expect you to keep the bargain."

Before she could stop him, he dumped one of her trunks on the ground. "What do you think you're doing?"

"Delivering your luggage."

"Don't you take another piece off that wagon." Surprising them both, Sarah grabbed his shirt and pulled him around to face her. "I insist you take me to my father's house immediately."

She wasn't just stupid, Jake thought. She was irritating. "Fine." He clipped her around the waist and hauled her over his shoulder.

At first she was too shocked to move. No man had ever touched her before. Now this, this *ruffian* had his hands all over her. And they were alone. Totally alone. Sarah began to struggle as he pushed open the door of the hut. Before she could draw the breath to scream, he was dropping her to her feet again.

"That good enough for you?"

She stared at him, visions of a hundred calamities that could befall a defenseless woman dancing in her brain. She stepped back, breathing hard, and prayed she could reason with him. "Mr. Redman, I have very little money of my own—hardly enough worth stealing."

Something came into his eyes that had her breath stopping altogether. He looked more than dangerous now. He looked fatal. "I don't steal." The light coming through the low doorway arched around him. She moistened her lips.

"Are you going to kill me?"

He nearly laughed. Instead, he leaned against the wall. Something about her was eating at him. He didn't know what or why, but he didn't like it. Not one damn bit.

"Probably not. You want to take a look around?" She just shook her head. "They told me he was buried around back, near the entrance of the mine. I'll go check on Matt's horses and water the team."

When he left, she continued to stare at the empty doorway. This was madness. Did the man expect her to believe her father had lived here, like this? She had letters, dozens of them, telling her about the house he'd been building, the house he'd finished, the house that would be waiting for her when she was old enough to join him.

The mine. If the mine was near, perhaps she could find someone there she could speak with. Taking a cautious look out the doorway, Sarah hurried out and rounded the house.

She passed what might have been the beginnings of a small vegetable garden, withered now in the sun. There was a shed that served as a stable and an empty paddock made of a few rickety pieces of wood. She walked beyond it to where the ground began to rise with the slope of the mountain.

The entrance to the mine was easily found, though it was hardly more than a hole in the rock wall. Above it was a crudely etched plank of wood.

SARAH'S PRIDE

She felt the tears then. They came in a rush that she had to work hard to hold back. There were no workmen here, no carts shuttling along filled with rock, no picks hacking out gold. She saw it for what it was, the dream of a man who had had little else. Her father had never been a successful prospector or an important landowner. He'd been a man digging in rock and hoping for the big strike.

She saw the grave then. They had buried him only a few yards from the entrance. Someone had been kind enough to fashion a cross and carve his name on it. She knelt and ran her palm along the rubble that covered him.

He'd lied. For twelve years he'd lied to her, telling her stories about rich veins and the mother lode. He'd spun fantasies about a big house with a parlor and fine wooden floors. Had he needed to believe it? When he'd left her he'd made her a promise.

"You'll have everything your heart desires, my sweet, sweet Sarah. Everything your mother would have wanted for you."

He had kept his promise—except for one thing. One vital thing. He hadn't given her himself. All those years, all she'd really wanted had been her father.

He'd lived like this, she thought, in a mud house in the middle of nowhere, so that she could have pretty dresses and new stockings. So that she could learn how to serve tea and waltz. It must have taken nearly everything he'd managed to dig out of the rock to keep her in school back east.

Now he was dead. She could barely remember his face, and he was dead. Lost to her.

"Oh, Papa, didn't you know how little it mattered?" Lying across the grave, she let the tears come until she'd wept her heart clean.

She'd been gone a long time. Too long, Jake thought. He was just about to go after her when he saw her coming over the rise from the direction of the old mine. She paused there, looking down at the house her father had lived in for more than a decade. She'd taken off her bonnet, and she was holding it by the ribbons. For a moment she stood like a statue in the airless afternoon, her face marble-pale, her body slim and elegant. Her hair was pinned up, but a few tendrils had escaped to curl around her face. The sun slanted over it so that it glowed richly, reminding him of the hide of a young deer.

Jake blew out the last of the smoke from the cigarette he'd rolled. She was a hell of a sight, silhouetted against the bluff. She made him ache in places he didn't care to think about. Then she saw him. He could almost see her chin come up as she started down over the rough ground. Yeah, she was a hell of a sight.

"Mr. Redman." The grief was there in her red-rimmed eyes and her pale cheeks, but her voice was strong. "I apologize for the scene I caused earlier."

That tied his tongue for a moment. The way she said it, they might have been talking over tea in some cozy parlor. "Forget it. You ready to go back?"

"I beg your pardon?"

He jerked his thumb toward the wagon. Sarah noted that all her trunks were neatly stacked on it again. "I said, are you ready to go back?"

She glanced down at her hands. Because the palms of her gloves were grimy, she tugged them off. They'd never be the same, she mused. Nothing would. She drew a long, steadying breath.

"I thought you understood me. I'm staying in my father's house."

"Don't be a fool. A woman like you's got no business out here."

"Really?" Her eyes hardened. "Be that as it may, I'm not leaving. I'd appreciate it if you'd move my trunks inside." She breezed by him.

"You won't last a day."

She stopped to look over her shoulder. Jake was forced to admit that he'd faced men over the barrel of a gun who'd had less determination in their eyes. "Is that your opinion, Mr. Redman?"

"That's a fact."

"Would you care to wager on it?"

"Look, Duchess, this is hard country even if you're born to it. Heat, snakes, mountain lions—not to mention Apaches."

"I appreciate you pointing all that out, Mr. Redman. Now my luggage."

"Damn fool woman," he muttered as he strode over to the wagon. "You want to stay out here, hell, it don't matter to me." He hefted a trunk into the house while Sarah stood a few feet back with her hands folded.

"Your language, Mr. Redman, is quite unnecessary."

He only swore with more skill as he carried in the second trunk. "Nobody's going to be around when it gets dark and you change your mind."

"I won't change my mind, but thank you so much for your concern."

"No concern of mine," he muttered, ignoring her sarcasm. He scooped up the rest of her boxes and dumped them inside the doorway. "Hope you got provisions in there, as well as fancy dresses."

"I assure you I'll be fine." She walked to the doorway herself and turned to him. "Perhaps you could tell me where I might get water."

"There's a stream half a mile due east."

Half a mile? she thought, trying not to show her dismay. "I see." Shading her eyes, she looked out. Jake mumbled another oath, took her by the shoulders and pointed in the opposite direction. "That way's east, Duchess."

"Of course." She stepped back. "Thank you again, Mr. Redman, for all your help. And good day," she added before she closed the door in his face.

She could hear him swearing at her as he unhitched the horses. If she hadn't been so weary, she might have been amused. She was certainly too exhausted to be shocked by the words he used. If she was going to stay, she was going to have to become somewhat accustomed to rough manners. She peeled off her jacket. And, she was going to stay.

If this was all she had left, she was going to make the best of it. Somehow.

She moved to the rounded opening beside the door

that served as a window. From there she watched Jake ride away. He'd left her the wagon and stabled the rented horses with her father's two. For all the good it did her, Sarah thought with a sigh. She hadn't the vaguest idea of how to hitch a team, much less how to drive one.

She continued to watch Jake until he was nothing but a cloud of dust fading in the distance. She was alone. Truly alone. She had no one, and little more than nothing.

No one but herself, she thought. And if she had only that and a mud hut, she'd find a way to make the best of it. Nobody—and certainly not Jake Redman—was going to frighten her away.

Turning, she unbuttoned her cuffs and rolled up her sleeves. The good sisters had always claimed that simple hard work eased the mind and cleansed the soul. She was about to put that claim to the test.

She found the letters an hour later. When she came across them in the makeshift loft that served as a bedroom she wiped her grimy hands as best as she could on the embroidered apron she'd dug out of one of her trunks.

He'd kept them. From the first to the last she'd written, her father had kept her letters to him. The tears threatened again, but she willed them back. Tears would do neither of them any good now. But, oh, it helped more than she could ever have explained that he'd kept her letters. To know now, when she would never see him again, that he had thought of her as she had thought of him.

He must have received the last, the letter telling him she was coming to be with him, shortly before his death. Sarah hadn't mailed it until she'd been about to board the train. She'd told herself it was because she wanted to surprise him, but she'd also wanted to be certain he wouldn't have time to forbid her to come.

Would you have, Papa? she wondered. Or would you finally have been willing to share the truth with me? Had he thought her too weak, too fragile, to share the life he'd chosen? Was she?

Sighing, she looked around. Four bedrooms, and a parlor with the windows facing west, she thought with a quiet laugh. Well, according to Jake Redman, the window did indeed face west. The house itself was hardly bigger than the room she'd shared with Lucilla at school. It was too small, certainly, for all she'd brought with her from Philadelphia, but she'd managed to drag the trunks into one corner. To please herself, she'd taken out a few of her favorite things—one of her wildflower sketches, a delicate blue glass perfume bottle, a pretty petit-point pillow and the china-faced doll her father had sent her for her twelfth birthday.

They didn't make it home, not yet. But they helped.

Setting the letters back in the tin box beside the bed, she rose. She had practical matters to think about now. The first was money. After paying the five dollars, she had only twenty dollars left. She hadn't a clue to how long that would keep her, but she doubted it would be very long. Then there was food. That was of more immediate concern. She'd found some flour, a few cans of beans, some lard and a bottle of whiskey. Pressing a hand to her stomach, Sarah decided she'd have to make do with the beans. All she had to do now was to figure out how to start a fire in the battered-looking stove.

She found a few twigs in the wood box, and a box of

matches. It took her half an hour, a lot of frustration and a few words the sisters would never have approved of before she was forced to admit she was a failure.

Jake Redman. Disgusted, she scowled at the handful of charred twigs. The least the man could have done was to offer to start a cook fire for her and fetch some water. She'd already made the trip down to the stream and back once, managing to scrounge out half a bucket from its stingy trickle.

She'd eat the beans cold. She'd prove to Jake Redman that she could do very well for herself, by herself.

Sarah unsheathed her father's bowie knife, shuddered once at the sight of the vicious blade, then plunged it into the lid of the can until she'd made an opening. Too hungry to care, she sat beside the small stone hearth and devoured the beans.

She'd think of it as an adventure, she told herself. One she could write about to her friends in Philadelphia. A better one, she decided as she looked around the tiny, clean cabin, than those in the penny dreadfuls Lucilla had gotten from the library and hidden in their room.

In those, the heroine had usually been helpless, a victim waiting for the hero to rescue her in any of a dozen dashing manners. Sarah scooped out more beans. Well, she wasn't helpless, and as far as she could tell there wasn't a hero within a thousand miles.

No one would have called Jake Redman heroic— though he'd certainly looked it when he'd ridden beside the coach. He was insulting and ill-mannered. He had cold eyes and a hot temper. Hardly Sarah's idea of a hero. If she had to be rescued—and she certainly didn't—she'd prefer someone smoother, a cavalry officer, perhaps. A man who carried a saber, a gentleman's weapon.

When she'd finished the beans, she hiccuped, wiped her mouth with the back of her hand and leaned back against the hearth only to lose her balance when a stone gave way. Nursing a bruised elbow, she shifted. She would have replaced the stone, but something caught her eye. Crouching again, she reached into the small opening that was now exposed and slowly pulled out a bag.

With her lips caught tight between her teeth, she poured gold coins into her lap. Two hundred and thirty dollars. Sarah pressed both hands to her mouth, swallowed, then counted again. There was no mistake. She hadn't known until that moment how much money could mean. She could buy decent food, fuel, whatever she needed to make her way.

She poured the coins back into the bag and dug into the hole again. This time she found the deed to Sarah's Pride.

What an odd man he must have been, she thought. To hide his possessions beneath a stone.

The last and most precious item she discovered in the hiding place was her father's journal. It delighted her. The small brown book filled with her father's cramped handwriting meant more to Sarah than all the gold coins in Arizona. She hugged it to her as she'd wanted to hug her father. Before she rose with it, she replaced the gold and the deed under the stone.

She would read about one of his days each evening. It would be like a gift, something that each day would bring her a little closer to this man she'd never really known. For now she would go back to the stream, wash as best she could and gather water for the morning.

Jake watched her come out of the cabin with a pail in one hand and a lantern in the other. He'd made himself as comfortable as he needed to be among the rocks. There had been enough jerky and hardtack in his saddlebag to make a passable supper. Not what he'd planned on, exactly, but passable.

He'd be damned if he could figure out why he'd decided to keep an eye on her. The lady wasn't his problem. But even as he'd been cursing her and steering his horse toward town, he'd known he couldn't just ride off and leave her there alone.

Maybe it was because he knew what it was to lose everything. Or because he'd been alone himself for more years then he cared to remember. Or maybe, damn her, it had something to do with the way she'd looked coming down that bluff with her bonnet trailing by the ribbons and tears still drying on her face.

He hadn't thought he had a weak spot. Certainly not where women were concerned. He shoved himself to his feet. He just didn't have anything better to do.

He stayed well behind her. He knew how to move silently, over rock, through brush, in sunlight or in the dark of the moon. That was both a matter of survival and a matter of blood. In his youth he'd spent some years with his grandmother's people and he'd learned more than any white man could have learned in a lifetime about tracking without leaving a mark, about hunting without making a sound.

As for the woman, she was still wearing that fancy skirt with the bustle and shoes that were made for city sidewalks rather than rough ground. Twice Jake had to stop and wait, or even at a crawl he'd have caught up with her.

Probably break an ankle before she was through, he thought. That might be the best thing that could happen to her. Then he'd just cart her on back to town. Couldn't say he'd mind too much picking her up again. She felt good—maybe too good. He had to grin when she shrieked and landed on her fancy bustle because a rabbit darted across her path.

Nope, the pretty little duchess from Philadelphia wasn't going to last a day.

With a hand to her heart, Sarah struggled to her feet. She'd never seen a rabbit that large in her life. With a little sound of distress, she noted that she'd torn the hem of her skirt. How did the women out here manage? she wondered as she began to walk again. In this heat, a corset felt like iron and a fashionable skirt prevented anything but the most delicate walking.

When she reached the stream, she dropped down on a rock and went to work with her buttonhook. It was heaven, absolute heaven, to remove her shoes. There was a blister starting on her heel, but she'd worry about that later. Right now all she could think about was splashing some cool water on her skin.

She glanced around cautiously. There couldn't be anyone there. The sensation of being watched was a natural one, she supposed, when a woman was alone in the wilderness and the sun was going down. She unpinned the cameo at her throat and placed it carefully in her skirt pocket. It was the one thing she had that had belonged to her mother.

Humming to keep herself company, she unbuttoned her blouse and folded it over a rock. With the greatest relief, she unfastened her corset and dropped it on top of the blouse. She could breathe, really breathe, for the first time all day. Hurrying now, she stripped down to her chemise, then unhooked her stockings.

Glorious. She closed her eyes and let out a low sound of pleasure when she stepped into the narrow, ankle-deep stream. The water, trickling down from the mountains, was cold and clear as ice.

What the hell did she think she was doing? Jake let out a low oath and averted his eyes. He didn't need this aggravation. Who would have thought the woman would strip down and play in the water with the night coming on? He glanced back to see her bend down to splash her face. There was nothing between the two of them but shadows and sunlight.

Water dampened the cotton she wore so that it clung here and there. When she bent to scoop up more water, the ruffles at the bodice sagged to tease him. Crouching behind the rock, he began to curse himself instead of her.

His own fault. Didn't he know minding your own business, and only your own, was the best way to get by? He'd just had to be riding along when the Apaches had hit the stage. He'd just had to be the one to tell her about her father. He'd just had to feel obliged to drive her out here. And then to stay.

What he should be doing was getting good and drunk at Carlotta's and spending the night in a feather bed wrestling with a woman. The kind of woman who knew what a man needed and didn't ask a bunch of fool questions. The kind of woman, Jake thought viciously, who didn't expect you to come to tea on Sunday.

He glanced back to see that one of the straps of Sarah's chemise had fallen down her arm and that her legs were gleaming and wet. Her shoulders were pale and smooth and bare.

Too long on the trail, Jake told himself. Too damn long, when a man started to hanker after skinny city women who didn't know east from west.

Sarah filled the pail as best she could, then stepped out of the stream. It was getting dark much more quickly than she'd expected. But she felt almost human again. Even the thought of the corset made her ribs ache, so she ignored it. After slipping on her blouse, she debated donning her shoes and stockings again. There was no one to see or disapprove. Instead, she hitched on her skirt and made a bundle of the rest. With the water sloshing in the pail, she made her way gingerly along the path.

She had to fight the urge to hurry. With sunset, the air was cooling rapidly. And there were sounds. Sounds she didn't recognize or appreciate. Hoots and howls and rustles. Stones dug into her bare feet, and the lantern spread more shadow than light. The half mile back seemed much, much longer than it had before.

Again she had the uncomfortable sensation that someone was watching her. Apaches? Mountain lions? Damn Jake Redman. The little adobe dwelling looked like a haven to her now. Half running, she went through the door and bolted it behind her.

The first coyote sent up a howl to the rising moon.

Sarah shut her eyes. If she lived through the night, she'd swallow her pride and go back to town.

In the rocks not far away, Jake bedded down.

Chapter 3

Soon after sunrise, Sarah awoke, stiff and sore and hungry. She rolled over, wanting to cling to sleep until Lucilla's maid brought the morning chocolate. She'd had the most awful dream about some gray-eyed man carrying her off to a hot, desolate place. He'd been handsome, the way men in dreams were supposed to be, but in a rugged, almost uncivilized way. His skin had been like bronze, taut over his face. He'd had high, almost exotic cheekbones, and the dark shadow of a beard. His hair had been untidy and as black as coal—but thick, quite thick, as it had swept down past his collar. She'd wondered, even in the dream, what it would be like to run her hands through it.

There had been something familiar about him, almost as if she'd known him. In fact, when he'd forced her to kiss him, a name had run through her mind. Then he hadn't had to force her any longer.

Drowsy, Sarah smiled. She would have to tell Lucilla about the dream. They would both laugh about it before they dressed for the day. Lazily she opened her eyes.

This wasn't the rose-and-white room she used whenever she visited Lucilla and her family. Nor was it the familiar bedroom she had had for years at school.

Her father's house, she thought, as everything came back to her. This was her father's house, but her father was dead. She was alone. With an effort, she resisted the urge to bury her face in the pillow and weep again. She had to decide what to do, and in order to decide she had to think clearly.

For some time last night she'd been certain the best thing would be for her to return to town and use the money she had found to book passage east again. At best, Lucilla's family would welcome her. At worst, she could return to the convent. But that had been before she'd begun reading her father's journal. It had taken only the first two pages, the only two she'd allowed herself, to make her doubt.

He'd begun the journal on the day he'd left her to come west. The love and the hope he'd felt had been in every word. And the sadness. He'd still been raw with grief over the death of Sarah's mother.

For the first time she fully understood how devastated he had been by the loss of the woman they'd both shared so briefly. And how inadequate he'd felt at finding himself alone with a little girl. He'd made a promise to his wife on her deathbed that he would see that their daughter was well cared for.

She remembered the words her father had written on the yellowed paper.

She was leaving me. There was nothing I could do to stop it. Toward the end there was so much pain I prayed for God to take her quickly. My Ellen, my tiny, delicate Ellen. Her thoughts were all for me, and our sweet Sarah. I promised her. The only comfort I could give was my promise. Our daughter would have everything Ellen wanted for her. Proper schooling and church on Sunday. She would be raised the way my Ellen would have raised her. Like a lady. One day she'd have a fine house and a father she could be proud of.

He'd come here to try, Sarah thought as she tossed back the thin blanket. And she supposed he'd done as well as he could. Now she had to figure what was best. And if she was going to think, first she needed to eat.

After she'd dressed in her oldest skirt and blouse, she took stock of the cupboard again. She could not, under any circumstances, face another meal of cold beans. Perhaps he had a storage cellar somewhere, a smoke-house, anything. Sarah pushed open the door and blinked in the blinding sunlight.

At first she thought it was a mirage. But mirages didn't carry a scent, did they? This one smelled of meat roasting and coffee brewing. And what she saw was Jake Redman sitting cross-legged by a fire ringed with stones. Gathering up her skirt, she forgot her hunger long enough to stride over to him.

"What are you doing here?"

He glanced up and gave her the briefest of nods. He poured coffee from a small pot into a dented tin cup. "Having breakfast."

"You rode all the way out here to have breakfast?" She didn't know what it was he was turning on the spit, but her stomach was ready for just about anything.

"Nope." He tested the meat and judged it done. "Never left." He jerked his head in the direction of the rocks. "Bedded down over there."

"There?" Sarah eyed the rocks with some amazement. "Whatever for?"

He looked up again. The look in his eyes made her hands flutter nervously. It made her feel, though it was foolish, that he knew how she looked stripped down to her chemise. "Let's say it was a long ride back to town."

"I hardly expect you to watch over me, Mr. Redman. I explained that I could take... What is that?"

Jake was eating with his fingers and with obvious enjoyment. "Rabbit."

"Rabbit?" Sarah wrinkled her nose at the idea, but her stomach betrayed her. "I suppose you trapped it on my property."

So it was her property already. "Might've."

"If that's the case, the least you could do is offer to share."

Jake obligingly pulled off a hunk of meat. "Help yourself."

"Don't you have any... Never mind." When in Rome, Sarah decided. Taking the meat and the coffee he offered, she sat down on a rock.

"Get yourself some supper last night?"

"Yes, thank you." Never, never in her life, had she tasted anything better than this roast rabbit in the already-sweltering morning. "You're an excellent cook, Mr. Redman."

"I get by." He offered her another hunk. This time she didn't hesitate.

"No, really." She caught herself talking with her mouth full, and she didn't care. "This is delightful." Because she doubted that his saddlebags held any linens, she licked her fingers.

"Better than a can of cold beans, anyway."

She glanced up sharply, but he wasn't even looking at her. "I suppose." She'd never had breakfast with a man before, and she decided it would be proper to engage in light conversation. "Tell me, Mr. Redman, what is your profession?"

"Never gave it much thought."

"But surely you must have some line of work."

"Nope." He leaned back against a rock and, taking out his pouch of tobacco, proceeded to roll a cigarette. She looked as fresh and neat as a daisy, he thought. You'd have thought she'd spent the night in some high-priced hotel instead of a mud hut.

Apparently making conversation over a breakfast of roasted rabbit took some skill. Patiently she smoothed her skirts and tried again. "Have you lived in Arizona long?"

"Why?"

"I—" The cool, flat look he sent her had her fumbling. "Simple curiosity."

"I don't know about back in Philadelphia." Jake took out a match, scraped it on the rock and lit the twisted end of his cigarette, studying her all the while. "But around here people don't take kindly to questions."

"I see." Her back had stiffened. She'd never encountered anyone to whom rudeness came so easily. "In a civilized society, a casual question is merely a way to begin a conversation."

"Around here it's a way to start a fight." He drew on the cigarette. "You want to fight with me, Duchess?"

"I'll thank you to stop referring to me by that name."

He grinned at her again, but lazily, the brim of his hat shadowing his eyes. "You look like one, especially when you're riled."

Her chin came up. She couldn't help it. But she answered him in calm, even tones. "I assure you, I'm not at all riled. Although you have, on several occasions already, been rude and difficult and annoying. Where I come from, Mr. Redman, a woman is entitled to a bit more charm and gallantry from a man."

"That so?" Her mouth dropped open when he slowly drew out his gun. "Don't move."

Move? She couldn't even breathe. She'd only called him rude and, sweet Mary, he was going to shoot her. "Mr. Redman, I don't—"

The bullet exploded against the rock a few inches away from her. With a shriek, she tumbled into the dirt. When she found the courage to look up, Jake was standing and lifting something dead and hideous from the rock.

"Rattler," he said easily. When she moaned and started to cover her eyes, he reached down and hauled her to her feet. "I'd take a good look," he suggested, still holding the snake in front of her. "If you stay around here, you're going to see plenty more."

It was the disdain in his voice that had her fighting off the swoon. With what little voice she had left, she asked, "Would you kindly dispose of that?"

With a muttered curse, he tossed it aside, then began to smother the fire. Sarah felt her breakfast rising uneasily and waited for it to settle. "It appears you saved my life."

"Yeah, well, don't let it get around."

"I won't, I assure you." She drew herself up straight, hiding her trembling hands in the folds of her skirts. "I appreciate the meal, Mr. Redman. Now, if you'll excuse me, I have a number of things to do."

"You can start by getting yourself into the wagon. I'll drive you back to town."

"I appreciate the offer. As a matter of fact, I would be grateful. I need some supplies."

"Look, there's got to be enough sense in that head of yours for you to see you don't belong out here. It's a two-hour drive into town. There's nothing out here but rattlers and coyotes."

She was afraid he was right. The night she'd spent in the cabin had been the loneliest and most miserable of her life. But somewhere between the rabbit and the snake she'd made up her mind. Matt Conway's daughter wasn't going to let all his efforts and his dreams turn to dust. She was staying, Lord help her.

"My father lived here. This place was obviously important to him. I intend to stay." She doubted Jake Redman had enough heart to understand her reasons.

"Now, if you'd be good enough to hitch up the wagon, I'll go change."

"Change what?"

"Why, my dress, of course. I can hardly go into town like this."

He cast a glance over her. She already looked dolled-up enough for a church social in her crisp white blouse and gingham skirt. He'd never known gingham to look quite so good on a woman before.

"Lone Bluff ain't Philadelphia. It ain't anyplace. You want the wagon hitched, I'll oblige you, but you'd better watch how it's done, because there's not going to be anyone around to do it for you next time." With that, he slung his saddlebags over his shoulder and walked away.

Very well, she thought after one last deep breath. He was quite right. It was time she learned how to do things for herself. The sooner she learned, the sooner she'd have no more need of him.

With her head held high, she followed him. She watched him guide the team out. It seemed easy enough. You simply hooked this and tied that and the deed was done. Men, she thought with a little smile. They always exaggerated the most basic chores.

"Thank you, Mr. Redman. If you'll wait just a moment, I'll be ready to go."

Didn't the woman know anything? Jake tipped his hat forward. He'd driven her out of town yesterday. If he drove her back this morning her reputation would be ruined. Even Lone Bluff had its standards. Since she'd decided to stay, at least temporarily, she'd need all the support she could get from the town women.

"I got business of my own, ma'am."

"But—" He was already moving off to saddle his own horse. Setting her teeth, Sarah stamped inside. She added another twenty dollars to what she carried in her reticule. As an afterthought she took down the rifle her father had left on the wall. She hadn't the least idea how to use it, was certain she wouldn't be able to in even the most dire circumstances, but she felt better having it.

Jake was mounted and waiting when she came out. "The road will lead you straight into town," he told her as she fastened her bonnet. "If you give Lucius a dollar he'll drive back out with you, then take the wagon and team back to the livery. Matt's got two horses of his own in the stables. Someone from town's been keeping an eye on them."

"A dollar." As if it were spun glass, she set the rifle in the wagon. "You charged me five."

He grinned at her. "I'm not Lucius." With a tip of his hat, he rode off.

It didn't take her long to climb up into the wagon. But she had to gather her courage before she touched the reins. Though she considered herself an excellent horse-woman, she'd never driven a team before. You've ridden behind them, she reminded herself as she picked up the reins. How difficult can it be?

She took the horses—or they took her—in a circle three times before she managed to head them toward the road.

Jake sat on his horse and watched her from a ridge. It was the best laugh he'd had in months.

* * *

By the time she reached Lone Bluff, Sarah was sweating profusely, her hands felt raw and cramped and her lower back was on fire. In front of the dry goods store she climbed down on legs that felt like water. After smoothing her skirts and patting her forehead dry, she spotted a young boy whittling a stick.

"Young man, do you know a man named Lucius?"

"Everybody knows old Lucius."

Satisfied, Sarah drew a coin out of her bag. "If you can find Lucius and tell him Miss Sarah Conway wishes to see him, you can have this penny."

The boy eyed it, thinking of peppermint sticks. "Yes, ma'am." He was off at a run.

At least children seemed about the same, east or west.

Sarah entered the store. There were several customers milling around, looking over the stock and gossiping. They all stopped to stare at Sarah before going back to their business. The young woman behind the counter came around to greet her.

"Good morning. May I help you?"

"Yes, I'm Sarah Conway."

"I know." When the pretty brunette smiled, dimples flashed in her cheeks. She was already envying Sarah her bonnet. "You arrived on the stage yesterday. I'm very sorry about your father. Everyone liked Matt."

"Thank you." Sarah found herself smiling back. "I'm going to need a number of supplies."

"Are you really going to stay out there, at Matt's place? Alone?"

"Yes. At least for now."

"I'd be scared to death." The brunette gave her an appraising look, then offered a hand. "I'm Liza Cody. No relation."

"I beg your pardon?"

"To Buffalo Bill. Most people ask. Welcome to Lone Bluff."

"Thank you."

With Liza's help. Sarah began to gather supplies and introductions. Within twenty minutes she'd nodded to half the women in Lone Bluff, been given a recipe for biscuits and been asked her opinion of the calico fabric just arrived from St. Joe.

Her spirits rose dramatically. Perhaps the women dressed less fashionably than their counterparts in the East, but they made her feel welcome.

"Ma'am."

Sarah turned to see Lucius, hat in hand. Beside him, the young boy was nearly dancing in anticipation of the penny. The moment it was in his hand, he raced to the jars of hard candy and began to negotiate.

"Mr...."

"Just Lucius, ma'am."

"Lucius, I was told you might be willing to drive my supplies back for me, then return the wagon and team to the livery."

He pushed his chaw into his cheek and considered. "Well, now, maybe I would."

"I'd be willing to give you a dollar for your trouble."

He grinned, showing a few yellowed—and several missing—teeth. "Glad to help, Miss Conway."

"Perhaps you'd begin by loading my supplies."

Leaving him to it, Sarah turned back to Liza. "Miss Cody."

"Liza, please."

"Liza, I wonder if you might have any tea, and I would dearly love some fresh eggs."

"Don't get much call for tea, but we've got some in the back." Liza opened the door to the rear storeroom. Three fat-bellied puppies ran out. "John Cody, you little monster. I told you to keep these pups outside."

Laughing, Sarah crouched down to greet them. "Oh, they're adorable."

"One's adorable, maybe," Liza muttered. As usual, her young brother was nowhere in sight when she needed him. "Three's unmanageable. Just last night they chewed through a sack of meal. Pop finds out, he'll take a strap to Johnny."

A brown mutt with a black circle around his left eye jumped into Sarah's lap. And captured her heart. "You're a charmer, aren't you?" She laughed as he bathed her face.

"A nuisance is more like it."

"Will you sell one?"

"Sell?" Liza stretched to reach the tea on a high shelf. "My pop'd pay you to take one."

"Really?" With the brown pup cradled in her arms, Sarah stood again. "I'd love to have one. I could use the company."

Liza added the tea and eggs to Sarah's total. "You want that one, you take it right along." She grinned when the pup licked Sarah's face again. "He certainly seems taken with you."

"I'll take very good care of him." Balancing the dog,

she took out the money to pay her bill. "Thank you for everything."

Liza counted out the coins before she placed them in the cash drawer and took out Sarah's change. Pop would be pleased, she thought. Not only because of the pup, but because Miss Conway was a cash customer. Liza was pleased because Sarah was young and pretty and would surely know everything there was to know about the latest fashions.

"It's been nice meeting you, Miss Conway."

"Sarah."

Liza smiled again and walked with Sarah to the door. "Maybe I'll ride out and see you, if you don't mind."

"I'd love it. Any time at all."

Abruptly Liza lifted a hand to pat her hair. "Good morning, Mr. Carlson."

"Liza, you're looking pretty as ever." She blushed and fluttered, though Carlson's eyes were on Sarah.

"Samuel Carlson, this is Sarah Conway."

"Delighted." Carlson's smile made his pale, handsome face even more attractive. It deepened the already-brilliant blue of his eyes. When he lifted Sarah's hand to his lips in a smooth, cavalier gesture, she was doubly glad she'd come into town.

Apparently Lone Bluff had some gentlemen after all. Samuel Carlson was slim and well dressed in a beautiful black riding coat and a spotless white shirt. His trim mustache was the same rich brown as his well-groomed hair. He had, as a gentleman should, swept off his hat at the introduction. It was a particularly fine hat, Sarah thought, black like his coat, with a silver chain for a band.

"My deepest sympathies for your loss, Miss Conway. Your father was a fine man and a good friend."

"Thank you. It's been comforting for me to learn he was well thought of."

The daughter was certainly a pretty addition to a dust hole like Lone Bluff, he thought. "Word around town is that you'll be staying with us for a while." He reached over to scratch the puppy's ears and was rewarded with a low growl.

"Hush, now." Sarah smiled an apology. "Yes, I've decided to stay. At least for the time being."

"I hope you'll let me know if there's anything I can do to help." He smiled again. "Undoubtedly life here isn't what you're used to."

The way he said it made it clear that it was a compliment. Mr. Carlson was obviously a man of the world, and of some means. "Thank you." She handed the puppy to Lucius and was gratified when Carlson assisted her into the wagon. "It was a pleasure to meet you, Mr. Carlson."

"The pleasure was mine, Miss Conway."

"Goodbye, Liza. I hope you'll come and visit soon." Sarah settled the puppy on her lap. She considered it just her bad luck that she glanced across the street at that moment. Jake was there, one hand hooked in his pocket, leaning against a post, watching. With an icy nod, she acknowledged him, then stared straight ahead as Lucius clucked to the horses.

When the wagon pulled away, the men studied each other. There was no nod of acknowledgment. They simply watched, cool and cautious, across the dusty road.

* * *

Sarah felt positively triumphant. As she stored her supplies, the puppy circled her legs, apparently every bit as pleased as she with the arrangement. Her nights wouldn't be nearly so lonely now, with the dog for company. She'd met people, was perhaps even on the way to making friends. Her cupboard was full, and Lucius had been kind enough to show her how to fire up the old cookstove.

Tonight, after supper, she was going to write to Lucilla and Mother Superior. She would read another page or two from her father's journal before she curled up under the freshly aired blanket.

Jake Redman be damned, she thought as she bent to tickle the pup's belly. She was making it.

With a glass of whiskey at his fingertips, Jake watched Carlotta work the room. She sure was something. Her hair was the color of gold nuggets plucked from a riverbed, and her lips were as red as the velvet drapes that hung in her private room.

She was wearing red tonight, something tight that glittered as it covered her long, curvy body and clung to her smooth white breasts. Her shoulders were bare. Jake had always thought that a woman's shoulders were enough to drive a man to distraction.

He thought of Sarah, standing ankle-deep in a stream with water glistening on her skin.

He took another gulp of whiskey.

Carlotta's girls were dressed to kill, as well. The men in the Silver Star were getting their money's worth. The piano rang out, and the whiskey and the laughter poured.

The way he figured it, Carlotta ran one of the best houses in Arizona. Maybe one of the best west of the Mississippi. The whiskey wasn't watered much, and the girls weren't bad. A man could almost believe they enjoyed their work. As for Carlotta, Jake figured she enjoyed it just fine.

Money came first with her. He knew, because she'd once had enough to drink to tell him that she took a healthy cut of all her girls' pay. If the man one of her girls was with decided to slip her a little extra, that was just fine with Carlotta. She took a cut of that, as well.

She had dreams of moving her business to San Francisco and buying a place with crystal chandeliers, gilt mirrors and red carpets. Carlotta favored red. But for now, like the rest of them, Carlotta was stuck in Lone Bluff.

Tipping back more whiskey, Jake watched her. She moved like a queen, her full red lips always smiling, her cool blue eyes always watching. She was making sure her girls were persuading the men to buy them plenty of drinks. What the bartender served the working girls was hardly more than colored water, but the men paid, and paid happily, before they moved along to one of the narrow rooms upstairs.

Hell of a business, Jake thought as he helped himself to one of the cigars Carlotta provided for her paying customers. She had them shipped all the way from Cuba, and they had a fine, rich taste. Jake had no doubt she added to the price of her whiskey and her girls to pay for them. Business was business.

One of the girls sidled over to light the cigar for him. He just shook his head at the invitation. She was warm and ripe and smelled like a bouquet of roses. For the life of him he couldn't figure out why he wasn't interested.

"You're going to hurt the girls' feelings." Perfume trailing behind her, Carlotta joined Jake at the table. "Don't you see anything you like?"

He tipped his chair back against the wall. "See plenty I like."

She laughed and lifted a hand in a subtle signal. "You going to buy me a drink, Jake?" Before he could answer, one of the girls was bringing over a new bottle and a glass. No watered-down liquor for Carlotta. "Haven't seen you around in a while."

"Haven't been around."

Carlotta took a drink and let it sweep through her system. She'd take liquor over a man any day. "Going to stay around?"

"Might."

"Heard there was a little trouble on the stage yesterday. It's not like you to do good deeds, Jake." She drank again and smiled at him. In a movement as smooth as the liquor she drank, she dropped a hand to his thigh. "That's what I like about you."

"Just happened to be there."

"Also heard Matt Conway's daughter's in town." Smiling, she took the cigar from him and took a puff. "You working for her?"

"Why?"

"Word around is that you drove her on out to his place." She slowly blew out a stream of smoke from between her painted lips. "Can't see you digging in rock for gold, Jake, when it's easier just to take it."

"Far as I remember, there was never enough gold in that rock to dig for." He took the cigar back and clamped it between his teeth. "You know different?"

"I only know what I hear, and I don't hear much about Conway." She poured a second drink and downed it. She didn't want to talk about Matt Conway's mine or about what she knew. Something in the air tonight, she decided. Made her restless. Maybe she needed more than whiskey after all. "Glad you're back, Jake. Things have been too quiet around here."

Two men hankering after the same girl started to scuffle. Carlotta's tall black servant tossed them both out. She just smiled and poured a third drink. "If you're not interested in any of my girls, we could make other arrangements." She lifted the small glass in a salute before she knocked it back. "For old times' sake."

Jake looked at her. Her eyes glittered against her white skin. Her lips were parted. Above the flaming red of her dress, her breasts rose and fell invitingly. He knew what she could do to a man, with a man, when the mood was on her. It baffled and infuriated him that she didn't stir him in the least.

"Maybe some other time." He rose and, after dropping a few coins on the table, strolled out.

Carlotta's eyes hardened as she watched him. She only offered herself to a privileged few. And she didn't like to be rejected.

* * *

With the puppy snoozing at her feet, Sarah closed her father's journal. He'd written about an Indian attack on the wagon train and his own narrow escape. In simple, often stark terms, he'd written of the slaughter, the terror and the waste. Yet even after that he'd gone on, because he'd wanted to make something of himself. For her.

Shivering a bit despite her shawl, she rose to replace the book beneath the stone. If she had read those words while still in Philadelphia, she would have thought them an exaggeration. She was coming to know better.

With a half sigh, she looked down at her hands. They were smooth and well tended. They were, she was afraid, woefully inadequate to the task of carving out a life here.

It was only the night that made her feel that way, Sarah told herself as she moved to check the bolt on the door. She'd done all she could that day, and it had been enough. She'd driven to town alone, stocked the cabin and replanted the vegetable garden. Her back ached enough to tell her she'd put in a full day. Tomorrow she'd start again.

The lonely howl of a coyote made her heart thud. Gathering the puppy to her breast, she climbed up for bed.

She was in her night shift when the dog started to bark and growl. Exasperated, she managed to grab him before he could leap from the loft.

"You'll break your neck." When he strained against her hold and continued to yelp, she took him in her arms. "All right, all right. If you have to go out, I'll let you out, but you might have let me know before I went to bed." Nuzzling him, she climbed down from the loft again. She saw the fire through the window and ran to the door. "Oh, my God."

The moment she yanked it open the puppy ran out, barking furiously. With her hands to her cheeks, Sarah watched the fire rise up and eat at the old, dry wood of the shed. A scream, eerily like a woman's, pierced the night.

Her father's horses. Following instinct alone, she ran.

The horses were already wild-eyed, stamping and screaming in their stalls. Muttering a prayer, Sarah dragged the first one out and slapped its flank. The fire was moving fast, racing up the walls and onto the roof. The hay had already caught and was burning wildly.

Eyes stinging from the smoke, she groped her way to the second stall. Coughing, swearing, she fought the terrified horse as it reared and shoved against her. Then she screamed herself when a flaming plank fell behind her. Fire licked closer and closer to the hem of her shift.

Whipping off her shawl, she tossed it over the horse's eyes and dragged them both out of the shed.

Blinded by smoke, she crawled to safety. Behind her she could hear the walls collapse, could hear the roar of flames consuming wood. Gone. It was gone. She wanted to beat her fists in the dirt and weep.

It could spread. The terror of that had her pushing up onto her hands and knees. Somehow she had to prevent the fire from spreading. She caught the sound of a horse running hard and had nearly gained her feet when something slammed into her.

Chapter 4

The night was clear, with a sharp-edged half-moon and white pinpoint stars. Jake rode easily, arguing with himself.

It was stupid, just plain stupid, for him to be heading out when he could be snuggled up against Carlotta right this minute. Except Carlotta didn't snuggle. What she did was more like devouring. With her, sex was fast and hot and uncomplicated. After all, business was business.

At least he knew what Carlotta was and what to expect from her. She used men like poker chips. That was fine with Jake. Carlotta wouldn't expect posies or boxes of chocolates or Sunday calls.

Sarah Conway was a whole different matter. A woman like that wanted a man to come courting wearing a stiff collar. And probably a tie. He snorted and kicked his mount into a trot. You'd have to see that your boots were shined so you could sit around making fancy talk. With her, sex would be… He swore viciously, and the mustang pricked up his ears. You didn't have sex with a woman like that. You didn't even think about it. And even if you did…

Well, he just wasn't interested.

So what the hell was he doing riding out to her place in the middle of the night?

"Stupid," he muttered to his horse.

Overhead, a nighthawk dived and killed with hardly a sound. Life was survival, and survival meant ruthlessness. Jake understood that, accepted it. But Sarah… He shook his head. Survival to her was making sure her ribbons matched her dress.

The best thing he could do was to turn around now and head back to town. Maybe ride right on through town and go down to Tombstone for a spell. He could pick up a job there if he had a mind to. Better yet, he could travel up to the mountains, where the air was cool and smelled of pine. There wasn't anything or anyone holding him in Lone Bluff. He was a free agent, and that was the way he intended to stay.

But he didn't turn his horse around.

When he got back from the mountains, he mused—if he got back—Miss Sarah Conway, with her big brown eyes and her white shoulders, would be long gone. Just plain stubbornness was keeping her here now, anyway. Even stubbornness had to give way sometime. If she was gone, maybe he'd stop having this feeling that he was about to make a big mistake.

As far as he could see, the biggest mistakes men made were over three things—money, whiskey and women. None of the three had ever meant enough to him to worry or fight over. He didn't plan on changing that.

Even if this woman *was* different. Somehow. That was what bothered him the most. He'd always been able to figure people. It had helped keep him alive all these years. He couldn't figure Sarah Conway, or what it was about her that made him want to see that she was safe. Maybe he was getting soft, but he didn't like to think so.

He couldn't help feeling for her some, traveling all this way just to find out her father was dead. And he had to admire the way she was sticking it out, staying at the old mine. It was stupid, he mused, but you had to admire it.

With a shrug, he kept riding. He was nearly to the Conway place, anyway. He might as well take a look and make sure she hadn't shot her foot off with her daddy's rifle.

He smelled the fire before he saw it. His head came up, like a wolf's when it scents an enemy. In a similar move, the mustang reared and showed the whites of his eyes. When he caught the first flicker of flame, he kicked the horse into a run. What had the damn fool woman done now?

There had only been a few times in his life when he had experienced true fear. He didn't care for the taste of it. And he tasted it now, as his mind conjured up the image of Sarah trapped inside the burning house, the oil she'd undoubtedly spilled spreading the fire hot and fast.

Another image came back to him, an old one, an image of fire and weeping and gunplay. He'd known fear then, too. Fear and hate, and an anguish he'd sworn he'd never feel again.

There was some small relief when he saw that it was the shed burning and not the house. The heat from it roared out as the last of the roof collapsed. He slowed his horse when he spotted two riders heading up into the rocks. His gun was already drawn, his blood already cold, before he saw Sarah lying on the ground. His horse was still moving when he slid from the saddle and ran to her.

Her face was as pale as the moon, and she smelled of smoke. As he knelt beside her, a small brown dog began to snarl at him. Jake brushed it aside when it nipped him.

"If you were going to do any guarding, you're too late."

His mouth set in a grim line, he pressed a hand to her heart. Something moved in him when he felt its slow beat. Gently he lifted her head. And felt the blood, warm on his fingers. He looked up at the rocks again, his eyes narrowed and icy. As carefully as he could, he picked her up and carried her inside.

There was no place to lay her comfortably but the cot. The puppy began to whine and jump at the ladder after Jake carried her up. Jake shushed him again and, grateful that Sarah had at least had the sense to bring in fresh water, prepared to dress her wound.

Dazed and aching, Sarah felt something cool on her head. For a moment she thought it was Sister Angelina, the soft-voiced nun who had nursed her through a fever when she had been twelve. Though she hurt, hurt all over, it was comforting to be there, safe in her own bed, knowing that someone was there to take care of her and make things right again. Sister would sometimes sing to her and would always, when she needed it, hold her hand.

Moaning a little, Sarah groped for Sister Angelina's hand. The one that closed over hers was as hard as iron. Confused, fooled for a minute into thinking her father had come back for her, Sarah opened her eyes.

At first everything was vague and wavering, as though she were looking through water. Slowly she focused on a face. She remembered the face, with its sharp lines and its taut, bronzed skin. A lawless face. She'd dreamed of it, hadn't she? Unsure, she lifted a hand to it. It was rough, unshaven and warm. Gray eyes, she thought dizzily. Gray eyes and a gray hat. Yes, she'd dreamed of him.

She managed a whisper. "Don't. Don't kiss me."

The face smiled. It was such a quick, flashing and appealing smile that she almost wanted to return it. "I guess I can control myself. Drink this."

He lifted the cup to her lips, and she took a first greedy sip. Whiskey shot through her system. "That's horrible. I don't want it."

"Put some color back in your cheeks." But he set the cup aside.

"I just want to…" But the whiskey had shocked her brain enough to clear it. Jake had to hold her down to keep her from scrambling out of bed. Her shift tangled around her knees and drooped over one shoulder.

"Hold on. You stand up now, you're going to fall on that pretty face of yours."

"Fire." She coughed, gasping from the pain in her

throat. To balance herself, she grabbed him, then dropped her head weakly on his chest. "There's a fire."

"I know." Relief and pleasure surged through him as he stroked her hair. Her cheek was nestled against his heart as if it belonged there. "It's pretty well done now."

"It might spread. I've got to stop it."

"It's not going to spread." He eased her back with a gentleness that would have surprised her if she'd been aware of it. "Nothing to feed it, no wind to carry it. You lost the shed, that's all."

"I got the horses out," she murmured. Her head was whirling and throbbing. But his voice—his voice and the stroke of his hands soothed her everywhere. Comforted, she let her eyes close. "I wasn't sure I could."

"You did fine." Because he wanted to say more and didn't know how, he passed the cloth over her face. "You'd better rest now."

"Don't go." She reached for his hand again and brought it to her cheek. "Please don't go."

"I'm not going anywhere." He brushed the hair away from her face while he fought his own demons. "Go on to sleep." He needed her to. If she opened her eyes and looked at him again, if she touched him again, he was going to lose.

"The puppy was barking. I thought he needed to go out, so I—" She came to herself abruptly. He could see it in the way her eyes flew open. "Mr. Redman! What are you doing here? Here," she repeated, scandalized, as she glanced around the loft. "I'm not dressed."

He dropped the cloth back in the bowl. "It's been a trial not to notice." She was coming back, all right, he thought as he watched her eyes fire up. It was a pleasure to watch it. With some regret, he picked up the blanket and tossed it over her. "Feel better?"

"Mr. Redman." Her voice was stiff with embarrassment. "I don't entertain gentlemen in my private quarters."

He picked up the cup of whiskey and took a drink himself. Now that she seemed back to normal, it hit him how scared he'd been. Bone-scared. "Ain't much entertaining about dressing a head wound."

Sarah pushed herself up on her elbows, and the room reeled. With a moan, she lifted her fingers to the back of her neck. "I must have hit my head."

"Must have." He thought of the riders, but said nothing. "Since I picked you up off the ground and carted you all the way up here, don't you figure I'm entitled to know what happened tonight?"

"I don't really know." With a long sigh, she leaned back against the pillow she'd purchased only that morning. He was entitled to the story, she supposed. In any case, she wanted to tell someone. "I'd already retired for the night when the puppy began to bark. He seemed determined to get out, so I climbed down. I saw the fire. I don't know how it could have started. It was still light when I fed the stock, so I never even had a lamp over there."

Jake had his own ideas, but he bided his time. Sarah lifted a hand to her throbbing head and allowed herself the luxury of closing her eyes. "I ran over to get the horses out. The place was going up so fast. I've never seen anything like it. The roof was coming down, and the horses were terrified. They wouldn't come out. I'd read somewhere that horses are so frightened by fire they just panic and burn alive. I couldn't have stood that."

"So you went in after them."

"They were screaming." Her brows drew together as she remembered. "It sounded like women screaming. It was horrible."

"Yeah, I know." He remembered another barn, another fire, when the horses hadn't been so lucky.

"I remember falling when I got out the last time. I think I was choking on the smoke. I started to get up. I don't know what I was going to do. Then something hit me, I guess. One of the horses, perhaps. Or perhaps I simply fell again." She opened her eyes and studied him. He was sitting on her bed, his hair disheveled and his eyes dark and intense. Beautiful, she thought. Then she wondered if she was delirious. "Then you were here. Why are you here?"

"Riding by this way. Saw the fire." He looked into the cup of whiskey. If he was going to sit here much longer, watching what the lamplight did to her skin, he was going to need more than a cupful. "I also saw two riders heading away."

"Away?" Righteous indignation had her sitting up again, despite the headache. "You mean someone was here and didn't try to help?"

Jake gave her a long, even look. She looked so fragile, like something you put behind glass in a parlor. Fragile or not, she had to know what she was up against. "I figure they weren't here to help." He watched as the realization seeped in. There was a flicker of fear. That was what he'd expected. What he hadn't counted on and was forced to admire was the passion in her eyes.

"They came on my land? Burned down my shed? Why?"

She'd forgotten that she was wearing no more than a shift, forgotten that it was past midnight and that she was alone with a man. She sat up, and the blanket dropped to pool at her waist. Her small, round breasts rose and fell with her temper. Her hair was loose. He'd never seen it that way before. Until that moment he hadn't taken the time or the trouble to really look. A man's hands could get lost in hair like that. The thought ran through his mind and was immediately banished. It glowed warm in the lamplight, sliding over her right shoulder and streaming down her back. Anger had brought the color back to her face and the golden glow back to her eyes.

He finished off the whiskey, reminding himself that he'd do well to keep his mind on the business at hand. "Seems logical to figure they wanted to give you some trouble, maybe make you think twice about keeping this place."

"That doesn't make any sense." She leaned forward. Jake shifted uncomfortably when her thin lawn gown gapped at the throat. "Why should anyone care about an adobe house and a few sagging sheds?"

Jake set the cup down again. "You forgot the mine. Some people'll do a lot more than set a fire for gold."

With a sound of disgust, Sarah propped her elbows on her knees. "Gold? Do you think my father would have lived like this if there'd been any significant amount of gold?"

"If you believe that, why are you staying?"

The brooding look left her eyes as she glanced back at him. "I don't expect you to understand. This is all I have. All I have left of my father is this place and a gold watch." She took the watch from the tilting table beside the bed and closed her hand around it. "I intend to keep what's mine. If someone's played a nasty joke—"

Jake interrupted her. "Might've been a joke. It's more likely somebody thinks this place is worth more than you say. Trying to burn horses alive and hitting women isn't considered much of a joke. Even out here."

She lifted a hand to the wound on her head. He was saying someone had struck her. And he was right, she acknowledged with a quick shudder. He was undoubtedly right. "No one's going to scare me off my land. Tomorrow I'll report this incident to the sheriff, and I'll find a way to protect my property."

"Just what way is that?"

"I don't know." She tightened her grip on the watch. The look in her eyes said everything. "But I'll find it."

Maybe she would, he thought. And maybe, since he didn't care much for people setting fires, he'd help her. "Someone might be offering to buy this place from you," Jake murmured, thinking ahead.

"I'm not selling. And I'm not running. If and when I return to Philadelphia, it will be because I've decided that's what I want to do, not because I've been frightened away."

That was an attitude he could respect. "Fair enough. Since it appears you're going to have your hands full tomorrow, you'd best get some sleep."

"Yes." Sleep? How could she possibly close her eyes? What if they came back?

"If it's all the same to you, I'll bunk down outside."

Her eyes lifted to his and held them. The quiet understanding in them made her want to rest her head on his shoulder. He'd take care of her. She had only to ask. But she couldn't ask.

"Of course, you're welcome to. Mr. Redman…" She remembered belatedly to drag the blanket up to her shoulders. "I'm in your debt again. It seems you've come to my aid a number of times in a very short acquaintance."

"I didn't have to go out of my way much." He started to rise, then thought better of it. "I got a question for you."

Because she was feeling awkward again, she offered him a small, polite smile. "Yes?"

"Why'd you ask me not to kiss you?"

Her fingers tightened on the blanket. "I beg your pardon?"

"When you were coming to, you took a good, long look at me, and then you told me not to kiss me."

She could feel the heat rising to her cheeks. Dignity, she told herself. Even under circumstances like these, a woman must keep her dignity. "Apparently I wasn't in my right senses."

He thought that through and then unnerved her by smiling. For his own satisfaction, he reached out to touch the ends of her hair. "A man could take that two ways."

She sputtered. The lamplight shifted across his face. Light, then shadow. It made him look mysterious, exciting. Forbidden. Sarah found it almost as difficult to breathe as she did when her stays were too tight. "Mr. Redman, I assure you—"

"It made me think." He was close now, so close that she could feel his breath flutter over her lips. They parted, seemingly of their own volition. He took the time—a heartbeat, two—to flick his gaze down to them. "Maybe you've been wondering about me kissing you."

"Certainly not." But her denial lacked the ring of truth. They both knew it.

"I'll have to give it some thought myself." The trouble was, he'd been giving it too much thought already. The way she looked right now, with her hair loose around her shoulders and her eyes dark, just a little scared, made him not want to think at all. He knew that if he touched her, head wound or not, he'd climb right in the bed with her and take whatever he wanted.

He was going to kiss her. Her head swam with the idea. He had only to lean closer and his mouth would be on hers. Hard. Somehow she knew it would be hard, firm, masterful. He could take her in his arms right now and there would be nothing she could do about it. Maybe there was nothing she wanted to do about it.

Then he was standing. For the first time she noticed that he had to stoop so that his head didn't brush the roof. His body blocked the light. Her heart was thudding so hard that she was certain he must hear it. For the life of her, she couldn't be sure if it was fear or excitement. Slowly he leaned over and blew out the lamp.

In the dark, he moved down from the loft and out into the night.

Shivering, Sarah huddled under the blanket. The man was— She didn't have words to describe him.

The only thing she was certain of was that she wouldn't sleep a wink.

She went out like a light.

When Sarah woke, her head felt as though it had been split open and filled with a drum-and-bugle corps. Moaning, she sat on the edge of the cot and cradled her aching head in her hands. She wished she could believe it had all been a nightmare, but the pounding at the base of her skull, and the rust-colored water in the bowl, said differently.

Gingerly she began to dress. The best she could do for herself at the moment was to see how bad the damage was and pray the horses came back. She doubted she could afford two more on her meager budget. In deference to her throbbing head, she tied her hair back loosely with a ribbon. Even the thought of hairpins made her grimace.

The power of the sun had her gasping. Small red dots danced in front of her eyes and her vision wavered and dimmed. She leaned against the door, gathering her strength, before she stepped out.

The shed was gone. In its place was rubble, a mass of black, charred wood. Determined, Sarah crossed over to it. She could still smell the smoke. If she closed her eyes she could hear the terrifying sound of fire crackling over dry wood. And the heat. She'd never forget the heat—the intensity of it, the meanness of it.

It hadn't been much of a structure, but it had been hers. In a civilized society a vandal was made to pay for the destruction of property. Arizona Territory or Philadelphia, she meant to see that justice was done here. But for now she was alone.

Alone. She stood in the yard and listened. Never before had she heard such quiet. There was a trace of wind, hot and silent. It lacked the strength to rustle the scrub that pushed its way through the rocks. The only sound she heard was the quick breathing of the puppy, who was sitting on the ground at her feet.

The horses had run off. So, Sarah thought as she turned in a circle, had Jake Redman. It was better that way, she decided—because she remembered, all too clearly, the way she had felt when he had sat on the cot in the shadowy lamplight and touched her hair. Foolish. It was hateful to admit it, but she'd felt foolish and weak and, worst of all, willing.

There was no use being ashamed of it, but she considered herself too smart to allow it to happen again. A man like Jake Redman wasn't the type a woman could flirt harmlessly with. Perhaps she didn't have a wide and worldly experience with men, but she recognized a dangerous one when she saw him.

There were some, she had no doubt, who would be drawn to his kind. A man who killed without remorse or regret, who came and went as he pleased. But not her. When she decided to give her heart to a man, it would be to one she understood and respected.

With a sigh, she bent down to soothe the puppy, who was whimpering at her feet. There was a comfort in the way he nuzzled his face against hers. When she fell in love and married, Sarah thought, it would be to a man of dignity and breeding, a man who would cherish her, who would protect her, not with guns and fists but with honor. They would be devoted to each other, and to the family they made between them. He would be educated and strong, respected in the community.

Those were the qualities she'd been taught a woman looked for in a husband. Sarah stroked the puppy's head and wished she could conquer this strange feeling that what she'd been taught wasn't necessarily true.

What did it matter now? As things stood, she had too much to do to think about romance. She had to find a way to rebuild the shed. Then she'd have to bargain for a new wagon and team. She stirred some of the charred wood with the toe of her shoe. She was about to give in to the urge to kick it when she heard horses approaching.

Panic came first and had her spinning around, a cry for help on her lips. The sunbaked dirt and empty rocks mocked her. The Lord helped those who help themselves, she remembered, and raced into the house with the puppy scrambling behind her.

When she came out again her knees were trembling, but she was carrying her father's rifle in both hands.

Jake took one look at her, framed in the doorway, her eyes mirroring fear and fury. It came to him with a kind of dull, painful surprise that she was the kind of woman a man would die for. He slid from his horse.

"I'd be obliged, ma'am, if you'd point that some-place else."

"Oh." She nearly sagged with relief. "Mr. Redman. I thought you'd gone." He merely inclined his head and took another meaningful look at the rifle. "Oh," she said again, and lowered it. She felt foolish, not because of the gun but because when she'd looked out and seen him all her thoughts about what she wanted and didn't want had shifted ground. There he was, looking dark and reckless, with guns gleaming at his hip. And there she was, fighting back a driving instinct to run into his arms.

"You…found the horses."

He took his time tying the team to a post before he approached her. "They hadn't gone far." He took the rifle from her and leaned it against the house. The stock was damp from her nervous hands. But he'd seen more than nerves in her eyes. And he wondered.

"I'm very grateful." Because she felt awkward, she leaned down to gather the yapping puppy in her arms. Jake still hadn't shaved, and she remembered how his face had felt against the palm of her hand. Fighting a blush, she curled her fingers. "I'm afraid I don't know what to do with them until I have shelter again."

What was going on in that mind of hers? Jake wondered. "A lean-to would do well enough for the time being. Just need to rig one over a corner of the paddock."

"A lean-to, yes." It was a relief to deal with something practical. Her mind went to work quickly. "Mr. Redman, have you had breakfast?"

He tipped his hat back on his head. "Not to speak of."

"If you could fashion a temporary shelter for the horses, I'd be more than glad to fix you a meal."

He'd meant to do it anyway, but if she wanted to bargain, he'd bargain. "Can you cook?"

"Naturally. Preparing meals was a very important part of my education."

He wanted to touch her hair again. And more.

Instead, he hooked his thumb in his pocket. "I ain't worried about you preparing a meal. Can you cook?"

She tried not to sigh. "Yes."

"All right, then."

When he walked away and didn't remount his horse, Sarah supposed a deal had been struck. "Mr. Redman?" He stopped to look over his shoulder. "How do you prefer your eggs?"

"Hot," he told her, then continued on his way.

She'd give him hot, Sarah decided, rattling pans. She'd give him the best damn breakfast he'd ever eaten. She took a long breath and forced herself to be calm. His way of talking was beginning to rub off on her. That would never do.

Biscuits. Delighted that she'd been given a brand-new recipe only the day before, she went to work.

Thirty minutes later, Jake came in to stand in the doorway. The scents amazed him. He'd expected to find the frying pan smoking with burnt eggs. Instead, he saw a bowl of fresh, golden-topped biscuits wrapped in a clean bandanna. Sarah was busy at the stove, humming to herself. The pup was nosing into corners, looking for trouble.

Jake had never thought much about a home for himself, but if he had it would have been like this. A woman in a pretty dress humming by the stove, the smells of good cooking rising in the air. A man could do almost anything if the right woman was waiting for him.

Then she turned. One look at her face, the elegance of it, was a reminder that a man like him didn't have a woman like her waiting for him.

"Just in time." She smiled, pleased with herself. Conquering the cookstove was her biggest accomplishment to date. "There's fresh water in the bowl, so you can wash up." She began to scoop eggs onto an ironstone plate. "I'm afraid I don't have a great deal to offer. I'm thinking of getting some chickens of my own. We had them at school, so I know a bit about them. Fresh eggs are such a comfort, don't you think?"

He lifted his head from the bowl, and water dripped down from his face. Her cheeks were flushed from cooking, and her sleeves were rolled up past her elbows, revealing slender, milk-white arms. Comfort was the last thing on his mind. Without speaking, he took his seat.

Sarah wasn't sure when he made her more nervous, when he spoke to her or when he lapsed into those long silences and just looked. Gamely she tried again. "Mrs. Cobb gave me the recipe for these biscuits yesterday. I hope they're as good as she claimed."

Jake broke one, and the steam and fragrance poured out. Watching her, he bit into it. "They're fine."

"Please, Mr. Redman, all this flattery will turn my head." She scooped up a forkful of eggs. "I was introduced to several ladies yesterday while I was buying supplies. They seem very hospitable."

"I don't know much about the ladies in town." At least not the kind Sarah was speaking of.

"I see." She took a bite of biscuit herself. It was more than fine, she thought with a pout. It was delicious. "Liza Cody—her family runs the dry goods store. I found her very amiable. She was kind enough to let me have one of their puppies."

Jake looked down at the dog, who was sniffing at his boot and thumping his tail. "That where you got this thing?"

"Yes. I wanted the company."

Jake broke off a bite of biscuit and dropped it to the dog, ignoring Sarah's muttered admonition about feeding animals from the table. "Scrawny now, but he's going to be a big one."

"Really?" Intrigued, she leaned over to look. "How can you tell?"

"His paws. He's clumsy now because they're too big for him. He'll grow into them."

"I fancy it's to my advantage to own a large dog."

"Didn't do you much good last night," he pointed out, but pleased both the pup and Sarah by scratching between the dog's floppy ears. "You give him a name yet?"

"Lafitte."

Jake paused with his fork halfway to his lips. "What the hell kind of name is that for a dog?"

"After the pirate. He had that black marking around his eye, like a patch."

"Pretty fancy name for a mutt," Jake said over a mouthful of eggs. "Bandit's better."

Sarah lifted a brow. "I'd certainly never give him a name like that."

"A pirate's a bandit, isn't he?" Jake dived into another biscuit.

"Be that as it may, the name stands."

Chewing, Jake looked down at the puppy, who was groveling a bit, obviously hoping for another handout. "Bet it makes you feel pretty stupid, doesn't it, fella?"

"Would you care for more coffee, Mr. Redman?" Frustrated, Sarah rose and, wrapping a cloth around the handle, took the pot from the stove. Without waiting for an answer, she stood beside Jake and poured.

She smelled good, he thought. Soft. Kind of subtle, like a field of wildflowers in early spring. At the ends of her stiff white sleeves, her hands were delicate. He remembered the feel of them on his cheek.

"They taught you good," he muttered.

"I beg your pardon?" She looked down at him. There was something in his eyes, a hint of what she'd seen in them the night before. It didn't make her nervous, as she'd been certain it would. It made her yearn.

"The cooking." Jake put a hand over hers to straighten the pot and keep the coffee from overflowing the cup. Then he kept it there, feeling the smooth texture of her skin and the surprisingly rapid beating of her pulse. She didn't back away, or blush, or snatch her hand from his. Instead, she simply looked back at him. The question in her eyes was one he wanted badly to answer.

She moistened her lips but kept her eyes steady. "Thank you. I'm glad you enjoyed it."

"You take too many chances, Sarah." Slowly, when he was certain she understood his meaning, he removed his hand.

With her chin up, she returned the pot to the stove. How dare he make her feel like that, then toss it back in her face? "You don't frighten me, Mr. Redman. If you were going to hurt me, you would have done so by now."

"Maybe, maybe not. Your kind wears a man down."

"My kind?" She turned, the light of challenge in her eyes. "Just what kind would that be?"

"The soft kind. The soft, stubborn kind who's right on the edge of stepping into a man's arms."

"You couldn't be more mistaken." Her voice was icy now in defense against the blood that had heated at his words. "I haven't any interest in being in your arms, or any man's. My only interest at the moment is protecting my property."

"Could be I'm wrong." He rocked back in his chair. She was a puzzle, all right, and he'd never known how pleasurable it could be to get a woman's dander up. "We'll both find out sooner or later. Meanwhile, just how do you plan to go about protecting this place?"

Not much caring whether he was finished or not, she began to stack the plates. "I'm going to alert the sheriff, of course."

"That's not going to hurt, but it's not going to help much, either, if you get more trouble out here. The sheriff's ten miles away."

"Just what do you suggest?"

He'd already given it some thought, and he had an answer. "If I were you, I'd hire somebody to help out around here. Somebody who can give you a hand with the place, and who knows how to use a gun."

A thrill sprinted through her. She managed, just barely, to keep her voice disinterested. "Yourself, I suppose."

He grinned at her. "No, Duchess, I ain't looking for that kind of job. I was thinking of Lucius."

Frowning, she began to scrub out the frying pan. "He drinks."

"Who doesn't? Give him a couple of meals and a place to bunk down and he'll do all right for you. A woman staying out here all alone's just asking for trouble. Those men who burned your shed last night might've done more to you than give you a headache."

His meaning was clear enough, clearer still because she'd thought of that possibility herself. She'd prefer him—though only because she knew he was capable, she assured herself. But she did need someone. "Perhaps you're right."

"No perhaps about it. Someone as green as you doesn't have the sense to do more than die out here."

"I don't see why you have to insult me."

"The plain truth's the plain truth, Duchess."

Teeth clenched, she banged dishes. "I told you not to—"

"I got a question for you," he said, interrupting her easily. "What would you have done this morning if it hadn't been me bringing back the horses?"

"I would have defended myself."

"You ever shot a Henry before?"

She gave him a scandalized look. "Why in the world would I have shot anyone named Henry?"

With a long sigh, he rose. "A Henry rifle, Duchess. That's what you were pointing at my belt buckle before you fixed my eggs."

Sarah wiped the pan clean, then set it aside. "No, I haven't actually fired one, but I can't imagine it's that complicated. In any case, I never intended to shoot it."

"What did you have in mind? Dancing with it?"

She snatched up a plate. "Mr. Redman, I'm growing

weary of being an amusement to you. I realize that someone like you thinks nothing of shooting a man dead and walking away. I, however, have been taught— rightfully—that killing is a sin."

"You're wrong." Something in his voice had her turning toward him again. "Surviving's never a sin. It's all there is."

"If you believe that, I'm sorry for you."

He didn't want her pity. But he did want her to stay alive. Moving over, he took the plates out of her hands. "If you see a snake, are you going to kill it or stand there and let it bite you?"

"That's entirely different."

"You might not think it's so different if you stay out here much longer. Where's the cartridges for the rifle?"

Wiping her hands on her apron, Sarah glanced at the shelf behind her. Jake took the cartridges down, checked them, then gripped her arm. "Come on. I'll give you a lesson."

"I haven't finished cleaning the dishes."

"They'll keep."

"I never said I wanted lessons," she told him as he pulled her outside.

"If you're going to pick up a gun, you ought to know how to use it." He hefted the rifle and smiled at her. "Unless you're afraid you can't learn."

Sarah untied her apron and laid it over the rail. "I'm not afraid of anything."

Chapter 5

He'd figured a challenge would be the best way to get her cooperation. Sarah marched along beside him, chin up, eyes forward. He didn't think she knew it, but when she'd held the rifle that morning she'd been prepared to pull the trigger. He wanted to make sure that when she did she hit what she aimed at.

From the rubble of the burned shed, Jake selected a few pieces of charred wood and balanced three of them against a pile of rocks.

"First thing you do is learn how to load it without shooting off your foot." Jake emptied the rifle's chamber, then slowly reloaded. "You've got to have respect for a weapon, and not go around holding it like you were going to sweep the porch with it."

To prove his point, he brought the rifle up, sighted in

and fired three shots. The three pieces of scrap wood flew backward in unison. "Bullets can do powerful damage to a man," he told her as he lowered the gun again.

She had to swallow. The sound of gunfire still echoed. "I'm aware of that, Mr. Redman. I have no intention of shooting anyone."

"Most people don't wake up in the morning figuring on it." He went to the rocks again. This time he set up the largest piece of wood. "Unless you're planning on heading back to Philadelphia real soon, you'd better learn how to use this."

"I'm not going anywhere."

With a nod, Jake emptied the rifle and handed her the ammo. "Load it."

She didn't like the feel of the bullets in her hands. They were cold and smooth. Holding them, she wondered how anyone could use them against another. Metal against flesh. No, it was inconceivable.

"You going to play with them or put them in the gun?"

Because he was watching her, Sarah kept her face impassive and did as he told her.

He pushed the barrel away from his midsection. "You're a quick study."

It shouldn't have pleased her, but she felt the corners of her mouth turn up nonetheless. "So I've been told."

Unable to resist, he brushed the hair out of her eyes. "Don't get cocky." Stepping behind her, he laid the gun in her hands, then adjusted her arms. "Balance it and get a good grip on it."

"I am," she muttered, wishing he wouldn't stand quite so close. He smelled of leather and sweat, a combination that, for reasons beyond her comprehension, aroused her. One hand was firm on her arm, the other on her shoulder. Hardly a lover's touch, and yet she felt her system respond as it had never responded to the gentle, flirtatious hand-holding she'd experienced in Philadelphia. She had only to lean back the slightest bit to be pressed close against him.

Not that she wanted to be. She shifted, then grumbled under her breath when he pushed her into place again.

"Hold still. Not stiff, woman, still," he told her when her body went rigid at his touch.

"There's no need to snap at me."

"You stand like that when you fire, you're going to get a broken shoulder. Loosen up. You see the sight?"

"That little thing sticking up there?"

He closed his eyes for a moment. "Yeah, that little thing sticking up there. Use it to sight in the target. Bring the stock up some." He leaned over. Sarah pressed her lips together when his cheek brushed hers. "Steady," he murmured, resisting the urge to turn his face into her hair. "Wrap your finger around the trigger. Don't jerk it, just pull it back, slow and smooth."

She shut her eyes and obeyed. The rifle exploded in her hands and would have knocked her flat on her back if he hadn't been there to steady her. She screamed, afraid she'd shot herself.

"Missed."

Breathing hard, Sarah whirled around. Always a cautious man, Jake took the rifle from her. "You might have warned me." She brought her hand up to nurse her bruised shoulder. "It felt like someone hit me with a rock."

"It's always better to find things out firsthand. Try it again."

With her teeth clenched, Sarah took the rifle and managed to get back into position.

"This time use your arm instead of your shoulder to balance it. Lean in a bit."

"My ears are ringing."

"You'll get used to it." He put a steadying hand on her waist. "It helps if you keep your eyes open. Sight low. Good. Now pull the trigger."

This time she was braced for the kick and just staggered a little. Jake kept a hand at her waist and looked over her head. "You caught a corner of it."

"I did?" She looked for herself. "I did!" Laughing, she looked over her shoulder at him. "I want to do it again." She lifted the rifle and didn't complain when Jake pushed the barrel three inches to the right. She kept her eyes wide open this time as she pressed her finger down on the trigger. She let out a whoop when the wood flew off the rocks. "I hit it."

"Looks like."

"I really hit it. Imagine." When he took the gun from her, she shook her hair back and laughed. "My arm's tingling."

"It'll pass." He was surprised he could speak. The way she looked when she laughed made his throat slam shut. He wasn't a man for pretty words, not for saying them or for thinking them. But just now it ran through his head that she looked like an angel in the sunlight, with her hair the color of wet wheat and her eyes like gold dust.

And he wanted her, as he'd wanted few things in his life.

Slowly, wanting to give himself time to regain control, he walked over to the rocks to pick up the target. She had indeed hit it. The hole was nearly at the top, and far to the right of center, but she'd hit it. He walked back to drop the wood in Sarah's hands and watched her grin about it.

"Trouble is, most things you shoot at don't sit nice and still like a block of wood."

He was determined to spoil it for her, Sarah thought, studying his cool, unreadable eyes. The man was impossible to understand. One moment he was going to the trouble to teach her how to shoot the rifle, and the next he couldn't even manage the smallest of compliments because she'd learned well. The devil with him.

"Mr. Redman, it's very apparent that nothing I do pleases you." She tossed the block of wood aside. "Isn't it fortunate for both of us that it doesn't matter in the least?" With that she gathered up her skirts and began to stamp back toward the house. She managed no more than a startled gasp as he spun her around.

She knew that look, she thought dazedly as she stared at him. It was the same one she'd first seen on his face, when he'd ridden beside the stage, firing his pistol over his shoulder. She hadn't a clue as to how to deal with him now, so she took the only option that came to mind.

"Take your hands off me."

"I warned you, you took too many chances." His grip only tightened when she tried to shrug him off. "It's not smart to turn your back on a man who's holding a loaded gun."

"Did you intend to shoot me in the back, Mr. Redman?" It was an unfair remark, and she knew it. But she wanted to get away from him, quickly, until that look faded from his eyes. "I wouldn't put that, or anything else, past you. You're the rudest, most ill-mannered, most ungentlemanly man I've ever met. I'll thank you to get back on your horse and ride off my land."

He'd resisted challenges before, but he'd be damned if he'd resist this one. From the first time he'd seen her she'd started an itch in him. It was time he scratched it.

"Seems to me you need another lesson, Duchess."

"I neither need nor want anything from you. And I won't be called by that ridiculous name." Her breath came out in a whoosh when he dragged her against him. He saw her eyes go wide with shock.

"Then I won't call you anything." He was still holding the rifle. With his eyes on hers, he slid his hand up her back to gather up her hair. "I don't much like talking, anyway."

She fought him. At least she needed to believe she did. Despite her efforts, his mouth closed over hers. In that instant the sun was blocked out and she was plunged, breathless, into the deepest, darkest night.

His body was like iron. His arm bonded her against him so that she had no choice, really no choice, but to absorb the feel of him. He made her think of the rifle, slim and hard and deadly. Through the shock, the panic and the excitement she felt the fast, uneven beating of his heart against hers.

Her blood had turned into some hot, foreign liquid that made her pulse leap and her heart thud. The rough stubble of his beard scraped her face, and she moaned. From the pain, she assured herself. It couldn't be from pleasure.

And yet… Her hands were on his shoulders, holding on now rather than pushing away.

He wondered if she knew she packed a bigger kick than her father's rifle. He'd never known that anything so sweet could be so potent. That anything so delicate could be so strong. She had him by the throat and didn't even know it. And he wanted more. In a move too desperate to be gentle, he dragged her head back by the hair.

She gasped in the instant he allowed her to breathe, dragging in air, unaware that she'd been stunned into holding her breath. Then his mouth was on hers again, his tongue invading, arousing in a way she hadn't known she could be aroused, weakening in a way she hadn't believed she could be weakened.

She moaned again, but this time there was no denying the pleasure. Tentatively, then boldly, she answered the new demand. Savoring the hot, salty taste of his lips, she ran her hands along the planes of his face and into his hair. Glorious. No one had ever warned her that a kiss could make the body burn and tremble and yearn. A sound of stunned delight caught in her throat.

The sound lit fires in him that he knew could never be allowed to burn free. She was innocent. Any fool could see that. And he…he hadn't been innocent since he'd drawn his first breath. There were lines he crossed, laws he broke. But this one had to be respected. He struggled to clear his mind, but she filled it. Her arms were around his neck, pulling him closer, pulling him in. And her mouth… Sweet Lord, her mouth. His heart was hammering in his head, in his loins…all from the taste of her. Honeyed whiskey. A man could drown in it.

Afraid he would, and even more afraid he'd want to, he pushed her away. Her eyes were dark and unfocused—the way they'd been last night, when she'd started to come to. It gave him some satisfaction to see it, because he felt as though he'd been knocked cold, himself.

"Like I said, you learn fast, Sarah." His hand was shaking. Infuriated, he curled it into a fist. He had a flash, an almost painful one, of what it would be like to drag her to the ground and take everything from her. Before he could act, one way or the other, he heard the sound of an approaching wagon. "You got company coming." He handed her the rifle and walked away.

What had he done to her? Sarah put a hand to her spinning head. He'd…he'd forced himself on her. Forced her until…until he hadn't had to force her any longer. Until it had felt right to want him. Until wanting him had been all there was.

Just like the dream. But this wasn't a dream, Sarah told herself, straightening her shoulders. It was more than real, and now he was walking away from her as if it hadn't mattered to him in the least. Pride was every bit as dangerous an emotion as anger.

"Mr. Redman."

When he turned, he saw her standing there with the rifle. If the look in her eyes meant anything, she'd have dearly loved to use it.

"Apparently you take chances, too." She tilted her head. There was challenge in the gesture, as well as a touch of fury and a stab of hurt. "This rifle's still loaded."

"That's right." He touched the brim of his hat in a

salute. "It's a hell of a lot harder to pull the trigger when you're aiming at flesh and blood, but go ahead. It'd be hard to miss at this range."

She wished she could. She wished she had the skill to put a bullet between his feet and watch him jump. Lifting her chin, she walked toward the house. "The difference between you and me, Mr. Redman, is that I still have morals."

"There's some truth in that." He strode easily beside her. "Seeing as you fixed me breakfast and all, why don't you call me Jake?" He swung up into the saddle as a buggy rumbled into the yard.

"Sarah?" With her hands still on the reins, Liza cast an uncertain glance at her new friend, then at the man in the saddle. She knew she wasn't supposed to approve of men like Jake Redman. But she found it difficult not to when he looked so attractive and exciting. "I hope you don't mind us coming out." A young boy jumped out of the buggy and began to chase the puppy, who was running in circles.

"Not at all. I'm delighted." Sarah shaded her eyes with her hand so that she could see Jake clearly. "Mr. Redman was just on his way."

"Those sure are some pretty guns you got there, mister." Young John Cody put a hand on the neck of Jake's gray mustang and peered up at the smooth wooden grip of one of the Colt .45s he carried. He knew who Jake Redman was—he'd heard all the stories—but he'd never managed to get this close before.

"Think so?" Ignoring the two women, Jake shifted in his saddle to get a better look at the boy. No more than ten, he figured, with awe in his eyes and a smudge of dirt on his cheek.

"Yessiree. I think that when you slap leather you're just about the fastest there is, maybe in the whole world."

"John Cody." Liza stayed in the buggy, wringing her hands. "You oughtn't to bother Mr. Redman."

Jake shot her a quick, amused look. Did she think he'd shoot the kid for talking to him? "No bother, ma'am." He glanced down at Johnny again. "You can't believe everything you hear."

But Johnny figured he knew what was what. "My ma says that since you saved that stage there's probably some good in you somewhere."

This time Liza called her brother's name in a strained, desperate whisper. Jake had to grin. He shifted his attention to Sarah long enough to see that she was standing as stiff as a rod, with one eyebrow arched.

"That's right kind of her. I'll tell the sheriff about your trouble…Miss Conway. I reckon he'll be out to see you."

"Thank you, Mr. Redman. Good day."

He tipped his hat to her, then to Liza. "See you around, Johnny." He turned his horse in a half circle and rode away.

"Yessir," Johnny shouted after him. "Yessiree."

"John Cody." Liza collected herself enough to climb out of the buggy. Johnny just grinned and raced off after the puppy again, firing an imaginary Peacemaker. "That's my brother."

"Yes, I imagined it was."

Liza gave Johnny one last look of sisterly disgust before going to Sarah. "Ma's tending the store today.

She wanted you to have this. It's a loaf of her cinnamon bread."

"Oh, how kind of her." One whiff brought memories of home. "Can you stay?"

Liza gave Sarah the bread and a quick, dimpled smile. "I was hoping I could."

"Come in, please. I'll fix us some tea."

While Sarah busied herself at the stove, Liza looked around the tiny cabin. It was scrubbed clean as a whistle. "It's not as bad as I thought it would be." Instantly she lifted a hand to her mouth. "I'm sorry. Ma always says I talk too much for my own good."

"That's all right." Sarah got out two tin cups and tried not to wish they were china. "I was taken by surprise myself."

At ease again, Liza sat at the table. "I didn't expect to run into Jake Redman out here."

Sarah brought the knife down into the bread with a thwack. "Neither did I."

"He said you had trouble."

Unconsciously Sarah lifted a finger to her lips. They were still warm from his, and they tingled as her arms had from the kick of the Henry. She had trouble, all right. Since she couldn't explain the kiss to herself, she could hardly explain it to Liza. "Someone set fire to my shed last night."

"Oh, Sarah, no! Who? Why?"

"I don't know." She brought the two cups to the table. "Fortunately, Mr. Redman happened to be riding by this way."

"Do you think he might have done it?"

Sarah's brow rose as she considered the possibility. She remembered the way he'd bathed her face and tended her hurts. "No, I'm quite certain he didn't. I believe Mr. Redman takes a more direct approach."

"I guess you're right about that. I can't say he's started any trouble here in Lone Bluff, but he's finished some."

"What do you know about him?"

"I don't think anyone knows much. He rode into town about six months ago. Of course, everybody's heard of Jake Redman. Some say he's killed more than twenty men in gunfights."

"Killed?" Stunned, Sarah could only stare. "But why?"

"I don't know if there always is a why. I did hear that some rancher up north hired him on. There'd been trouble...rustling, barn-burning."

"Hired him on," Sarah murmured. "To kill."

"That's what it comes down to, I suppose. I do know that plenty of people were nervous when he rode in and took a room at Maggie O'Rourke's." Liza broke off a corner of the slice of bread Sarah had served her. "But he didn't seem to be looking for trouble. About two weeks later he found it, anyway."

A hired killer, Sarah thought, her stomach churning. And she'd kissed him, kissed him in a way no lady kissed a man who wasn't her husband. "What happened?"

"Jim Carlson was in the Bird Cage. That's one of the saloons in town."

"Carlson?"

"Yes, he's Samuel Carlson's brother. You wouldn't know it," Liza continued, pursing her lips. "Jim's nothing like Samuel. Full of spit, that one. Likes to brag and swagger and bully. Cheats at cards, but nobody had the nerve to call him on it. Until Jake." Liza drank more tea and listened with half an ear to her brother's war whoops in the yard. "The way I heard it, there were some words over the card table. Jim was drunk and a little careless with his dealing. Once Jake called him on it, some of the other men joined in. Word is, Jim drew. Everybody figured Jake would put a bullet in him there and then, but he just knocked him down."

"He didn't shoot him?" She felt a wave of relief. Perhaps he wasn't what people said he was.

"No. At least, the way I heard it, Jake just knocked him silly and gave Jim's gun to the bartender. Somebody had already hightailed it for the sheriff. By the time he got there, Jake was standing at the bar having himself a drink and Jim was picking himself up off the floor. I think Barker was going to put Jim in a cell for the night until he sobered up. But when he took hold of him, Jim pulled the gun from the sheriff's holster. Instead of getting a bullet in the back, Jake put one in Jim Carlson, then turned around and finished his drink."

Dead's dead. "Did he kill him?"

"No, though there's some in town wished he had. The Carlsons are pretty powerful around here, but there were enough witnesses, the sheriff included, to call it self-defense."

"I see." But she didn't understand the kind of justice that had to be meted out with guns and bullets. "I'm surprised Jake—Mr. Redman—hasn't moved on."

"He must like it around here. What about you? Doesn't it scare you to stay out here alone?"

Sarah thought of her first night, shivering under the blanket and praying for morning. "A little."

"After living back east." Liza gave a sigh. To her, Philadelphia sounded as glamorous and foreign as Paris or London. "All the places you've seen, the pretty clothes you must have worn."

Sarah struggled with a quick pang of homesickness. "Have you ever been east?"

"No, but I've seen pictures." Liza eyed Sarah's trunks with longing. "The women wear beautiful clothes."

"Would you like to see some of mine?"

Liza's face lit up. "I'd love to."

For the next twenty minutes Liza oohed and aahed over ruffles and lace. Her reaction caused Sarah to appreciate what she had always taken for granted. Crouched on the cabin floor, they discussed important matters such as ribbons and sashes and the proper tilt of a bonnet while Johnny was kept occupied with a hunk of bread and the puppy.

"Oh, look at this one." Delighted, Liza rose, sweeping a dress in front of her. "I wish you had a looking glass."

It was the white muslin with the rosebuds on the skirt. The dress she'd planned to wear for her first dinner with her father. He'd never see it now. She glanced at the trunks. Or any of the other lovely things he'd made certain she had in her life.

"What's wrong?" With the dress still crushed against her, Liza stepped forward. "You look so sad."

"I was thinking of my father, of how hard he worked for me."

Liza's fascination with the clothes was immediately outweighed by her sympathy. "He loved you. Often when he came in the store he'd talk about you, about what you'd written in one of your letters. I remember how he brought in this picture of you, a drawing in a little frame. He wanted everyone to see how pretty you were. He was so proud of you, Sarah."

"I miss him." With a shake of her head, Sarah blinked back tears. "It's strange, all those years we were separated. Sometimes I could barely remember him. But since I've been here I seem to know him better, and miss him more."

Gently Liza laid a hand on her shoulder. "My pa sure riles me sometimes, but I guess I'd about die if anything happened to him."

"Well, at least I have this." She looked around the small cabin. "I feel closer to him here. I like to think about him sitting at that table and writing to me." After a long breath she managed to smile. "I'm glad I came."

Liza held out a hand. "So am I."

Rising, Sarah fluffed out the sleeves of the dress Liza was holding. "Now, let me be your looking glass. You're taller and curvier than I…" With her lips pursed, she walked in a circle around Liza. "The neckline would flatter you, but I think I'd do away with some of the ruffles in the bodice. A nice pink would be your color. It would show off your hair and eyes."

"Can you imagine me wearing a dress like that?" Closing her eyes, Liza turned in slow circles. "It would have to be at a dance. I'd have my hair curled over my shoulder and wear a velvet ribbon around my throat. Will Metcalf's eyes would fall right out."

"Who's Will Metcalf?"

Liza opened her eyes and giggled. "Just a man. He's a deputy in town. He'd like to be my beau." Mischief flashed across her face. "I might decide to let him."

"Liza loves Will," Johnny sang through the window.

"You hush up, John Cody." Rushing to the window, Liza leaned out. "If you don't, I'll tell Ma who broke Grandma's china plate."

"Liza loves Will," he repeated, unconcerned, then raced off with the puppy.

"Nothing more irritating than little brothers," she muttered. With a sigh of regret, she replaced the dress in the trunk.

Tapping a finger on her lips, Sarah came to a quick decision. She should have thought of it before, she reflected. Or perhaps it had been milling around in her mind all along. "Liza, would you like a dress like that…in pink, like that pretty muslin I saw in your store yesterday?"

"I guess I'd think I'd gone to heaven."

"What if I made it for you?"

"Made it for me?" Wide-eyed, Liza looked at the trunk, then back at Sarah. "Could you?"

"I'm very handy with a needle." Caught up in the idea, Sarah pushed through her trunks to find her measuring tape. "If you can get the material, I'll make the dress. If you like it, you can tell the other women who come in your store."

"Of course." Obediently Liza lifted her arms so that Sarah could measure her. "I'll tell everyone."

"Then some of those women might want new

dresses, fashionable new dresses." Looking up, she caught the gleam of understanding in Liza's eyes.

"You bet they would."

"You get me that material and I'll make you a dress that will have Will Metcalf standing on his head."

Two hours later Sarah was pouring water over her vegetable garden. In the heat of the afternoon, with her back smarting from the chores and sun baking the dirt almost as fast as she could dampen it, she wondered if it was worth it. A garden out here would require little less than a miracle. And she would much prefer flowers.

You couldn't eat flowers, she reminded herself, and poured the last of the water out. Now she would have to walk back to the stream and fill the pail again to have water for cooking and washing.

A bath, she thought as she wiped the back of her hand over her brow. What she wouldn't give for a long bath in a real tub.

She heard the horses. It pleased her to realize that she was becoming accustomed to the sound—or lack of sound—that surrounded her new home. With her hand shading her eyes, she watched two riders come into view. It wasn't until she recognized one as Lucius that she realized she'd been holding her breath.

"Lafitte!" she called, but the dog continued to race around the yard, barking.

"Miss Conway." Sheriff Barker tipped his hat and chuckled at the snarling pup. "Got yourself a fierce-looking guard dog there."

"Makes a ruckus, anyhow," Lucius said, swinging

down from his horse. Lafitte sprang at him, gripping the bottom of his pant leg with sharp puppy teeth. Bending, Lucius snatched him up by the cuff of the neck. "You mind your manners, young fella." The second he was on the ground again, Lafitte ran to hide behind Sarah's skirts.

"Heard you had some trouble out here." Barker nodded toward the remains of the shed. "This happen last night?"

"That's right. If you'd like to come inside, I was just about to get some water. I'm sure you'd like some coffee after your ride."

"I'll fetch you some water, miss," Lucius said, taking the pail from her. "Hey, boy." He grinned down at the pup. "Why don't you come along with me? I'll keep you out of trouble." After a moment's hesitation, Lafitte trotted along after him.

"Are you thinking about hiring him on?"

With her lip caught between her teeth, Sarah watched Lucius stroll off. "I was considering it."

"You'd be smart to do it." Barker took out a bandanna and wiped his neck. "Lucius has a powerful affection for the bottle, but it doesn't seem to bother him. He's honest. Did some soldiering a while back. He's amiable enough, drunk or sober."

Sarah managed a smile. "I'll take that as a recommendation, Sheriff Barker."

"Well, now." The sheriff looked back at the shed. "Why don't you tell me what happened here?"

As clearly as she could, Sarah told him everything she knew. He listened, grunting and nodding occasionally. Everything she said jibed with the story Jake had given him. But she didn't add, because she didn't know, that Jake had followed the trail of two riders into the rocks, where he'd discovered the ashes of a campfire.

"Any reason you can think of why somebody'd want to do this?"

"None at all. There's nothing here that could mean anything to anyone other than myself. Did my father have any enemies?"

Barker spit tobacco juice in the dirt. "I wouldn't think so right off. I got to tell you, Miss Conway, there ain't much I can do. I'll ask some questions and poke around some. Could be some drifters passed through and wanted to raise some hell. Begging your pardon." But he didn't think so.

"I'd wondered the same myself."

"You'll feel safer having old Lucius around."

She glanced over to see him coming back with the pail and the puppy. "I suppose you're right." But he didn't look like her idea of a protector. It was unfortunate for her that her idea of one had taken the form of Jake Redman. "I'm sure we'll do nicely," she said with more confidence than she felt.

"I'll ride out now and again and see how you're getting on." Barker pulled himself onto his horse. "You know, Miss Conway, Matt tried to grow something in that patch of dirt for as long as I can recollect." He spit again. "Never had any luck."

"Perhaps I'll have better. Good afternoon, Sheriff."

"Good day, ma'am." He lifted a hand to Lucius as he turned for home.

Chapter 6

Within a week Sarah had orders for six dresses. It took all her creativity and skill to fashion them, using her wardrobe and her imagination instead of patterns. She set aside three hours each day and three each evening for sewing. Each night when she climbed up to bed her eyes and fingers ached. Once or twice, when the exhaustion overwhelmed her, she wept herself to sleep. The grief for her father was still too raw, the country surrounding her still too rugged.

But there were other times, and they were becoming more common, when she fell asleep with a sense of satisfaction. In addition to the dresses, she'd made pretty yellow curtains for the windows and a matching cloth for the table. It was her dream, when she'd saved enough from her sewing, to buy planks for a real floor. In the meantime, she made do with what she had and was more grateful than she'd ever imagined she could be for Lucius.

He'd finished building a new shed and he was busy repairing the other outbuildings. Though he'd muttered about it, he'd agreed to build Sarah the chicken coop she wanted. At night he was content to sleep with the horses.

Sometimes he watched, tickling Lafitte's belly, as she took her daily rifle practice.

She hadn't seen Jake Redman since the day he'd given her a shooting lesson. Just as well, Sarah told herself as she pulled on her gloves. There was no one she wanted to see less. If she thought about him at all— and she hated to admit she had—it was with disdain.

A hired gun. A man with no loyalty or morals. A drifter, moving from place to place, always ready to draw his weapon and kill. To think she'd almost begun to believe there was something special about him, something good and admirable. He'd helped her, there was no denying that. But he'd probably done so out of sheer boredom. Or perhaps, she thought, remembering the kiss, because he wanted something from her. Something, she was ashamed to admit, she had nearly been willing to give.

How? Sarah picked up her hand mirror and studied her face, not out of vanity but because she hoped to see some answers there. How had he managed to make her feel that way in just a few short days, with just one embrace? Now, time after time, in the deepest part of the night, she brought herself awake because she was dreaming of him. Remembering, she thought, experiencing once again that stunning moment in the sun when his mouth had been on hers and there had been no doubt in her mind that she belonged there.

A momentary madness, she told herself, placing the mirror facedown on the table. Sunstroke, perhaps. She would never, could never, be attracted to a man who lived his life the way Jake Redman lived his.

It was time to forget him. Perhaps he had already moved on and she would never see him again. Well, it didn't matter one way or the other. She had her own life to see to now, and with a little help from Liza it appeared she had her own business. Picking up the three bundles wrapped in brown paper, Sarah went outside.

"You real sure you don't want me to drive you to town, Miss Conway?"

Sarah put the wrapped dresses in the back of the wagon while Lucius stood at the horses' heads. "No, thank you, Lucius."

She was well aware that her driving skills were poor at best, but she'd bartered for the wagon with the owner of the livery stable. He had two daughters that she'd designed gingham frocks for, and she intended to deliver them herself. For Lucius she had a big, sunny smile.

"I was hoping you'd start on the chicken coop today. I'm going to see if Mrs. Miller will sell me a dozen young chicks."

"Yes'm." Lucius shuffled his feet and cleared his throat. "Going to be a hot, dry day."

"Yes." What day wasn't? "I have a canteen, thank you."

He waited until Sarah had gained the seat and smoothed out her skirts. "There's just one thing, Miss Conway."

Anxious to be on her way, Sarah took the reins. "Yes, Lucius, what is it?"

"I'm plumb out of whiskey."

Her brow rose, all but disappearing under the wispy bangs she wore. "And?"

"Well, seeing as you're going into town and all, I thought you could pick some up for me."

"I? You can hardly expect me to purchase whiskey."

He'd figured on her saying something of the kind. "Maybe you could get somebody to buy a bottle for you." He gave her a gap-toothed smile and was careful not to spit. "I'd be obliged."

She opened her mouth, ready to lecture him on the evils of drink. With a sigh, she shut it again. The man worked very hard for very little. It wasn't her place to deny him his comforts, whatever they might be.

"I'll see what can be done."

His grizzled face brightened immediately. "That's right kind of you, miss. And I sure will get started on that coop." Relieved, he spit in the dirt. "You look real pretty today, miss. Just like a picture."

Her lips curved. If anyone had told her a week ago that she would grow fond of a smelly, whiskey-drinking creature like Lucius, she'd have thought them mad. "Thank you. There's chicken and fresh bread in the cabin." She held her breath and snapped the reins.

Sarah had dressed very carefully for town. If she was going to interest the ladies in ordering fashionable clothes from her, then it was wise to advertise. Her dress was a particularly flattering shade of moss green with a high neckline she'd graced with her cameo. The trim of rose-colored ribbon and the rows of flounces at the skirt made it a bit flirtatious. She'd added a matching bonnet, tilted low as much for dash as for added shade. She felt doubly pleased with her choice when her two young customers came running out of the livery and goggled at it.

Sarah left them to race home and try on their new dresses while she completed her errands.

"Sarah." Liza danced around the counter of the dry goods store to take both of her hands. "Oh, what a wonderful dress. Every woman in town's going to want one like it."

"I was hoping to tempt them." Laughing, Sarah turned in a circle. "It's one of my favorites."

"I can see why. Is everything all right with you? I haven't been able to get away for days."

"Everything's fine. There's been no more trouble." She wandered over to take a look at the bolts of fabric. "I'm certain it was just an isolated incident. As the sheriff said, it must have been drifters." Glancing over, she smiled. "Hello, Mrs. Cody," she said as Liza's mother came in from the stockroom.

"Sarah, it's nice to see you, and looking so pretty, too."

"Thank you. I've brought your dress."

"Well, that was quick work." Anne Cody took the package in her wide, capable hands and went immediately to the cash drawer.

"Oh, I don't want you to pay for it until you look and make sure it's what you wanted."

Anne smiled, showing dimples like her daughter's. "That's good business. My Ed would say you've got a head on your shoulders. Let's just take a look, then." As she unwrapped the package, two of her customers moved closer to watch.

"Why, Sarah, it's lovely." Clearly pleased, Anne held it up. The dress was dove gray, simple enough to wear for work behind the counter, yet flatteringly feminine, with touches of lace at the throat and sleeves. "My goodness, honey, you've a fine hand with a needle." Deliberately she moved from behind the counter so that the rest of her customers could get the full effect. "Look at this work, Mrs. Miller. I'll swear you won't see better."

Grinning, Liza leaned over to whisper in Sarah's ear. "She'll have a dozen orders for you in no time. Pa always says Ma could sell a legless man new boots."

"Here you are, Sarah." Anne passed her the money. "It's more than worth every penny."

"Young lady." Mrs. Miller peered through her spectacles at the stitches in Anne's new dress. "I'm going to visit my sister in Kansas City next month. I think a traveling suit of this same fabric would be flattering to me."

"Oh, yes, ma'am." Sarah beamed, ignoring the fact that very little would be flattering to Mrs. Miller's bulky figure. "You have a good eye for color. This fabric trimmed in purple would be stunning on you."

By the time she was finished, Sarah had three more orders and an armful of fabric. With one hand muffling her giggles, Liza walked out with her. "Imagine you talking that old fuddy-duddy Mrs. Miller into two dresses."

"She wants to outshine her sister. I'll have to make sure she does."

"It won't be easy, considering what you have to work with. And she's overcharging you for those chicks."

"That's all right." Sarah turned with a grin. "I'm going to overcharge her for the dresses. Do you have time to walk with me? I'd like to go down and see if this blue-and-white stripe takes Mrs. O'Rourke's fancy."

They started down the walkway. After only a few steps, Liza stopped and swept her skirts aside. Sarah watched the statuesque woman approach. In all her life she'd never seen hair that color. It gleamed like the brass knob on Mother Superior's office door. The vivid blue silk dress she wore was too snug at the bodice and entirely too low for day wear. Smooth white breasts rose out of it, the left one adorned with a small beauty mark that matched another at the corner of her red lips. She carried an unfurled parasol and strolled, her hips swaying shamelessly.

As she came shoulder-to-shoulder with Sarah, the woman stopped and looked her up and down. The tiny smile she wore became a smirk as she walked on, rolling her hips.

"My goodness." Sarah could think of little else to say as she rubbed her nose. The woman's perfume remained stubbornly behind.

"That was Carlotta. She runs the Silver Star."

"She looks...extraordinary."

"Well, she's a—you know."

"A what?"

"A woman of ill repute," Liza said in a whisper.

"Oh." Sarah's eyes grew huge. She'd heard, of course. Even in Philadelphia one heard of such women.

But to actually pass one on the street… "Oh, my. I wonder why she looked at me that way."

"Probably because Jake Redman's been out your way a couple times. Jake's a real favorite with Carlotta." She shut her mouth tight. If her mother heard her talking that way she'd be skinned alive.

"I should have known." With a toss of her head Sarah started to walk again. For the life of her she didn't know why she felt so much like crying.

Mrs. O'Rourke greeted her with pleasure. Not only had it been a year since she'd had a new dress, she was determined to know all there was to know about the woman who was keeping Jake so churned up.

"I thought you might like this striped material, Mrs. O'Rourke."

"It's right nice." Maggie fingered the cotton with a large, reddened hand. "No doubt it'll make up pretty. Michael…my first husband was Michael Bailey, he was partial to a pretty dress. Died young, did Michael. Got a little drunk and took the wrong horse. Hung him for a horse thief before he sobered up."

Not certain what response was proper, Sarah murmured something inaudible. "I'm sure the colors would flatter you."

Maggie let out a bray of laughter. "Girl, I'm past the age where I care about being flattered. Buried me two husbands. Mr. O'Rourke, rest his soul, was hit by lightning back in '63. The good Lord doesn't always protect fools and drunkards, you know. Save me, I'm not in the market for another one. The only reason a woman decks herself out is to catch a man or keep one." She ran her shrewd eyes over Sarah. "Now you've got a rig on this day, you do."

Deciding to take the remark as a compliment, Sarah offered a small smile. "Thank you. If you'd prefer something else, I could—"

"I wasn't saying I didn't like the goods."

"Sarah can make you a very serviceable dress, Mrs. O'Rourke," Liza put in. "My ma's real pleased with hers. Mrs. Miller's having her make up two for her trip to Kansas City."

"That so?" Maggie knew what a pinchpenny the Miller woman was. "I reckon I could do with a new dress. Nothing fancy, mind. I don't want any of my boarders getting ideas in their heads." She let out a cackle.

"If a man got ideas about you, Maggie, he'd lose them quick enough after a bowl of your stew."

Sarah's fingers curled into her palms when she heard Jake's voice. Slowly, her body braced, she turned to face him. He was halfway down the stairs.

"Some men want something more from a woman than a bowl of stew," Maggie told him, and cackled again. "You ladies want to be wary of a man who smiles like that," she added, pointing a finger at Jake. "I ought to know, since I married two of them." As she spoke, she watched the way Jake and Sarah looked at each other. Someone had lit a fire there, she decided. She wouldn't mind fanning it a bit. "Liza, all this talk about cooking reminds me. I need another ten pounds of flour. Run on up and fetch it for me. Have your ma put it on my account."

"Yes, ma'am."

Anxious to be off, Sarah picked up the bolt of material again. "I'll get started on this right away, Mrs. O'Rourke."

"Hold on a minute. I've got a dress upstairs you can use for measuring. Needs some mending, too. I'm no hand with a needle. Liza, I can use two pounds of coffee." She motioned at the girl with the back of her hand. "Go on, off with you."

"I'll just be a minute," Liza promised as she walked out the door. Pleased with her maneuvering, Maggie started up the stairs.

"You're about as subtle as a load of buckshot," Jake murmured to her.

With the material still in her hands, Sarah watched Jake approach her. Though she was standing in the center of the room, she had the oddest sensation that her back was against the wall. He was staring at her in that way he had that made her stomach flutter and her knees shake. She promised herself that if he touched her, if he even looked as though he might touch her, she would slap him hard enough to knock his hat off.

He had images of touching her. Of tasting her. Of rolling around on the ground and filling himself with her. Seeing her now, looking like some flower that had sprung up out of the sand, he had to remind himself that they could only be images.

He figured that was no reason he couldn't needle her a bit.

"Morning, Duchess. You come by to see me?"

"Certainly not."

He couldn't help but enjoy the way her eyes fired up. Casually he brushed a finger over the fabric she held and felt her jolt. "Mighty pretty, but I like the dress you've got on better."

"It isn't for me." There was no reason in the world she should feel flattered, Sarah reminded herself. No reason at all. "Mrs. O'Rourke expressed interest in having a dress made."

"So you sew, too." His gaze traveled over her face, lingering on her mouth too long for comfort. "You're full of surprises."

"It's an honest way to make a living." Deliberately she looked down at the gun on his hip. "It's a pity not everyone can say the same."

It was difficult to say what the cool, disapproving tone made him feel. Rage, familiar and bitter-tasting. Futility, with its cold, hollow ring. Both emotions and flickers of others showed in his eyes as he stared down at her.

"So you heard about me," he said before she could follow her first impulse and lay a soothing hand on his arm. "I'm a dangerous man, Sarah." He took her chin in his hand so that her eyes stayed on his. "I draw my gun and leave women widows and children orphans. The smell of gunsmoke and death follows me wherever I go. I got Apache blood in my veins, so I don't look on killing the way a white man might. I put a bullet in a man the same way a wolf rips out throats. Because it's what I was made for. A woman like you had best keep her distance."

She heard the fury licking at his words. More, she heard frustration, a deep, raw frustration. Before he could reach the door, she was calling after him.

"Mr. Redman. Mr. Redman, please." Gathering up her skirts, she hurried after him. "Jake."

He stopped and turned as she came through the doorway. They were outside only a step, but that was enough to have the heat and dust rising around them.

"You'd do better to stay inside until Maggie comes down for you."

"Please, wait." She laid a hand on his arm. "I don't understand what you do, or who you are, but I do know you've taken the trouble to be a help to me. Don't tell me to forget it," she said quickly. "Because I won't."

"You've got a talent for tying a man up in knots," he murmured.

"I don't mean—"

"No, I don't reckon you do. Anything else you want to say?"

"Actually, I—" She broke off when she heard a burst of wild laughter from the next building. As she looked, a man was propelled headfirst through a pair of swinging doors. He landed in a heap in the dust of the road. Even as Sarah started forward, Jake shifted to block her.

"What do you think you're doing?"

"That man might be hurt."

"He's too drunk to be hurt."

Her eyes wide, Sarah looked past Jake's shoulder and saw the drunk struggle to his feet and stagger back inside. "But it's the middle of the day."

"Just as easy to get drunk in the daylight as it is when the sun's down."

Her lips primmed. "It's just as disgraceful." Whiskey might be the work of the devil, Sarah thought, but she had promised Lucius. "I wonder if I might ask you another favor?"

"You can ask."

"I need a bottle of whiskey."

Jake took off his hat and smoothed back his hair, then replaced the hat. "I thought you didn't care for it much."

"It's not for me. It's for Lucius." She was certain she heard the sound of breaking glass from the neighboring saloon as she reached for her reticule. "I'm afraid I don't know the price."

"Lucius is good for it. Go back inside," he told her, then passed through the swinging doors.

"Quite a man, isn't he?"

Sarah lifted a hand to her heart. "Mrs. O'Rourke, you startled me."

Grinning, Maggie stepped outside. "Your mind was elsewhere." She handed Sarah a bundle. "Good-looking, Jake is. Strong back, good hands. A woman can hardly ask for more." Maggie glanced over as the din from the saloon grew louder. "You don't have a fella back east, do you?"

"A what?" Distracted, Sarah inched closer to the saloon. She hated to admit it, but she was dying to see inside. "Oh, no. At least there was no one I cared for enough to marry."

"A smart woman knows how to bring a man around to marriage and make him think it was his idea all along. You take Jake—" Maggie broke off when Sarah squealed. Two men burst through the swinging doors and rolled into the street, fists flying.

"My goodness." Her mouth hanging open, Sarah watched the two men kick and claw and pummel each other.

"I thought I told you to go inside." Jake strolled out, carrying a bottle of whiskey by the neck.

"I was just—Oh!" She saw blood fly as a fist connected with a nose. "This is dreadful. You have to stop them."

"Like hell I do. Where's your wagon?"

"But you must," Sarah insisted. "You can't simply stand here and watch two men beat each other like this."

"Duchess, if I try to break that up, both of them are going to start swinging at me." He passed her the bottle of whiskey. "I don't feel much like killing anybody today."

With a huff, Sarah thrust the bottle back into his hands and followed it with the fabric and Maggie's bundle. "Then I'll stop them myself."

"It's going to be a shame when you lose some of those pretty teeth."

Taking time only to glare at him, Sarah bent down and scooped up the spittoon Maggie kept beside her doorway. Her skirts in one hand, weapon in the other, she marched toward the middle of the melee.

"That's some woman," Maggie said with a grin. Jake merely grunted. "Got grit."

"Go water down your stew."

Maggie just laughed. "She's got you, too. Hope I'm around when she figures it out."

A little breathless, Sarah dodged the rolling bodies. The men were groaning and hissing as they struggled to land punches. The smell of stale whiskey and sweat rose from both of them. She had to scramble a bit for aim before she brought the brass down with a thunk on one head and then the other. A roar of laughter, then a few cheers, poured out the doorway of the saloon. Ignoring the sound, Sarah looked down at the two men, who were frowning at her and rubbing their heads.

"You should be ashamed of yourselves," she told them, in a tone that would have made Mother Superior proud. "Fighting in the street like a couple of school-boys. You've done nothing but bloody your faces and make a spectacle of yourselves. Now stand up." Both men reached for their hats and struggled to their feet. "I'm sure whatever disagreement you have can be better solved by talking it out." Satisfied, Sarah nodded politely, then glided back across the street to where Jake and Maggie stood.

"There." She handed Maggie the spittoon. Her self-satisfied smirk was for Jake alone. "It was only a matter of getting their attention, then applying reason."

He glanced over her head to where the two men were wrestling in the dirt again. "Yes, ma'am." Taking her arm, he started up the street before she could get it in her head to do something else. "Did you learn to swing like that in your fancy school?"

"I had occasion to observe the nuns' techniques for handling disagreements."

"Ever get knocked on the head with a spittoon?"

She tilted her head, her eyes laughing under the cover of her lashes. "No, but I know what a wooden ruler feels like." Sarah glanced in the dry goods as she stopped by her wagon. Inside, she could see Liza flirting with a thin, gangly man with straw-colored hair and shiny brown boots.

"Is that Will Metcalf?"

Jake stowed the rest of her things in the back of the wagon. "Yeah."

"I think Liza's quite taken with him." She bit back a

sigh. Romance was as far away from her right now as the beautiful house her father had built for her in his mind. Turning, she bumped into Jake's chest. His hands came up to steady her and stayed on her arms. Not so far away, she thought again. It wasn't far away at all when it could reach out and touch you.

"You got to watch where you're going."

"I usually do. I used to." He was going to kiss her again, right there in the center of town. She could feel it. She could almost taste it.

He wanted to. He wanted five minutes alone with her, though he knew there was no use, it was no good. "Sarah—"

"Good morning, Jake." Twirling her parasol, Carlotta sauntered up to the wagon. Smiling slightly she ignored the warning look he sent her and turned her attention to Sarah. She'd already decided to hate her, for what she was, for what she had. Her smile still in place, she skimmed her gaze up and down Sarah. Pure and proper and dull, she decided. Jake would be tired of her in a week. But in the meantime it would give her pleasure to make the little priss uncomfortable.

"Aren't you going to introduce me to your friend?"

Jake ignored her and kept a hand on Sarah's arm to steer her to the front of the wagon.

Sarah didn't recognize the basic female urge, the primal urge, to face the enemy down. She only knew she wouldn't have the woman smirking at her back. "I'm Sarah Conway." She didn't offer her hand, she simply nodded. It was as much of an insult as Carlotta's sneering scrutiny.

"I know who you are." Carlotta smiled, fully, even

as her eyes turned to blue ice. "I knew your pa. I knew him real well."

The blow hit home. Carlotta was delighted to see it. But when her eyes skimmed up to meet Jake's, most of the pleasure she felt died. She'd seen him look at men that way when they'd pushed him too far. With a toss of her head, she turned away. He'd come around, she told herself. Men always did.

His mouth grim, Jake reached for Sarah's arm again to help her into the wagon. The moment his fingers brushed her, she jerked away.

"Don't touch me." She had to turn, to grip the edge of the wagon, until she caught the breath Carlotta had knocked out of her. All of her illusions were shattered now. The idea of her father, her own father, with a woman like that was more than she could take.

He'd have preferred to walk away. Just turn and keep going. Infuriated, he dug his hands into his pockets. "Let me help you into the damn wagon, Sarah."

"I don't want your help." She whirled back to face him. "I don't want anything from you. Do you understand?"

"No, but then I don't figure I'm supposed to."

"Do you kiss her the same way you kissed me? Did you think of me the same way you think of her and women like her?"

His hand shot out to stop her before she could scramble into the wagon. "I wasn't thinking at all when I kissed you, and that was my mistake."

"Miss Conway." Samuel Carlson stopped his horse at the head of the wagon. His eyes stayed on Jake's as he dismounted. "Is there a problem?"

"No." Instinctively she stepped between the men. Carlson's gun had a handle of polished ivory, and it looked deadly and beautiful below his silver brocade vest. It no longer shocked her to realize that even a man as obviously cultured and educated as he wouldn't hesitate to use a weapon. "Mr. Redman's been an invaluable help to me since I arrived."

"I heard you'd had some trouble."

Sarah discovered she was digging her nails into her palms. Slowly, stiffly, she uncurled her fingers, but she could do nothing about the tension that was pounding at the base of her throat. It sprang, she knew, from the men, who stood on either side of her, watching each other, ready, almost eager.

"Yes. Fortunately, the damage wasn't extensive."

"I'm glad to hear that." At last Carlson shifted his gaze to Sarah. She heard her own sigh of relief. "Did you ride into town alone, Miss Conway?"

"Yes, I did. As a matter of fact, I'd better be on my way."

"I'd be obliged if you'd allow me to drive you back. It's a long ride for a woman alone."

"That's kind of you, Mr. Carlson. I couldn't impose."

"No imposition at all." Taking her arm, he helped her into the seat. "I've been meaning to ride out, pay my respects. I'd consider it a favor if you'd allow me to drive you."

She was about to refuse again when she looked at Jake. There was ice in his eyes. She imagined there would be a different look in them altogether when he looked at Carlotta.

"I'd love the company," she heard herself say, and she

waited while Carlson tied his horse to the rear of the wagon. "Good day, Mr. Redman." Folding her hands in her lap, she let Carlson guide her team out of town.

They talked of nothing important for most of the drive. The weather, music, the theater. It was a pleasure, Sarah told herself, to spend an hour or two in the company of a man who understood art and appreciated beauty.

"I hope you won't take offense if I offer some advice, Miss Conway."

"Advice is always welcome." She smiled at him. "Even if it's not taken."

"I hope you'll take mine. Jake Redman is a dangerous man, the kind who brings trouble to everyone around him. Stay away from him, Miss Conway, for your own good."

She said nothing for a moment, surprised by the strength of the anger that rose up in her. Carlson had said nothing but the truth, and nothing she hadn't already told herself. "I appreciate your concern."

His voice was calm and quiet and laced with regret. "But you won't take my advice."

"I don't think it will be necessary. It's unlikely I'll be seeing Mr. Redman now that I've settled in."

Carlson shook his head and smiled. "I have offended you."

"Not at all. I understand your feelings for Jake—" She corrected herself carefully. "Mr. Redman. I'm sure the trouble between him and your brother was very distressing for you."

Carlson's mouth thinned. "It pains me to say that Jim

brought that incident on himself. He's young and a bit wild yet. Redman's a different matter. He lives by his gun and his reputation with it."

"That sounds like no life at all."

"Now I've stirred your sympathies. That certainly wasn't my intention." He touched a hand lightly to hers. "You're a beautiful, sensitive woman. I wouldn't want to see you hurt."

She hadn't been called beautiful in what felt like a very long time. Since a waltz, she remembered, at a ball at Lucilla's big house. "Thank you, but I assure you I'm learning very quickly to take care of myself."

As they drove into the yard, the puppy bounded up, racing around the wagon and barking. "He's grown some," Carlson commented as Lafitte snapped at his ankles.

"Hush, now." Lafitte snarled when Carlson lifted Sarah from the wagon. "He has the makings of an excellent guard dog, I think. And, thank heaven, he gets along well with Lucius. May I offer you some coffee?"

"I'd like that." Once inside, Carlson took a long look. "I've had some difficulty picturing you here. A drawing room with flowered wallpaper and blue draperies would suit you."

She laughed a little as she put the coffee on. "I think it will be some time yet before I put up wallpaper and draperies. I'd like a real floor first. Please sit down."

From the tin on the shelf she took a few of the sugar cookies she'd baked earlier in the week. It pleased her to be able to offer him a napkin she'd sewed out of scrap material.

"It must be a lonely life for you."

"I haven't had time to be lonely, though I admit it's not what I'd hoped for."

"It's a pity your father never made the mine pay."

"It gave him hope." She thought of the journal she was reading. "He was a man who needed hope more than food."

"You're right about that." Carlson sipped at the coffee she served him. "You know, I offered to buy this place from him some time back."

"You did?" Sarah took the seat across from him. "Whatever for?"

"Sentiment." Carlson sent her an embarrassed smile. "Foolish, really. My grandfather once owned this land. He lost it in a poker game when I was a boy. It always infuriated him." He smiled again and sampled a cookie. "Of course, he had the ranch. Twelve hundred acres, with the best water that can be had in these parts. But he grumbled about losing that old mine until the day he died."

"There must be something about it that holds a man. It certainly held my father."

"Matt bought it from the gambler and dived right in. He always believed he'd find the mother lode, though I don't think there is one. After the old man died and I took over, I thought it might be fitting somehow for me to bring it back into the family. A tribute. But Matt, he wouldn't part with it."

"He had a dream," Sarah murmured. "It killed him, eventually."

"I'm sorry. I've upset you. I didn't mean to."

"It's nothing. I still miss him. I suppose I always will."

"It might not be healthy for you to stay here, so close to where he died."

"It's all I have."

Carlson reached over to pat her hand. "As I said, you're a sensitive woman. I was willing to buy this place from Matt. I'd be willing to buy it from you if you feel you'd like to sell."

"Sell?" Surprised, she looked over. The sun was streaming through the yellow curtains at the window. It made a stream of gold on the floor. Before long, the strength of it would fade the material. "That's very generous of you, Mr. Carlson."

"I'd be flattered if you'd call me Samuel."

"It's very generous, and very kind, Samuel." Rising, she walked to the window. Yes, the sun would bleach it out, the same way it bleached the land. She touched a hand to the wall. The adobe stayed cool. It was a kind of miracle, she thought. Like the endurance that kept men in this place. "I don't think I'm ready to give up here."

"You don't have to decide what you want now." He rose, as well, and moved over to lay a gentle hand on her shoulder. She smiled at the gesture. It was comforting to have friends who cared.

"It's been difficult, adjusting here. Yet I feel as though I can't leave, that in leaving I'd be deserting my father."

"I know what it is to lose family. It takes time to think straight again." He turned her to face him. "I can say that I feel I knew Matt enough to be sure he'd want the best for you. If you decide you want to let it go, all you have to do is tell me. We'll leave it an open offer."

"Thank you." She turned and found herself flustered when he lifted both her hands to his lips.

"I want to help you, Sarah. I hope you'll let me."

"Miss Conway."

She jolted, then sighed when she saw Lucius in the doorway. "Yes?"

He eyed Carlson, then turned his head to spit. "You want me to put this team away?"

"Please."

Lucius stayed where he was. "How about the extra horse?"

"I'll be riding out. Thank you for the company, Sarah."

"It was a pleasure."

As they stepped outside, Carlson replaced his hat. "I hope you'll let me call again."

"Of course." Sarah was forced to snatch up the dog when he came toward her guest, snarling and snapping. "Goodbye, Samuel."

She waited until he'd started out before she put the puppy down and walked over to Lucius.

"Lucius." She leaned over to speak to him as he unhitched the horses. "You were quite rude just now."

"If you say so, miss."

"Well, I do." Frustrated, she ducked under the horses to join him. "Mr. Carlson was considerate enough to drive me back from town. You looked at him as though you wanted to shoot him in the head."

"Maybe."

"For heaven's sake. Why?"

"Some snakes don't rattle."

Casting her eyes to the sky, she gave up. Instead, she

snatched the bottle of whiskey from the wagon and watched his eyes light up. "If you want this, take off your shirt."

His mouth dropped as if she'd hit him with a board. "Beg pardon, ma'am?"

"The pants, too. I want you to strip right down to the skin."

He groped at his neckcloth. "Mind if I ask why you'd be wanting me to do that, Miss Conway?"

"I'm going to wash your clothes. I've tolerated the smell of them—and you—quite long enough. While I'm washing them, you can take that extra cake of soap I bought and do the same with yourself."

"Now, miss, I—"

"If, and only if, you're clean, I'll give you this bottle. You get a pail of water and the soap and go into that shed. Toss your clothes out."

Not sure he cared for the arrangement, Lucius shifted his feet. "And if I don't?"

"Then I'll pour every drop of this into the dirt."

Lucius laid a hand on his heart as she stamped off. He was mortally afraid she'd do it.

Chapter 7

Sarah rolled up the sleeves of her oldest shirtwaist, hitched up her serviceable black skirt and went to work.

They'd be better off burned, she thought as she dunked Lucius's stiff denim pants into the stream. The water turned a mud brown instantly. With a sound of disgust, she dunked them again. It would take some doing to make them even marginally acceptable, but she was determined.

Cleanliness was next to godliness.

That had been one of the proverbs cross-stitched on Mother Superior's office wall. Well, she was going to get Lucius as close to God as was humanly possible. Whether he liked it or not.

Leaving the pants to soak, she picked up his faded blue shirt by the tips of her fingers. Deplorable, she decided as she dampened and scrubbed and soaked. Absolutely deplorable. She doubted the clothes had seen clean water in a year. Which meant Lucius's skin had been just as much in need of washing. She'd soon fix that.

She began to smile as she worked. The expression on his face when she'd threatened to empty out the whiskey had been something to see. Poor Lucius. He might look tough and crusty, but underneath he was just a sweet, misguided man who needed a woman to show him the way.

Most men did. At least that was what Lucilla had always said. As she beat Lucius's weathered shirt against the rocks, Sarah wondered what her friend would think of Jake Redman. There was certainly nothing sweet about him, no matter how deep down a woman might dig. Though he could be kind. It baffled her that time and time again he had shown her that streak of good-heartedness. Always briefly, she added, her lips thinning. Always right before he did something inexcusable.

Like kissing the breath out of her. Kissing her until her blood was hot and her mind was empty and she wanted something she didn't even understand. He'd had no right to do it, and still less to walk away afterward, leaving her trembling and confused.

She should have slapped him. With that thought in mind, Sarah slapped the shirt on the water and gave a satisfied nod at the sound. She should have knocked the arrogance right out of him, and then it should have been she who walked away.

The next time… There would be no next time, she assured herself. If Jake Redman ever touched her again, she'd…she'd…melt like butter, she admitted. Oh, she hated him for making her wish he would touch her again.

When he looked at her, something happened, something frantic, something she'd never experienced before. Her heart beat just a little too fast, and dampness sprang out on the palms of her hands. A look was all that was necessary. His eyes were so dark, so penetrating. When he looked at her it was as if he could see everything she was, or could be, or wanted to be.

It was absurd. He was a man who lived by the gun, who took what he wanted without regret or compunction. All her life she'd been taught that the line between right and wrong was clear and wide and wasn't to be crossed.

To kill was the greatest sin, the most unforgivable. Yet he had killed, and would surely kill again. Knowing it, she couldn't care for him. But care she did. And want she did. And need.

Her hands were wrist-deep in water when she brought herself back. She had no business even thinking this way. Thinking about him. If she had to think of a man, she'd do better to think of Samuel Carlson. He was well-mannered, polished. He would know the proper way to treat a lady. There would be no wild, groping kisses from a man like him. A woman would be safe, cherished, cared for.

But she wished Jake had offered to drive her home.

This was nonsense. Sarah wrung out the shirt and rubbed her nose with the back of her damp hand. She'd had enough nonsense for the time being. She would wash thoughts of Jake away just as she washed the grime and grit and the good Lord knew what from Lucius's shirt.

She wanted her life to be tidy. Perhaps it wouldn't be as grand as she'd once imagined, but it would be tidy. Even here. Sitting back on her heels, she looked around. The sun was heading toward the buttes in the west. Slowly, like a big golden ball in a sky the color of Indian paintbrush. The rocks towered, their odd, somewhat mystical shapes rising up and up, some slender as needles, others rough and thick.

There was a light smell of juniper here, and the occasional rustle that didn't alarm her as it once would have. She watched an eagle soar, its wings spread wide. King of the sky. Below, the stream gurgled, making its lazy way over the rocks.

Why, it was beautiful. She lifted a hand to her throat, surprised to discover that it was aching. She hadn't seen it before, or hadn't wanted to. There was a wild, desolate, marvelous beauty here that man hadn't been able to touch. Or hadn't dared. If the land was lawless, perhaps it deserved to be.

For the first time since she had arrived, she felt a sense of kinship, of belonging. Of peace. She'd been right to stay, because this was home. Hers. At long last, hers.

When she rose to spread the shirt over a rock, she was smiling. Then she saw the shadow, and she looked up quickly.

There were five of them. Their black hair was loose past their bare shoulders. All but one sat on a horse. It was he who stepped toward her, silent in knee-length moccasins. There was a scar, white and puckered, that ran from his temple, catching the corner of his eye, then curving like a sickle down his cheek. She saw that, and the blade of the knife he carried. Then she began to scream.

Lucius heard the rider coming and strapped his gunbelt on over his long underwear. With soap still lathered all over his face, he stepped out of the shed. Jake pulled up his mount and took a long, lazy look.

"Don't tell me it's spring already."

"Damn women." Lucius spit expertly.

"Ain't that the truth?" After easing off his horse, Jake tossed the reins over the rail. Lafitte immediately leaped up to rest his paws on his thigh. In the way dogs have, he grinned and his tongue lolled. "Going to a dance or something?"

"No, I ain't going anywhere." Lucius cast a vicious look toward the house. "She threatened me. Yes, sir, there's no two ways about it, it was a threat. Said less'n I took myself a bath and let her wash my clothes she'd pour out every last drop of whiskey in the bottle she brought."

With a grin of his own, Jake leaned against the rail and rolled a cigarette. "Maybe she's not as stupid as she looks."

"She looks okay," Lucius muttered. "Got a streak of stubborn in her, though." He wiped a soapy hand on the thigh of his long underwear. "What are you doing out here?"

"Came out to talk to you."

"Like hell. I got eyes. She ain't in there," he said when Jake continued to stare at the house.

"I said I came to talk to you." Annoyed, Jake flicked a match and lit his cigarette. "Have you done any checking in the mine?"

"I've taken a look. She don't give a body much free time." He picked up a rock and tossed it so that the puppy would have something to chase. "Always wanting something built or fixed up. Cooks right good, though." He patted his belly. "Can't complain about that."

"See anything?"

"I saw where Matt was working some, right enough. And the cave-in." He spit again. "Can't say I felt real good about digging my way past it. Now, maybe if you told me what it was I was supposed to be looking for."

"You'll know if you find it." He looked back at the house. She'd put curtains on the windows. "Does she ever go up there?"

"Goes up, not in. Sits by his grave sometimes. Breaks your heart."

"Sounds like you're going soft on her, old man." He reached down to give Lafitte a scratch on the head.

"Wouldn't talk if I was you." He only laughed when Jake looked at him. There weren't many men who would have dared. "Don't go icing up on me, boy. I've known you too long. Might interest you to know that Samuel Carlson paid a call."

Jake blew out smoke with a shrug. "I know." He waited, took another drag, then swore under his breath. "Did he stay long?"

"Long enough to make up to her. Kissing her hands, he was. Both of them."

"Is that so?" The fury burned low in his gut and spread rapidly. Eyes narrowed, he flicked the cigarette away, half finished, and watched it smolder. "Where is she?"

"Down to the stream, I imagine."

Lucius smothered a laugh and bent down to pick up Lafitte before the puppy could scramble after Jake. "I wouldn't, if'n I was you, young fella. There's going to be fireworks fit for Independence Day."

Jake wasn't sure what he was going to do, but he didn't think Sarah was going to like it. He hoped she didn't. She needed a short rein, he decided. And he was going to see to it himself. Letting Carlson paw all over her. Just the thought of it made small, jagged claws of jealousy slice through him.

When he heard her scream, both guns were out of their holsters and in his hands in a heartbeat. He took the last quarter of a mile at a run, her screams and the sound of running horses echoing in his head.

When he reached the stream he saw the dust the ponies had kicked up. Even at a distance he recognized Little Bear's profile. There was a different kind of fire in him now. It burned ice-cold as he holstered his weapons. Lafitte came tearing down the path, snarling.

"You're too late again," Jake told the dog as he sniffed the ground and whined. He turned as Lucius came running in nothing more than his gunbelt and long johns.

"What happened?" Jake said nothing. Hunkering down, Lucius studied the marks left by the struggle. "'Paches." He saw his shirt, freshly washed and drying in the sun. "Damn it all to hell." Still swearing, he raced down the path toward Jake. "Let me get on my spare shirt and my boots. They don't have much of a lead."

"I'm going alone."

"There was four of them, maybe more."

"Five." Jake strode back into the clearing. "I ride alone."

"Listen, boy, even if it was Little Bear, that don't give you no guarantees. You weren't no more than kids last time, and you chose different ways."

"It was Little Bear, and I'm not looking for guarantees." He swung into the saddle. "I'm going to get her back."

Lucius put a hand on the saddle horn. "See that you do."

"If I'm not back tomorrow sundown, go get Barker. I'll leave a trail even he can follow." He kicked his horse into a gallop and headed north.

She hadn't fainted, but she wasn't so sure that was a blessing. She'd been tossed roughly onto the back of a horse, and she was forced to grip its mane to keep from tumbling off. The Indian with the scar rode behind her, calling out to his companions occasionally and gesturing with a new government-issue Winchester. He'd dragged her by her hair to get her astride the horse, and he still seemed fascinated by it. When she felt him push his nose into it, she closed her eyes, shuddered and prayed.

They rode fast, their ponies apparently tireless and obviously surefooted, as they left the flats for the rocks and the hills. The sun was merciless here. She felt it beating down on her head as she struggled not to weep. She didn't want to die weeping. They would undoubtedly kill her. But what frightened her more than whatever death was in store for her was what they would do to her first.

She'd heard stories, horrible, barbaric stories, about what was done to captive white women. Once she'd thought them all foolishness, like the stories of bogeymen conjured up to frighten small children. Now she feared that the stories were pale reflections of reality.

They climbed higher, to where the air cooled and the mountains burst to life with pine and fast-running streams. When the horses slowed, she slumped forward, her thighs screaming from the effort of the ride. They talked among themselves in words that meant nothing to her. Time had lost all meaning, as well. It had been hours. She was only sure of that because the sun was low and just beginning to turn the western sky red. Blood red.

They stopped, and for one wild moment she thought about kicking the horse and trying to ride free. Then she was being dragged to the ground. With the breath knocked from her, she tried to get her bearings.

Three of the men were filling water skins at the stream. One seemed hardly more than a boy, but she doubted age mattered. They watered their mounts and paid no attention to her.

Pushing herself up on her elbows, she saw the scarfaced Indian arguing with one she now took to be the leader. He had a starkly beautiful face, lean and chiseled and cold. There was an eagle feather in his hair, and around his neck was a string of what looked like small bleached bones. He studied her dispassionately, then signaled to the other man.

She began to pray again, silently, desperately, as the scarfaced brave advanced on her. He dragged her to her feet and began to toy with her hair. The leader barked out an order that the brave just snarled at. He reached for her throat. Sarah held her breath as he ripped the cameo from her shirtwaist. Apparently satisfied for the moment, he pushed her toward the stream and let her drink.

She did, greedily. Perhaps death wasn't as close as

she'd feared. Perhaps somehow, somehow, she could evade it. She wouldn't despair, she told herself as she soothed her burning skin with the icy water. Someone would come after her. Someone.

Jake.

She nearly cried out his name when she was dragged to her feet again. Her captor had fastened her brooch to his buckskin vest. Like a trophy, she thought. Her mother's cameo wouldn't be a trophy for a savage. Furious, she reached for it, and was slapped to the ground. She felt the shirtwaist rip away from her shoulder as she was pulled up by it. Instinctively she began to fight, using teeth and nails. She heard a cry of pain, then rolling masculine laughter. As she kicked and squirmed, her hands were bound together with a leather strap. She was sobbing now, but with rage. Tossed astride the pony again, she felt her ankles bound tight under its belly.

There was the taste of blood in her mouth, and tears in her eyes. They continued to climb.

She dozed somehow. When the pain in her arms and legs grew unbearable, it seemed the best escape. The height was dizzying. They rode along the edge of a narrow canyon that seemed to drop forever. Into hell, she thought as her eyes drooped again. Straight into hell.

Wherever they were taking her, it was a different world, one of forests and rivers and sheer cliffs. It didn't matter. She would die or she would escape. There was nothing else.

Survival. That's all there is.

She hadn't understood what Jake had meant when

he'd said that to her. Now she did. There were times when there was nothing but life or death. If she could escape, and had to kill to do so, then she would kill. If she could not escape, and they were planning what she feared they were, she would find a way to kill herself.

They climbed. Endlessly, it seemed to Sarah, they rode up a winding trail and into the twilight. Around her she could hear the call of night birds, high and musical, accented by the hollow hooting of an owl. The trees glowed gold and red, and as the wind rose it sounded through them. The air chilled, working through the torn shirtwaist. Only her pride remained as she shivered in silence.

Exhaustion had her dreaming. She was riding through the forest with Lucilla, chatting about the new bonnet they had seen that morning. They were laughing and talking about the men they would fall in love with and marry. They would be tall and strong and devastatingly handsome.

She dreamed of Jake—of a dream kiss, and a real one. She dreamed of him riding to her, sweeping her up on his big gray mount and taking her away. Holding her, warming her, keeping her safe.

Then the horses stopped.

Her heart was too weary even for prayer as her ankle bonds were cut. She was pulled unresisting from the horse, then sprawled on the ground when her legs buckled under her. There was no energy left in her for weeping, so she lay still, counting each breath. She must have slept, because when she came to again she heard the crackling of a fire and the quiet murmuring of men at a meal.

Biting back a moan, she tried to push herself up. Before she could, a hand was on her shoulder, rolling her onto her back.

Her captor leaned over her, his dark eyes gleaming in the firelight. He spoke, but the words meant nothing to her. She would fight him, she promised herself. Even knowing she would lose, she would fight. He touched her hair, running his fingers through it, lifting it and letting it fall. It must have pleased him, for he grinned at her before he took out his knife.

She thought, almost hoped, that he would slit her throat and be done with it. Instead, he began to cut her skirt away. She kicked, as viciously as she could, but he only parried the blows, then locked her legs with his own. Hearing her skirt rip, she struck out blindly with her bound hands. As he raised his own to strike her, there was a call from the campfire. Her kidnappers rose, bows and rifles at the ready.

She saw the rider come out of the gloom and into the flickering light. Another dream, she thought with a little sob. Then he looked at her. Strength poured back into her body, and she scrambled to her feet.

"Jake!"

She would have run to him, but she was yanked ruthlessly back. He gave no sign, barely glanced her way as he walked his horse toward the group of Apaches. He spoke, but the words were strange, incomprehensible to her.

"Much time has passed, Little Bear."

"I felt breath on my back today." Little Bear lowered his rifle and waited. "I thought never to see you again, Gray Eyes."

Slowly, ignoring the rage bubbling inside him, Jake dismounted. "Our paths have run apart. Now they come together again." He looked steadily into eyes he knew as well as he knew his own. There was between them a love few men would have understood. "I remember a promise made between boys. We swore in blood that one would never lift a hand against the other."

"The promise sworn in blood has not been forgotten." Little Bear held out his hand. They gripped firm, hand to elbow. "Will you eat?"

With a nod, Jake sat by the fire to share the venison. Out of the corner of his eye, he saw Sarah huddled on the ground, watching. Her face was pale with fear and exhaustion. He could see bruises of fatigue under eyes that were glazed with it. Her clothes were torn, and he knew, as he ate and drank, that she must be cold. But if he wanted her alive, there were traditions to be observed.

"Where is the rest of our tribe?"

"Dead. Lost. Running." Little Bear stared broodingly into the fire. "The long swords have cut us down like deer. Those who are left are few and hide in the mountains. Still they come."

"Crooked Arm? Straw Basket?"

"They live. North, where the winters are long and the game is scarce." He turned his head again, and Jake saw a cold, depthless anger—one he understood. "The children do not laugh, Gray Eyes, nor do the women sing."

They talked, as the fire blazed, of shared memories, of people both had loved. Their bond was as strong as it had been when Jake had lived and learned and felt like an Apache. But they both knew that time had passed.

When the meal was over, Jake rose from the fire. "You have taken my woman, Little Bear. I have come to take her back."

Little Bear held up a hand before the scarred man beside him could speak. "She is not my prisoner, but Black Hawk's. It is not for me to return her to you."

"Then the promise can be kept between us." He turned to Black Hawk. "You have taken my woman."

"I have not finished with her." He put a hand on the hilt of his knife. "I will keep her."

He could have bargained with him. A rifle was worth more than a woman. But bargaining would have cost him face. He had claimed Sarah as his, and there was only one way to take her back.

"The one who lives will keep her." He unstrapped his guns, handing them to Little Bear. There were few men he would have trusted with his weapons. "I will speak with her." He moved to Sarah as Black Hawk began to chant in preparation for the fight.

"I hope you enjoyed your meal," she said, sniffing. "I actually thought you might have come to rescue me."

"I'm working on it."

"Yes, I could see that. Sitting by the fire, eating, telling stories. My hero."

His grin flashed as he hauled her against him for a long, hard kiss. "You're a hell of a woman, Sarah. Just sit tight and let me see what I can do."

"Take me home." Pride abandoned, she gripped the front of his shirt. "Please, just take me home."

"I will." He squeezed her hands as he removed them from his shirt. Then he rose, and he, too, began to chant. If there was magic, he wanted his share.

They stood side by side in the glow of the fire as the youngest warrior bound their left wrists together. The glitter of knives had Sarah pushing herself to her feet. Little Bear closed a hand over her arm.

"You cannot stop it," he said in calm, precise English.

"No!" She struggled as she watched the blades rise. "Oh, God, no!" They came down, whistling.

"I will spill your white blood, Gray Eyes," Black Hawk murmured as their blades scraped, edge to edge.

Locked wrist to wrist, they hacked, dodged, advanced. Jake fought in grim silence. If he lost, even as his blood poured out, Black Hawk would celebrate his victory by raping Sarah. The thought of it, the fury of it, broke his concentration, and Black Hawk pushed past his guard and sliced down his shoulder. Blood ran warm down his arm. Concentrating on the scent of it, he blocked Sarah from his mind and fought to survive.

In the frigid night air, their faces gleamed with sweat. The birds had flown away at the sound of blades and the smell of blood. The only sound now was the harsh breathing of the two men locked in combat, intent on the kill. The other men formed a loose circle around them, watching, the inevitability of death accepted.

Sarah stood with her bound hands at her mouth, holding back the need to scream and scream until she had no air left. At the first sight of Jake's blood she had closed her eyes tight. But fear had had them wide again in an instant.

Little Bear still held her arm, his grip light but inescapable. She already understood that she was to be a kind of prize for the survivor. As Jake narrowly deflected Black Hawk's blade, she turned to the man beside her.

"Please, if you stop it, let him live, I'll go with you willingly. I won't fight or try to escape."

For a moment, Little Bear took his eyes away from the combat. Gray Eyes had chosen his woman well. "Only death stops it now."

As she watched, both men tumbled to the ground. She saw Black Hawk's knife plunge into the dirt an inch from Jake's face. Even as he drew it out, Jake's knife was ripping into his flesh. They rolled toward the fire.

Jake didn't feel the heat, only an ice-cold rage. The fire seared the skin on his arm before he yanked free. The hilt of his knife was slick with his own sweat but the blade dripped red with his opponent's blood.

The horses whinnied and shied when the men rolled too close. Then they were in the shadows. Sarah could see only a dark blur and the sporadic gleam of a knife. But she could hear desperate grunts and the scrape of metal. Then she heard nothing but the sound of a man breathing hard. One man. With her heart in her throat, she waited to see who would come back into the light.

Bruised, bloodied, Jake walked to her. Saying nothing, he cut through her bonds with the blade of the stained knife. Still silent, he pushed it into his boot and took his guns back from Little Bear.

"He was a brave warrior," Little Bear said.

With pain and triumph singing through him, Jake

strapped on his gunbelt. "He died a warrior's death." He offered his hand again. "May the spirits ride with you, brother."

"And with you, Gray Eyes."

Jake held out a hand for Sarah. When he saw that she was swaying on her feet, he picked her up and carried her to his horse. "Hold on," he told her, swinging up into the saddle behind her. He rode out of camp without looking back, knowing he would never see Little Bear again.

She didn't want to cry, but she couldn't stop. Her only comfort was that her tears were silent and he couldn't hear them. Or so she thought. They'd ridden no more than ten minutes at a slow walk when he turned her around in the saddle to cradle her against him.

"You've had a bad time, Duchess. Go on and cry for a while."

So she wept shamelessly, her cheeks pressed against his chest, the movement of the horse lulling her. "I was so afraid." Her voice hitching, she clung to him. "He was going to—"

"I know. You don't want to think about it." He didn't. If he did, he'd lose the already-slippery grip he had on his control. "It's all over now."

"Will they come after us?"

"No."

"How can you be sure?" As the tears passed, the fear doubled back.

"It wouldn't be honorable."

"Honorable?" She lifted her head to look at him. In the moonlight his face looked hard as rock. "But they're Indians."

"That's right. They'll stand by their honor a lot longer than any white man."

"But—" She had forgotten for a moment the Apache in him. "You seemed to know them."

"I lived with them five years. Little Bear, the one with the eagle feather, is my cousin." He stopped and dismounted. "You're cold. I'll build a fire and you can rest awhile." He pulled a blanket out of his saddlebag and tossed it over her shoulders. Too tired to argue, Sarah wrapped it tight around herself and sat on the ground.

He had a fire burning quickly and started making coffee. Without hesitation, Sarah bit into the jerky he gave her and warmed her hands over the flames.

"The one you…fought with. Did you know him?"

"Yeah."

He'd killed for her, she thought, and had to struggle not to weep again. Perhaps it had been a member of his own family, an old friend. "I'm sorry," she managed.

"For what?" He poured coffee into a cup, then pushed it into her trembling hands.

"For all of it. They were just there, all at once. There was nothing I could do." She drank, needing the warmth badly. "When I was in school, we would read the papers, hear stories. I never really believed it. I was certain that the army had everything under control."

"You read about massacres," he said with a dull fury in his voice that had her looking up again. "About settlers slaughtered and wagon trains attacked. You read about savages scalping children. It's true enough. But did you read any about soldiers riding into camps and butchering, raping women, putting bullets in babies long after treaties were signed and promises made? Did you hear stories about poisoned food and contaminated blankets sent to the reservations?"

"But that can't be."

"The white man wants the land, and the land isn't his—or wasn't." He took out his knife and cleaned it in the dirt. "He'll take it, one way or the other."

She didn't want to believe it, but she could see the truth in his eyes. "I never knew."

"It won't go on much longer. Little Bear and men like him are nearly done."

"How did you choose? Between one life and the other?"

He moved his shoulders. "There wasn't much choice. There's not enough Apache in me to have been accepted as a warrior. And I was raised white, mostly. Red man. That's what they called my father when he was coming up outside an army post down around Tucson. He kept it. Maybe it was pride, maybe it wasn't."

He stopped, annoyed with himself. He'd never told anyone so much.

"You up to riding?"

She wanted him to go on, to tell her everything there was to tell about himself. Instinct held her back. If she pushed, she might never learn. "I can try." Smiling, she reached out to touch his arm. "I want to— Oh, you're bleeding."

He glanced down. "Here and there."

"Let me see. I should have tended these already." She was up on her knees, pulling away the rent material of his sleeve.

"Nothing a man likes better than to have his clothes ripped off by a pretty woman."

"I'll thank you to behave yourself," she told him, but she couldn't muffle a chuckle.

It was good to hear her laugh, even if only a little. Most of the horror had faded from her eyes. But he wanted it gone, all of it. "Heard you made Lucius strip down to the skin. He claimed you threatened him."

This time her laughter was warmer. "The man needed to be threatened. I wish you'd seen his face when I told him to take off his pants."

"I don't suppose you'd like me to do the same."

"Just the shirt should do. This arm certainly needs to be bandaged." She rose and, modesty prevailing, turned her back before she lifted the hem of her skirt to rip her petticoat.

"I'm obliged." He eased painfully out of his shirt. "I've been wondering, Duchess, just how many of those petticoats do you wear?"

"That's certainly not a subject for discussion. But it's fortunate that I..." She turned back to him, and the words slipped quietly down her throat. She'd never seen a man's chest before, had certainly never thought a man could be so beautiful. But he was firm and lean, with the dark skin taut over his rib cage and gleaming in the firelight. She felt the heat flash inside her, pressing and throbbing in her center and then spreading through her like a drug.

An owl hooted behind her and made her jolt. "I'll need some water." She was forced to clear her throat. "Those wounds should be cleaned."

With his eyes still on hers, he lifted the canteen. Saying nothing, she knelt beside him again to tend the cut that ran from his shoulder to his elbow.

"This is deep. You'll want a doctor to look at it."

"Yes, ma'am."

Her eyes flicked up to his, then quickly away. "It's likely to scar."

"I've got others."

Yes, she could see that. His was the body of a hero, scarred, disciplined and magnificent. "I've caused you a great deal of trouble."

"More than I figured on," he murmured as her fingers glided gently over his skin.

She tied the first bandage, then gave her attention to the slice in his side. "This one doesn't look as serious, but it must be painful."

Her voice had thickened. He could feel the flutter of her breath on his skin. He winced as she cleaned the wound, but it was the firelight on her hair that was making him ache. He held his breath when she reached around him to secure the bandage.

"There are some nicks," she murmured. Fascinated, she touched her palm to his chest. "You'll need some salve."

He knew what he needed. His hand closed over her wrist. Her pulse jumped, but she only stared, as if she were mesmerized by the contrast of his skin against hers. Dazed, she watched her own fingers spread and smooth over the hard line of his chest.

The fire had warmed it, warmed her. Slowly she lifted her head and looked at him. His eyes were dark, darker than she'd ever seen them. Storm clouds, she thought. Or gunsmoke. She thought she could hear her heart pounding in her head. Then there was no sound. No sound at all.

He reached for her face, just to rub his palm over her cheek. Nothing in his life had ever seemed so soft or looked so beautiful. The fire was in her eyes, glowing, heating. There was passion there. He knew enough of women to recognize it. Her cheeks, drained of color by fatigue, were as delicate as glass.

He leaned toward her, his eyes open, ready for her to shy away.

She leaned toward him, her pulse pounding, waiting for him to take.

An inch apart, they hesitated, his breath merging with hers. Softly, more softly than either of them would have thought he could, he brushed his lips over hers. And heard her sigh. Gently, with hands more used to molding the grips of guns, he drew her to him. And felt her give. Her lips parted, as they would only for him.

Boldly, as she had never known she could, she ran her hands up his chest. Was he trembling? She murmured to him, lost in the wonder of it. His body was rigid with tension, even as he took the kiss deeper, gloriously deeper. She tasted the hot flavor of desire on his lips as they moved, restless and hungry, over hers.

Eager for more, she pressed against him, letting her arms link tight behind him, and her mouth tell him everything.

He felt the need burst through him like wildfire, searing his mind and loins and heart. Her name tore out of him as he twisted her in his arms and plundered her mouth. The flames beside them leaped, caught by the wind, and sent sparks shooting into the air. He felt her body strain against his, seeking more. Desperate, he tugged at the torn neck of her blouse.

She could only gasp when he covered her breast with his hand. His palm was rough with calluses, and the sensation made her arch and ache. Then his mouth was on her, hot and wet and greedy as it trailed down. Helpless, she dragged her hands through his hair.

She had faced death. This was life. This was love.

His lips raced over her until she was a mass of nerves and need. Recklessly she dragged his mouth back to hers and drove them both toward delirium. His hands were everywhere, pressing, bruising, exciting. With her breath hammering in and out of her lungs, she began to tremble.

His mouth was buried at her throat. The taste of her had seeped into him, and now it was all he knew, all he wanted to know. She was shuddering. Over and over, beneath his own, her body shook. Jake dug his fingers into the dirt as he fought to drag himself back. He'd forgotten what he was. What she was. Hadn't he proven that by nearly taking her on the ground? He heard her soft, breathless moan as he rolled away from her.

She was dizzy, dazed, desperate. With her eyes half closed, she reached out. The moment she touched him, he was moving away, standing.

"Jake."

He felt as though he'd been shot, low in the gut, and would bleed for the rest of his life. In silence, he smothered the fire and began to break camp.

Sarah suddenly felt the cold, and she wrapped her arms around herself. "What's wrong?"

"We've got to ride."

"But…" Her skin still tingled where his hands had scraped over it. "I thought…that is, it seemed as though…"

"Damn it, woman, I said we've got to ride." He yanked a duster out of his saddlebag and tossed it to her. "Put that on."

She held it against her as she watched him secure his saddlebags again. She wouldn't cry. Biting her lip hard to make sure, she vowed she would never cry over him. He didn't want her. It had just been a whim. He preferred another kind of woman. After dragging the duster around her shoulders, she walked to the horse.

"I can mount," she said coldly when he took her arm.

With a nod, he stepped back, then vaulted into the saddle behind her.

Chapter 8

The crack of the rifle echoed over the rock and sent a lone hawk wheeling. Sarah gritted her teeth, cocked the lever and squeezed again. The empty whiskey bottle exploded. She was improving, she decided as she mopped her brow and reloaded. And she was determined to get better still.

Lucius wandered over, Lafitte dancing at his heels. "You got a good eye there, Miss Sarah."

"Thank you." She lowered the rifle to give the pup a scratch. Jake was right. He was going to be a big one. "I believe I do."

No one was going to have to rescue her again, not from a rattlesnake, not from Apache marauders, not from the wrath of God himself. In the two weeks since Jake had dropped her, without a word and apparently without a thought, on her doorstep, she'd increased her daily rifle practice. Her aim had sharpened a great deal since she'd taken to imagining that the empty bottles and cans were Jake's grinning face.

"I told you, Lucius, there's no need for you to watch my every move. What happened before wasn't your fault."

"I can't help feeling it was. You hired me on to keep a lookout around here. Then the first time my pants're down—so to speak, Miss Sarah—you're in trouble."

"I'm back now, and unharmed."

"And I'm mighty grateful for it. If Jake hadn't just ridden up…I'd have tried to get you back, Miss Sarah, but he was the man for it."

She bit back the unkind remark that sprang to mind. He had saved her, had risked his life to do so. Whatever had happened afterward couldn't diminish that.

"I'm very grateful to Mr. Redman, Lucius."

"Jake just done what he had to."

She remembered the knife fight with a shudder. "I sincerely hope he won't be required to do anything like it again."

"That's why I'm going to keep a better eye on you. I tell you the God's truth now, Miss Sarah, worrying after a woman's a troublesome thing. I ain't had to bother since my wife died."

"Why, Lucius, I never knew you'd been married."

"Some years back. Quiet Water was her name. She was mighty dear to me."

"You had an Indian wife?" Wanting to hear more, Sarah sat down on a rock, spreading her skirts.

He didn't talk about it often, at least not when he was

sober. But he found he was making himself comfortable and telling his tale. "Yes, ma'am. She was Apache, one of Little Bear's tribe. Fact is, she'd've been some kind of aunt to him. I met her when I'd come out here to do some soldiering. Fought Cheyenne, mostly. That would have been back in '62. Didn't mind the fighting, but I sure got tired of the marching. I headed south some to do a little prospecting. Anyways, I met up with John Redman. That was Jake's pa."

"You knew Jake's father?"

"Knew him right well. Partnered up for a while. He and his missus had hit some hard times. Lot of people didn't care much for the idea of him being half-Apache." With a little laugh, he shrugged. "He told me once that some of his tribe didn't care much for the idea of him being half-white. So there you go."

"What kind of man was he?"

"Hardheaded, but real quiet. Didn't say much less'n you said something first. Could be funny. Sometimes it wouldn't occur to you for a minute or two that he'd made a joke. He was good for a laugh. Guess he was the best friend I ever had." He took out his bottle and was relieved when Sarah said nothing. "John had in mind to do some ranching, so I lent a hand here and there. That's how I came to meet Quiet Water."

Casually Sarah pleated her skirt. "I suppose you knew Jake as a boy."

"I'll say I did." Lucius let go a whistling laugh. "Tough little cuss. Could look a hole right through you. Ain't changed much. He was spending some time with his grandma's people. Would've thought he was one of them then, 'cept for the eyes. Course, he wasn't. They knew it and he knew it. Like John said, it's hard not being one or the other. I used to wonder what would've happened if Quiet Water and me had had kids."

"What happened to her, Lucius?"

"I had gone off looking for gold." His eyes narrowed as he stared off into the sun. "Seems a regiment rode through early one morning. Some settler claimed his stock was stolen, and that the Apaches had done it. So the soldiers came in, looking for trouble, hating Indians. Killed most everybody but those who made it up into the rocks."

"Oh, Lucius. Lucius, I'm so sorry." Unable to find words, she took both his hands in hers.

"When I come back, it was done. I was half-crazy, I guess. Rode around for days, not going anywhere. I guess I was hoping somebody'd come along and shoot me. Then I headed to the Redman place. They'd been burned out."

"Oh, dear God."

"Nothing left but charred wood and ashes."

"How horrible." She tightened her grip on his hands. "Oh, Lucius, it wasn't the soldiers?"

"No. Leastwise they weren't wearing uniforms. Seemed like some men from town got liquored up and decided they didn't want no breed that close by. John and his missus had had trouble before, like I said, but this went past hard words and threats. They started out to burn the barn, raise hell. One of them started shooting. Maybe they'd meant to all along, there's no saying. When it was over, they'd burned them out and left the family for dead."

Horror made her eyes dark and huge. "Jake. He would have been just a boy."

"Thirteen, fourteen, I reckon. But he was past being a boy. I found him where he'd buried his folks. He was just sitting there, between the two fresh graves. Had his pa's hunting knife in his hands. Still carries it."

She knew the knife. She'd seen it stained with blood, for her. But now all she could think of was the boy. "Oh, the poor child. He must have been so frightened."

"No, ma'am. I don't believe frightened's the word. He was chanting, like in a trance the Indians sometimes use. War chant, it was. He figured on going into town and finding the men who killed his folks."

"But you said he was only thirteen."

"I said he was past being a boy. Best I could do was talk him out of it for a time, till he learned to handle a gun better. He learned mighty fast. I ain't never seen a man do with a gun what Jake can do."

Though it was hot out, she rubbed the chill from her arms. "Did he…go back for them?"

"I don't rightly know. I never asked. I thought it best we move on until he had some years on him, so we headed south. Didn't know what to do for him. Bought him a horse, and we rode together awhile. I always figured he'd hook up with the wrong kind, but Jake was never much for hooking up with anybody. He'd've been about sixteen when we parted ways. Heard about him off and on. Then he rode into Lone Bluff a few months back."

"To lose everything that way." A tear ran down her cheek. "It's a wonder he's not filled with hate."

"He's got it in him, but it's cold. Me, I use the bottle,

wash it away now and then. Jake uses something in here." He tapped his temple. "That boy holds more inside than anybody should have to. He ever lets it out, people better stand back."

She understood what he meant. Hadn't she seen it, that flat, dangerous look that came into his eyes? That expressionless stare that was more passionate than fury, more deadly than rage.

"You care for him."

"He's all I got that you might call family. Yeah, I got an affection for the boy." Lucius squinted over at her. "I figure you do, too."

"I don't know what I feel for him." That was a lie. She knew very well what she felt, how she felt. She was even coming to understand why she felt. He wasn't the man she had once imagined she would love, but he was the only man she ever would. "It doesn't matter what I feel," she said, "if he doesn't feel it back."

"Maybe he does. It might be hard for him to say it right out, but I always figure a woman's got a sense about those things."

"Not always." With a little sigh, she rose. "There's work to be done, Lucius."

"Yes'm."

"There is one question. What have you been doing in the mine?"

"The mine, Miss Sarah?"

"You said yourself I have a good eye. I know you've been going in there. I'd like to know why."

"Well, now." Fabricating wasn't Lucius's strong suit.

He coughed and shifted his feet and peered off at nothing. "Just having a look around."

"For gold?"

"Could be."

"Do you think you'll find any?"

"Matt always figured there was a rich vein in that rock, and when Jake—" He broke off.

"When Jake what? Asked you to look?"

"Maybe he might have suggested it sometime."

"I see." Sarah looked up to the top of the ridge. She had always wondered what Jake wanted, she thought, her heart shattering. Perhaps she knew now. Gold seemed to pull at the men she loved. "I have no objection to you working the mine, Lucius. In fact, I think it's an excellent idea. You must let me know if you require any tools." When she looked back at him, her eyes were as cool and hard as any man's. "The next time you ride into town, you might mention to Jake that Sarah's Pride is mine."

"Yes, ma'am, if you'd like."

"I insist." She looked toward the road. "There's a buggy coming."

Lucius spit and hoped it wasn't Carlson. As far as he was concerned, the man had been too free with his visits to Sarah in the past few weeks.

It wasn't Carlson. As the buggy drew closer, Sarah saw it was a woman holding the reins. Not Liza, she realized with a pang of disappointment. The woman was dark and delicate and a stranger to her.

"Good morning." Sarah set the rifle against the wall of the house.

"Good morning, ma'am." The young woman sat in

the buggy and sent Sarah a nervous smile. "You sure live a ways out."

"Yes." Since her visitor didn't seem in a hurry to alight, Sarah walked to the buggy. "I'm Sarah Conway."

"Yes, ma'am, I know. I'm Alice. Alice Johnson." She gave the puppy a bright, cheerful smile, then looked at Sarah again. "Pleased to meet you."

"It's nice to meet you, too, Miss Johnson. Would you like to come in for some tea?"

"Oh, no, ma'am, I couldn't."

Baffled by Alice's horrified expression, Sarah tried again. "Perhaps you're lost?"

"No, I've come to talk with you, but I couldn't come in. It wouldn't be fitting."

"Oh? Why?"

"Well, you see, Miss Conway, I'm one of Carlotta's girls."

Carlotta? Wide-eyed, Sarah looked her visitor over again. She was hardly more than a girl, a year or more younger than Sarah herself. Her face was scrubbed clean, and her dress was certainly modest. As Sarah stared, thick lashes lowered over her dark eyes and a blush rushed into her cheeks.

"Do you mean you work at the Silver Star?"

"Yes, ma'am, for nearly three months now."

"But—" Sarah swallowed the words when she saw Alice bite her lip. "Miss Johnson, if you've come to see me, I suggest we talk inside. It's much too hot to stand in the sun."

"I couldn't. Really, it wouldn't be fitting, Miss Conway."

"Fitting or not, I don't wish sunstroke on either of us. Please, come in." Leaving the decision in the hands of her visitor, Sarah walked inside.

Alice hesitated. It didn't feel right, not when Miss Conway was a real lady. But if she went back and couldn't tell Carlotta that she'd done what she'd been sent for, she'd get slapped around for sure. Carlotta always knew when you lied. And you always paid for it.

Sarah heard the timid footsteps as she put water on to boil. Before she could turn and offer Alice a seat, the girl was bubbling.

"Oh, my, isn't this pretty? You've got a real nice place here, Miss Conway. Curtains and all."

"Thank you." Her smile was full and genuine. It was the first time she'd had company who had thought so. "I'm more and more at home here. Please, sit down, Miss Johnson. I'm making tea."

"It's real kind of you, but I don't feel right, you giving me tea. It ain't proper."

"This is my house, and you're my guest. Of course it's proper. I hope you'll enjoy these cookies. I made them only yesterday."

With her fingers plucking nervously at her skirt, Alice sat. "Thank you, ma'am. And don't worry. I won't tell a soul I came in and sat at your table."

Intrigued, Sarah poured the tea. "Why don't you tell me what brought you out to see me?"

"Carlotta. She's been looking at all the dresses you've been making for the ladies in town. They're real pretty, Miss Conway."

"Thank you."

"Just the other day, after Jake left—"

"Jake?"

"Yes'm." Hoping she was holding the cup properly, Alice drank. "He comes into the Silver Star pretty regular. Carlotta's real fond of him. She don't work much herself, you know. Unless it's somebody like Jake."

"Yes, I see." She waited for what was left of her heart to break. Instead, it swelled with fury. "I suppose she might find a man like him appealing."

"She surely does. All the girls got a fondness for Jake."

"I'm sure," she murmured.

"Well, like I was saying, Carlotta got it into her head one day after he left that we should have us some new clothes. Something classy, like ladies would wear. She told me Jake said you could sew some up for us."

"Did he?"

"Yes, ma'am. She said she thought Jake had a real fine idea there, and she sent me on out to see about it. I got me all the measurements."

"I'm sorry, Miss Johnson, I really couldn't. Be sure to tell Carlotta that I appreciate the offer."

"There's eight of us girls, miss, and Carlotta said she'd pay you in advance. I got the money."

"That's generous, but I can't do it. Would you like more tea?"

"I don't—" Confused, Alice looked at her cup. She didn't know anyone who'd ever said no to Carlotta. "If it's not too much trouble." She wanted to stretch out her visit, though she knew that, and the message she'd be taking back, would make Carlotta box her ears.

"Miss Johnson—"

"You can call me Alice, Miss Conway. Everybody does."

"Alice, then. Would you mind telling me how it was you came to work for Carlotta? You're very young to be…on your own."

"My daddy sold me off."

"*Sold* you?"

"There was ten of us at home, and another on the way. Every time he got drunk he whipped one of us or made another. He got drunk a lot. Few months back, a man passed through and Daddy sold me for twenty dollars. I ran off as soon as I could. When I got to Lone Bluff I went to work for Carlotta. I know it ain't right and proper, but it's better than what I had. I get my meals and a bed to myself when I'm finished work." She gave a quick, uncomfortable shrug. "Most of the men are all right."

"Your father had no right to sell you, Alice."

"Sometimes there's right and there's what's done."

"If you wanted to leave Carlotta, I'm sure there would be other work for you in town. Proper work."

"Begging your pardon, Miss Conway, but that ain't true. None of the town ladies would hire me for anything. And they shouldn't. Why, how would they know if I'd been with one of their husbands?"

It was sound thinking, but Sarah shook her head. "If you decide to leave, I'll find work for you."

Alice stared at her, wide-eyed. "That's kind of you. I knew you were a real lady, Miss Conway, and I'm obliged. I'd better be heading back."

"If you'd like to visit again, I'd be happy to see you," Sarah told her as she walked her out.

"No, ma'am, that wouldn't be proper. Thank you for the tea, Miss Conway."

Sarah thought a great deal about Alice's visit. That night, as she read her father's journal by lamplight, she tried to imagine what it had been like. To be sold, she thought with an inward shudder. By her own father, like a horse or a steer. It was true that she, too, had spent years of her life without a real family, but she had always known her father loved her. What he had done, he had done with her best interests at heart.

Once she would have condemned Alice's choice out of hand. But now she thought she understood. It was all the girl knew. The cycle had begun with her father's callousness, and the girl was caught in it, helplessly moving in the same circle, selling herself time after time because she knew nothing else.

Had it been the same for Jake? Had the cruelty he'd lived through as a child forced him into a life of restlessness and violence? The scars he carried must run deep. And the hate. Sarah looked into the soft glow of the lamp. As Lucius had said, the hate ran cold.

She should have hated him. She wanted to, she wished the strong, destructive emotion would come, filling all the cracks in her feelings, blocking out everything else. With hate, a coolheaded, sharply honed hate, she would have felt in control again. She needed badly to feel in control again. But she didn't hate him. She couldn't.

Even though she knew he had spent the night with another woman, kissing another woman's lips, touching another woman's skin, she couldn't hate him. But she could grieve for her loss, for the death of a beauty that had never had a chance to bloom fully.

She had come to understand what they might have had together. She had almost come to accept that they belonged together, whatever their differences, whatever the risks. He would always live by his gun and by his own set of rules, but with her, briefly, perhaps reluctantly, he had shown such kindness, such tenderness.

There was a place for her in his heart. Sarah knew it. Beneath the rough-hewn exterior was a man who believed in justice, who was capable of small, endearing kindnesses. He'd allowed her to see that part of him, a part she knew he'd shared with few others.

Then why, the moment she had begun to soften toward him, to accept him for what and who he was, had he turned to another woman? A woman whose love could be bought with a handful of coins?

What did it matter? With a sigh, she closed her father's journal and prepared for bed. She had only fooled herself into believing he could care for her. Whatever kindness Jake had shown her would always war with his lawless nature and his restless heart. She wanted a home, a man by her side and children at her feet. As long as she loved Jake, she would go on wanting and never having.

Somehow, no matter how hard it was, no matter how painful, she would stop loving him.

Jake hated himself for doing it, but he rode toward Sarah's place, a dozen excuses forming in his head. He wanted to talk to Lucius and check on the progress in the mine. He wanted to make sure she hadn't been bitten by a snake. He'd wanted a ride, and her place was as good as any.

They were all lies.

He just wanted to see her. He just wanted to look at her, hear her talk, smell her hair. He'd stayed away from her for two weeks, hadn't he? He had a right…. He had no rights, he told himself as he rode into the yard. He had no rights, and no business thinking about her the way he was thinking about her, wanting her the way he wanted her.

She deserved a man who could make her promises and keep them, who could give her the kind of life she'd been born to live.

He wasn't going to touch her again. That was a promise he'd made himself when he'd ridden away from her the last time. If he touched her, he wouldn't pull back. That would only cause them both more misery.

He'd hurt her. He had seen that plain enough when he'd left her. But that was nothing compared to what he would have done if he'd stayed.

It was quiet. Jake pulled up his mount and took a long, cautious look around, his hand hovering over the butt of his gun. The dog wasn't yapping, nor was there any smoke rising from the chimney. The saddle creaked as he dismounted.

He didn't knock, but pushed open the door and listened. There wasn't a sound from inside. He could see, as his eyes scanned from one corner to the next, that the cabin was empty and as tidy as a church. The curtains she'd sewed had already begun to fade, but they moved prettily in the hot wind. His shoulders relaxed.

She'd done something here. That was something else he had to admire about her. She'd taken less than nothing and made it a home. There were pictures on the walls. One was a watercolor of wildflowers in soft, dreamy hues. It looked like her, he thought as he took a closer study. All dewy and fresh and delicate. Flowers like that would wither fast if they weren't tended.

He moved to the next, his brows drawing together as he scanned it. It was a pencil drawing—a sketch, he figured she'd call it. He recognized the scene, the high, arrogant buttes, the sun-bleached rock. If you looked west from the stream you'd see it. It wasn't an empty place. The Apache knew the spirits that lived there. But oddly, as he studied the lines and shadows, he thought Sarah might know them, too. He would never have imagined her taking the time to draw something so stark and strong, much less hang it on the wall so that she would see it every time she turned around.

Somehow—he couldn't quite figure out the why of it—it suited her every bit as much as the wildflowers.

Annoyed with himself, he turned away. She knew something about magic, he figured. Didn't the cabin smell of her, so that his stomach kept tying itself in knots? He'd be better off out in the air—fifty miles away.

A book caught his eye as he started out. Without giving a thought to her privacy, he opened it. Apparently she'd started a diary. Unable to resist, he scanned the first page.

She'd described her arrival in Lone Bluff. He had to grin as he read over her recounting of the Apache raid and his timely arrival. She'd made him sound pretty impressive, even if she'd noted what she called his "infuriating and unchristian behavior."

There was a long passage about her father, and her feelings about him. He passed it by. Grief was to be respected, unless it needed to be shared. He chuckled out loud as she described her first night, the cold can of beans and the sounds that had kept her awake and trembling until morning. There were bits and pieces he found entertaining enough about the townspeople and her impressions of life in the West. Then he caught his name again.

"Jake Redman is an enigma." He puzzled over the word, sure he'd never heard it before. It sounded a little too fancy to be applied to him.

I don't know if one might call him a diamond in the rough, though rough he certainly is. Honesty forces me to admit that he has been of some help to me and shown glimmers of kindness. I can't resolve my true feelings about him, and I wonder why I find it necessary to try. He is a law unto himself and a man wholly lacking in manners and courtesy. His reputation is distressing, to say the least. He is what is referred to as a gunslinger, and he wears his weapons as smoothly as a gentleman wears a watch fob. Yet I believe if one dug deeply enough one might discover a great deal of goodness there. Fortunately, I have neither the time nor the inclination to do the digging.

Despite his manner and his style of living there is a certain, even a strong, attractiveness about him. He has fine eyes of clear gray, a mouth that

some women might call poetic, particularly when
he smiles, and truly beautiful hands.

He stopped there to frown down at his hands. They'd
been called a lot of things, but beautiful wasn't one of
them. He wasn't sure he cared for it. Still, she sure did
have a way with words.

He turned the page and would have read on, but the
slightest of sounds at his back had him whirling, his
guns gripped firmly in his hands.

Lucius swore long and skillfully as he lowered his
own pistol. "I ain't lived this long to have you blow
holes in me."

Jake slipped his guns home. "You'd better be careful
how you come up on a man. Didn't you see my horse?"

"Yeah, I saw it. Just making sure. Didn't expect to
find you poking around in here." He glanced down at
the book. Without a word, Jake shut it.

"I didn't expect to find the place deserted."

"I've been up to the mine." Lucius pulled a small
bottle of whiskey from his pocket.

"And?"

"It's interesting." He took a long pull, then wiped his
mouth with the back of his hand. "I can't figure how
Matt got himself caught in that cave-in. He was pretty
sharp, and I recollect them beams being secure enough.
Looks to me like someone worked pretty hard to bring
them down."

With a nod, Jake glanced at the watercolor on the
wall. "Have you said anything to her yet?"

"Nope." He didn't think it was the best time to tell

"You're strong-willed. I find that very attractive."

He took her hand again. Before she could decide how to respond, a man strode into the house. He was shorter and leaner than Carlson, but there was enough of a resemblance around the mouth and eyes for her to recognize him. His hat was pushed back so that it hung around his neck by its strap. Yellow dust coated his clothes. He hooked his thumbs in the pockets of his pants and looked at her in a way that made her blood chill.

"Well, now, what have we got here?"

"Miss Conway." There was a warning, mild but definite, in Carlson's voice. "My brother Jim. You'll have to excuse him. He's been working the cattle."

"Sam handles the money, I handle the rest. You didn't tell me we were having company." He swaggered closer. He carried the scents of leather and tobacco, but she found nothing appealing about it. "Such nice-looking company."

"I invited Miss Conway to lunch."

"And it was lovely, but I really should be getting back." And away, she thought, from Jim Carlson.

"You don't want to rush off the minute I get in." Grinning, Jim laid a dirty hand on the polished surface of a small table. "We don't get enough company here, at least not your kind. You're just as pretty as a picture." He glanced at his brother with a laugh Sarah didn't understand. "Just as pretty as a picture."

"You'd better wash up." Though his voice was mild, Carlson sent him a hard look. "We have some business to discuss when I get back."

"It's all business with Sam." Jim winked at Sarah. "Now, me, I got time for other things."

Sarah swallowed a sigh of relief when Carlson took her elbow again. "Good day, Mr. Carlson."

Jim watched her retreating back. "Yeah, good day to you. A real good day."

"You'll have to excuse him." Carlson helped Sarah into the waiting buggy. "Jim's a bit rough around the edges. I hope he didn't upset you."

"No, not at all," she said, struggling to keep a polite smile. With her hands folded in her lap, she began to chat about whatever came to mind.

"You seem to be adjusting well to your new life," Carlson commented.

"Actually, I'm enjoying it."

"For selfish reasons, I'm glad to hear it. I was afraid you'd lose heart and leave." He let the horses prance as he turned to smile at her. "I'm very glad you're staying." He pulled up so that they could have a last look at the ranch from the rise. The house spread out, rising two stories, glowing pink in the sunlight, its small glass windows glimmering. Neat paddocks and outbuildings dotted the land, which was cut through by a blue stream and ringed by hills.

"It's lovely, Samuel. You must be very proud of it."

"Pride isn't always enough. A place like this needs to be shared. I've regretted not having a family of my own to fill it. Until now I'd nearly given up hoping I'd find a woman to share it with me." He took her hand and brought it to his lips. "Sarah, nothing would make me happier than if that woman were you."

She wasn't sure she could speak, though she could hardly claim to be surprised. He'd made no secret about the fact that he was courting her. She studied his face in silence. He was everything she had dreamed of. Handsome, dashing, dependable, successful. Now he was offering her everything she had dreamed of. A home, a family, a full and happy life.

She wanted to say yes, to lift a hand to his cheek and smile. But she couldn't. She looked away, struggling to find the right words.

She saw him then. He was hardly more than a silhouette on the horizon. An anonymous man on horseback. But she knew without seeing his face, without hearing his voice, that it was Jake. That knowledge alone made her pulse beat fast and her body yearn.

Deliberately she turned away. "Samuel, I can't begin to tell you how flattered I am by your offer."

He sensed refusal, and though anger tightened within him, he only smiled. "Please, don't give me an answer now. I'd like you to think about it. Believe me, Sarah, I realize we've known each other only a short time and your feelings might not be as strong as mine. Give me a chance to change that."

"Thank you." She didn't object when he kissed her hand again. "I will think about it." That she promised herself. "I'm very grateful you're patient. There's so much on my mind right now. I've nearly got my life under control again, and now that I'm going to open the mine—"

"The mine?" His hand tightened on hers. "You're going to open the mine?"

"Yes." She gave him a puzzled look. "Is something wrong?"

"No, no, it's only that it's dangerous." It was a

measure of his ambition that he was able to bring himself under control so quickly. "And I'm afraid doing so might distress you more than you realize. After all, the mine killed your father."

"I know. But it also gave him life. I feel strongly that he would have wanted me to continue there."

"Will you do something for me?"

"I'll try."

"Think about it carefully. You're too important to me. I would hate to have you waste yourself on an empty dream." With another smile, he clucked to the horses. "And if you marry me, I'll see that the mine is worked without causing you any heartache."

"I will think about it." But her mind was crowded with other thoughts as she looked over her shoulder at the lone rider on the hill.

Chapter 9

Sarah had never been more excited about a dance in her life. Nor had she ever worked harder. The moment the plans had been announced for a town dance to celebrate Independence Day, the orders for dresses began to pour in. She left all the chores to Lucius and sewed night and day.

Her fingers were cramped and her eyes burned, but she had earned enough to put through an order for the wood floor she wanted so badly.

After the floor, Sarah thought, she would order glass for the windows and a proper set of dishes. Then, when time and money allowed, she was going to have Lucius build her a real bedroom. With a little laugh, she closed her eyes and imagined it. If the mine came through, she would have that house with four bedrooms and a parlor, but for now she'd settle for a real floor beneath her feet.

Soon, she thought. But before floors and windows came the dance.

She might have made every frock as pretty and as fashionable as her skill allowed, but she wasn't about to be outdone. On the afternoon of the dance she took out her best silk dress. It was a pale lavender blue, the color of moonbeams in a forest. White lace flirted at the square-cut bodice that accented the line of her throat and a hint of shoulder. There were pert bows of a deeper lavender at the edge of each poufed sleeve.

She laced her stays so tightly that her ribs hurt, telling herself it would be worth it. With her hand mirror, she struggled to see different parts of herself and put them together in her mind for a complete image. The flounced skirt with the bows was flattering, she decided, and the matching velvet ribbon at her throat was a nice touch. She would have pinned her cameo to it, but that, like so much else, had been lost.

She wouldn't think about that tonight, she told herself as she patted her hair. She'd swept it up, and its weight had caused her to use every hairpin she could find. But, she thought with a nod, it looked effortless, curling ever so slightly at her ears and temples.

It was important that she look her best. Very important, she added, pulling on her long white gloves. If Jake was there, she wanted him to see just what he'd tossed aside. She swept on her white lace shawl, checked the contents of her reticule, then stepped outside.

"Glory be." Lucius stood by the wagon with his hat

in his hand. He'd cleaned up without her having to remind him, and had even taken a razor to his chin. When she smiled at him, he decided that if he'd been ten years younger he'd have given Jake a run for his money.

"Lucius, how handsome you look."

"Hell, Miss Sarah. I mean—" He cleared his throat. "You sure look a sight."

Recognizing that as a compliment, Sarah smiled and held out a hand. With as much style as he could muster, Lucius helped her into the wagon.

"You're going to set them on their ears."

"I hope so." At least she hoped she set one person on his ear. "You're going to save a dance for me, aren't you, Lucius?"

"I'd be pleased to. If I do say so, I dance right well, drunk or sober."

"Perhaps you'll try it sober tonight."

Jake saw them ride into town. He was sitting at his window, smoking and watching some of the cowboys racing in the streets, waving their hats, shooting off guns and howling.

Independence Day, he thought, blowing smoke at the sky. Most of them figured they had a right to freedom and the land they'd claimed. He'd come to accept that they, and others like them, would take the Arizona Territory and the rest of the West. Black Hawk, and others like him, would never stop the rush.

And he was neither invader nor invaded.

Maybe that was why he had never tried to put his mark on the land. Not since he'd lost what his father had tried to build. It was better to keep whatever you owned light, light enough that it fit on your horse.

The town was full of noise and people. Most of the cowhands were going to get three-quarters drunk, and they were liable to end up shooting themselves instead of the targets Cody had set up for the marksmanship contest. He didn't much care. He just sat at the window and watched.

Then he saw her. It hurt. Unconsciously he rubbed a hand over his heart, where the ache centered. She laughed. He could hear the sound float right up to him and shimmer like water over his skin. The wanting, the pure strength of it, made him drag his eyes away. For survival.

But he looked back, unable to stop himself. She stepped out of the wagon and laughed again as Liza Cody ran out of her father's store. She twirled in a circle for Liza, and he saw all of her, the white skin of her throat, the hint of high, round breasts, the tiny waist, the glow in her eyes. The cigarette burned down to his fingers, and he cursed. But he didn't stop looking.

"You going to sit in the window all day or take me down like you promised?" Maggie came farther into the room, her hands on her hips. The boy hadn't heard a word. She tugged on his shoulder, ignored the name he called her and repeated herself.

"I never promised to do anything."

"You promised, all right, the night I poured you into that bed when you came in so drunk you couldn't stand."

He remembered the night clearly enough. It had been a week after he'd brought Sarah back from the mountains. A week since he'd been going to the Silver Star, trying to work up enough interest to take Carlotta or any other woman to bed. Drinking had been simpler, but getting blind drunk was something he'd never done before and didn't intend to do again.

"I could have gotten myself into bed well enough."

"You couldn't even crawl up the stairs. If there's one thing I know, it's a man who's too drunk to think. Now, are you going to take me down or are you going to back down?"

He grumbled but pushed himself away from the window. "Nothing worse than a nagging woman."

She only grinned and handed him his hat.

They had no more than stepped outside when John Cody came racing up. "Mr. Redman. Mr. Redman. I've been waiting for you."

"Yeah?" He pulled the boy's hat over his face. "Why's that?"

Delighted with the attention, Johnny grinned. "The contest. My pa's having a contest. Best shooting gets a brand-new saddle blanket. A red one. You're going to win, ain't you?"

"I wasn't figuring on it."

"How come? Nobody shoots better'n you. It's a real nice blanket, too."

"Go on, Jake." Maggie gave him a slap on the arm. "The boy's counting on you."

"I don't shoot for sport." He meant to walk on, but he saw Johnny's face fall. "A red blanket?"

The boy's eyes lit instantly. "Yessiree, about the prettiest one I ever seen."

"I guess we could look." Before the sentence was complete, Johnny had him by the hand and was pulling him across the street.

At the back of the store Cody had set up empty bottles and cans of varying sizes. Each contestant stood behind a line drawn in the dirt and took his best six shots. Broken glass littered the ground already.

"It costs two bits to enter," Johnny told him. "I got a short bit if you need it."

Jake looked at the dime the boy offered. The gesture touched him in a way that only those who had been offered very little through life would have understood. "Thanks, but I think I got two bits."

"You can shoot better than Jim Carlson. He's winning now." Johnny glanced over to where Jim was showing off a fancy railman's spin with his shiny new Smith & Wesson .44. "Can you do that?"

"Why? It doesn't help you shoot any better." He flipped a quarter to Johnny. "Why don't you go put my name down?"

"Yessir. Yessiree." He took time out to have a friendly shoving match with another boy, then raced away.

"Going to shoot for the blanket?" Lucius asked from behind him.

"Thinking about it." But he was watching Jim Carlson. He remembered that Jim rode a big white gelding. Jake had seen the gleam of a white horse riding away the night Sarah's shed had burned.

Lucius tipped his hat to Maggie. "Ma'am."

"That you, Lucius? I don't believe I've ever seen you with that beard shaved."

He colored up and stepped away. "I guess a man can shave now and then without a body gawking at him."

"I forgot you had a face under there," Jake commented as he watched Will Metcalf hit four out of six bottles. "You looking for a new red blanket, too?"

"Nope. Just thought I'd come around and tell you Burt Donley rode into town."

Only his eyes changed. "Is that so? I thought he was in Laramie."

"Not anymore. He came this way while you were in New Mexico. Started working for Carlson."

In an easy move, Jake turned and scanned the area behind him. "Donley doesn't punch cattle."

"Hasn't been known to. Could be Carlson hired him to do something else."

"Could be," Jake murmured, watching Donley walk toward the crowd.

He was a big man, burly at the shoulders, thick at the waist. He wore his graying hair long, so long it merged with his beard. And he was fast. Jake had good reason to know just how fast. If the law hadn't stepped in two years before, one of them would be dead now.

"Heard you had some trouble a while back."

"Some." Through the crowd, Jake's eyes met Donley's. They didn't need words. There was unfinished business between them.

As she stood beside Liza, Sarah watched Jake. And shivered. Something had come into his eyes. Something cold and deadly and inevitable. Then the crowd roared when the next contestant shattered all six bottles.

"Oh, look." Liza gave Sarah a quick shake. "Jake's

going to shoot. I know it's wrong, but I've always wanted to see how he does it. You hear such stories. There was one—" Her mouth fell open when he drew his right hand and fired.

"I didn't even see him take it out," she whispered. "It was just in his hand, quick as a blink."

"He hit them all." Sarah wrapped her shawl tighter around her. He had hardly moved. His gun was still smoking when he slid it back in place.

Donley strode over, flipped a quarter and waited until more targets were set. Sarah watched his big hand curl over the butt of his gun. Then he drew and fired.

"Goodness. He hit all of them, too. That leaves Dave Jeffrey, Jim Carlson, Jake and Burt Donley."

"Who is he?" she asked, wondering why Jake looked like he wanted to kill him. "The big man in the leather vest."

"Donley? He works for Samuel Carlson. I've heard talk about him, too. The same kind of talk as you hear about Jake. Only…"

"Only?"

"Well, you know how I told you Johnny's been tagging after Jake, pestering him and talking his ear off? I can't say it worries me any. But if he got within ten feet of Burt Donley I'd skin him alive."

The crowd shifted as Cody brought the line back five feet. When the first man aimed and fired, missing two bottles, Sarah saw Johnny tug on Jake's arm and whisper something. To her surprise, Jake grinned and ruffled the boy's hair. There it was again, she thought. That goodness. That basic kindness. Yet she remembered the look that had come into his eyes only moments before.

Who are you? she wanted to ask.

As if he'd heard her, Jake turned his head. Their eyes met and held. She felt a flood of emotions rise up uncontrollably and again wished she could hate him for that alone.

"You keep looking at her like that," Maggie murmured at his side, "you're going to have to marry her or ride fast in the other direction."

"Shut up, Maggie."

She smiled as sweetly as if he'd kissed her cheek. "Just thought you'd like to know that Sam Carlson ain't too pleased by the way you two are carrying on."

Jake's gaze shifted and met Carlson's. He had come up to stand behind Sarah and lay a proprietary hand on her shoulder. Jake considered allowing himself the pleasure of shooting him for that alone. "He's got no claim."

"Not for lack of trying. Better move fast, boyo."

The onlookers cheered again as Jim Carlson nipped five out of six targets.

Taking his time, Jake reloaded his pistol, then moved to the line. The six shots sounded almost like one. When he lowered his Colt, six bottles had been shattered.

Donley took his place. Six shots, six hits.

The line was moved farther back.

"They can't do it from here," Liza whispered to Sarah. "No one could."

Sarah just shook her head. It wasn't a game anymore. There was something between the two men, something much deeper, much darker, than a simple contest of skill. Others sensed it, too. She could hear the murmur of the crowd and see the uneasy looks.

Jake moved behind the line. He scanned the targets, judging the distance, taking mental aim. Then he did what he did best. He drew and fired on instinct. Bottles exploded, one by one. There was nothing left but a single jagged base. Without pausing, he drew his other gun and shattered even that.

There was silence as Donley stepped forward. He drew, and the gun kicked in his hand with each shot. When he was done, a single bottle remained unbroken.

"Congratulations, Redman." Cody brought the blanket over, hoping to dispel some of the tension. Relief made him let out his breath audibly when Sheriff Barker strolled over.

"That was some shooting, boys." He gave each man a casual nod. Will Metcalf stood at his shoulder as directed. "Good to get it out of your system with a few bottles. Either one of you catches a bullet tonight, there's sure no way I can doubt who put it there."

The warning was given with a smile that was friendly enough. Behind Sarah, Carlson gave a quick shake of his head. Without speaking, Donley made his way through the crowd, which parted for him.

"I ain't never seen nobody shoot like that." Johnny looked up at Jake with awe and wonder in his eyes.

Jake tossed the blanket to him. "There you go."

His eyes widened even farther. "I can have it?"

"You got a horse, don't you?"

"Yes, sir, I got me a bay pony."

"Red ought to look real nice on a bay. Why don't you go see?"

With a whoop, Johnny raced off, only to be caught by his mother. After a minor scuffle, he turned back, grinning. "Thanks, Mr. Redman. Thanks a lot."

"You sure did please that boy pink," Barker commented.

"I don't need a blanket."

Barker only shook his head. "You're a puzzle, Jake. I can't help but have a liking for you."

"That's a puzzle to me, Sheriff. Most lawmen got other feelings."

"Maybe so. Either way, I'd be obliged if you'd keep those guns holstered tonight. You wouldn't want to tell me what there is between you and Donley?"

Jake sent him an even look. "No."

"Didn't figure you would." He spit out tobacco juice. "Well, I'm going to have me some chicken and dance with my wife."

There were a dozen tables lined up along one side of the big canvas tent. Even before the music started, more than half of the food was gone. Women, young and old, were flirting, pleased to be shown off in their best dresses. When the fiddle started, couples swarmed onto the floor. Liza, in her pink muslin, grabbed Will's hand and pulled him with her. Carlson, dashing in his light brown suit and string tie, bowed to Sarah.

"I'd be honored if you'd step out with me, Sarah."

With a little laugh, she gave him a formal curtsy. "I'd be delighted."

The music was fast and cheerful. Despite the heat, the dancing followed suit. At the front of the tent the musicians fiddled and plucked and strummed tirelessly, and the caller wet his whistle with free beer. Couples swung and sashayed and kicked up their heels in a reel. It was different from the dances Sarah had attended in Philadelphia. Wonderfully different, she thought as she twirled in Lucius's arms. Hoots and hollers accompanied the music, as well as hand-clapping, foot-stamping and whistles.

"You were right, Lucius." Laughing, she laid a hand on her speeding heart when the music stopped.

"I was?"

"Yes, indeed. You're a fine dancer. And this is the best party I've ever been to." She leaned over impulsively and kissed his cheek.

"Well, now." His face turned beet red with embarrassed pleasure. "Why don't I fetch you a cup of that punch?"

"That would be lovely."

"Sarah!" Liza's face was nearly as pink as Lucius's when she rushed over and grabbed Sarah's arm.

"My goodness, what's wrong?"

"Nothing. Nothing in the world is wrong." Impatient, Liza dragged Sarah to a corner of the tent. "I just got to tell somebody or bust."

"Then tell me. I'd hate to see you rip the seams of that dress."

"I was just outside, taking a little air." She looked quickly right, then left. "Will came out after me. He kissed me."

"He did?"

"Twice. I guess my heart just about stopped."

One brow lifted, Sarah struggled with a smile. "I suppose that means you've decided to let him be your beau."

"We're getting married," Liza blurted out.

"Oh, Liza, really? That's wonderful." Delighted, Sarah threw her arms around her friend. "I'm so happy for you. When?"

"Well, he's got to talk to Pa first." Liza chewed her lip as she glanced toward her father. "But I know it's going to be all right. Pa likes Will."

"Of course he does. Liza, I can't tell you how happy I am for you."

"I know." When her eyes filled, Liza blinked and sniffled. "Oh, Lordy, I don't want to cry now."

"No, don't, or I'll start."

Laughing, Liza hugged her again. "I can't wait. I just can't wait. It'll be your turn before long. The way Samuel Carlson can't take his eyes off you. I have to admit, I used to have a crush on him." She gave a quick, wicked smile. "Mostly, I thought about using him to make Will jealous."

"I'm not going to marry Samuel. I don't think I'm ever going to get married."

"Oh, nonsense. If not Samuel, there's bound to be a man around here who'll catch your eye."

The musicians began to play again. A waltz. Half smiling, Sarah listened. "The trouble is," she heard herself saying, "one has, but he isn't the kind who thinks about marriage."

"But who—" Liza broke off when she saw Sarah's

eyes go dark. "Oh, my," she said under her breath as she watched Jake come into the tent and cross the room.

There might have been no one else there. No one at all. The moment he'd walked in everything had faded but the music, and him. She didn't see Carlson start toward her to claim the waltz. Nor did she see his jaw clench when he noted where her attention was focused. She only saw Jake coming toward her.

He didn't speak. He just stopped in front of her and held out a hand. Sarah flowed like water into his arms.

She thought it must be a dream. He was holding her, spinning her around and around the room while the music swelled in her head. His eyes never left hers. Without thinking, she lifted her hand from his shoulder to touch his face. And watched his eyes darken like storm clouds.

Flustered by her own behavior, she dropped her hand again. "I didn't imagine you would dance."

"My mother liked to."

"You haven't—" She broke off. It was shameless. The devil with it. "You haven't been by to see me."

"No."

He was never any help, Sarah thought. "Why?"

"You know why." He was crazy to be doing even this. Holding her, torturing himself. She had lowered her eyes at his words, but she raised them again now. The look was clear and challenging.

"Are you afraid to see me?"

"No." That was a lie, and he didn't lie often. "But you should be."

"You don't frighten me, Jake."

"You haven't got the sense to be scared, Sarah." When the music stopped, he held her a moment longer. "If you did, you'd run like hell any time I got close."

"You're the one doing the running." She drew out of his arms and walked away.

It was difficult to hold on to her composure, difficult not to fume and stamp and scream as she would have liked. With her teeth gritted, she stood up for the next dance with the first man who asked her. When she looked again, Jake was gone.

"Sarah." Carlson appeared at her side with a cup of lemonade.

"Thank you." Her small silk fan was hardly adequate for the July heat. "It's a lovely party, isn't it?"

"Yes. More so for me because you're here."

She sipped, using the drink as an excuse not to respond.

"I don't want to spoil your evening, Sarah, but I feel I must speak my mind."

"Of course. What is it?"

"You're stepping on very dangerous ground with Jake Redman."

"Oh." Her dander rose, and she fought it down again. "How is that, Samuel?"

"You must know him for what he is, my dear. A killer, a hired gun. A man like that will treat you with no more respect than he would a woman who was…less of a lady."

"Whatever you think of him, Samuel, Mr. Redman has come to my aid a number of times. If nothing else, I consider him a friend."

"He's no one's friend. Stay away from him, Sarah, for your own sake."

Her spine shot ramrod-straight. "That doesn't sound like advice any longer, but like a demand."

Recognizing the anger in her eyes, he shifted ground. "Consider it a request." He took her hand. "I like to think we have an understanding, Sarah."

"I'm sorry." Gently she took her hand from his. "We don't. I haven't agreed to marry you, Samuel. Until I do I feel no obligation to honor a request. Now, if you'll excuse me, I'd like some air. Alone."

Knowing she had been unnecessarily short with him, she hurried out of the tent.

The moon was up now, and nearly full. Taking the deep, long breaths Sister Madeleine had always claimed would calm an unhealthy temper, she studied it. Surely the moon had been just as big and white in the East. But it had never seemed so. Just as the sky had never seemed so vast or so crowded with stars. Or the men as impossible.

The breathing wasn't going to work, she discovered. She'd walk off her anger instead. She'd taken no more than five steps when the shadow of a man brought her up short. She watched Jake flick away a cigarette.

"It's a hot night for walking."

"Thank you for pointing that out," she said stiffly, and continued on her way.

"There's a lot of drinking going on tonight. A lot of men in town who don't get much chance to see pretty women, much less hold on to one. Walking alone's not smart."

"Your advice is noted." She stormed away, only to have her arm gripped.

"Do you have to be so ornery?"

"Yes." She yanked her arm free. "Now, if that's all you have to say, I'd like to be alone."

"I got more to say." He bit off the words, then dug into his pocket. "This belongs to you."

"Oh." She took the cameo, closing her fingers around it. "I thought it was gone. The Apache with the scar. He'd taken it. He was wearing it when—" When you killed him, she thought.

"I took it back. I've been meaning to give it to you, but it slipped my mind." That was another lie. He'd kept it because he'd wanted to have something of her, even for a little while.

"Thank you." She opened her bag and slipped the cameo inside. "It means a great deal to me." The sound of high, wild feminine laughter tightened her lips. Apparently there was a party at the Silver Star tonight, as well. She wouldn't soften toward him, not now, not ever again. "I'm surprised you're still here. I'd think a dance would be a bit tame for your tastes. Don't let me keep you."

"Damn it, I said I don't want you walking around alone."

Sarah looked down at the hand that had returned to her arm. "I don't believe I'm obliged to take orders from you. Now let go of me."

"Go back inside."

"I'll go where I want, when I want." She jerked free a second time. "And with whom I want."

"If you're talking about Carlson, I'm going to tell you now to stay away from him."

"Are you?" The temper that had bubbled inside her when one man had warned her boiled over at the nerve of this one. "You can tell me whatever you choose, but *I* don't choose to listen. I'll see Samuel when it pleases me to see him."

"So he can kiss your hand?" The anger he was keeping on a short rein strained for freedom. "So you can have the town talking about you spending the day at his place?"

"You have quite a nerve," she whispered. "You, who spends your time with—that woman. Paying her for attention. How dare you insinuate that there's anything improper in my behavior?" She stepped closer to stab a finger at his chest. "If I allow Samuel to kiss my hand, that's my affair. He's asked me to marry him."

The last thing she expected was to be hauled off her feet so that her slippers dangled several inches from the ground. "What did you say?"

"I said he asked me to marry him. Put me down."

He gave her a shake that sent hairpins flying. "I warn you, Duchess, you think long and hard about marrying him, because the same day you're his wife, you're his widow. That's a promise."

She had to swallow her heart, which was lodged in her throat. "Is a gun your answer for everything?"

Slowly, his eyes on hers, he set her down. "Stay here."

"I don't—"

He shook her again. "By God, you'll stay here. Right here, or I'll tie you to a rail like a bad-tempered horse."

Scowling after him, she rubbed the circulation back into her arms. Of all the rude, high-handed— Then her eyes grew wide. Oh, dear Lord, she thought. He's going to kill someone. Flinging a hand to her throat, she started to run. He caught her on his way back, when she was still two feet from the tent.

"Don't you ever listen?"

"I thought—I was afraid—"

"That I was going to put a bullet in Carlson's heart?" His mouth thinned. So she cared that much, to come running to save him. "There's time for that yet." Taking a firmer grip on her arm, he pulled her with him.

"What are you doing?"

"Taking you home."

"You are not." She tried and failed to dig in her heels. "I'm not going with you, and I'm not ready to go home."

"Too bad." Impatient with her struggles, he swooped her up.

"Stop this at once and put me down. I'll scream."

"Go right ahead." He dumped her on the wagon seat. She scrambled for the reins, but he was faster.

"Lucius will take me home when I choose to go home."

"Lucius is staying in town." Jake cracked the reins. "Now why don't you sit back and enjoy the ride? And keep quiet," he added when she opened her mouth. "Or I swear I'll gag you."

Chapter 10

Dignity. Despite the circumstances... No, Sarah thought, correcting herself, *because* of the circumstances, she would maintain her dignity. It might be difficult at the speed Jake was driving, and given the state of her own temper, but she would never, never forget she was a lady.

She wished she were a man so she could knock him flat.

Control. Jake kept his eyes focused over the horses' heads as they galloped steadily and wished it was as easy to control himself. It wasn't easy, but he'd used his control as effectively as he had his Colts for most of his life. He wasn't about to lose it now and do something he'd regret.

He thought it was a shame that a man couldn't slug a woman.

In stony silence, they drove under the fat, full moon. Some might consider it a night for romance, Sarah thought with a sniff. Not her. She was certain she'd never see another full moon without becoming furious. Dragging her off in the middle of a party, she fumed, trying to give her orders on her personal affairs. Threatening to tie her up like—like a horse, she remembered. Of all the high-handed, arrogant, ill-mannered— Taking a long, cautious breath, she blocked her thoughts.

She'd lose more than her dignity if she allowed herself to dwell on Jake Redman.

The dog sent up a fast, frantic barking as they drove into the yard. He scented Sarah and the tall man who always scratched him between the ears. Tongue lolling, he jumped at the side of the wagon, clearly pleased to have his mistress home. One look had him subsiding and slinking off again. She'd worn that same look when he'd tried to sharpen his teeth on one of her kid slippers.

The moment Jake had pulled the horses up in front of the house, Sarah gathered her skirts to step down. Haste and temper made her careless, and she caught the hem. Before she could remind herself about her dignity, she was tugging it free. She heard the silk rip.

"Now see what you've done."

Just as angry, but without the encumbrances, Jake climbed down from the opposite side. "If you'd have held on a minute, I'd have given you a hand."

"Oh, really?" With her chin lifted, she marched around the front of the wagon. "You've never done a gentlemanly thing in your life. You eat with your hat on, swear and ride in and out of here without so much as a good day or a goodbye."

He decided she looked much more likely to bite than her scrawny dog. "Those are powerful faults."

"Faults?" She lifted a brow and stepped closer. "I haven't begun to touch on your faults. If I began, I'd be a year older before I could finish. How dare you toss me in the wagon like a sack of meal and bring me back here against my wishes?"

She was stunning in the moonlight, her cheeks flushed with anger, her eyes glowing with it. "I got my reasons."

"Do you? I'd be fascinated to hear them."

So would he. He wasn't sure what had come over him, unless it was blind jealousy. That wasn't a thought he wanted to entertain. "Go to bed, Duchess."

"I have no intention of going anywhere." She grabbed his arm before he could lead the horses away. "And neither will you until you explain yourself. You accosted me, manhandled me and threatened to kill Samuel Carlson."

"It wasn't a threat." He took her hand by the wrist and dragged it away from his arm. "The next time he touches you, I'll kill him."

He meant it, Sarah realized. She stood rooted to the spot. The ways of the West might still be new to her, but she recognized murder when she saw it in a man's eyes. With her shawl flying behind her, she raced after him.

"Are you mad?"

"Maybe."

"What concern is my relationship with Samuel Carlson to you? I assure you that if I didn't wish Samuel, or any man, to touch me, I would not be touched."

"So you like it?" The horses shied nervously when he spun around to her. "You like having him hold you, put his hands over you, kiss you."

She would have suffered the tortures of hell rather than admit that Carlson had done no more than kiss her fingers. And that the only man who had done more was standing before her now. She stepped forward until she was toe-to-toe with him.

"I'll risk repeating myself and say that it's none of your business."

The way she lifted that chin, he thought, she was just asking to have it punched. "I figure it is." He dragged the horses inside the shed to unharness them.

"You figure incorrectly." Sarah followed him inside. Dignified or not, she was going to have her say. "What I do is my business, and mine alone. I've done nothing I'm ashamed of, and certainly nothing I feel requires justification to you. If I allow Samuel to court me, you have no say in the matter whatsoever."

"Is that what you call it?" He dragged the first horse into its stall. "Courting?"

She went icily still. "Have you another name for it?"

"Maybe I've been wrong about you." He took the second horse by the bridle as he studied Sarah. "I thought you were a bit choosier. Then again, you didn't pull back when I put my hands on you." He grabbed her wrist before she could have the satisfaction of slapping his face.

"How dare you?" Her breath heaved through her lips. "How dare you speak to me that way?" When she jerked free, her shawl fell to the ground unnoticed. "No, I didn't object when you touched me. By God, I wish I had. You make me feel—" The words backed up in her throat. Sarah dug her fingers into her palms until she could choke them free. "You made me feel things I still don't understand. You made me trust you, and those feelings, when it was all a lie. You made me want you when you didn't want me back. After you'd done that, you turned away as though it had meant nothing."

Pain clawed through his gut. What she was saying was true. The hurt shining from her eyes was real. "You're better off," he said quietly as he led the horse into a stall.

"I couldn't agree more." She wanted to weep. "But if you think that gives you any right to interfere in my life, you're wrong. Very wrong."

"You jumped mighty fast from my arms to his." Bitterness hardened the words even as he cursed himself for saying them.

"I?" It was too much—much more than she could bear. Driven by fury, she grabbed his shirt with both hands. "It wasn't I who jumped, it was you. You left me here without a word, then rode straight to the Silver Star. You kissed me, then rubbed my taste from your mouth so that you could kiss her."

"Who?" He caught her by the shoulder before she could rush back outside. "Who?"

"I have nothing more to say to you."

"You started it. Now finish it. Whose bed do you have me jumping in, Sarah?"

"Carlotta's." She threw the name at him with all the hurt and fury that was bottled up inside of her. "You left me to go to her. If that wasn't enough hurt and humiliation, you told her to hire me."

"Hire you?" Shock had his fingers tightening, bruising her flesh. "What the hell are you talking about?"

"You know very well you told her she should hire me to sew dresses for her and her—the others."

"Sew?" He didn't know if he should laugh or curse. Slowly he released his grip and let his hands fall to his sides. "Whatever else you think about me, you should know I'm not stupid."

"I don't know what I think about you." She was fighting back tears now, and it infuriated her.

It was the gleam of those tears that had him explaining when he would have preferred to keep silent. "I never told Carlotta to hire you, for anything. And I haven't been with—" He broke off, swearing. Before he could stride out, she snatched his arm again. She'd conquered her tears, but she couldn't stop her heart from pounding.

"Are you telling me that you haven't been to the Silver Star?"

"No. I'm not telling you that."

"I see." With a bitter little laugh, she rubbed her temple. "So you've simply found, and bought, another woman who suits you. Poor Carlotta. She must be devastated."

"It would take a hell of a lot more than that. And I haven't bought anything in the Silver Star but whiskey since you—since I got back to town."

"Why?" She had to force even a whisper through her lips.

"That's my business." Cursing himself, he started out again, only to have her rush to stop him.

"I asked you a question."

"I gave you my answer." He scooped up her shawl and pushed it into her hands. "Now go to bed."

She tossed the filmy lace on the ground again. "I'm not going anywhere, and neither are you until you tell me why you haven't been with her, or anyone."

"Because I can't stop thinking about you." Enraged, he shoved her back against the wall with a force that had pins scattering and her hair tumbling wild and free to her waist. He wanted to frighten her, frighten her half as much as she frightened him. "You're not safe with me, Duchess." He leaned close to her, dragging a hand roughly through her hair. "Remember that."

She pressed her damp hands against the wall. It wasn't fear she felt. The emotion was strong and driving, but it wasn't fear. "You don't want me."

"Wanting you's eating holes in me." His free hand slid up to circle her neck. "I'd rather be shot than feel the way you make me feel."

"How do I make you feel?" she murmured.

"Reckless." It was true, but it wasn't everything. "And that's not smart, not for either of us. I'll hurt you." He squeezed lightly, trying to prove it to them both. "And I won't give a damn. So you better run while I still have a mind to let you."

"I'm not running." Even if she had wanted to, it would have been impossible. Her legs were weak and trembling. She was already out of breath. "But you are." Knowing exactly what she was doing, what she was risking, she raised her chin. "Threats come easily to you. If you were the kind of man you say you are, and you wanted me, you'd take me. Right here, right now."

His eyes darkened. They were almost black as they bored into hers. She didn't wince as his fingers tightened painfully in her hair. Instead, she kept her chin up and dared him.

"Damn you." He brought his mouth down hard on hers. To scare her, he told himself as he pressed her back against the wall and took his fill. To make her see once and for all what he was. Ruthless, knowing she would bruise, he dragged his hands over her. He touched her the way he would have touched a girl at the Silver Star. Boldly, carelessly. He wanted to bring her to tears, to make her sob and tremble and beg him to leave her alone.

Maybe then he would be able to.

He heard her muffled cry against his mouth and tried to pull back. Her arms circled him, drawing him in.

She gave herself totally, unrestrainedly, to the embrace. He was trying to hurt her, she knew. But he couldn't. She would make him see that being in his arms would never cause her pain. She gasped, forced to grip him tighter to keep her balance, when his mouth roamed down her throat, spreading luxuriant heat. The scraping of his teeth against her skin had her moaning. Too aroused to be shocked by her own actions, she tugged at his shirt. She wanted to touch his skin again, wanted to feel the warmth of it.

He was losing himself in her. No, he was already lost. Her scent, the fragility of it, had his senses spinning. Her mouth, the hunger of it, clawed at his control. Then she said his name—it was a sigh, a prayer—and broke the last bonds.

He pulled her down into the hay, desperate for her.

The silk of her dress rustled against his hands as he dragged it from her shoulders. A wildness was on him, peeling away right and wrong as he tore the silk away to find her.

Terror rose up to grab her by the throat. But it wasn't terror of him. It was terror of the need that had taken possession of her. It ruled her, drove her beyond what could and could not be. As ruthless as he, she ripped at his shirt.

He was yanking at her laces, cursing them, cursing himself. Impatient with encumbrances, he shrugged out of his shirt, then sucked in his breath when her fingers dug into his flesh to pull him closer.

Hot, quick kisses raced over her face. She couldn't catch her breath, not even when he tore her laces loose. They rolled over on the hay as they fought to free themselves, and each other, of the civilized barrier of clothing. She arched when he filled his hands with her breasts, too steeped in pleasure to be ashamed of her nakedness. Her pulse hammered at dozens of points, making her thoughts spin and whirl and center only on him.

She was willow-slim, soft as the silk he'd torn, delicate as glass. For all her fragility, he couldn't fight her power over him. He could smell the hay, the horses, the night. He could see her eyes, her hair, her skin, as the moonlight pushed through the chinks in the shed to shimmer over them. Once more, just once more, he tried to bring himself to sanity. For her sake. For his own.

Then she lifted her arms to him and took him back.

He was lean and firm and strong. Sarah tossed her common sense aside and gave herself to the need, to the love. His eyes were dark, dangerously dark. His skin gleamed like copper in the shadowed light. She saw the scar that ran down his arm. As his mouth came bruisingly back to hers, she ran a gentle finger over it.

There was no turning back for either of them. The horses scraped the ground restlessly in their stalls. In the hills, a coyote sent up a wailing, lonesome song. They didn't hear. She heard her name as he whispered it. But that was all.

The hay scratched her bare skin as he covered her body with his own. She only sighed. He felt the yielding, gloried in it. He tasted the heat and the honey as he drew her breast into his mouth. A breathless moan escaped her at this new intimacy. Then his tongue began to stroke, to tease.

The pleasure built, painful, beautiful, tugging at her center as his teeth tugged at her nipples. It was unbearable. It was glorious. She wanted to tell him, wanted to explain somehow, but she could only say his name over and over.

He felt her thigh tremble when he stroked a hand along it. Then he heard her gasp of surprise, her moan of desire, when he touched what no man had ever dared to touch.

His. He took her as gently as his grinding need would allow toward her first peak. She was his. She cried out, her body curving like a bow as she crested. The breath burned in his lungs as he crushed his mouth to hers and took her flying again.

She held on, rocked, dazed and desperate. So this was love. This was what a man and woman brought to each other in the privacy of the night. It was more, so much more, than she had ever dreamed. Tears streamed from her eyes to mix with the sweat that slicked her body and his.

"Please," she murmured against his mouth, unsure of what she was asking. "Please."

He didn't want to hurt her. With that part of his mind that still functioned he prayed he could take her painlessly. His breathing harsh and ragged, he entered her slowly, trying to soothe her with his mouth and his hands.

Lights exploded behind her eyes, brilliant white lights that flashed into every color she'd ever seen or imagined. The heat built and built until she was gasping from it, unaware that her nails had scraped down his back and dug in.

Then she was running, racing, speeding, toward something unknown, something urgently desired. Like life. Like breath. Like love. Instinct had her hips moving. Joy had her arms embracing.

She lost her innocence in a wild burst of pleasure that echoed endlessly.

The moonlight slanted across her face as she slept. He watched her. Though his body craved sleep, his mind couldn't rest. She looked almost too beautiful to be real, curled into the hay, her hair spread out, her skin glowing, covered by nothing more than the thin velvet ribbon around her neck.

He'd recognized the passion in her from the beginning. He had suppressed his own for too long not to recognize it when it was suppressed in another. She'd come to him openly, honestly, innocently. And of all the sins he'd ever committed, the greatest had been taking that innocence from her.

He'd had no right. He pressed his fingers against his

eyes. He'd had no choice. The kind of need he'd felt for her—still felt, he realized—left no choice.

He was in love with her. He nearly laughed out loud. That kind of thinking was dangerous. Dangerous to Sarah. The things he loved always seemed to end up dead, destroyed. His gaze shifted. Her dress was bundled in a heap near her feet. On the pale silk lay his gunbelt.

That said it all, Jake decided. He and Sarah didn't belong together any more than his Colts and her silk dress did. He didn't belong with anyone.

He shifted, started to rise, but Sarah stirred and reached for his hand. "Jake."

"Yeah." Just the way she said his name made desire quicken in him.

Slowly, a smile curving her lips, she opened her eyes. She hadn't been dreaming, she thought. He was here, with her. She could smell the hay, feel it. She could see the glint of his eyes in the shadowed light. Her smile faded.

"What's wrong?"

"Nothing's wrong." Turning away, he reached for his pants.

"Why are you angry?"

"I'm not angry." He yanked his pants over his hips as he rose. "Why the hell should I be angry?"

"I don't know." She was determined to be calm. Nothing as beautiful as what had happened between them was going to be spoiled by harsh words. She found her chemise, noted that one shoulder strap was torn and slipped it on. "Are you going somewhere?"

He picked up his gunbelt because it troubled him to

see it with her things. "I don't think I'd care to walk back
to town, and Lucius has my horse."

"I see. Is that the only reason you're staying?"

He turned, ready to swear at her. She was standing
very straight, her hair drifting like clouds around her
face and shoulders. Her chemise skimmed her thighs
and dipped erotically low at one breast. Because his
mouth had gone dry, he could only shake his head.

She smiled then, and held out a hand. "Come to the
house with me. Stay with me."

It seemed he still had no choice. He closed his
hand over hers.

Sarah awoke with Lafitte licking her face. "Go
away," she muttered, and turned over.

"You asked me to stay." Jake hooked an arm around
her waist. He watched her eyes fly open, saw the shock,
the remembering and the pleasure.

"I was talking to the dog." She snuggled closer. Surely
there was no more wonderful way to wake up than in the
arms of the man you loved. "He figured out how to climb
up, but he hasn't figured out how to get down."

Jake leaned over to pat Lafitte's head. "Jump," he
said, then rolled Sarah on top of him.

"Is it morning?"

"Nope." He slid a hand up to cup her breast as he
kissed her.

"But the sun's up— Oh…" It dimmed as his hands
moved over her.

Day. Night. Summer. Winter. What did time matter?
He was here, with her, taking her back to all those won-

derful places he had shown her. She went willingly at dawn, as she had on the blanket of hay and then again and again on the narrow cot as the moon had set.

He taught her everything a woman could know about the pleasures of love, about needs stirred and needs met. He showed her what it was like to love like lightning and thunder. And he showed her what it was to love like soft rain. She learned that desire could be a pain, burning hot through the blood. She learned it could be a joy, rushing sweet under the skin.

But, though she was still unaware of it, she taught him much more, taught him that there could be beauty, and comfort, and hope.

They came together with the sun rising higher and the heat of the day chasing behind it.

Later, when she was alone in the cabin, Sarah cooled and bathed her skin. This was how it could be, she thought dreamily. Early every morning she would heat the coffee while he fed the stock and fetched fresh water from the stream. She would cook for him and tend the house. Together they would make something out of the land, out of their lives. Something good and fine.

They would start a family. She pressed a hand lightly against her stomach and wondered if one had already begun. What a beautiful way to make a child, she thought, running her fingers over her damp skin. What a perfect way.

She caught herself blushing and patted her skin dry. It wasn't right to think that way, not when they weren't married. Not when he hadn't even asked her. Would he? Sarah slipped on her shirtwaist and buttoned it quickly. Hadn't she herself said he wasn't the kind of man who thought of marriage?

And yet… Could he love her the way he had loved her and not want to spend his life with her?

What had Mrs. O'Rourke said? Sarah thought back as she finished dressing. It had been something about a smart woman bringing a man around to marriage and making him think it had been his idea all along. With a light laugh, she turned toward the stove. She considered herself a very smart woman.

"Something funny?"

She glanced around as Jake walked in. "No, not really. I guess I'm just happy."

He set a basket of eggs on the table. "I haven't gathered eggs since my mother—for a long time."

As casually as she could, she took the eggs and started preparations for breakfast. "Did your mother have chickens when you were a boy?"

"Yeah. Is that coffee hot?"

"Sit down. I'll pour you some."

He didn't want to talk about his past, she decided. Perhaps the time wasn't right. Yet.

"I was able to get a slab of bacon from Mr. Cobb." She sliced it competently while the pan heated. "I've thought about getting a few pigs. Lucius is going to grumble when I ask him to build a sty, but I don't think he'd complain about eating ham. I don't suppose you know anything about raising pigs?"

Would you listen to her? Jake thought as he tilted back in her chair. The duchess from Philadelphia talking about raising pigs. "You deserve better," he heard himself say.

The bacon sizzled as she poured the coffee. "Better than what?"

"Than this place. Why don't you go back east, Sarah, and live like you were meant to?"

She brought the cup to him. "Is that what you want, Jake? You want me to go?"

"It's not a matter of what I want."

She stood beside him, looking down. "I'd like to hear what you want."

Their eyes held. He'd had some time to think, and think clearly. But nothing seemed clear enough when he looked at her. "Coffee," he said, taking the cup.

"Your wants are admirably simple. Take your hat off at my table." She snatched it off his head and set it aside.

He just grinned, running a hand through his hair. "Yes, ma'am. Good coffee, Duchess."

"It's nice to know I do something that pleases you." She let out a yelp when he grabbed her from behind and spun her around.

"You do a lot that pleases me." He kissed her, hard and long. "A whole lot."

"Really?" She tried to keep her tone aloof, but her arms had already wound around his neck. "A pity I can't say the same."

"I guess that was some other woman who had her hands all over me last night." Her laugh was muffled against his lips. "I brought your things over from the shed. Dress is a little worse for wear. Four petticoats." He nipped her earlobe. "I hope you don't pile that many on every day around here."

"I don't intend to discuss—"

"And that contraption you lace yourself into. Lucky you don't pass out. Can't figure you need it. Your waist's no bigger around than my two hands. I ought to know." He proved it by spanning her. "Why do you want to strap yourself into that thing?"

"I have no intention of discussing my undergarments with you."

"I took them off you. Seems I should be able to talk about them."

Blushing to the roots of her hair, she struggled away. "The bacon's burning."

He took his seat again and picked up his coffee. "How many of those petticoats do you have on now?"

After rescuing the bacon, she sent him a quick, flirtatious look over her shoulder. "You'll just have to find out for yourself." Pleased at the way his brows shot up, she went back to her cooking.

He was no longer certain how to handle her. With breakfast on the table, the scents wafting cozily in the air, and Sarah sitting across from him, Jake searched his mind for something to say.

"I saw your pictures on the wall. You draw real nice."

"Thank you. I've always enjoyed it. If I'd known that my father was living here—that is, if I'd known how a few sketches would brighten the house up—I would have sent him some. I did send a small watercolor." She frowned a little. "It was a self-portrait from last Christmas. I thought he might like to know what I looked like since I'd grown up. It's strange. He had all the letters I'd written to him in that little tin box in the loft, but the sketch is nowhere to be found. I've been meaning to ask the sheriff if he might have forgotten to give it to me."

"If Barker had it, he'd have seen you got it back." He didn't care for the direction his thoughts were taking. "You sure it got this far? Mail gets lost."

"Oh, yes. He wrote me after he received it. Liza also mentioned that my father had been rather taken with it and had brought it into the store to show around."

"Might turn up."

"I suppose." She shrugged. "I've given this place a thorough cleaning, but I might not have come across it. I'll look again when Lucius puts in the floor."

"What floor?"

"The wooden floor. I've ordered boards." She broke off a bite of biscuit. "Actually, I ordered extra. I have my heart set on a real bedroom. Out the west wall, I think. My sewing money's coming in very handy."

"Sarah, last night you said something about Carlotta telling you I'd given her some idea about having you sew for her." He watched her stiffen up immediately. "When did you talk to her?"

"I didn't. I have no intention of talking to that woman."

He rolled his tongue into his cheek. He doubted Sarah would be pleased to know that her tone amused him. "Where did you hear that from?"

"Alice Johnson. She works in…that place. Apparently Carlotta had her drive out here to negotiate for my services."

"Alice?" He cast his mind back, juggling faces with names. "She's the little one—dark hair, big eyes?"

Sarah drew in a quiet, indignant breath. "That's an

accurate description. You seem to know the staff of the Silver Star very well."

"I don't know as I'd call them staff, but yeah, I know one from the other."

Rising, she snatched up his empty plate. "And I'm sure they know you quite well." When he just grinned, she had to fight back the urge to knock the look off his face with the cast-iron skillet. "I'll thank you to stop smirking at me."

"Yes, ma'am." But he went right on. "You sure are pretty when you get fired up."

"If that's a compliment," she said, wishing it didn't make her want to smile, "you're wasting your breath."

"I ain't much on compliments. But you're pretty, and that's a fact. I guess you're about the prettiest thing I've ever seen. Especially when you're riled."

"Is that why you continue to go out of your way to annoy me?"

"I expect. Come here."

She smoothed down her skirt. "I will not."

He rose slowly. "You're ornery, too. Can't figure why it appeals to me." He dragged her to him. After a moment's feigned struggle, she laughed up at him.

"I'll have to remember to stay ornery and annoyed, then."

He said nothing. The way she'd looked up at him had knocked the breath out of his body. He pulled her closer, holding on, wishing. Content, Sarah nuzzled his shoulder. Before he could draw her back, she framed his face with her hands and brushed her lips over his.

"You're still tying me up in knots," he muttered.

"That's good. I don't intend to stop."

He stepped back, then gripped her hands with his. "Which one did he kiss?"

"I don't know what you mean."

"Carlson." She gave a surprised gasp when his fingers tightened on hers. "Which hand did he kiss?"

Sarah kept her eyes on his. "Both."

She watched the fury come then, and was amazed at how quickly, how completely, he masked it. But it was still there. She could feel it rippling through him. "Jake—"

He shook his head. Then, in a gesture that left her limp, he brought her hands to his lips. Then he dropped them, obviously uncomfortable, and dug his own hands into his pockets.

"I don't want you to let him do it again."

"I won't."

Her response should have relaxed him, but his tension doubled. "Just like that?"

"Yes, just like that."

He turned away and began to pace. Her brow lifted. She realized she'd never before seen him make an unnecessary movement. If he took a step, it was to go toward or away.

"I've got no right." There was fury in his voice. The same kind she heard outside the tent the night before. In contrast, hers was soft and soothing.

"You have every right. The only right. I'm in love with you."

Now he didn't move at all. He froze as a man might when he heard a trigger cocked at the back of his head. She simply waited, her hands folded at her waist, her eyes calm and clear.

"You don't know what you're saying," he managed at last.

"Of course I do, and so do you." With her eyes on his, she walked to him. "Do you think I could have been with you as I was last night, this morning, if I didn't love you?"

He stepped back before she could touch him. It had been so long since he'd been loved that he'd forgotten what it could feel like. It filled him like a river, and its currents were strong.

"I've got nothing for you, Sarah. Nothing."

"Yourself." She reached a hand to his cheek. "I'm not asking for anything."

"You're mixing up what happened last night with—"

"With what?" she challenged. "Do you think because you were the first man that I don't know the difference between love and…lust? Can you tell me it's been like that for you before, with anyone? Can you?"

No, he couldn't. And he couldn't tell her it would never be that way with anyone but her. "Lucius will be back soon," he said instead. "I'll go down and get the water you wanted before I leave."

And that was all? she thought. Damn him for turning his back on her again. He didn't believe her, she thought. He thought she was just being foolish and romantic…. But no, no, that wasn't right, she realized. That wasn't it at all.

It came to her abruptly and with crystalline clarity. He did believe her, and that was why he had turned away. He was as frightened and confused by her love as she had been by the land. It was just as foreign to him. Just as difficult to understand and accept.

She could change that. Taking a long, cleansing

breath, she turned to her dishes. She could change that in the same way she had changed herself. She embraced the land now, called it her own. One day he would do the same with her.

She heard the door open again, and she turned, smiling. "Jake—"

But it was Burt Donley who filled the doorway.

Chapter 11

"Where's Redman?"

Panic came first, and it showed in her wide, wild eyes. She was still holding the skillet, and she had one mad thought of heaving it at his head. But his hand was curled over the butt of his gun. She saw in his eyes what she had never seen in Jake's, what she realized she'd never seen in any man's, not even in those of the Apache who had kidnapped her. A desire, even an eagerness, to kill.

He stepped inside, and through the thickness of his beard she saw that he was smiling. "I asked you, where's Redman?"

"He's not here." It surprised her how calm a voice could sound even when a heart was pounding. She had a man to protect. The man she loved. "I don't believe I asked you in."

His smile widened into a grin. "You ain't going to tell me he brought you all the way out here last night and then left a pretty thing like you all alone?"

She was terrified Jake would come back. And terrified he wouldn't. She had no choice but to hold her ground. "I'm not telling you anything. But as you can see, I'm alone."

"I can see that, real plain. Funny, 'cause his horse is in town and he ain't." He picked up a biscuit from the bowl on the table with his wide, blunt-edged fingers, studied it, then bit in. "Word is he spends time out here."

"Mr. Redman occasionally visits. I'll be sure to tell him you were looking for him, if and when I see him."

"You do that. You be sure and do that." He took another bite, chewing slowly, watching her.

"Good day, then."

But he didn't leave. He only walked closer. "You're prettier than I recollect."

She moistened her lips, knowing they were trembling. "I don't believe we've met."

"No, but I've seen you." She strained backward when he put a hand to her hair. "You don't favor your pa none."

"You'll have to excuse me." She tried to step to the side, but he blocked her.

"He sure did set some store by you. A man can see why." He pushed the rest of the biscuit into his mouth, chewing as he reached down to toy with the small bow at her collar. "Too bad he got himself killed over that mine and left you orphaned. Smart man would've kept himself alive. Smart man would've seen the sense in that."

She shifted again, and was again blocked. "He could hardly be blamed for an accident."

"Maybe we'll talk about that later." Enjoying her trembling, he tugged the little bow loose. "You look smarter than your pa was."

Lafitte burst in, snarling. Donley had his hand on the butt of his gun when Sarah grabbed his arm. "No, please. He's hardly more than a puppy." Moving quickly, she gathered the growling dog up. "There's no need for you to hurt him. He's harmless."

"Donley likes killing harmless things." Jake spoke from the doorway. The men stood ten feet apart, Jake backed by sun, Donley by shadow. "There was a man in Laramie—more of a boy, really. Daniel Little Deer was harmless, wasn't he, Donley?"

"He was a breed." Donley's teeth gleamed through his beard. "I don't think no more of killing a breed than a sick horse."

"And it's easier when it's back-shooting."

"I ain't shooting at your back, Redman."

"Move aside, Sarah."

"Jake, please—"

"Move aside." He was over the sick fear he'd felt when he'd seen Donley's horse outside the house. He was cold, killing-cold. His guns hung low on his hips, and his hands were limber and ready.

Donley shifted, settling his weight evenly. "I've waited a long time for this."

"Some of us get lucky," Jake murmured, "and wait a long time to die."

"When I've killed you, I'm going to have the woman,

and the gold." His hand slapped the butt of his gun. The .44 was aimed heart-high. He was fast.

The sound of a gunshot exploded, ripping through the still morning air. Sarah watched in horror as Donley stumbled, forward, then back. A red stain spread across his shirt and his leather vest before he fell by the stone hearth and lay still.

Jake stood in the doorway, his face expressionless, his mind calm and cold. He'd never once felt the rush some men spoke of that came from killing. To him it was neither power nor curse. It was survival.

"Oh, God." Pressed back against the wall, Sarah stared. Lafitte leaped out of her limp arms to crouch, growling, by Donley's gun hand. Her vision grayed, wavered, then snapped back when Jake gripped her arms.

"Did he hurt you?"

"No, I—"

"Get outside."

Hysteria bubbled up in her throat. A man was dead, lying dead on her floor, and the one holding her looked like a stranger. "Jake—"

"Get outside," he repeated, doing his best to shield her from the man he'd killed. "Go on into the shed or down to the stream." When she only continued to stare, he pulled her to the door and shoved her out. "Do what I tell you."

"What—what are you going to do?"

"I'm going to take him into town."

Giving in to weakness, she leaned on the rail, dragging in gulps of the hot, dusty air as though it were water. "What will they do to you? You killed him."

"Barker'll take me at my word. Or he'll hang me."

"No, but—" Nausea was churning now, coating her skin with a thin, clammy sweat. "He wanted to kill you. He came looking for you."

"That's right." He took both her arms again because he wanted her to look at him, really look. "And tomorrow, next week, next month, there'll be someone else who comes looking for me. I got fast hands, Sarah, and somebody's always going to want to prove they got faster. One day they'll be right."

"You can change. It can change. It has to." She struggled out of his hold, only to throw her arms around him. "You can't want to live this way."

"What I want and what is have always been two different things." He pushed her away. "I care about you." It was easy to mean it, hard to say it. "That's why I'm telling you to walk away."

He'd just killed a man in front of her eyes. And killed him coldly. Even through her horror she'd seen that. But it hadn't left him untouched. What she saw now was the frustration and anger of a man caught in a trap. He needed someone to offer him a way out, or at least the hope of one. If she could do nothing else, she could give him hope.

"No." She stepped forward to frame his face with her hands. "I can't. I won't."

Her hands were trembling. Cold and trembling, he thought as he reached for them. "You're a damn fool."

"Yes. I'm quite sure you're right. But I love you."

He couldn't have begun to tell her what it did to him inside when she said that. When he looked into her eyes and saw that she meant it. He pulled her against him for a rough, hungry kiss. "Go away from the house. I don't want you here when I bring him out."

She nodded, took a long breath and stepped back. The sickness had passed, though the raw feeling inside remained. "Once I was sure there was only right and wrong, and that to kill another person was the greatest wrong. But there isn't only right and wrong, Jake. What you did, what you had to do, kept you alive. There's nothing more important to me than that." She paused and touched his hand. "Come back."

He watched her, as he had watched her once before, start up the rise to her father's grave. When she was gone, he went back inside.

Two days passed, and Sarah tried to follow her daily routine and not to wonder why Jake hadn't ridden back to her. It seemed everyone else had paid her a visit, but not Jake. Barker had come out and, in his usual take-your-time way, questioned her about Burt Donley. It seemed no more than a token investigation to Sarah. Barker, either because he was lazy or because he was a shrewd judge of character, had taken Jake at his word.

The story had spread quickly. Soon after Barker, Liza and Johnny had driven up to hear the details and eat oatmeal cookies. Before she had left, Liza had chased Johnny outside to pester Lucius so that she could spend an hour talking about Will and her upcoming wedding. She was to have a new dress, and she had already ordered the pink silk and the pattern from Santa Fe.

The following morning, the sound of a rider approaching had Sarah rushing out of the chicken coop, eggs banging dangerously against each other in the basket she carried. She struggled to mask her disappointment when she saw Samuel Carlson.

"Sarah." He dismounted quickly, and would have taken her hand, but she used both to grip the handle of the basket. "I've been worried about you."

"There's no need." She smiled as he tied his horse at the rail.

"I was shocked to learn that Donley and Redman had drawn guns right here in your house. It's a miracle you weren't injured."

"I'm sure I would have been if Jake hadn't come back when he did. Donley was...very threatening."

"I feel responsible."

"You?" She stopped in front of the house. "Why?"

"Donley worked for me. I knew what kind of man he was." There was a grimness around his eyes and mouth as he spoke. "I can't say I had any trouble with him until Redman came back to town."

"It was Donley who sought Jake out, Samuel." Her voice sharpened with the need to defend him. "It was he who deliberately provoked a fight. I was there."

"Of course." He laid a soothing hand on her arm. Manners prevented him from stepping inside the house without an invitation. He was shrewd enough to see that something had changed, and that he wouldn't get one. "I detest the fact that you were forced to witness a killing, and in your own home. It must distress you to stay here now."

"No." She glanced over her shoulder. It had been difficult, the first time she had gone inside afterward. There were still traces of dried blood in the dirt, the sight of which had given Johnny ghoulish pleasure. But it was her home. "I'm not as frail as that."

"You're a strong woman, Sarah, but a sensitive one. I'm concerned about you."

"It's kind of you to be. Your friendship is a great comfort to me."

"Sarah." He touched a gentle hand to her cheek. "You must realize that I want to be much more than your friend."

"I know." Regret was in her eyes, in her voice. "It's not possible, Samuel. I'm sorry."

She saw the anger mar his face, and was surprised by the depth of it before he brought it under control again. "It's Redman, isn't it?"

She felt it would be dishonorable, and insulting, to lie to him. "Yes."

"I thought you were more sensible, Sarah. You're an intelligent, gently bred woman. You must understand that Redman is a dangerous man, a man without scruples. He lives by violence. It's part of him."

She smiled a little. "He describes himself the same way. I believe you're both wrong."

"He'll only hurt you."

"Perhaps, but I can't change my feelings. Nor do I wish to." Regret had her reaching out to touch his arm. "I'm sorry, Samuel."

"I have faith that in time you'll get over this infatuation. I can be patient."

"Samuel, I don't—"

"Don't distress yourself." He patted her hand. "Along with patience, I have confidence. You were meant to belong to me, Sarah." He stepped back to untie his horse. Inside, he was boiling with rage. He wanted this woman, and what belonged to her—and he intended to have them, one way or the other.

When he turned to stand beside his mount with his reins in his hands, his face was touched only with affection and concern. "This doesn't change the fact that I worry about you, living out here all alone."

"I'm not alone. I have Lucius."

Carlson cast a slow, meaningful look around the yard.

"He's up in the mine," Sarah explained. "If there was trouble, he'd come down quickly enough."

"The mine." Carlson cast his eyes up at the rock. "At least promise me that you won't go inside. It's a dangerous place."

"Gold doesn't lure me." She smiled again, relieved that they would remain friends.

He swung gracefully into the saddle. "Gold lures everyone."

She watched him ride off. Perhaps he was right, she mused. Gold had a lure. Even though in her heart she didn't believe she'd ever see the mine pay, it was exciting knowing there was always a chance. It kept Lucius in the dark and the dust for hours on end. Her father had died for it.

Even Jake, she thought, wasn't immune. It was he who had asked Lucius to pick up where her father had left off. She had yet to discover why. With death on his mind, Donley's last words had been… A glimmer of suspicion broke into her mind.

I'm going to have the woman, and the gold.

Why should a man like Donley speak of gold before he drew his gun? Why would a worthless mine be on his mind at such a time? Or was it worthless?

Her promise to Samuel forgotten, she started toward the rise.

A movement caught her eye and, turning around again, she scanned the road. Someone was coming, on foot. Even as she watched, the figure stumbled and fell. Sarah had her skirts in her hand and was running before the figure struggled to stand again.

"Alice!" Sarah quickened her pace. The girl was obviously hurt, but until Sarah reached her, catching her before she fell again, she couldn't see how badly.

"Oh, dear Lord." Gripping the sobbing girl around the waist, she helped her toward the house. "What happened? Who did this to you?"

"Miss Conway..." Alice could hardly speak through her bruised and bloodied lips. Her left eye was blackened and swollen nearly shut. There were ugly scratches, like the rake of fingernails, down her cheek, and every breath she took came out with a hitch of pain.

"All right, don't worry, just lean on me. We're nearly there."

"Didn't know where else to go," Alice managed. "Shouldn't be here."

"Don't try to talk yet. Let me get you inside. Oh, Lucius." Half stumbling herself, Sarah looked up with relief as he came hurrying down the rocks. "Help me get her inside, up to bed. She's badly hurt."

"What in the holy hell—?" Wheezing a bit from the

exertion, he picked Alice up in his scrawny arms. "You know who this girl is, Miss Sarah?"

"Yes. Take her up to my bed, Lucius. I'll get some water."

Alice swooned as he struggled to carry her up the ladder to the loft. "She's done passed out."

"That may be a blessing for the moment." Moving quickly, Sarah gathered fresh water and clean cloths. "She must be in dreadful pain. I can't see how she managed to get all the way out here on foot."

"She's taken a mighty beating."

He stepped out of the way as best he could when Sarah climbed the stairs to sit on the edge of the bed. Gently she began to bathe Alice's face. When she loosened the girl's bodice, he cleared his throat and turned his back.

"Oh, my God." With trembling hands, Sarah unfastened the rest of the buttons. "Help me get this dress off of her, Lucius. It looks as though she's been whipped."

His sense of propriety was overcome by the sight of the welts on Alice's back and shoulders. "Yeah, she's been whipped." The cotton of her dress stuck to the raw, open sores. "Whipped worse'n a dog. I'd like to get my hands on the bastard who done this."

Sarah found her own hands were clenched with fury. "There's some salve on the shelf over the stove, Lucius. Fetch it for me." She did her best to bathe and cool the wounds. As Alice's eyes fluttered open and she moaned, Sarah soothed her in a low, calming voice. "Try not to move, Alice. We're going to take care of you. You're safe now. I promise you you're safe."

"Hurts."

"I know. Oh, I know." There were tears stinging her eyes as she took the salve from Lucius and began to stroke it over the puffy welts.

It was a slow, painful process. Though Sarah's fingers were light and gentle, Alice whimpered each time she touched her. Her back was striped to the waist with angry red lines, some of which had broken open and were bleeding. With sweat trickling down her face, Sarah tended and bandaged, talking, always talking.

"Would you like another sip of water?"

"Please." With Sarah's hand cradling her head, Alice drank from the cup. "I'm sorry, Miss Conway." She lay back weakly as Sarah held a cool cloth to her swollen eye. "I know I shouldn't have come here. It ain't right, but I wasn't thinking straight."

"You did quite right by coming."

"You was—were—so nice to me before. And I was afraid if I didn't get away…"

"You aren't to worry." Sarah applied salve to her facial scratches. "In a few days you'll be feeling much better. Then we can think about what's to be done. For now, you'll stay right here."

"I can't—"

"You can and you will." Setting the salve aside, Sarah took her hand. "Do you feel strong enough to tell us what happened? Did a man—one of your customers— do this to you?"

"No, ma'am." Alice moistened her swollen lips. "It was Carlotta."

"Carlotta?" Sarah's eyes narrowed to slits. "Are you saying that Carlotta beat you like this?"

"I ain't never seen her so mad. Sometimes she gets mean if something don't go her way, or if she's been drinking too much you get a slap or two. She went crazy. I think she might've killed me if the other girls hadn't broke in the door and started screaming."

"Why? Why would she hurt you like this?"

"I can't say for sure. I done something wrong." Her voice slurred, and her eyes dropped shut. "She was mad, powerful mad, after Jake came by. They had words. Nancy, she's one of the other girls, listened outside of Carlotta's office. He said something to set her off, I expect. Nancy said she was yelling. Said something about you, Miss Conway, I don't rightly know what. When he left she went crazy. Started smashing things. I went on up to my room. She came after me, beat me worse'n Pa ever did. Eli, he brought me out."

"Eli's the big black Carlotta has working for her," Lucius explained.

"He drove me out as far as he could. She finds out, she'll make him sorry. Took a belt to me," she murmured as sleep took her under. "Kept hitting me and hitting me, saying it was my fault Jake don't come around no more."

"Bitch," Lucius said viciously. Then he wiped his mouth. "'Scuse me, Miss Sarah."

"No excuse necessary. I couldn't agree more." There was a rage running through her, hotter and huger than anything she'd ever experienced. She stared at the girl asleep in her bed, her small, pretty face bruised and swollen. She remembered each welt she'd tended. "Hitch up the wagon, Lucius."

"Yes'm. You want me to go somewheres?"

"No, I'm going. I want you to stay with Alice."

"I'll hitch it up, Miss Sarah, but if you're thinking about talking to the sheriff, it won't do much good. Alice here ain't going to talk to him like she done with you. She'd be too scared."

"I'm not going to the sheriff, Lucius. Just hitch up the wagon."

She pushed the horses hard, pleased that the fury didn't subside as she approached town. She wanted the fury. Since she'd come west she'd learned to accept many things—the grief, the violence, the labor. Perhaps the land was lawless, but there were times and reasons, even here, for justice.

Johnny raced out of the dry goods as Sarah rode by, then raced back in again to complain to Liza that Sarah hadn't waved at him. She hadn't even seen him. There was only one face in her mind now. She drew up in front of the Silver Star.

Three women lounged in what might have been called a parlor. The late-morning heat had them half dozing in their petticoats and their feathered wraps. The room itself was dim and almost airless. Vivid red drapes hung limp at the windows. Gold leaf glowed dull and dusty on the frames of the mirrors.

As Sarah entered, a heavy-eyed redhead popped up from her sprawled position on a settee. She plopped back again with a howling laugh. "Well, look here, girls, we got ourselves some company. Get out the teacups."

The others looked over. One of them hitched her

wrap up around her shoulders. Her hands folded, Sarah stood in the doorway and took it all in.

So this was a bordello. She couldn't say she saw anything remotely exciting. It looked more like a badly furnished parlor in need of a good dusting. There was a heavy floral scent of mixed perfumes that merged, none too appealingly, with plain sweat. Carefully, finger by finger, Sarah drew off her driving gloves.

"I'd like to speak with Carlotta, please. Will someone tell her I'm here?"

No one moved. The women merely exchanged looks. The redhead went back to examining her nails. After a long breath, Sarah tried another tactic.

"I'm here to speak with her about Alice." That caught their attention. Every one of the women looked over at her. "She'll be staying with me until she's well."

Now the redhead rose. Her flowered wrap slid down her shoulders with the movement. "You took Alice in?"

"Yes. She needs care, Miss—"

"I'm Nancy." She took a quick look behind her. "How come somebody like you's going to see to Alice?"

"Because she needs it. I'd be grateful to you if you would tell Carlotta I'd like to speak with her."

"I reckon I could do that." The redhead pulled her wrap up. "You tell Alice we was asking about her."

"I'll be glad to."

While Nancy disappeared up the stairs, Sarah tried to ignore the other women's stares. She had changed to one of her best day dresses. Sarah thought the dove gray very distinguished, particularly with its black trim.

Her matching hat had been purchased just before her trip west and was the latest Paris fashion. Apparently it wasn't proper attire for a bordello, she thought as she watched Carlotta descend the stairs.

The owner of the Silver Star was resplendent in her trademark red. The silk slithered down her tall, curvaceous body, clinging, shifting, swaying. Her high white breasts rose like offerings from the scalloped bodice, which was threaded with silver threads. In her hand she carried a matching fan. As she flicked it in front of her face, the heavy scent of roses filled the room.

Despite her feelings, Sarah couldn't deny that the woman was stunning. In another place, another time, she could have been a queen.

"My, my, this is a rare honor, Miss Conway."

She'd been drinking. Sarah caught the scent of whiskey under the perfume. "This is hardly a social call."

"Now you disappoint me." Her painted mouth curved. "I can always use a new girl around here. Isn't that right…ladies?"

The other women shifted uncomfortably and remained tactfully silent.

"I thought maybe you'd come in looking for work." Still waving the fan, she strolled around Sarah, sizing her up. "Little scrawny," she said. "But some men like that. Could use some fixing up, right, girls? Little more here." She patted Sarah's unrouged cheek. "Little less there." She flicked a hand at the neckline of Sarah dress. "You might make a tolerable living."

"I don't believe I'd care to…work for you, Carlotta."

"That so?" Her eyes, already hardened by the

whiskey, iced over. "Too much of a lady to take pay for it, but not too much of a lady to give it away."

Sarah curled her fingers into a fist, then forced them to relax again. She would not resort to violence, or be driven to it. "No. I wouldn't care to work for anyone who beats their employees. Alice is with me now, Carlotta, and she'll stay with me. If you ever put your hands on her again, I'll see to it that you're thrown in jail."

"Oh, will you?" An angry flush darkened cheeks already bright with rouge. "I'll put my hands on who I please." She stabbed the fan into Sarah's chest. "No prim-faced bitch from back east is going to come into my place and tell me different."

With surprising ease, Sarah reached out and snapped the fan in two. "I just have." She had only an instant to brace herself for the slap. It knocked her backward. To balance herself she grabbed a table and sent a statuette crashing to the floor.

"Your kind makes me sick." Carlotta's voice was high and brittle as she leaned toward Sarah. Whiskey and anger had taken hold of her and twisted her striking face. "Looking as though they wouldn't let a man touch them. But you'll spread your legs as easy as any. You think because you went to school and lived in a big house that makes you special? You're nothing out here, nothing." She scooped up a fat plaster cherub and sent it crashing into the wall.

"The fact that I went to school and lived in a house isn't all that separates us." Sarah's voice was a sharp contrast to Carlotta's in its calmness. "You don't make me sick, Carlotta. You only make me sorry."

"I don't need pity from you. I made this place. I got something, and nobody handed it to me. Nobody ever gave me money for fine dresses and fancy hats. I earned it." Breasts heaving, she stepped closer. "You think you got Jake dangling on a string, honey, you're wrong. Soon as he's had his fill of you, he'll be back. What he's doing to you on these hot, sweaty nights, he'll be doing to me."

"No." Amazingly, Sarah's voice was still calm. "Even if he comes back and puts your price in your hands, you'll never have what I have with him. You know it," Sarah said quietly. "And that's why you hate me." With her eyes on Carlotta, she began to pull on her gloves again. Her hands would tremble any moment. She knew it, and she wanted to be on her way first. "But the issue here is Alice, not Jake. She is no longer in your employ."

"I'll tell that slut when she's through here."

It happened so quickly, Sarah was hardly aware of it. She had managed to hold her temper during Carlotta's insulting tirade against her own person. But to hear Alice called by that vile name while the girl was lying helpless and hurt was too much. Her ungloved hand shot out and connected hard with the side of Carlotta's face.

The three women, and the one who had come creeping down the stairs to look in on the commotion, let out gasps of surprise in unison. Sarah barely had time to feel the satisfaction of her action when Carlotta had her by the hair. They tumbled to the floor in a flurry of skirts.

Sarah shrieked as Carlotta tried to pull her hair out by the roots. She had handfuls of it, tugging and ripping while she cursed wildly. Fighting the pain, Sarah swung out and connected with soft flesh. She heard Carlotta grunt, and they rolled across the rug. Crockery smashed as they collided with a table, each trying to land a blow or defend against one. Sarah took a fist in the stomach with a gasp, but managed to evade a lethal swipe of Carlotta's red-tipped nails.

There was hate in Carlotta's eyes, a wild, almost mad hate. Sarah grabbed her wrist and twisted, knowing that if the other woman got her hands on her throat she'd squeeze until all her breath was gone.

She had no intention of being strangled, or pummeled. Her own rage had her rolling on top of her opponent and grabbing a handful of dyed hair. When she felt teeth sink into her arm, she cried out and yanked with all her strength, jerking Carlotta's head back and bringing out a howl of rage and pain. Other screams rose up, but Sarah was lost in the battle. She yanked and clawed and tore as viciously as Carlotta. They were equals now, with no barriers of class or background. A lamp shattered in a shower of glass as the two writhing bodies careened into another table.

"What in the hell is going on here?" Barker burst into the parlor. He took one look at the scene on the floor and shut his eyes. He'd rather have faced five armed, drunken cowboys than a pair of scratching women. "Break it up," he ordered as the two of them tumbled across the floor. "Somebody's going to get hurt here." He shook his head and sighed. "Most likely me."

He stepped into the melee just as Jake strode through the parlor doors.

"Let's pull them apart," Barker said heavily. "Take your pick." But Jake was already hauling Sarah up off the floor. She kicked out, her breath hissing as she tried to struggle away.

"Pull in your claws, Duchess." He clamped an arm around her waist as Barker restrained Carlotta.

"Get her out of here." Carlotta shoved away from Barker and stood, her dress ripped at both shoulders, her hair in wild tufts. "I want that bitch out of here and in jail. She came in here and started breaking up my place."

"Now, that don't seem quite logical," Barker mused. "Miss Sarah, you want to tell me what you're doing in a place like this?"

"Business." She tossed her hair out of her eyes. "Personal business."

"Well, looks to me like you've finished with your business here. Why don't you go on along home now?"

Sarah drew on her dignity like a cape over her torn dress. "Thank you, Sheriff." She cast one last look at Carlotta. "I am quite finished here." She glided toward the door to the secret admiration of Carlotta's girls.

"Just one damn minute." Jake took her arm the second she stepped outside. She had time now for embarrassment when she noted the size of the crowd she'd drawn.

"If you'll excuse me," she said stiffly, "I must get home." She reached up to tidy her tousled hair. "My hat."

"I think I saw what was left of it back in there." Jake ran his tongue over his teeth as he looked at her. She had a bruise beginning under her eye. It would make up to be a pretty good shiner by the end of the day. Her fashionable gray dress was ripped down one arm, and her hair looked as though she'd been through a windstorm.

Thoughtfully, he tucked his hands in his pockets. Carlotta had looked a hell of a lot worse.

"Duchess, a man wouldn't know it to look at you, but you're a real firebrand."

Grimly she brushed at her rumpled skirts. "I can see that amuses you."

"I have to say it does." He smiled, and her teeth snapped together. "I guess I'm flattered, but you didn't have to get yourself in a catfight over me."

Her mouth dropped open. The man looked positively delighted. She was scratched and bruised and aching and humiliated, and he looked as though his grin might just split his face. Over him? she thought, and made herself return the smile.

"So you think I fought with Carlotta over you, because I was jealous?"

"Can't think of another reason."

"Oh, I'll give you a reason." She brought her fist up and caught him neatly on the jaw. He was holding a hand to his face and staring after her when Barker strolled out.

"She's got what you might call a mean right hook." In the street, people howled and snickered as Sarah climbed into the wagon and drove off. "Son," Barker said with a hand on Jake's shoulder, "you're the fastest hand I ever saw with those Colts of yours. You play a fine game of poker, and you hold your whiskey like a man. But you got a hell of a lot to learn about women."

"Apparently," Jake murmured. He walked across to O'Riley's and untied his horse.

Sarah seethed as she raced the wagon toward

home. She'd made a spectacle of herself. She'd engaged in a crude, despicable sparring match with a woman with no morals. She'd brought half the town out into the street to stare and snicker at her. And then, to top it all off, she'd had to endure Jake Redman's grinning face.

She'd shown him. Sarah tossed her head up and spurred the horses on. Her hand might possibly be broken, but she'd shown him. The colossal conceit of the man, to believe that she would stoop to such a level out of petty jealousy.

She wished she'd torn Carlotta's brass-colored hair out by its black roots.

Not over him, she reminded herself. At least not very much over him.

She heard the rider coming up fast and looked over her shoulder. With a quick gasp of alarm, she cracked the reins. She would not speak to him now. Jake Redman could go to the devil, as far as she was concerned. And he could take his grin with him.

But her sturdy workhorses were no match for his mustang. Nor was her driving skill a match for his riding. Even as she cursed him, he came up beside her. She had a flash, clear as a bell, of how he'd looked when he'd raced beside the stagecoach, firing over his shoulder. He looked just as untamed and dangerous now.

"Stop that damn thing."

Chin up, she cracked the reins again.

One of these days somebody was going to teach her to listen, Jake thought. It might just be today. He judged the timing and rhythm, then leaped from his horse into the wagon. Surefooted, he stepped over onto the seat, and though she fought him furiously he pulled the horses in.

"What the hell's got into you, woman?" He scrambled for a hold as she shoved him aside and tried to jump out.

"Take your hands off me. I won't be handled this way."

"Handling you is a sight more work than I care for." He snatched his hand out of range before she could bite him. "Haven't you had enough scratching for one day? Sit down before you hurt yourself."

"You want the blasted wagon, take it. I won't ride with you."

"You'll ride with me, all right." Out of patience, he twisted her into his lap and silenced her. She squirmed and pushed and held herself as rigid as iron. Then she melted. He felt the give, slow, easy, inevitable. In her. In himself. As her lips parted for his, he forgot about keeping her quiet and just took what he kept trying to tell himself he couldn't have.

"You pack a punch, Duchess." He drew her away to rub a hand over his chin. "In a lot of ways. You want to tell me what that was for?"

She pulled away, furious that she'd gone soft with just one kiss. "For assuming that I was jealous and would fight over any worthless man."

"So now I'm worthless. Well, that may be, but you seem to like having me around."

She did her best to straighten what was left of her dress. "Perhaps I do."

He needed to know it more than he'd imagined. Jake took her chin in his hand and turned her to face him. "You change your mind?"

Again she softened, this time because she saw the doubt in his eyes. "No, I haven't changed my mind." She drew a long breath. "Even though you didn't come back and you've been to the Silver Star to see Carlotta."

"You sure do hear things. Can't imagine what you'd know if you lived closer to town. Stay in the wagon." He recognized the look in her eye by now. "Stay in the wagon, Sarah, until I get my horse tied on. I'll just catch you again if you run."

"I won't run." She brought her chin up again and stared straight ahead. When he'd joined her again, she continued her silence. Jake clucked to the horses and started off.

"I like to know why a woman's mad at me. Why don't you tell me how you know I've been to Carlotta's?"

"Alice told me."

"Alice Johnson?"

"That's right. Your friend Carlotta nearly beat her to death."

He brought the horses up short. "What?"

Her fury bounded back and poured over him. "You heard what I said. She beat that poor girl as cruelly as anyone can be beaten. Eli helped Alice get out of town. Then she walked the rest of the way to my place."

"Is she going to be all right?"

"With time and care."

"And you're going to give it to her?"

"Yes." Her eyes dared him. "Do you have any objections?"

"No." He touched her face, gently, in a way that was

new to him. Abruptly he snatched his hand back and snapped the reins again. "You went into the Silver Star to have it out with Carlotta over Alice."

"I've never been so furious." Sarah lifted a hand to where Jake had touched her. "Alice is hardly more than a child. No matter what she did, she didn't deserve that kind of treatment."

"Did she tell you why Carlotta did it?"

"She didn't seem to know, only that she must have made some kind of mistake. Alice did say that Carlotta was in a temper after you had been there."

He said nothing for a moment as he put the pieces together. "And she took it out on Alice."

"Why did you go? Why did you go to Carlotta? If there's something you…" She hadn't any idea how to phrase it properly. "If I don't know enough about your needs… I realize I don't have any experience in these matters, but I—"

She found her mouth crushed again in a kiss that was half hungry, half angry. "There's never been anyone else who's known so much about what I need." He watched her face clear into a smile. "I went to see Carlotta to tell her I don't care much for having my name used as a reference."

"So she took it out on Alice, because Alice was the one who'd come to talk to me." Sarah shook her head and tried not to let her temper take over again. "Alice only told me what Carlotta wanted her to tell me. It didn't work the way she'd planned, and Alice paid for it."

"That's about the size of it."

Sarah linked her fingers again and set them in her lap. "Is that the only reason you went to Carlotta?"

"No." He waited for the look. The look of passionate fury. "I went for that, and to tell her to stay away from you. Of course, I didn't know at the time that you were going to go and bloody her lip."

"Did I?" She tried and failed to bank down the pleasure she felt at the news. "Did I really?"

"And her nose. Guess you were a little too involved to notice."

"I've never struck anyone before in my life." She tried to keep her voice prim, then gave up. "I liked it."

With a laugh, Jake pulled her to his side. "You're a real wildcat, Duchess."

Chapter 12

Jake learned something new when he watched Sarah with Alice. He had always assumed that a woman who had been raised in the sheltered, privileged world would ignore, even condemn, one who lived as Alice lived. There were many decent women, as they called themselves, who would have turned Alice away as if she were a rabid dog.

Not Sarah.

And it was more than what he supposed she would have called Christian charity. He'd run into his share of people who liked to consider themselves good Christians. They had charity, all right, unless they came across somebody who looked different, thought different. There had been plenty of Christian women who had swept their skirts aside from his own mother because she'd married a man of mixed blood.

They went into church on Sundays and quoted the Scriptures and professed to love their neighbor. But when their neighbor didn't fit their image of what was right, love turned to hate quickly enough.

With Sarah it wasn't just words. It was compassion, caring, and an understanding he hadn't expected from her. He could hear, as he sat at the table, the simple kindness in her voice as she talked to the girl and tended her wounds.

As for Alice, it was obvious the girl adored Sarah. He'd yet to see her, as Sarah claimed her patient wasn't up to visitors. But he could hear the shyness and the respect in her voice when she answered Sarah's questions.

She'd fought for Alice. He couldn't quite get over that. Most people wouldn't fight for anything unless it was their own, or something they wanted to own. It had taken pride, and maybe what people called valor, for her to walk into a place like the Silver Star and face Carlotta down. And she'd done it. He glanced up toward the loft. She'd more than done it. She'd held her own.

Rising, he walked outside to where Lucius was doing his best to teach an uncooperative Lafitte to shake hands.

"Damn it, boy, did I say jump all over me? No, you flea-brained mongrel, I said shake." Lucius pushed the dog's rump down and grabbed a paw. "Shake. Get it?" Lafitte leaped up again and licked Lucius's face.

"Doesn't appear so," Jake commented.

"Fool dog." But Lucius rubbed the pup's belly when he rolled over. "Grows on you, though." He squinted up at Jake. "Something around here seems to be growing on you, too."

"Somebody had to bring her back."

"Reckon so." He waited until Jake crouched to scratch the puppy's head. "You want to tell me how Miss Sarah came to look like she'd been in a fistfight?"

"She looked like she was in a fistfight because she was in a fistfight."

Lucius snorted and spit. "Like hell."

"With Carlotta."

Lucius's cloudy eyes widened, and then he let out a bark of laughter that had Lafitte racing in circles. "Ain't that a hoot? Are you telling me that our Miss Sarah went in and gave Carlotta what for?"

"She gave her a bloody nose." Jake looked over with a grin. "And pulled out more than a little of her hair."

"Sweet Jesus, I'd've given two pints of whiskey to've seen that. Did you?"

Chuckling, Jake pulled on Lafitte's ears. "The tail end of it. When I walked in, the two of them were rolling over the floor, spitting like cats. I figure Carlotta outweighs Sarah by ten pounds or more, but Sarah was sitting on her, skirts hiked up and blood in her eye. It was one hell of a sight."

"She's got spunk." Lucius pulled out his whiskey and toasted Sarah with a healthy gulp. "I knew she had something in her head when she tore out of here." Feeling generous, he handed the bottle to Jake. "Never would have thought she'd set her mind on poking a fist into Carlotta. But nobody ever deserved it more. You seen Alice?"

"No." Jake let the whiskey spread fire through him. "Sarah's got the idea that it's not fitting for me to talk to the girl until she's covered up or something."

"I carried her in myself, and I don't mind saying I ain't seen no woman's face ever smashed up so bad. Took a belt to her, too, from the looks of it. Her back and shoulders all come up in welts. Jake, you wouldn't whup a dog the way that girl was whupped. That Carlotta must be crazy."

"Mean and crazy's two different things." He handed Lucius the bottle. "Carlotta's just mean."

"Reckon you'd know her pretty well."

Jake watched Lucius take another long sip. "I paid for her a few times, sometime back. Doesn't mean I know her."

"Soon plop my ass next to a rattler's." Lucius handed the bottle back to Jake again, then fell into a fit of coughing. "Miss Sarah, I didn't hear you come out."

"So I surmised," she said with a coolness that had Lucius coughing again. "Perhaps you gentlemen have finished drinking whiskey and exchanging crude comments and would like to wash for supper. If not, you're welcome to eat out here in the dirt." With that she turned on her heel, making certain she banged the door shut behind her.

"Ooo-whee." Lucius snatched back the bottle and took another drink. "She's got a mighty sharp tongue for such a sweet face. I tell you, boy, you'll have to mind your step if'n you hitch up with her."

Jake was still staring at the door, thinking how beautiful she'd looked, black eye and all, standing there like a queen addressing her subjects. "I ain't planning on hitching up with anyone."

"Maybe you are and maybe you ain't." Lucius rose

and brushed off his pants. A little dirt and she'd have them off him again and in the stream. "But she's got plans, all right. And a woman like that's hard to say no to."

Sarah spoke politely at supper, as if she were entertaining at a formal party. Her hair was swept up and tidied, and she'd changed her dress. She was wearing the green one that set off her hair and eyes. The stew was served in ironstone bowls, but the way she did it, it could have been a restaurant meal on fancy china.

It made him think, as he hadn't in years, of his mother and how she had liked to fuss over Sunday supper.

She said nothing about the encounter in town, and it was clear that she didn't care to have the subject brought up. It was hard to believe she was the same woman he'd dragged off the floor in the Silver Star. But he noticed that she winced now and then. He bit into a hunk of fresh bread and held back a grin. She was hurting, all right, and more than her pride, from the look of it. As he ate he entertained thoughts of how he would ease those hurts when the sun went down.

"Would you like some more stew, Lucius?"

"No, ma'am." He patted his belly. "Full as a tick. If it's all the same to you, I'll just go take a walk before I feed the stock and such. Going to be a pretty night." He sent them both what he thought was a bland look. "I'll sleep like a log after a meal like this. Yessir. I don't believe I'll stir till morning." He scraped back his chair and reached for his hat. "Mighty fine meal, Miss Sarah."

"Thank you, Lucius."

Jake tipped back his chair. "I wouldn't mind a walk myself."

Sarah had to smile at the way Lucius began to whistle after he'd closed the door. "You go ahead."

He took her hand as she rose. "I'd like it better if you went with me."

She smiled. He'd never asked her to do something as ordinary, and as romantic, as going for a walk. Thank goodness she hadn't forgotten how to flirt. "Why, that's nice of you, but I have to see to the dishes. And Alice may be waking soon. I think she could eat a bit now."

"I imagine I could occupy myself for an hour or two. We'll take a walk when you're done."

She sent him a look from under lowered lashes. "Maybe." Then she laughed as he sent her spinning into his lap. "Why, Mr. Redman. You are quite a brute."

He ran a finger lightly over the bruise under her eye. "Then you'd best be careful. Kiss me, Sarah."

She smiled when her lips were an inch from his. "And if I don't?"

"But you will." He traced her bottom lip with his tongue. "You will."

She did, sinking into it, into him. Her arms wound around him, slender and eager. Her mouth opened like a flower in sunlight. They softened against him even as they heated. They yielded even as they demanded.

"Don't be long," he murmured. He kissed her again, passion simmering, then set her on her feet. She let out a long, shaky breath when he closed the door behind him.

With Alice settled for the night and the day's work behind her, Sarah stepped out into the quieting light of early evening. It was still too warm to bother with a shawl, but she pushed her sleeves down past her elbows and buttoned the cuffs. There were bruises on her arms that she didn't care to dwell on.

From where she stood she could hear Lucius in the shed, talking to Lafitte. He'd become more his dog than hers, Sarah thought with a laugh. Or perhaps they'd both become something of hers.

As the land had.

She closed her eyes and let the light breeze flutter over her face. She could, if she concentrated hard enough, catch the faintest whiff of sage. And she could, if she used enough imagination, picture what it would be like to sit on the porch she envisioned having, watching the sun go down every evening while Jake rolled a cigarette and listened with her to the music of the night.

Bringing herself back, she looked around. Where was he? She stepped farther out into the yard when she heard the sound of hammer against wood. She saw him, a few yards from the chicken coop, beating an old post into the ground. He'd taken his shirt off, and she could see the light sheen of sweat over his lean torso and the rippling and bunching of his muscles as he swung the heavy hammer down.

Her thoughts flew back to the way his arms had swung her into heat, into passion. The hands that gripped the thick, worn handle of the hammer now had roamed over her, touching, taking whatever they chose.

And she had touched, wantonly, even greedily, that long, limber body, taking it, accepting it as her own.

Her breath shuddered out as she watched him bend and lift and pound. Was it wrong to have such thoughts, such wonderful, exciting visions? How could it be, when she loved so completely? She wanted his heart, but oh, she wanted his body, as well, and she could find no shame in it.

His head came up quickly, as she imagined an animal's might when it caught a scent. And he had. Though she was several yards away, he had sensed her, the trace of lilac, the subtlety of woman. He straightened, and just as she had looked her fill of him, he looked his of her.

She might have stepped from a cool terrace to walk in a garden. The wind played with her skirts and her hair, but gently. The backdrop of the setting sun was like glory behind her. Her eyes, as she walked toward him, were wide and dark and aware.

"You've got a way of moving, Duchess, that makes my mouth water."

"I don't think that's what the good sisters intended when they taught me posture. But I'm glad." She moved naturally to his arms, to his lips. "Very glad."

For the first time in his life he felt awkward with a woman, and he drew her away. "I'm sweaty."

"I know." She pulled a handkerchief from her pocket and dabbed at his face. "What are you doing?"

She made him feel like a boy fumbling over his first dance. "You said you wanted pigs. You need a pen." He picked up his shirt and shrugged it on. "What are you doing?"

"Watching you." She put a hand to his chest, where the shirt lay open. "Remembering. Wondering if you want me as much as you did."

He took her hand before she could tear what was

inside of him loose. "No, I don't. I want you more."
He picked up his gunbelt, but instead of strapping it
on he draped it over his shoulder. "Why don't we go
for that walk?"

Content, she slipped her hand into his. "When I first
came here I wondered what it was that had kept my
father, rooted him here. At first I thought it was only for
me, because he wanted so badly to provide what he
thought I'd need. That grieved me. I can't tell you how
much." She glanced up as they passed the rise that led to
his grave. "Later I began to see that even though that was
part of it, perhaps the most important part to him, he was
also happy here. It eases the loss to know he was happy."

They started down the path to the stream she had
come to know so well.

"I didn't figure you'd stick." Her hand felt right, easy
and right, tucked in his. "When I brought you out here
the first time, you looked as if someone had dropped you
on your head."

"It felt as though someone had. Losing him… Well,
the truth is, I'd lost him years and years ago. To me, he's
exactly the same as he was the day he left. Maybe
there's something good about that. I never told you he
had spun me a tale." At the stream she settled down on
her favorite rock and listened to the water's melody. "He
told me of the fine house he'd built after he'd struck the
rich vein of gold in Sarah's Pride. He painted me a
picture of it with his words. Four bedrooms, a parlor
with the windows facing west, a wide porch with big
round columns." She smiled a little and watched the sun
glow over the buttes. "Maybe he thought I needed that,

and maybe I did, to see myself as mistress of a fine, big house with curving stairs and high, cool walls."

He could see it, and her. "It was what you were made for."

"It's you I was made for." Rising, she held out her hands.

"I want you, Sarah. I can't offer you much more than a blanket to spread on the ground."

She glanced over at the small pile of supplies he'd already brought down to the stream. She moved to it and lifted the blanket.

It was twilight when they lowered to it. The air had softened. The wind was only a rustle in the thin brush. Overhead the sky arched, a deep, ever-darkening blue. Under the wool of the blanket the ground was hard and unforgiving. She lifted her arms to him and they left the rest behind.

It was as it had been the first time, and yet different. The hunger was there, and the impatient pull of desire. With it was a knowledge of the wonder, the magic, they could make between them. A little slower now, a little surer, they moved together.

There was urgency in his kiss. She could feel it. But beneath it was a tenderness she had dreamed of, hoped for. Seduced by that alone, she murmured his name. Beneath her palm, his cheek was rough. Under her fingers, his skin was smooth. His body, like his mind, like his heart, was a contrast that drew her, compelled her to learn more.

A deep, drugging languor filled her as he began to undress her. There was no frantic rush, as there had been before. His fingers were slow and sure as they moved down the small covered buttons. She felt the air whisper against her skin as he parted the material. Then it was his mouth, warmer, sweeter, moving over her. Her sigh was like music.

He wanted to give her something he'd never given another woman. The kind of care she deserved. Tenderness was new to him, but it came easily now as he peeled off layer after layer to find her. He sucked in his breath as her fingers fumbled with the buttons at his waist. Her touch wasn't hesitant, but it was still innocent. It would always be. And her innocence aroused him as skill never could have.

She removed the layers he'd covered himself with. Not layers of cotton or leather, but layers of cynicism and aloofness, the armor he'd used to survive, just as he'd used his pistols. With her he was helpless, more vulnerable than he had been since childhood. With her he felt more of a man than he had ever hoped to be.

She felt the change, an explosion of feelings and needs and desires, as he dragged her up into his arms to crush his mouth against hers. What moved through him poured into her, leaving her breathless, shaken and impossibly strong. Without understanding, without needing to, she answered him with everything in her heart.

Then came the storm, wild, windy, wailing. Rocked by it, she cried out as he drove her up, up, into an airless, rushing cloud of passion. Sensations raced through her—the sound of her own desperate moans, the scrape of his face against her skin as he journeyed down her trembling body, the taste of him that lingered on her lips, on her tongue, as he did mad, unspeakably wonderful things to her. Lost, driven beyond reason, she pressed his head closer to her.

She was like something wild that had just been unchained. He could feel the shocked delight ripple through her when he touched her moist heat with his tongue. He thought her response was like a miracle, though he'd long ago stopped believing in them. There was little he could give her besides the pleasures of her own body. But at least that, he would do.

Sliding upward, he covered her mouth with his. And filled her.

Long after her hands had slipped limply from his back, long after their breathing had calmed and leveled, he lay over her, his face buried in her hair. She'd brought him peace, and though he knew it wouldn't last, for now she'd brought him peace of mind, of body, of heart.

He hadn't wanted to love, hadn't dared to risk it. Even now, when it was no longer possible to hide it from himself, he couldn't tell her.

"Lucius was right," she murmured against his ear.

"Mmm?"

"It's a pretty night." She ran her hands up his back. "A very pretty night."

"Am I hurting you?"

"No." She gripped her own wrists so that she could hold him closer. "Don't move yet."

"I'm heavy, and you've got some colorful bruises."

If she'd had the energy, she might have laughed. "I'd forgotten about them."

"I put some on you myself last night." He lifted his head to look down at her. "I don't know much about going easy."

"I'm not complaining."

"You should." Fascinated, he stroked a finger down her cheek. "You're so beautiful. Like something I made up."

She turned her lips into his palm as her eyes filled. "You've never told me you thought I was beautiful."

"Sure I did." He shifted then, frustrated by his own lack of words. "I should have."

She curled comfortably against his side. "I feel beautiful right now."

They lay in contented silence, looking up at the sky.

"What's an enigma?" he asked her.

"Hmm? Oh, it's a puzzle. Something difficult to understand. Why?"

"I guess I heard it somewhere." He thought of her diary, and her description of him, but couldn't see how it applied. He'd always seen himself as being exactly what he appeared to be. "You're getting cold."

"A little."

Sitting up, he pushed through her discarded undergarments for her chemise. She smiled, lifting her arms over her head. Her lips curved when she saw his gaze slide over her skin. When he pulled the cotton over her, she linked her hands behind his neck.

"I was hoping to stay warm a different way."

With a laugh, he slid a hand down over her hip. "I remember telling you once before you were a quick study." Experimentally he pushed the strap of her chemise off her shoulder. "You want to do something for me?"

"Yes." She nuzzled his lips. "Very much."

"Go on over and stand in that stream."

Confused, she drew back. "I beg your pardon?"

"Nobody says that better than you, Duchess. I'll swear to that." He kissed her again, in a light, friendly manner that pleased and puzzled her.

"You want to go wading?"

"Not exactly." He toyed with the strap. Women wore the damnedest things. Then they covered them all up anyhow. "I thought you'd go stand in the stream wearing just this little thing. Like you did that first night."

"What first night?" Her puzzled smile faded as he traced his fingertip along the edge of her bodice. "That first— You! You were watching me while I—"

"I was just making sure you didn't get yourself into any trouble."

"That's disgraceful." She tried to pull away, but he held her still.

"I started thinking then and there how much I'd like to get my hands on you. Had some trouble sleeping that night." He lowered his lips to the curve of her throat and began to nibble. "Fact is, I haven't had a good night's sleep since I set eyes on you."

"Stop it." She turned her head, but it only made it easier for him to find her mouth.

"Are you going to go stand in the stream?"

"I am not." She smothered a laugh when he rolled her onto the blanket again. "I'm going to get dressed and go back to the house to check on Alice."

"No need. Lucius is keeping an eye on her."

"Oh, I see. You've already decided that for me."

"I guess you could put it like that. You're not going anywhere but this blanket. And maybe the stream, once I talk you into it."

"You won't talk me into it. I have no intention of sleeping outside."

"I don't figure on sleeping much at all." He stretched out on his back again and gathered her close. "Haven't you ever slept outside before, looked at the sky? Counted stars?"

"No." But, of course, tonight she would. She wanted nothing more. She turned her head to study his profile. "Have you ever counted stars, Jake?"

"When I was a kid." He stroked a hand lazily up and down her arm. "My mother used to say there were pictures. She'd point them out to me sometimes, but I could never find them again."

"I'll show you one." Sarah took his hand and began to draw in the air. "It's a horse. A winged horse. Pegasus," she added. Then she caught her breath. "Look, a shooting star." She watched, his hand held in hers, as it arced across the sky. She closed her eyes quickly, then made a wish. "Will you tell me about your mother?"

For a long moment he said nothing, but continued to stare up at the sky. The arc of light was gone, without a trace. "She was a teacher." Sarah's gaze flicked up quickly to his face. "She'd come out here from St. Louis."

"And met your father?"

"I don't know much about that. He wanted to learn to read and write, and she taught him. She set a lot of store by reading."

"And while she was teaching him, they fell in love."

He smiled a little. It sounded nice the way she said it. "I guess they did. She married him. It wouldn't have been easy, with him being half Apache. They wanted to build something. I remember the way my father used to talk about taking the land and making it work for him. Leaving something behind."

She understood that, because it was what she wanted for herself. "Were they happy?"

"They laughed a lot. My mother used to sing. He always talked about buying her a piano one day, so she could play again like she did in St. Louis. She'd just laugh and say she wanted lace curtains first. I'd forgotten that," he murmured. "She wanted lace curtains."

She turned her face into his shoulder because she felt his pain as her own. "Lucius told me what happened to them. To you. I'm so sorry."

He hadn't known he needed to talk about it, needed to tell her. "They came in from town…eight, ten of them, I've never been sure." His voice was quiet now, his eyes on the sky. He could still see them, as he hadn't allowed himself to see them for years. "They lit the barn first. Maybe if my father had stayed in the house, let them shoot and shout and trample, they'd have left the rest. But they'd have come back. He knew it. He took his rifle and went out to protect what was his. They shot him right outside the door."

Sarah held him tighter, seeing it with him.

"We ran out. They tasted blood now, like wolves, wild-eyed, teeth bared. She was crying, holding on to my father and crying. Inside the barn, the horses were screaming. The sky was lit up so I could see their faces while they torched the rest."

And he could smell the smoke as he lay there, could hear the crackle of greedy flames and his mother's pitiful weeping.

"I picked up the rifle. That's the first time I ever wanted to kill. It's like a fever in the blood. Like a hand has ahold of you, squeezing. She started to scream. I saw one of the riders take aim at me. I had the rifle in my hands, but I was slow. Better with a bow or a knife back then. She threw herself up and in front of me so when he pulled the trigger the bullet went in her."

Sarah tightened her arms around him as tears ran fast and silent down her cheeks.

"One of them hit me with a rifle butt as he rode by. It was morning before I came to. They'd burned everything. The house was still smoking—even when it cooled there was nothing in it worth keeping. The ground was hard there, and I got dizzy a few times, so it took me all day to bury them. I slept there that night, between the two graves. I told myself that if I lived until morning I'd find the men who'd done it and kill them. I was still alive in the morning."

She said nothing, could say nothing. It wasn't necessary to ask what he'd done. He'd learned to use a gun, and use it well. And he had found the men, or some of them.

"When Lucius came, I told him what happened. That was the last time I told anyone."

"Don't." She turned to lay her body across his. "Don't think about it anymore."

He could feel her tears on his chest, the warmth of

them. As far as he knew, no one had ever cried for him before. Taking her hand, he kissed it. "Show me that picture in the sky, Sarah."

Turning, keeping her hand in his, she began to trace the stars. The time for tears, for regrets—and, she hoped, for revenge—was done. "The stars aren't as big in the East, or as bright." They lay quietly for a while, wrapped close, listening to the night sounds. "I used to jump every time I heard a coyote. Now I like listening for them. Every night, when I read my father's journal—"

"Matt kept a journal?" He sat up as he asked, dragging her with him.

"Why, yes." There was an intensity in his eyes that made her heart skip erratically. "What is it?"

"Have you read it?"

"Not all of it. I've been reading a few pages each night."

He suddenly realized that he was digging his fingers into her arms. He relaxed them. "Will you let me read it?"

Her heart was steady again, but something cold was inching its way over her skin. "Yes. If you tell me why you want to."

He turned away to reach casually in his saddlebag for his tobacco pouch and papers. "I just want to read it."

She waited while he rolled a cigarette. "All right. I trust you. When are you going to trust me, Jake?"

He struck a match on a rock. The flame illuminated his face. "What do you mean?"

"Why did you ask Lucius to work in the mine?"

He flicked the match out, then tossed it aside. The scent of tobacco stung the air. "Maybe I thought Matt would have liked it."

Determined, she put a hand to his face and turned it toward hers. "Why?"

"A feeling I had, that's all." Shifting away, he blew out a stream of smoke. "People usually have a reason for setting fires, Sarah. There was only one I could figure when it came to you. Somebody didn't want you there."

"That's ridiculous. I hardly knew anyone at that point. The sheriff said it was drifters." She curled her hands in her lap as she studied his face. "You don't think it was."

"No. Maybe Barker does, and maybe he doesn't. There's only one thing on this land that anyone could want. That's gold."

Impatient, Sarah sat back on her heels. "But there isn't any gold."

"Yes, there is." Jake drew deep on his cigarette and watched the range of expressions cross her face.

"What are you talking about?"

"Lucius found the mother lode, just the way Matt did." He glanced at the glowing tip of his cigarette. "You're going to be a rich woman, Duchess."

"Wait." She pressed a hand to her temple. It was beginning to throb. "Are you telling me that the mine is really worth something?"

"More than something, according to Lucius."

"I can't believe it." With a quick, confused laugh, she shook her head. "I never thought it was anything but a dream. Just this morning, I'd begun to wonder, but— How long have you known?"

"A while."

"A while?" she repeated, looking back at him. "And you didn't think it important enough to mention to me?"

"I figured it was important enough not to." He took a last drag before crushing the cigarette out. "I've never known a woman who could keep her mouth shut."

"Is that so?"

"Yes, ma'am."

"I'm perfectly capable of keeping my mouth shut, as you so eloquently put it. But why should I?"

There was no way to tell her but straight out. "Matt found the gold, and then he was dead."

"There was an accident…" she began. Suddenly cold, she hugged her elbows. He didn't have to speak for her to see what was in his mind. "You're trying to tell me that my father was murdered. That can't be." She started to scramble up, but he took her arms and held her still.

"Ten years he worked the mine and scratched a few handfuls of gold from it. Then he hits, hits big. The minute he does, there's a cave-in, and he's dead."

"I don't want to think about it."

"You're going to think about it." He gave her a quick shake. "The mine's yours now, and the gold in it. I'm not going to let what happened to Matt happen to you." His hands gentled and slid up to frame her face. "Not to you."

She closed her eyes. She couldn't take it in, not all at once. Fear, hysteria and fresh grief tangled within her. She lifted her hands to his wrists and held on until she felt herself calming. He was right. She had to think about it. Then she would act. When she opened her eyes, they were clear and steady.

"Tell me what you want me to do."

"Trust me." He touched his lips to hers, then laid her

back gently on the blanket. She'd given him peace early in the night. Now, as the night deepened, he would try to do the same for her.

Chapter 13

"I'm feeling lots better, Miss Conway." Alice took the tin cup and sipped gingerly.

She didn't want to complain about her back, or about the pain that still galloped along it despite the cooling salve. The morning light showed her facial bruises in heart-wrenching detail and caused the girl to look even younger and smaller and more vulnerable. Though the scratches on her cheeks were no longer red and angry, Sarah judged it would be several days before they faded.

"You look better." It wasn't strictly true, and Sarah vowed to keep her patient away from a mirror a bit longer. Though the swelling had eased considerably, she was still worried about Alice's eye and had already decided to drive into town later and talk with the doctor.

"Try a little of this soft-boiled egg. You need your strength."

"Yes, ma'am." Privately Alice thought the glossy wet yolk looked more like a slimy eye than food. But if Sarah had told her to eat a fried scorpion she'd have opened her mouth and swallowed. "Miss Conway?"

"Yes, Alice?" Sarah spooned up more egg.

"I'm beholden to you for taking me in like you did, and I can't— Miss Conway, you gave me your own bed last night. It ain't fitting."

Smiling a little, Sarah set the plate aside. "Alice, I assure you, I was quite comfortable last night."

"But, Miss Conway—"

"Alice, if you keep this up I'm going to think you're ungrateful."

"Oh!" Something close to horror flashed in Alice's eyes. "No, ma'am."

"Well, then." Because the response was exactly what she'd expected, Sarah rose. She remembered that the nuns had nursed with compassion tempered with brisk practicality. "You can show your gratitude by being a good patient and getting some more rest. If you're feeling up to it later, I'll have Lucius bring you down and we can sit and talk awhile."

"I'd like that. Miss Conway, if it hadn't been for you and Eli, I think I'd've died. I was hoping… Well, I got some money saved. It ain't much, but I'd like you to have it for all your trouble."

"I don't want your money, Alice."

The girl flushed and looked away. "I know you're probably thinking about where it comes from, but—"

"No." She took Alice's hand firmly in hers. "That has nothing to do with it." Pride, Sarah thought. She had plenty of her own. Alice was entitled to hers. "Alice, did Eli want money for driving you out of town?"

"No, but...he's a friend."

"I'd like to be your friend, if you'd let me. You rest now, and we'll talk about all this later." She gave Alice's hand a reassuring squeeze before she picked up the empty dishes and started down the ladder. She barely muffled a squeal when hands closed around her waist.

"Told you you didn't need that corset."

Sarah sent Jake what she hoped was an indignant look over her shoulder. "Is that why I couldn't find it when I dressed this morning?"

"Just doing you a favor." Before she could decide whether to laugh or lecture, he was whirling her around and kissing her.

"Jake, Alice is—"

"Not likely to faint if she figures out what I'm doing." But he set her aside, because he liked the way the sunlight streamed through the curtains and onto her hair. "You're mighty nice to look at, Duchess."

It was foolish to blush, but her color rose. "Why don't you sit down, and you can look at me some more while I fix you breakfast?"

"I'd like to, but I've got some things to see to." He touched her again, just a fingertip to the single wispy curl that had escaped from the neat bun on top of her head. "Sarah, will you let me have Matt's journal?"

Both the grief and the dread showed clearly in her eyes before she lowered them. During the night, after love and before sleep, she had thought of little else but what Jake had told her. Part of her wondered if she would be better off not knowing, not being sure. But another part, the same part that had kept her from turning back and going east again, had already accepted what needed to be done.

"Yes." She walked to the hearth to work the rock loose. "I found this the first night. His journal, what must have been his savings, and the deed to Sarah's Pride."

When she held the book out to him, Jake resisted the urge to open it there and then. If he found what he thought he would find, he would have business to take care of before he said anything else to her. "I'll take it along with me, if it's all the same to you."

She opened her mouth to object, wanting the matter settled once and for all. But he'd asked for her trust. Perhaps this was the way to show him he had it. "All right."

"And the deed? Will you let me hold on to it until we have some answers?"

In answer, she offered it to him, without hesitation, without question. For a moment they held the deed, and the dream, between them. "Just like that?" he murmured.

"Yes." She smiled and released her hold. "Just like that."

That her trust was so easily given, so total in her eyes, left him groping for words. "Sarah, I want…" What? he wondered as he stared down at her. To guard and protect, to love and possess? She was like something cool and sweet that had poured into him and washed away years of bitter thirst. But he didn't have the words, he thought. And he didn't have the right.

"I'll take care of this."

She lifted a brow. There had been something else, something in his eyes. She wanted it back, so that she could see it, understand it. "I thought *we* were going to take care of it."

"No." He cupped her chin in his hand. "You're going to leave this to me. I don't want anything to happen to you."

Her brow was still lifted as her lips curved. "Why?"

"Because I don't. I want you to—" Whatever he might have said was postponed. He moved to the window quickly. "You've got company coming." As he spotted the buggy, his shoulders relaxed. "Looks like Mrs. Cody and her girl."

"Oh." Sarah's hands shot up automatically to straighten her hair. "I must look— Oh, how would I know? I haven't had a chance to so much as glance in the mirror."

"Wouldn't matter much." Without glancing back, he pulled open the door. "Too bad you're so homely."

Muttering, she pulled off her apron and followed him outside. Then memory came flooding back and had her biting her lip. "I imagine they would have heard all about the, ah, incident yesterday."

"I expect." Jake secured the deed and the journal in the saddlebags that he'd tossed over the rail.

"You needn't look so amused." She fiddled nervously with the cameo at her throat, then put on her brightest smile. "Good morning, Mrs. Cody. Liza."

"Good morning, Sarah." Anne Cody brought the horses to a stop. "I hope you don't mind an early call."

"Not at all." But her fingers were busy pleating her

skirt. She was afraid there was a lecture coming. The good sisters had given Sarah more than what she considered her share over the past twelve years. "I'm always delighted to see you," she added. "Both of you."

Anne glanced over at the dog, who'd run out to bark at the horses. "My, he's grown some, hasn't he?" She held out a hand. "Mr. Redman?"

Jake stepped over to help her, then Liza, down, remaining silent until he'd slung his saddlebags over his shoulder. "I'd best be on my way." He touched a hand to his hat. "Ladies."

"Mr. Redman." Anne held up a hand in the gesture she used to stop her children from rushing out before their chores were finished. "Might I have a word with you?"

He shifted his bags until their weight fell evenly. "Yes, ma'am."

"My son John has been dogging your heels these last weeks. I'm surprised you put up with it."

Jake didn't imagine it pleased her, either, to have the boy spending time with him. "He hasn't made a pest of himself."

Curious, Anne studied his face. "That's a kind thing to say, Mr. Redman, when I'm sure he's done just that."

"Johnny was born a pest," Liza put in, earning a slow, measured look from her mother.

"It appears my children have that in common." With Liza effectively silenced, Anne turned back to Jake. "He's been going through what most boys his age go through, I expect. Fascinated with guns, gunfights. Gunfighters. I don't mind saying it's given me some worry."

"I'll keep my distance," Jake said, and turned to leave.

"Mr. Redman." Anne hadn't raised two willful children without knowing how to add the right tone of authority to her voice. "I'll have my say."

"Ma." Both Liza's cheeks and voice paled when she saw the look in Jake's eyes. Cold, she thought, and moistened her lips. She'd never seen eyes so cold. "Maybe we should let Mr. Redman be on his way."

"Your mother's got something to say," Jake said quietly. "I reckon she ought to say it."

"Thank you." Pleased, Anne drew off her riding gloves. "Johnny was real excited about what happened here between you and Burt Donley."

"Mrs. Cody," Sarah began, only to be silenced by a look from both her and Jake.

"As I was saying," Anne continued, "Johnny hardly talked about anything else for days. He figured having a shoot-out made a man a man and gave him something to strut about. Even started pestering his pa for a Peacemaker." She glanced down at the guns on Jake's hips. "Wooden grip, he said. Nothing fancy, like some of the glory boys wear. Just a good solid Colt. Mr. Cody and I had just about run clean out of patience with the boy. Then, just yesterday, he came home and told me something." She paused, measuring her words. "He said that killing somebody in a gunfight or any other way doesn't make a man grown-up or important. He said that a smart man doesn't look for trouble. He walks away from it when he can, and faces it when he can't."

For the first time, Anne smiled. "I guess I'd been telling him pretty near the same, but it didn't get through coming from me or his pa. Made me wonder who got him thinking that way." She offered her hand again. "I wanted to tell you I'm obliged."

Jake stared at the hand before taking it. It was the kind of gesture, one of gratitude, even friendship, that had rarely been made to him. "He's a smart boy, Mrs. Cody. He'd have come around to it."

"Sooner or later." Anne stepped toward the door of the house and then she turned back. "Maggie O'Rourke thinks a lot of you. I guess I found out why. I won't keep you any longer, Mr. Redman."

Not quite sure how to respond, he touched his hat before he started toward the paddock to saddle his horse.

"That's quite a man, Sarah," Anne commented. "If I were you, I'd want to go say a proper goodbye."

"Yes, I..." She looked at Anne, then back toward Jake, torn between manners and longings.

"You won't mind if I fix tea, will you?" Anne asked as she disappeared inside.

"No, please, make yourself at home." Sarah looked toward Jake again. "I'll only be a minute." Gathering her skirts, she ran. "Jake!" He turned, the saddle held in both hands, and enjoyed the flash of legs and petticoats. "Wait. I—" She stopped, a hand on her heart, when she realized she was not only out of breath but hadn't any idea what she wanted to say to him. "Are you... When will you be back?"

The mustang shifted and nickered softly as Jake settled the saddle in place. "Haven't left yet."

She hated feeling foolish, and hated even more the idea that he could swing onto his horse and ride out of her life for days at a time. Perhaps patience would do the job.

"I was hoping you'd come back for supper."

He tossed up a stirrup to tighten the cinch. "You asking me to supper?"

"Unless you've something else you'd rather be doing."

His hand snaked out, fast and smooth, to snag her arm before she could flounce away. "It's not often I get invitations to supper from pretty ladies." His grip firm, he glanced back toward the house. Things were changing, he decided, and changing fast, when he looked at the adobe cabin and thought of home. He still didn't know what the hell to do about it.

"If I'd known you'd need so long to think about it," Sarah said between her teeth, "I wouldn't have bothered. You can just—" But before she could tell him he swept her off her feet.

"You sure do get fired up easy." He brought his mouth down hard on hers to taste the heat and the honey. "That's one of the things I like about you."

"Put me down." But her arms encircled his neck. "Mrs. Cody might see." Then she laughed and kissed him again as he swung her down. "Well, will you come to supper or not?"

He vaulted into the saddle in one fluid, economical motion. His eyes were shadowed by the brim of his hat when he looked down at her. "Yeah, I'll come to supper."

"It'll be ready at seven," she called after him as he spurred his horse into a gallop. She watched until dust and distance obscured him. Gathering her skirts again, she ran back to the house. The laughter that was bubbling in her throat dried up when she heard Alice's weeping.

Liza stood by the stove, the kettle steaming in her

hand. "Sarah, Ma's..." But Sarah was already rushing up the ladder, ready to defend the girl.

Anne Cody held the weeping Alice in her arms, rocking her gently. One wide, capable hand was stroking the girl's dark hair.

"There now, honey, you cry it all out," she murmured. "Then it'll be behind you." Wanting quiet, she sent Sarah a warning glance. Her own eyes were damp. Slowly Sarah descended the ladder.

"Alice called for you," Liza explained, still holding the kettle. "Ma went up to see what she needed." Liza set the sputtering kettle aside. Tea was the last thing on her mind. "Sarah, what's going on?"

"I'm not sure I know."

Liza cast another look toward the loft and said in a low voice. "Was she...that girl...really beaten?"

"Yes." The memory of it had Sarah touching a fingertip to the bruise under her own eye. "Horribly. Liza, I've never known one person was capable of hurting another so viciously." She needed to be busy, Sarah decided. There was too much to think about. Her father, the mine, Jake, Alice. After running a distracted hand over her hair, she began to slice honey cake.

"Did she really work for Carlotta?"

"Yes. Liza, she's just a girl, younger than you and I."

"Really?" Torn between sympathy and fascination, Liza edged closer to Sarah. "But she... Well, I mean, at the Silver Star she must have..."

"She didn't know anything else." Sarah looked down at her hands. Honey cake and tea. There had been a time when she had thought life was as ordered and simple as that. "Her father sold her. Sold her to a man for twenty dollars."

"But that's—" The curiosity in Liza's eyes heated to fury. "Why, he's the one who should be beat. Her own pa. Somebody ought to—"

"Hush, Liza." Anne slipped quietly down the ladder. "No one deserves to be beat."

"Ma. Sarah says that girl's pa sold her. Sold her off for money, like a horse."

Anne paused in the act of brushing down her skirts. "Is that true, Sarah?"

"Yes. She ran away and ended up at the Silver Star."

Anne's lips tightened as she fought back words that even her husband had never heard her utter. "I'd dearly love that tea now."

"Oh, yes." Sarah hurried back to the stove. "I'm sorry. Please sit down." She set out the napkins she'd made out of blue checked gingham. "I hope you'll enjoy this honey cake. It's a recipe from the cook of a very dear friend of mine in Philadelphia." As she offered the plate, Philadelphia and everyone in it seemed years away.

"Thank you, dear." Anne waited for Sarah to sit down, then said, "Alice is sleeping now. I wasn't sure you'd done the right thing by taking her in here. Truth is, I drove out this morning because I was concerned."

"I had to take her in."

"No, you didn't." When Sarah bristled, Anne laid a hand on hers. "But you did what was right, and I'm proud of you. That girl needs help." With a sigh, she sat back and looked at her own daughter. Pretty Liza, she thought, always so bright and curious. And safe, she re-

flected, adding a quick prayer of thanksgiving. Her
children had always had a full plate and a solid roof over
their heads—and a father who loved them. She made up
her mind to thank her husband very soon.

"Alice Johnson has had nothing but hard times."
Anne took a sip of tea. Her mind was made up. She had
only to convince her husband. At that thought her lips
curved a little. It was never hard to convince a man
whose heart was soft and open. The other ladies in town
would be a bit more difficult, but she'd bring them
around. The challenge of it made her smile widen and
the light of battle glint in her eyes.

"What that girl needs is some proper work and a real
home. When she's on her feet again, I think she should
come work at the store."

"Oh, Mrs. Cody."

Anne brushed Sarah's stunned gratitude aside.
"Once Liza's married to Will I'm going to need new
help. She can take Liza's room in the house, as
well…as part of her wage."

Sarah fumbled for words, then gave up and simply
leaned over to wrap her arms around Anne. "It's kind
of you," she managed. "So kind. I've spoken with Alice
about just that, but she pointed out that the women in
town wouldn't accept her after she'd worked at the
Silver Star."

"You don't know Ma." Pride shimmered in Liza's
voice. "She'll bring the ladies around, every one.
Won't you, Ma?"

Anne patted her hair. "You can put money on it."
Satisfied, she broke off a corner of the honey cake.

"Sarah, now that we've got that settled, I feel I have to talk to you about the…visit you paid to the Silver Star yesterday."

"Visit?" Though she knew it was hopeless, Sarah covered the bruise under her eyes with her fingers.

"You know, when you tangled with Carlotta," Liza put in. "Everyone in town's talking about how you wrestled with her and even punched Jake Redman. I wish I'd seen it." She caught her mother's eye and grimaced. "Well, I do."

"Oh, Lord." This time Sarah covered her entire face. "Everyone?"

"Mrs. Miller was standing just outside when the sheriff went in." Liza took a healthy bite of cake. "You know how she loves to carry tales."

When Sarah just groaned, Anne shook her head at Liza. "Honey, you eat some more of that cake and keep your mouth busy. Now, Sarah." Anne pried Sarah's hands away from her face. "I have to say I was a mite surprised to hear that you'd gone in that place and had a hair-pulling match with that woman. Truth is, a nice young girl like you shouldn't even know about places and people like that."

"Can't live in Lone Bluff two days and not know about Carlotta," Liza said past a mouthful of cake. "Even Johnny—"

"Liza." Anne held up a single finger. "Chew. Seeing as you're without kin of your own, Sarah, I figured I'd come on out and speak to you about it." She took another sip of tea while Sarah waited to be lectured. "Well, blast it, now that I've seen that girl up there, I wished I'd taken a good yank at Carlotta, myself."

"Ma!" Delighted, Liza slapped both hands to her mouth. "You wouldn't."

"No." Anne flushed a little and shifted in her chair. "But I'd like to. Now, I'm not saying I want to hear about you going back there, Sarah."

"No." Sarah managed a rueful smile. "I think I've finished any business I might have at the Silver Star."

"Popped you a good one, did she?" Anne commented studying Sarah's eye.

"Yes." Sarah grinned irrepressibly. "But I gave her a bloody nose. It's quite possible that I broke it."

"Really. Oh, I do wish I'd seen that." Ready to be impressed, Liza leaned forward, only to straighten again at a look from Anne. "Well, it's not as if I'd go inside myself."

"Not if you want to keep the hide on your bottom," Anne said calmly. She smoothed her hair, took another sip of tea, then gave up. "Well, darn it, are you going to tell us what it looks like in there or not?"

With a laugh, Sarah propped her elbows on the table and told them.

Scheming came naturally to Carlotta. As she lay in the wide feather bed, she ran through all the wrongs that had been done to her and her plans for making them right. The light was dim, with only two thin cracks appearing past the sides of the drawn shades. It was a large room by the Silver Star's standards. She'd had the walls between two smaller rooms removed to fashion her own private quarters, sacrificing the money one extra girl would have made her for comfort.

For Carlotta, money and comfort were one and the same. She wanted plenty of both.

Though it was barely nine, she poured a glass of whiskey from the bottle that was always at her bedside. The hot, powerful taste filled the craving she awoke with every morning. Sipping and thinking, she cast her eyes around the room.

The walls were papered in a somewhat virulent red-and-silver stripe she found rich and elegant. Thick red drapes, too heavy for the blistering Arizona summers, hung at the windows. They made her think, smugly, of queens and palaces. The carpet echoed the color and was badly in need of cleaning. She rarely noticed the dirt.

On the mirrored vanity, which was decorated with painted cherubs, was a silver brush set with an elaborate *C* worked into the design. It was the only monogram she used. Carlotta had no last name, at least none she cared to remember.

Her mother had always had a man in her bed. Carlotta had gone to sleep most nights on a straw pallet in the corner, her lullaby the grunts and groans of sex. It had made her sick, the way men had pounded themselves into her mother. But that had been nothing compared to the disgust she had felt for her mother's weeping when the men were gone.

Crying and sniveling and begging God's forgiveness, Carlotta thought. Her mother had been the whore of that frigid little town in the Carolina mountains, but she hadn't had the guts to make it work for her.

Always claimed she was doing it to feed her little girl, Carlotta remembered with a sneer. She poured more whiskey into the glass. If that had been so, why had her little girl gone hungry so many nights? In the dim light, Carlotta studied the deep amber liquid. Because Ma was just as fond of whiskey as I am, she decided. She drank, and savored the taste.

The difference between you and me, Ma, she thought to herself, is that I ain't ashamed—not of the whiskey, not of the men. And I made something of myself.

Did you cry when I left? Carlotta laughed as she thought back to the night she'd left the smelly, window-less shack for the last time. She'd been fifteen and she'd saved nearly thirty dollars she'd made selling herself to trappers. Men paid more for youth. Carlotta had learned quickly. Her mother had never known her daughter was her stiffest competition.

She despised them all. Every man who'd pushed himself into her. She took their money, arched her hips and loathed them. Hate made a potent catalyst for passion. Her customers went away satisfied, and she saved every coin.

One night she'd packed her meager belongings, stolen another twenty dollars from the can her mother kept hidden in the rafters and headed west.

She'd worked saloons in the early years, enjoying the fancy clothes and bottles of paint. Her affair with whiskey had blossomed and helped her smile and seduce hungry-eyed cowboys and rough-handed drifters. She'd saved, keeping her mouth firmly shut about the bonuses she wheedled from men.

When she'd turned eighteen she had had enough to open her own place. A far cry from the Silver Star,

Carlotta remembered. Her first brothel had been hardly more than a shack in a stinking cattle town in east Texas. But she'd made certain her girls were as young and pretty as she could get.

She'd had a brief affair with a gambler who'd sported brocade vests and string ties. He'd filled her head with talk of crystal chandeliers and red carpets. When she'd moved on, she'd taken his pearl stickpin, two hundred in cash and her own profits.

Then she'd opened the Silver Star.

One day she'd move on again, on to California. But she intended to do it in style. She'd have those crystal chandeliers, she vowed. And a white porcelain tub with gold handles. Gold.

Carlotta felt a pleasure flow through her, a pleasure as fluid as the whiskey. It was gold she needed to bring her dream to full life. And gold she intended to have.

The man beside her was the tool she would use to gain it.

Jim Carlson. Carlotta looked down at his face. It was rough with several days' growth of beard and slack from sleep, sex and whiskey. She knew him for a fool, hot-tempered, small-minded and easily manipulated. Still, he was better-looking than many she had taken into her bed. His body was tough and lean, but she preferred young, limber bodies. Like Jake's.

Scowling, Carlotta took another drink. She'd broken her most important rule with Jake Redman. She'd let herself want him, really want him, in a way she'd never desired another man. Her body had responded to his so that for the first time in her life she hadn't feigned the ecstasy men wanted from a whore. She'd felt it. Now she craved it, as she craved whiskey, and gold, and power.

With Jake, desire was a hot, tight fist in her gut. Not just because he had a style in bed most men who came to her didn't feel obliged to employ. Because Jake Redman held something of himself back, something she sensed was powerful and exciting. Something she wanted for herself. And had been on her way to getting, she thought, before that pasty-faced bitch had come to town.

She had a lot to pay Miss Sarah Conway back for. Thoughtful, Carlotta touched a hand to her bruised cheek. A whole lot. Pay her back she would, and in doing so she would take Jake and the gold.

Jim Carlson, though he was unaware of it, was going to help her on all counts.

Setting the empty glass aside, Carlotta picked up a hand mirror. The bruises annoyed her, but they would fade. The faint lines fanning out from her eyes and bracketing her mouth would not. They would only deepen. She cursed and pushed the mirror aside. With a pleased smile, she ran both hands down her body. It was long, smooth-skinned and curvaceous.

It was her body men wanted and her body she had used, and would continue to use, to get what life had cheated her of.

She shifted, took Jim in her hand and brought him breathlessly awake.

"God Almighty, Carlotta." Groaning, he tried to roll over and into her.

"In a hurry, Jim?" She evaded him expertly, all the while using her skill to keep him aroused.

"Thought you'd burned the life out of me last night." He shuddered. "Glad to find out it ain't so."

"I want to talk to you, Jim."

"Talk." He filled his hands with her breasts. "Honey, I got better ways to spend my money than talk."

She let him suck and nuzzle, calculating how far she could let him go and keep him in line. Rooting about like a puppy, she thought in disgust while she stroked his hair.

"Your money ran out at dawn, sweetheart."

"I got more." He bit her, hard. Because she knew he expected it, she gave a soft moan of pleasure.

"House rules, Jim. Money first."

He swore at her and considered taking his pleasure as he chose. But if he forced her and managed to avoid getting tossed out by Eli, the doors of the Silver Star would be barred to him. He had money, he thought. And a need that was rock-hard.

When he started to shift, Carlotta trailed a finger down his arm. "Talk, Jim, and I'll…" With a long sigh, she arched back so that he could look his fill. "I'll give you the rest for free."

Sweat beaded on his upper lip as he studied her. "You don't do nothing for free."

Deliberately she ran a hand over her breast and down her rib cage and stroked the soft swell of her belly. "Talk. We're going to talk first." Her lips curved as she watched him swallow. "About gold." When he stiffened, her smile only widened. "Don't worry, Jim. I haven't told anyone, have I? I've never said a word about how you and Donley killed old Matt Conway."

"I was drunk when I told you about that." He wiped

a hand over the back of his mouth as fear and desire twined inside him. "A man says all kinds of things when he's drunk."

That made her laugh. She pillowed her head on her folded arms. "Nobody knows that better than a whore or a wife, Jim, honey. Relax. Who was the one who told you old Matt had finally hit? Who was the one who told you his daughter was coming and you had to move fast? Don't try dealing from the bottom with me, sweetheart. It's business, remember. Yours and mine."

After pushing himself up in bed, he reached bad-temperedly for the whiskey bottle. "I told you once Sam got things worked out you'd get your share."

"And what does Sam have to work out?" She let him take a swallow, two. It never hurt to loosen a man's tongue, but there were some who went from relaxed to mean with whiskey. With Jim the line was all too easily crossed. She took the bottle back.

"We've already been through this," he muttered. He no longer felt like having sex, and he sure as hell didn't want to talk.

"If Sam had some idea about getting that Conway bitch to the altar to get his hands on the deed, he's had time enough. Everybody in town knows she doesn't have her eye on your brother, but on Jake Redman."

"How about you?" He tapped a finger, none too gently, against her bruised cheekbone. "Who do you have those blue eyes on?"

"The main chance, sweetheart. Always the main chance." She ran her tongue over her lips, grimly pleased with the way Jim's eyes followed the movement. The surest way to lead a man, she knew, was from a point just below his gunbelt. She rose, knowing the shuttered light would be flattering to her skin. Slowly she ran her hands up her body, letting them linger on her breasts.

"You know, Jim," she began, slipping into a thin red negligee that was as transparent as glass, "I've always been drawn to men who take risks, who know what they want and take it." She left the negligee open as she walked back toward the bed. "That night you came in and told me how you and Donley had dragged Matt up to the mine and how you'd killed him because he wouldn't hand over the deed. You told me just how you'd killed him, how you'd hurt him first. Remember that night, Jim? You and me sure had ourselves a good time after we came upstairs."

He wet his lips. Her nipples were dark and just out of reach. "I remember."

"It was exciting. Knowing you'd just come from killing a man. Killing him to get what you wanted. I knew I was with a real man." The negligee fell carelessly off one shoulder. "Trouble is, nothing's happened since. I keep waiting."

"I told you. Sam's going—"

"The hell with Sam." She battled back her temper to smile at him. "He's too slow, too careful. A real man takes action. If he wants the Conway girl, why doesn't he just take her? Or you could take her for him." She moved closer, letting the idea take root. "She's all that's in the way, Jim. You deal with her—and I ain't talking about firing one of her sheds." The quick wariness in his eyes pleased her. "Hurt her, Jim. She'll hand over the deed quick enough. Then kill her." She murmured the words like a love song. "When she's dead, you come to me. We can do anything you want." She stood beside the bed, glorious and gleaming. "Anything. And it won't cost you a cent."

She didn't cry out when his hand clamped over her wrist. Their faces were close, each of them aroused in different ways, for different reasons.

"You'll take care of her?"

"Yes, damn you. Come here."

Carlotta smiled bitterly at the ceiling while Jim collapsed on top of her.

From her window an hour later, Carlotta watched as Jake rode into town. Her hands clenched into fists—from anger, yes, but also from a stab of desire. Soon, she thought, very soon, he'd come back to her.

She turned as Jim pulled up his pants. She was smiling.

"I think it's a real good time for you to pay Sarah Conway a visit."

Chapter 14

When Jake walked into Maggie's, she set her fisted hands on her hips and looked him up and down with a sniff.

"Fine time to be strolling in, boyo." What she wanted was gossip, and she hoped to annoy it out of him. "Can't figure why a man would be paying good money for a bed and never sleep in it."

"I pay for your chicken and dumplings, too, but I ain't stupid enough to eat them." He started resignedly up the stairs, knowing she would follow.

"You don't seem to be suffering any from lack of food." With the audacity she'd been born with, she poked a finger in his ribs. "Must be getting meals someplace."

"Must be."

"Sarah a good cook, is she?"

Saying nothing, he pushed open the door to his room.

"Don't go pokering up on me, Jake, my boy." Maggie swiped a dustcloth here and there. "It's too late. Every blessed soul in town saw the way you looked at her at the dance. Then there was the way you rode out of town after her when she socked you in the jaw." The dark, furious glint in his eyes had Maggie cackling. "That's more like it. Always said you could drop a man dead with a look as quick as with those guns of yours. No need to draw on me, though. I figure Sarah Conway's just what you need."

"Do you?" Jake tossed his saddlebags on the bed. He considered starting to strip to get rid of her. But he'd tried that before, and it hadn't budged her an inch. "I reckon you want to tell me why before you leave me the hell alone."

"Like to see the back of me, would you?" She just laughed again and patted his cheek. "More than one man's considered it my best side."

He barely managed to control a grin. He was damned if he knew why the nosy old woman appealed to him. "Why don't you get yourself another husband, Maggie? Then you could nag him."

"You'd miss me."

"I reckon some dogs miss the fleas once they manage to scratch them off." Then he sat by the window, propping his back against one side and his boot against the other.

"Somebody's got to bite at you. Might as well be me. I got something to say about you and Sarah Conway."

Staring out the window, he frowned. "It won't be anything I haven't said to myself. Go away, Maggie."

"Now listen to me, boy," she said in an abruptly

serious tone. "There's some who're born to the pretty. They slide out of their mothers and straight into silk and satin. Then there's others who have to fight and claw and scratch for every good thing. We know something about that, you and me."

Still frowning, he looked back at her. With a nod, she continued. "Some go hungry, and some have their bellies full. The sweet Lord himself knows why he set things up that way, and no one else. But he didn't make the one man better than the other. It's men themselves who decide if they're going to be strong or weak—and that's the same as good or bad. Sometimes there's a woman who shoves them one way or the other. You take ahold of Sarah Conway, Jake. She'll shove you right enough."

"Could work the other way around," he murmured. "A woman's easier to shove than a man."

Maggie's brows rose in two amused peaks. "Jake, my boy, you've got a lot to learn about women."

It was the second time in so many days he'd been told that, Jake mused when Maggie clicked the door shut behind her. But it wasn't a woman he had to think about now.

It was gold. And it was murder.

He took Matt Conway's journal and started to read.

Unlike Sarah, Jake didn't bother with the early pages. He scanned a few at the middle, where Matt had written of working the mine and of his hopes for a big strike. There were mentions of Sarah here and there, of Matt's regrets at leaving her behind, of his pride in the letters she wrote him. And always he wrote of his longing to send for her.

He had wanted to build her a home first, a real home, like the one he'd described to her. The mine would do it, or so he had thought. Throughout the pages, his confidence never wavered.

Each time I enter, I feel it. Not just hope, but certainty. Today. Each time I'm sure it will be today. There is gold here, enough to give my Sarah the life of a princess—the life I had wanted so badly to give her mother. How alike they are. The miniature Sarah sent me for Christmas might be my own lost, lovely Ellen. Looking at it each night before I sleep makes me grieve for the little girl I left behind and ache for the young woman my daughter has become.

So there had been a painting, Jake mused. Questions might be answered once it was found. He skipped on, toward the end.

In my years of prospecting, I've learned that success is as elusive as any dream. A man may have a map and tools, he may have skill and persistence. But there is one factor that cannot be bought, cannot be learned. Luck. Without it a man can dig and hammer for years with the vein he seeks always inches out of reach. As I have been. Sweet God, as I have been.

Was it the hand of chance that caused my own to slip, that had me sprawled in the dirt nursing my bruised and bloody fingers and cursing God as I learned to curse him so eloquently? And when I stumbled, half-blind with tears of frustration and pain, was it his hand that led me deeper into the tunnel, swinging my pick like a madman?

There it was, under my still-bleeding fingers. Glinting dull against the dark rock. It ran like a river, back, back into the dark mouth of the mine, narrow, then widening. I know it cannot be, yet to me it seemed to shimmer and pulse like a living thing. Gold. At long last.

I am not ashamed that I sat on the dusty floor of the mine, my lamp between my knees, and wept.

He'd found it, Jake thought as he frowned over the words. It was no longer just a hunch, a feeling, but fact. Matt Conway had found his gold, and he'd died. Perhaps there would be an answer to why and how in the remaining pages.

Do men grow more foolish with age? Perhaps. Perhaps. But then, whiskey makes fools of young and old. There need be no excuses. A man finds his heart's desire after years of sweat. To what does he turn? A woman, and a bottle. I found both at the Silver Star.

It had been my intention to keep my discovery to myself for a little longer. Sarah's letter changed that. She's coming. My own little girl is already on her way to join me. There is no way to prepare her for what she will find. Thank God I will soon be able to give her all that I promised.

It wasn't my intent to tell Carlotta of the gold, or of Sarah's arrival. Whiskey and weakness. Undoubtedly I paid for my lack of discretion with a vicious head the next morning. And the visit from Samuel Carlson.

Could it be coincidence that now, after all these years, he wants the mine? His offer was generous. Too generous for me to believe the purchase was to be made from sentiment on his part. Perhaps my suspicions are unfounded. He took my refusal in good temper, leaving the offer open. Yet there was something, something in the way he held his brother and his man Donley to silence—like holding wild dogs on a leash. Tomorrow I will ride into town and tell Barker about my discovery. It may be wise to hire a few men to help me work the mine. The sooner it is begun, the sooner I can build my Sarah the house she believes is already waiting for her.

It was the last entry. Closing the book, Jake rose. He had his answers.

"Miss Sarah, seeing as you're going into town and all…"

Sarah sighed as she adjusted her straw bonnet. "Again, Lucius?"

He scratched his grizzled beard. "A man gets powerful thirsty doing all this work."

"Very well." She'd managed to cure him of his abhorrence of water. Easing him away from his passion for whiskey would take a bit more time.

"I'm obliged, Miss Sarah." He grinned at her. In the weeks he'd been working for her he'd discovered she had a soft heart—and a tough mind. "You check on that wood you ordered. I'll be right pleased to put that floor in for you when it gets here."

Easily said, she mused, when the wood was still hundreds of miles away. "You might finish building the pen Jake started. I intend to inquire about buying some piglets while I'm in town."

"Yes'm." He spit. He'd build the cursed pen, but he'd be damned if he'd tend pigs. "Miss Sarah, I'm getting a mite low on tobacco."

Whiskey and tobacco, Sarah thought, rolling her eyes heavenward. What would Mother Superior have said? "I'll see to it. You look in on Alice regularly, Lucius. See that she has a bit of that broth and rests."

She heard him grumble about being a nursemaid and snagged her lip to keep it from curving. "I'll be back by three. I'm going to fix a very special meal tonight." She gave him a final glance. "You'll want to change your shirt." She cracked the reins and headed out before she allowed herself to laugh.

Life was glorious. Life was, she thought as she let the horses prance, magnificent. Perhaps she was rich, as Jake had said, but the gold no longer mattered. So many things that had seemed so important only a short time before really meant nothing at all.

She was in love, beautifully, wildly, in love, and all the gold in the world couldn't buy what she was feeling.

She would make him happy. It would take some time, some care and more than a little patience, but she would make Jake Redman see that together they could have everything two people could want. A home, children, roots, a lifetime.

What they had brought to each other had changed them both. She was not the same woman who had boarded the train in Philadelphia. How far she'd come, Sarah reflected as she scanned the distant buttes. Not just in miles. It was much more than miles. Only weeks before she'd been certain her happiness depended on having a new bonnet. She laughed as the hot wind tugged at the brim of the one she wore now. She had come to Lone Bluff with dreams of fine parties and china dishes. She hadn't found them. But she had found more, much more.

And she had changed him. She could see it in the way he looked at her, in the way he reached for her as he slept, just to hold her, to keep her close. Perhaps the words were difficult for him to say. She could wait.

Now that she had found him, nothing and no one would keep her from being with him.

She saw the rider coming, and for an instant her smile bloomed. But it wasn't Jake. Sarah watched Jim Carlson slow his horse to a trot as he crossed the road in front of her. She intended to ride by with a brief nod of greeting, but he blocked her way.

"Morning, ma'am." He shifted in his saddle to lean toward her. The stink of whiskey colored his words. "All alone?"

"Good morning, Mr. Carlson. I'm on my way to town, and I'm afraid I'm a bit pressed for time."

"That so?" It was going to be easier than he'd

thought. He wouldn't have to go through Lucius to get to her. "Now that's a shame, since I was just riding out to see you."

"Oh?" She didn't care for the look in his eyes, and the smell of whiskey on his breath didn't seem harmless, as it did with Lucius. "Is there something I can do for you, Mr. Carlson?"

"There sure is." Slowly, his eyes on hers, he drew his gun. "Step on out of the wagon."

"You must be mad." She'd frozen at the first sight of the barrel, but now, instinctively, her fingers inched toward her rifle.

"I wouldn't touch that rifle, ma'am. It'd be a shame for me to put a hole in that pretty white hand of yours. Now, I said get out of the wagon."

"Jake will kill you if you touch me."

He'd already thought that one through. That was the reason he was altering Carlotta's plan to suit himself. He wasn't going to kill Sarah here and now, unless she did something stupid. "Oh, I got plans for Redman, honey, don't you worry. You just step out of that wagon before I have to put a bullet in your horses."

She didn't doubt he would, or that he would shoot her in the back should she try to run. Trapped, she stepped down and stood stiffly beside the wagon.

"God Almighty, you got looks, Sarah. That's why Sam took to you." With his gun still in his hand, Jim slid out of the saddle. "You got those fine lady looks like our mama did. You saw her picture at the house. Sam, he's mighty fond of pictures." He grinned again. When he reached out to touch Sarah's face, she hissed and jerked it aside. "But you, you got some fire. Mama was just crazy. Plumb crazy." He stepped forward so that his body pushed hers against the side of the wagon. "Sam told you she was delicate, didn't he? That's the word he uses. Crazy was what she was, so that the old man would lock her up sometimes for days. One day when he opened up the door he found her hanging dead with a pretty pink silk scarf around her neck."

Horror leaped into her eyes and warred with fear. "Let me go. If Samuel finds out what you've done, he'll—"

"You think I run scared of Sam?" Laughing, Jim forced Sarah's face back to his. "Maybe you figure he's smoother than me, got more brains. But we're blood." His fingers bit into her skin. "Don't forget it. You ever let him get this close, let him do what he wanted? Or did you save yourself for that breed?"

She slapped him with all the force of her fear and rage. Then she was clawing at him, blindly, with some mad hope of getting to his horse. She felt the barrel of the gun press into the soft underside of her jaw and heard the click of the hammer.

"Try that again and I'll leave what's left of you here for the buzzards, gold or no gold. Your pa tried to get away, too." The stunned look in her eyes pleased him, gave him the edge he wanted. "You think on what happened to him and take care." He was breathing quickly, his finger trembling on the trigger. He'd lied when he'd said he wasn't scared of his brother. If it hadn't been for the rage Sam would heap on him, Jim would have sent a bullet into her. "Now you're going to do just like I say, and you'll stay alive a while longer."

* * *

"Interesting reading." Barker squinted down at Matt's journal while he fanned the hot, still air around his face with his hat. "Matt had a fine way of putting words on paper."

"Fine or not, it's plain enough." Jake fidgeted at the window, annoyed with himself for coming to the law with something he could, and should, have handled himself. Sarah's doing, he thought. He hadn't even felt the shove.

"It's plain that Matt thought he'd found gold."

"He'd found it. Lucius dug through to where Matt was working. It's there, just the way Matt wrote."

Thoughtful, Barker closed the book and leaned back in his chair. "Poor old Matt. Finally makes the big strike, then gets caught in a cave-in."

"He was dead before those beams gave way."

Taking his time, Barker pushed a cozy plug of tobacco in his cheek. "Well, now, maybe you think so, and maybe I'm doing some pondering on it, but this here journal isn't proof. It's not going to be easy to ride out to the Carlson ranch and talk to Sam about murder with no more than a book in my hand. Now hold on," he added when Jake snatched the book from the desk. "I didn't say I wasn't going out, I just said it wasn't going to be easy." Still fanning himself with his hat, he sat back in his chair. He wanted to think it through, and think it through carefully. The Carlson family had a long reach. He was more concerned about that than about the quick temper and gun of young Jim.

"Got a question for you, Jake. Why'd you bring me

that journal instead of riding on out and putting a hole in the Carlson brothers?"

Jake skimmed his eyes over Barker's comfortable paunch. "My deep and abiding respect for the law."

After a bark of laughter, the sheriff spit a stream of tobacco juice into the spittoon. "I once knew a woman— before Mrs. Barker—who lied as smooth as that. Couldn't help but admire her." With a sigh, he perched his hat on his head. "Whatever your reason, you brought it, so I'm duty-bound to do something about it. Got to tell you, nothing's more tiring than duty." He reached unenthusiastically for his gunbelt as the door burst open.

"Sheriff." Nancy stood, darting glances over her shoulder and tugging restlessly at the shoulder of her hastily donned dress. "I got to talk to you."

"You'll just have to hold on to it till I get back. One of them cowboys got a little too enthusiastic over at the Silver Star, I ain't getting worked up about it."

"You'd better listen." Nancy stood firm in front of the door. "I'm only doing this 'cause of Alice." She glanced at Jake then. "Carlotta'd strip my skin if she found out I come, but I figured Miss Conway done right by Alice, I ought to do right by her."

"Quit babbling. If you're hell-bent on talking, say it."

"It's Carlotta." Nancy kept her voice low, as if it might carry back to the Silver Star. "She's been feeling real mean since yesterday."

"Carlotta was born feeling mean," Barker muttered. Then he waved to Nancy to continue. "All right, finish it out."

"Last night she took Jim Carlson up. She don't

usually let men stay overnight in her room, but he was still there this morning. My room's next to hers, and I heard them talking."

Jake took her arm to draw her farther into the room. "Why don't you tell me what you heard?"

"She was talking about how Jim and Donley killed Matt Conway, and how he was supposed to take care of Matt's girl." She yelped when Jake's fingers bit into her arm. "I didn't have no part in it. I'm telling you what I heard 'cause she took Alice in after Carlotta near killed her."

"Looks like I'd better have a talk with Carlotta," Barker mused, straightening his hat.

"No, you can't." Fear for her own skin had her yanking free of Jake. "She'll kill me. That's the God's truth. Anyways, it's too late for that."

"Why?" Jake caught her again before she could dash out the door.

She'd gone this far, Nancy thought, dragging the back of her hand over her mouth. She might as well finish. "Carlotta said Jim was to scare Miss Conway good, hurt her. Then, when he had the deed to the mine, he was to kill her. He rode out an hour ago, and I couldn't get away till now."

Jake was already through the door and halfway to his horse when Barker caught up with him. "Will and me'll be right behind you."

There had been times when killing had come easily to Jake, so easily that after it was done he'd felt nothing. This time would be different. He knew it, felt it, as he sped down the road toward Sarah's house. If Jim

Carlson was ahead of him and he got within range, he would kill him without question. It would be easy. And it would be a pleasure.

He heard the horses behind him, but he didn't look back.

His own mount seemed to sense the urgency and lengthened his strides until his powerful legs were a blur and the dust was a yellow wall behind them.

When Jake saw the wagon, the cold rage dropped into his gut and turned into a hot, bubbling fear. He vaulted from the saddle beside the two horses, which stood slack-hipped and drowsy.

Surprisingly agile, Barker slipped down beside him. "Take it easy." He began to place a hand on Jake's shoulder, but then he thought better of it. "If he took her off somewhere, we'll track him." He held up a hand before any of the men with him could speak. Along with Will were three men from town, including John Cody, who still wore his store apron. "We take care of our own here, Jake. We'll get her back."

In silence, Jake bent down to pick up the cameo lying facedown in the road. Its slender pin was snapped. There were a few pale blue threads clinging to the broken point. The signs told him she'd struggled, and the picture of her frightened and fighting clawed at him. The signs also told him where she was being taken. With the broach in his pocket, he jumped into the saddle and rode hard for the Carlson ranch.

Her hands were bound together and tied to the saddle horn. If it had been possible, she would have jumped to the ground. Though there was nowhere to run, at least she would have had the satisfaction of making him sweat.

Everything Jake had said was true—about the gold, about her father's death. Sarah had no doubt that the man responsible for it all was sitting behind her.

At first she thought he was taking her into the hills, or to the desert, where he could kill her and leave her body hidden. But she saw, with some confusion, the graceful lines of the Carlson ranch house in the shallow valley below.

It was a peaceful scene, lovely despite the waves of radiant heat rising up from the ground. She heard a dog bark. As they approached, Samuel burst out of the house, hatless and pale, to stare at his brother.

"What in God's name have you done?"

Jim loosened the rope around the saddle horn, then lifted Sarah to the ground. "Brought you a present."

"Sarah, my dear." His mouth grim, Carlson tugged at her bonds. "I'm speechless. There's no way I could ever…" He let his words trail off and began to massage the raw skin of her wrists. "He must be drunk. Stable that horse, damn you," he shouted at Jim. "Then come inside. You've a great deal to answer for."

It stunned her, left her limp, when Jim merely shrugged and led his horse away. It must be a joke, a bizarre joke, she thought, bringing her trembling hands to her lips. But it wasn't. She knew it was much too deadly to be a joke.

"Samuel—"

"My dear, I don't know what to say." He slipped a supporting arm around her waist. "I can't begin to apologize for my brother's outrageous behavior. Are you hurt? Dear Lord, your dress is torn." He had her by the shoulders then, and the look in his eyes froze her blood. "Did he touch you, molest you?"

She managed to shake her head, once, then twice. Then the words came. "Samuel, he killed my father. It was for the gold. There's gold in the mine. He must have found out and he—he murdered my father."

She was breathless now, her hands clinging to his trim black vest. He only stared at her, stared until she wanted to scream. "Samuel, you must believe me."

"You're overwrought," he said stiffly. "And no wonder. Come in out of the heat."

"But he—"

"You needn't worry about Jim." He led her inside the thick adobe walls. "He won't bother you again. You have my word. I want you to wait in my office." His voice was quiet, soothing, as he led her past his mother's portrait and into a room. "Try to relax. I'll take care of everything."

"Samuel, please be careful. He might—he could hurt you."

"No." He patted her hand as he eased her into a chair. "He'll do exactly what I tell him."

When the door shut, she covered her face with her hands. For a moment she let the hysteria she'd fought off take control. He'd intended to kill her. She was certain of it, from the way he'd looked at her, the way he'd smiled at her. Why in God's name had he brought her here, where she would be protected by Samuel?

Protected. After letting out a shaky breath, she waited

until her heartbeat leveled and the need to scream passed. She was safe now. But it wasn't over. She closed her eyes briefly. It was far from over.

It was madness. Jim Carlson was as mad as his poor mother had been, but instead of killing himself he had killed her father. She wanted to weep, to let the new, aching grief come. But she couldn't. She couldn't weep, and she couldn't sit.

Rising, she began to pace. The room was small but beautifully furnished. There were delicate porcelain figurines and a painting in fragile pastels. It reflected Samuel's elegant taste and eye for beauty. How unalike the brothers were, she thought.

Cain and Abel.

With a hand on her heart, she rushed to the door. She could never have borne the guilt if one brother killed another over her.

But the door was locked. For a moment she thought it was only her nerves making her fumble. After a deep breath she tried the knob again. It resisted.

Whirling around, she stared at the room. Locked in? But why? For her own protection? Samuel must have thought she would be safer behind a locked door until he came back for her.

And if it was Jim who came back with the key? Her heart thudding in her throat, she began a frantic search for a weapon.

She pulled out desk drawers, pushing ruthlessly through papers. If not a pistol, she thought, then a knife, even a letter opener. She would not be defenseless. Not again. She tugged open the middle drawer, and the brass pulls knocked against the glossy mahogany. Her hand froze when she saw the miniature. Her miniature.

Like a sleepwalker, she reached for it, staring blindly.

It was the self-portrait that she had painted the year before, the one she had shipped to her father for Christmas. The one, Sarah realized as her fingers closed over it, that he had shown with pride to his friends in town. The one that had been missing from his possessions. Missing because it had been taken by his murderer.

When the key turned in the lock, she didn't bother to close the drawer or to hide what she held in her hand. Instead, she rose and faced him.

"It was you," she murmured as Samuel Carlson closed and locked the door behind him. "You killed my father."

An Important Message from the Editors

Dear Nora Roberts Fan,

*Because you've chosen to read one of our fine novels, we'd like to say "thank you!" And, as a **special** way to thank you, we're offering to send you a choice of <u>two more</u> of the books you love so well **plus** two exciting Mystery Gifts — absolutely <u>FREE</u>!*

Please enjoy them with our compliments...

Pam Powers

Peel off seal and place inside...

What's Your Reading Pleasure...
~~ROMANCE?~~ _OR_ **SUSPENSE?**

Do you prefer spine-tingling page turners OR heart-stirring stories about love and relationships? Tell us which type of books you enjoy – and you'll get 2 FREE "ROMANCE" BOOKS or 2 FREE "SUSPENSE" BOOKS with **no obligation to purchase anything.**

Choose **"ROMANCE"** and get **2 FREE BOOKS** that will fuel your imagination with intensely moving stories about life, love and relationships.

FREE!

FREE!

Choose **"SUSPENSE"** and you'll get **2 FREE BOOKS** that will thrill you with a spine-tingling blend of suspense and mystery.

Whichever category you select, your 2 free books have a combined cover price of $15.98 or more.

And remember. . . just for accepting the Editor's Free Gift Offer, we'll send you 2 books and 2 gifts, ABSOLUTELY FREE!

YOURS FREE! We'll send you two fabulous surprise gifts worth about $10, absolutely FREE, just for trying "Romance" or "Suspense"!

® and ™ are trademarks owned and used by the trademark owner and/or its licensee.

Visit us at

www.ReaderService.com

The Editor's "Thank You" Free Gifts Include:

- *2 Romance OR 2 Suspense books!*
- *2 exciting mystery gifts!*

Yes!
I have placed my Editor's "Thank You" seal in the space provided at right. Please send me 2 free books, which I have selected, and 2 fabulous mystery gifts. I understand I am under no obligation to purchase any books, as explained on the back of this card.

PLACE
FREE GIFT
SEAL
HERE

ROMANCE
193 MDL EW6H   393 MDL EW65

SUSPENSE
192 MDL EW55   392 MDL EW6T

FIRST NAME

LAST NAME

ADDRESS

APT.#

CITY

STATE/PROV.

ZIP/POSTAL CODE

Thank You!

Offer limited to one per household and not valid to current subscribers of Romance, Suspense or the Romance/Suspense Combo. **Your Privacy** - The Reader Service is committed to protecting your privacy. Our Privacy Policy is available online at www.eHarlequin.com or upon request from the Reader Service. From time to time we make our lists of customers available to reputable third parties who may have a product or service of interest to you. If you would prefer for us not to share your name and address, please check here☐.

▼ DETACH AND MAIL CARD TODAY! ▼

© 2008 HARLEQUIN ENTERPRISES LIMITED

(NR-RS-09R)

The Reader Service — Here's How It Works:

Accepting your 2 free books and 2 free gifts places you under no obligation to buy anything. You may keep the books and gifts and return the shipping statement marked "cancel." If you do not cancel, about a month later we'll send you 3 additional books and bill you just $5.74 each in the U.S. or $6.24 each in Canada. That is a savings of at least $2.25 off the cover price. It's quite a bargain! Shipping and handling is just 25 cents per book. You may cancel at any time, but if you choose to continue, every month we'll send you 3 more books, which you may either purchase at the discount price or return to us and cancel your subscription.

*Terms and prices subject to change without notice. Sales tax applicable in N.Y. Canadian residents will be charged applicable provincial taxes and GST. Offer not valid in Quebec. All orders subject to approval. Books received may vary. Credit or debit balances in a customer's account(s) may be offset by any other outstanding balance owed by or to the customer. Please allow 4 to 6 weeks for delivery. Offer available while quantities last.

If offer card is missing write to: The Reader Service, P.O. Box 1867, Buffalo, NY 14240-1867

BUSINESS REPLY MAIL
FIRST-CLASS MAIL   PERMIT NO. 717   BUFFALO, NY

POSTAGE WILL BE PAID BY ADDRESSEE

THE READER SERVICE
PO BOX 1341
BUFFALO NY 14240-8571

NO POSTAGE
NECESSARY
IF MAILED
IN THE
UNITED STATES

Chapter 15

Carlson crossed the room until only the desk was between them. "Sarah." His voice was almost a sigh, a sigh touched with patience. In his hand he carried a delicate cup filled with fragrant tea. But she noted that he had strapped on his gun. "I realize how upset you must be after Jim's inexcusable behavior. Now, why don't you sit down, compose yourself?"

"You killed my father," she repeated. It was rage she felt now, waves of it.

"That's ridiculous." The words were said gently. "I haven't killed anyone. Here, my dear. I've brought you some tea. It should help calm you."

The quiet sincerity in his eyes caused her to falter. He must have sensed it, because he smiled and stepped forward. Instantly she backed away. "Why was this in your desk?"

Carlson looked at the miniature in her hand. "A woman should never intrude on a man's personal belongings." His voice became indulgent as he set the cup on the desk. "But since you have, I'll confess. I can be faulted for being overly romantic, I suppose. The moment I saw it, I fell in love with you. The moment I saw your face, I wanted you." He held out a hand, palm up, as if he were asking for a dance. "Come, Sarah, you can't condemn me for that."

Confused, she shook her head. "Tell me how this came to be in your drawer when it belonged to my father."

Impatience clouded his face, and he dropped his hand to his side. "Isn't baring my soul enough for you? You knew, right from the beginning, you knew the way I felt about you. You deceived me." There was more than impatience in his face now. Something else was building in him. Something that had the bright, hot taste of fear clogging her throat.

"I don't know what you're talking about, Samuel." She spaced her words carefully and kept her eyes on his. "But you're right. I'm upset, and I'm not myself. I'd prefer to go home now and discuss all of this later." With the miniature still clutched in her hand, she stepped around the desk and toward the door. The violence with which he grabbed her and shoved her back against the wall had her head reeling.

"It's too late. Jim's interference has changed everything. His interference, and your prying. I was patient with you, Sarah. Now it's too late."

His face was close to hers—close enough for her to see clearly what was in his eyes. She wondered, as the blood drained slowly from her face, how it was that she'd never seen it before. The madness was bright and deadly. She tried to speak and found she had to swallow first.

"Samuel, you're hurting me."

"I would have made you a queen." He took one hand and brought it up to stroke her face. She cringed, but his eyes warned her not to move. "I would have given you everything a woman could want. Silk." He traced a finger over her cheekbone. "Diamonds." Then he ran it lightly down her throat. "Gold." His hand tightened abruptly around her windpipe. Before she could begin to struggle, it was loosened again. "Gold, Sarah. It belonged to me, truly to me. My grandfather had no right to lose that part of my heritage. And your father…he had no right to deny me what was already mine."

"He did it for me." Perhaps she could calm him, if only she could remain calm herself, before it was too late. "He only wanted to see that I was taken care of."

"Of course." He nodded, as if he were pleased that she understood. "Of course he did. As I do. It would have been yours as much as mine. I would never have let you suffer because I had taken it back. As my wife, you would have had every luxury. We would have gone back east together. That was always my plan. I was going to follow you back east and court you. But you stayed. You should never have stayed, Sarah. This isn't the place for you. I knew it the moment I saw your picture. It was there, in that miserable little cabin, beside the cot. I found it while I was looking for the deed to the mine."

His face changed again. He looked petulant now, like a boy who had been denied an extra piece of pie. "I was very annoyed that my brother and Donley killed Matt. Clumsy. They were only to…convince him to turn over the deed. Then, of course, it was up to me to think of causing the cave-in to cover up what they'd done. I never found the deed. But I found your picture."

She didn't think he was aware of how viciously his fingers were digging into her arms. She was almost certain he was no longer aware of how much he was telling her. She remained silent and still, knowing her only hope now was time.

"Delicate," he murmured. "Such a delicate face. The innocence shining in the eyes, the soft curve of the mouth. It was a lie, wasn't it, Sarah?" The violence sprang back into his face, and she could only shake her head and wait. "There was no delicacy, no innocence. You toyed with me, offering me smiles, only smiles, while you gave yourself to Redman like a whore. He should be dead for touching what belonged to me. You should both be dead."

She prepared to scream. She prepared to fight for what she knew was her life.

"Sam!" The banging on the door brought with it a mixture of fear and relief.

Swearing, Carlson dragged Sarah to the door to unlock it. "Goddamn it, I told you to go back and get rid of the wagon and team."

"Riders coming in." The sweat on Jim's face attested to the fact that he had already ridden, and ridden hard. "It's Redman and the sheriff, with some men from town." He glanced at Sarah. "They'll be looking for her."

When Sarah tried to break away, Samuel locked an arm around her throat. "You've ruined everything, bringing her here."

"I only did it 'cause you wanted her. I could've taken care of her back on the road. Hell, I could've taken care of her the night we torched her shed, but you said you didn't want her hurt none."

Carlson tightened his grip as Sarah clawed at his arm. Her vision grayed from lack of air. As if from a distance, she heard the voices, one mixing into the other.

"How long?"

"Ten minutes, no more... Kill her now."

"Not here, you idiot... Hold them off.... In the hills."

Sarah's last thought before she lost consciousness was that Jake was coming, but too late.

"You listen to me." Barker stopped the men on the rise above the Carlson ranch. But it was Jake he was looking at. "I know you'd like to ride in there hell-bent, but you take a minute to think. If they've got her, we've got to go slow."

"They've got her." In his mind, the Carlson brothers were already dead.

"Then let's make sure we get her back in one piece. Will, I want you to break off, ease on over to the barn. John, I'd be obliged if you'd circle around the back. I don't want any shooting until it's necessary." With a nod, he spurred his horse.

Jim watched them coming and wiped the sweat off his brow. His men were all out on the range. Not that they'd have been any good, he thought. The only one who'd have backed them against the sheriff was Donley. And he was dead. Wetting his lips, he levered the rifle in the window.

He had to wait until they got close. That was what Sam had told him. Wait until they got close. Then he was to kill as many as he could. Starting with Redman.

Sweat dripped down into his eyes. His fingers twitched.

Sam had sent Donley to kill Redman, Jim remembered. But it was Donley who'd been buried. Now he was going to do it. He wet his lips when he caught Jake in the sight. He was going to do it right. But nerves had his finger jerking on the trigger.

Jake felt the bullet whiz past his cheek. Like lightning, he kicked one foot free of the stirrup to slide halfway down the side of his horse. Gun drawn, he rode toward the house while Barker shouted orders. He could hear the men scrambling for cover and returning fire, but his mind was on one thing and one thing alone.

Getting inside to Sarah.

Outside the doors, he leaped off. When he kicked them open, his second gun was drawn. The hall and the foyer were empty. He could hear the shouts of men and peppering gunfire. With a quick glance for any sign of her, he started up the stairs.

Jim Carlson's back was to him when he broke open the door.

"Where is she?" Jake didn't flinch when a bullet from outside plowed into the wall beside him.

From his crouched position, Jim turned slowly. "Sam's got her." With a grin, he swung his rifle up. For months he'd wanted another chance to kill Jake Redman. Now he took it.

He was still grinning as he fell forward. Jake slid his smoking guns back in their holsters. Moving quickly, he began to search the house.

Barker met him on the steps. "She ain't here. I found this on the floor." In his hand he held Sarah's miniature.

Jake's eyes flicked up to Barker's. They held there only seconds, but Barker knew he would never forget the look in them. Later he would tell his wife it was the look of a man whose soul had gotten loose.

Turning on his heel, Jake headed outside, with Barker close behind.

"Oh, God." For the first time since Jake had known him, Barker moved with speed. Pushing past Jake, he raced to where two of his men were carrying Will Metcalf.

"He isn't dead." John Cody laid Will down and held his head. "But we have to get him back to town, to the doc."

Barker crouched down as Will's eyes fluttered open. "You're going to be all right, son."

"Took me by surprise," Will managed, struggling not to gasp at the pain as Cody pressed a pad to the hole in his shoulder. "Was Sam Carlson, Sheriff. He had her— I saw he had her on the horse. Think they headed west."

"Good job, Will." Barker used his own bandanna to wipe the sweat off his deputy's brow. "One of you men hitch up a wagon, get some blankets. You get this boy to the doctor, John. Redman and I'll go after Carlson."

But when he stood, all he saw of Jake was the dust his mustang kicked up as he galloped west.

* * *

Sarah came to slowly, nausea rising in her throat. Moaning, she choked it back and tried to lift a hand to her spinning head. Both wrists were bound tight to the saddle horn.

For a moment she thought she was still with Jim. Then she remembered.

The horse was climbing, picking its way up through dusty, dung-colored rock. She watched loose dirt and stones dislodged by the horse's hooves fall down a dizzying ravine. The man behind her was breathing hard. Fighting for calm, she tried to mark the trail they were taking and remember it. When she escaped—and she would—she didn't intend to wander helplessly through the rocks.

He stopped the horse near the edge of a canyon. She could see the thin silver line of a river far below. An eagle called as he swooped into the wide opening, then returned to a nest built in the high rock wall.

"Samuel, please—" She cried out when he pulled the rope from around her wrists and dragged her roughly to the ground. One look warned her that the calm, sane words she had meant to use would never reach him.

There was a bright, glazed light in his eyes. His face was pale and drenched with sweat. His hair was dark with it. She watched his eyes dart here and there, as if he expected something to leap out from behind a huddle of rock.

The man who had swept off his hat and kissed her fingers wasn't here with her now. If he had ever been part of Samuel Carlson, he had vanished. The man who stood over her was mad, and as savage as any beast that lived in the hills.

"What are you going to do?"

"He's coming." Still breathing rapidly, Carlson swiped a hand over his mouth. "I saw him behind us. When he comes for you, I'll be ready." He reached down to drag her to her feet. "I'm going to kill him, Sarah. Kill him like a dog." He pulled out his gun and rubbed the barrel against her cheek, gently, like a caress. "You're going to watch. I want you to watch me kill him. Then you'll understand. It's important that you understand. A man like that deserves to die by a gun. He's nothing, less than nothing. A crude gunslinger with Indian blood. He put his hands on you." A whimper escaped her as he dragged a hand through her hair. "I'm going to kill him for you, Sarah. Then we're going away, you and I."

"No." She wrenched free. The canyon was at her back when she faced him. If she had stumbled another step she would have fallen back into nothing. There was fear. The taste of it was bitter in her throat. But it wasn't for herself. Jake would come, she knew, and someone would die. "I won't go anywhere with you. It's over, Samuel. You must see that. They know what you've done, and they'll hunt you down."

"A potbellied sheriff?" He laughed and, before she could evade him, closed his hand over her arm. "Not likely. This is a big country, Sarah. They won't find us."

"I won't go with you." The pain when he squeezed her arm nearly buckled her knees. "I'll get away."

"If I must, I'll keep you locked up, the way my mother was locked up. For your own good."

She heard the horse even as he did and screamed out a warning. "No, Jake, he'll kill you!" Then she screamed again, this time in pain, as Carlson bent her arm behind her back. Calmly he put the gun to her temple.

"It's her I'll kill, Redman. Come out slow and keep your hands where I can see them, or the first bullet goes in her brain." He twisted her arm ruthlessly because he wanted Jake to hear her cry out again. He wanted Jake to hear the pain. "Now, Redman, or I'll kill her and toss her body over the edge."

"No. Oh, no." Tears blurred her vision as she watched Jake step out into the open. "Please don't. It won't gain you anything to kill him. I'll go with you." She tried to turn her head to look into Carlson's eyes. "I'll go anywhere you want."

"Not gain anything?" Carlson laughed again, and it echoed off the rocks and air. "Satisfaction, my dear. I'll gain satisfaction."

"Are you hurt?" Jake asked quietly.

"No." She shook her head, praying she could will him back behind the rock, back to safety. "No, he hasn't hurt me. He won't if you go back."

"But you're wrong, my dear, quite wrong." Carlson bent his head close to hers, amused by the quick fury in Jake's eyes when he brushed his lips over Sarah's hair. "I'll have to, you see, because you won't understand. Unless I kill him for you, you won't understand. Your gunbelt, Redman." Carlson drew back the hammer for emphasis and kept the gun tight against Sarah's temple. "Take it off, slowly, very slowly, and kick it aside."

"No!" She began to struggle, only to have him drag

her arm farther up her back. "I'll kill you myself." She wept in rage and fear. "I swear it."

"When I'm done here, my dear, you'll do exactly what I say, when I say. In time you'll understand this was for the best. Drop the belt, Redman." Carlson smiled at him and jerked his head to indicate that he wanted the guns kicked away. "That's fine." He took the gun away from Sarah's temple to point it at Jake's heart. "You know, I've never killed a man before. It always seemed more civilized to hire someone—someone like yourself." His smile widened. "But I believe I'm going to enjoy it a great deal."

"You might." Jake watched his eyes. He could only hope Sarah had the sense to run when it was over. Barker couldn't be far behind. "Maybe you'll enjoy it more when I tell you I killed your brother."

The muscles in Carlson's cheek twitched. "You bastard."

Sarah screamed and threw her weight against his gun hand. She felt the explosion, as if the bullet had driven into her. Then she was on her knees. Life poured out of her when she saw Jake sprawled on the ground, blood seeping from his side.

"No. Oh, God, no."

Carlson threw back his head and laughed at the sky. "I was right. I enjoyed it. But he's not dead yet. Not quite yet." His lips stretched back from his teeth as he lifted the gun again.

She didn't think. There was no room for thought in a mind swamped with grief. She reached out and felt the smooth grip of Jake's gun in her hand. Kneeling in the dirt, she balanced it and aimed. "Samuel," she murmured, and waited for him to turn his head.

The gun jumped in her hand when she fired. The sound of the shot echoed on and on and on. He just stared at her. Afraid she'd missed, Sarah drew back the hammer and calmly prepared to fire again.

Then he stumbled. He stared at her as his hand reached up to press against the blood that blossomed on his shirt-front. Without a sound, he fell back. He groped once in the air, then tumbled off the edge and into the canyon.

Her hand went limp on the gun. Then the shudders began, racking shudders, as she crawled to Jake. He'd pushed himself up on one elbow, and he held his knife in his hand. She was weeping as she tore at her petticoats to pad the wound in his side.

"I thought he'd killed you. You looked—" There was so much blood, she thought frantically as she tore more cloth. "You need a doctor. I'll get you on the horse as soon as—" She broke off again as her voice began to hitch. "It was crazy, absolutely crazy, for you to come out in the open like that. I thought you had more sense."

"So did I." The pain was searing, centering in his side and flowing out in waves of heat. He wanted to touch her, just once more, before he died. "Sarah…"

"Don't talk." Tears clogged her throat. His blood seeped through the pad and onto her hands. "Just lie still. I'm going to take care of you. Damn you, I won't let you die."

He couldn't see her face. Tired of the effort, he closed his eyes. He thought, but couldn't be sure, that he heard horses coming. "You're a hell of a woman," he murmured, and passed out.

* * *

When he awoke, it was dark. There was a bitter taste in his mouth and a hollow throbbing at the base of his skull. The pain in his side was still there, but dull now, and constant. He lay still and wondered how long he'd been in hell.

He closed his eyes again, thinking it didn't matter how long he'd been there, since he wouldn't be leaving. Then he smelled her, smelled the soft scent that was Sarah. Though it cost him dearly, he opened his eyes again and tried to sit up.

"No, don't." She was there, murmuring to him, pressing him gently back on a pillow, then laying a cool cloth against his hot face.

"How long—" He could only manage two whispered words before the strength leaked out of him.

"Don't worry." Cradling his head with her arm, she brought a cup to his lips. "Drink a little. Then you'll sleep again. I'm right here with you," she continued when he coughed and tried to turn his head away.

"Can't—" He tried to focus on her face, but saw only a silhouette. It was Sarah, though. "Can't be in hell," he murmured, then sank back into the darkness.

When he awoke again, it was daylight. And she was there, leaning over him, smiling, murmuring something he couldn't quite understand. But there were tears drying on her cheeks, cheeks that were too pale. She sat beside him, took his hand and held it against her lips. Even as he struggled to speak, he lost consciousness again.

She thought it would drive her mad, the way he drifted in and out of consciousness that first week, with the fever burning through him and the doctor giving her no hope. Hour after hour, day after day, she sat beside him, bathing his hot skin, soothing when the chills racked him, praying when he fell back into that deep, silent sleep.

What had he said that day when he'd awakened? Pacing to the window, the one Maggie had told her Jake had sometimes sat in, she drew the curtain aside to look down at the empty street. He'd said it couldn't be hell. But he'd been wrong, Sarah thought. It was hell, and she was mired in it, terrified each day that he would leave her.

So much blood. He'd lost so much blood. By the time Barker had ridden up she'd nearly managed to stop it, but the ride back to town had cost him more. She had stanched still more while the doctor had cut and probed into his side to remove the bullet. She hadn't known that watching the bullet come out of him would be as bad as watching it go in.

Then the fever had raced through him, vicious and merciless. In a week he'd been awake only a handful of minutes, often delirious, sometimes speaking in what Lucius had told her was Apache. If it didn't break soon, she knew, no matter how hard she prayed, no matter how hard she fought, it would take him.

Sarah moved back to the bed to sit beside him and watch over him in the pale light of dawn.

Time drifted, for her even as it did for him. She lost track of minutes, then hours, then days. When morning came she held his hand in hers and thought over the time they'd had together. His hands had been strong, she thought. Biting back a sob, she laid her forehead on his shoulder. And gentle, too, she remembered. When he'd touched her. When he'd taught her.

With him she'd found something lovely, something powerful. A sunrise. A fast river. A storm. She knew now that love, desire, passion and affection could be one emotion for one man. From that first frantic discovery in the hay to the soft, sweet loving by the stream, he'd given her more than most women had in a lifetime.

"But I'm greedy," she murmured to him. "I want more. Jake, don't leave me. Don't cheat me out of what we could have." She blinked back tears when she heard the door open behind her.

"How is he?"

"The same." Sarah rose and waited while Maggie set a tray on the bureau. She'd long ago stopped arguing about eating. It had taken her only a few days to realize that if she wanted the strength to stay with Jake she needed food.

"Don't worry none about this breakfast, because Anne Cody made it up for you."

Sarah dashed away the hated, weakening tears. "That was kind of her."

"She asked about our boy here, and wanted you to know that Alice is doing just fine."

"I'm glad." Without interest, she folded back the cloth so that steam rose fragrantly from the biscuits.

"Looks like Carlotta skipped town."

"It doesn't matter." With no more interest than she had in the biscuits, she looked at her own face in the mirror. Behind her reflection, she could see Jake lying motionless in the bed. "The damage is done."

"Child, you need sleep, and not what you get sitting up in that chair all night. You go on and use my room. I'll stay with him."

"I can't." Sarah ignored the biscuits and took the coffee. "Sometimes he calls for me, and I'm afraid if I'm not here he might…slip away. That's foolish, I suppose, but I just can't leave him, Maggie."

"I know." Because she did, Maggie set a comforting hand on Sarah's shoulder. The noise at the door had her turning back. "What are you doing sneaking around here, young John Cody?"

Johnny slipped into the doorway and stood with his hat crushed in his hands. "Just wanted to see him, is all."

"A sickroom ain't no place for nasty little boys."

"It's all right." Sarah waved him in and summoned up a smile. "I'm sure Jake would be pleased that you'd taken the time to visit him."

"He ain't going to die, is he, Sarah?"

"No." She found the confidence she'd lost during the night. "No, he isn't going to die, Johnny."

"Ma says you're taking real good care of him." He reached out a hand, then balled it at his side again.

"It's all right, boy," Maggie said, softening. "You can pet him as long as he don't know it. I do it myself."

Gingerly Johnny stroked a hand along Jake's forehead. "He's pretty hot."

"Yes, but the fever's going to break soon." Sarah laid a hand on Johnny's shoulder. "Very soon."

"Will's better," he said, giving Sarah a hopeful smile. "He's got his arm in a sling and all, but he's getting around just fine and dandy. Won't even let Liza fuss no more."

"Before long Jake won't let me fuss, either."

Hours later she dozed, lulled by the afternoon sun. She slept lightly, her head nestled against the wing of the chair and her hands in her lap on top of her journal. She'd written everything she felt, hoped, despaired of on those pages. Someone called her name, and she lifted a hand as if to brush the voice away. She only wanted to sleep.

"Sarah."

Now her eyes flew open, and she bolted out of the chair. Jake was half sitting up in bed, his brows drawn together in annoyance or confusion. And his eyes, she noted, were focused, alert and direct on hers.

"What the hell's going on?" he asked her. Then he watched, astonished, as she collapsed on the side of the bed and wept.

It was three weeks before he had the strength to do more than stand on his own feet. He had time to think—perhaps too much time—but when he tried to do anything he found himself weak as a baby.

It infuriated him, disgusted him. When he swore at Maggie twice in one morning, she told Sarah their patient was well on the road to recovery.

"He's a tough one, Jake is," Maggie went on as they climbed the steps to his room together. "Said he was damn sick and tired of having females poking him, pouring things into him and trying to give him baths."

"So much for gratitude," Sarah said with a laugh. Then she swayed and clutched the banister for support.

Maggie grabbed her arm. "Honey, are you all right?"

"Yes. Silly." Shrugging it off, Sarah waited for the dizziness to pass. "I'm just tired yet, I think." One look at Maggie's shrewd face had her giving up and sitting carefully on the riser.

"How far along are you?"

It surprised Sarah that the direct question didn't make her blush. Instead, she smiled. "About a month." She knew the exact moment when she had conceived Jake's child, on the riverbank under the moon. "I had the obvious sign, of course. Then, for the last few days, I haven't been able to keep anything down in the morning."

"I know." Pleased as a partridge, Maggie cackled. "Honey, I knew you were breeding three days ago, when you turned green at the sight of Anne Cody's flapjacks. Ain't Jake just going to fall on his face?"

"I haven't told him," Sarah said quickly. "I don't want him to know until he's…until we've…" She propped her chin in her hands. "Not yet, Maggie."

"That's for you to decide."

"Yes, and you won't say anything…to anyone?"

"Not a peep."

Satisfied, Sarah rose and started up the stairs again. "The doctor said he'd be up and around in a couple of days. We haven't been able to talk about anything important since he's been healing." She knocked on the door to his room before pushing it open.

The bed was empty.

"What— Maggie!"

"He was there an hour ago. I don't know where—" But she was talking to air, as Sarah was flying down the stairs again.

"Sarah! Sarah!" His hand wrapped around a licorice whip, Johnny raced toward her. "I just saw Jake riding out of town. He sure looked a lot better."

"Which way?" She grabbed the surprised boy by the shoulders. "Which way did he go?"

"That way." He pointed. "I called after him, but I guess he didn't hear me."

"Damned hardheaded man," Maggie muttered from the doorway.

"So he thinks he can just ride off," Sarah said between her teeth. "Well, Jake Redman is in for a surprise. I need a horse, Maggie. And a rifle."

He'd thought it through. He'd had nothing but time to think over the last weeks. She'd be mad, he figured. He almost smiled. Mad enough to spit, he imagined, but she'd get over it. In time she'd find someone who was right for her. Who was good for her.

Talking to her wouldn't have helped. He'd never known a more stubborn woman. So he'd saddled up and ridden out of Lone Bluff the way he'd ridden out of countless towns before. Only this time it hurt. Not just the pain from his still-healing wound, but an ache deeper, sharper, than anything that could be caused by a bullet.

He'd get over it, too, he told himself. He'd just been fooling himself, letting himself pretend that she could belong to him.

He'd never forget how she'd looked, kneeling in the dirt with his gun in her hand. His gun. And there had been horror in her eyes. He'd taught her to kill, and he wasn't sure he could live with that.

The way he figured it, she'd saved his life. The best he could do for her was return the favor and get out of hers.

She was rich now. Jake remembered how excited Lucius had been when he'd come to visit, talking on and on about the mine and how the gold was all but ready to fall into a man's hands. She could go back east, or she could stay and build that big house with the parlor she'd told him about.

And he would…he would go on drifting.

When he heard the rider coming, instinct had him wheeling his horse around and reaching for his gun. He swore, rubbing his hand on his thigh, as Sarah closed the distance between them.

"You bastard."

He acknowledged her with a nod. There was only one way to handle her now, one way to make certain she turned around and left. Before just looking at her made him want to crawl.

"Didn't know you could ride, Duchess. You come out all this way to tell me goodbye?"

"I have more than that to say." Her hands balled on the reins while she fought with her temper. "Not a word, Jake, to me, to anyone? Just saddle up and ride out?"

"That's right. When it's time to move on, you move."

"So you're telling me you have no reason to stay?"

"That's right." He knew the truth sometimes hurt, but he hadn't known a lie could. "You're a mighty pretty woman, Duchess. You'll be hard to top."

He saw the hurt glow in her eyes before her chin came up. "That's a compliment? Well, you're quite right, Jake. I'll be very hard to top. You'll never love another woman the way you love me. Or want one," she said, more quietly. "Or need one."

"Go on back, Sarah." He started to turn his horse but stopped short when she drew the rifle out of its holster and aimed it heart-high. "You want to point that someplace else?"

For an answer, she lowered it a few strategic inches, smiling when his brow lifted. "Ever hear the one about hell's fury, Jake?"

"I get the idea." He shifted slightly. "Duchess, if it's all the same to you, I'd rather you pointed it back at my chest."

"Get off your horse."

"Damn it, Sarah."

"I said off." She cocked the lever in two sharp movements. "Now."

He leaned forward in the saddle. "How do I know that's even loaded?"

"How do you know it's loaded?" She smiled, brought it up to her eye and fired. His hat flew off his head.

"Are you crazy?" Stunned, he dragged a hand through his hair. He could almost feel the heat. "You damn near killed me."

"I hit what I aim at. Isn't that what you said I should learn to do?" She cocked the rifle again. "Now get off that horse before I shoot something more vital off you."

Swearing, he slid down. "What the hell are you trying to prove with all this?"

"Just hold it right there." She dropped to the ground. Giddiness washed over her, and she had to lean one hand against her mount.

"Sarah—"

"I said hold it right there." She shook her head to clear it.

"Are you sick?"

"No." Steady again, she smiled. "I've never felt better in my life."

"Just crazy, then." He relaxed a little, but her pallor worried him. "Well, if you've a mind to kill me after spending the better part of a month keeping me alive, go ahead."

"You're damn right I kept you alive, and I didn't do it so you could leave me the minute you could stand up. I did it because I love you, because you're everything I want and everything I intend to have. Now you tell me, you stand there and tell me why you left."

"I already told you. It was time."

"You're a liar. Worse, you're a coward."

Her words had the effect she'd hoped for. The cool, almost bored look in his eyes sizzled into heat. "Don't push me, Sarah."

"I haven't begun to push you. I'll start by telling you why you got on that horse and rode away. You left because you were afraid. Of me. No, not even of me, of yourself and what you feel for me." Her chin was up, a challenge in her eyes as she dared him to say it was untrue. "You loved me enough to stand unarmed in front of a madman, but not enough to face your own heart."

"You don't know what I feel."

"Don't I? If you believe that, you're a fool, as well as a liar." The fresh flash of fury in his eyes delighted her. "Don't you think I knew every time you touched me, every time you kissed me?" He was silent, and she drew a long breath. "Well, you can get on that horse and you can ride, you can run into the hills, to the next town. You can keep running until you're hundreds of miles away. Maybe you'll be fast enough, just fast enough to get away from me. But before you do you're going to tell me."

"Tell you what?"

"I want you to tell me you love me."

He studied her. Her eyes glowed with determination, and her cheeks were flushed with anger. Her hair, caught by the wind, was blowing back. He should have known then and there that he'd never had anywhere to run.

"A man'll say most anything when a woman's pointing a rifle at his belly."

"Then say it."

He bent to pick up his hat, slapping it against his thighs twice to loosen the dust. Idly he poked his finger through the hole in the crown.

"I love you, Sarah." He settled the hat on his head. "Now do you want to put that thing away?"

The temper went out of her eyes, and with it the glint of hope. Without a word, she turned to secure the rifle in the holder. "Well, I had to threaten it out of you, but at least I heard you say it once. Go ahead and ride off. I won't stop you. No one's holding a gun on you now."

She wouldn't cry. No, she swore to herself she wouldn't hold him with tears. Fighting them back, she tried to struggle back into the saddle. He touched her arm, lightly, not holding, when he wanted more than anything he'd ever wanted in his life to hold her.

"I love you, Sarah," he said again. "More than I should. A hell of a lot more than I can stand."

She closed her eyes, praying that what she did now would be right for both of them. Slowly she turned toward him, but she kept her hands at her sides. "If you ride away now, I'll come after you. No matter where you go, I'll be there. I'll make your life hell, I swear it."

He couldn't stop the smile any more than he could stop his hand from reaching up to touch her face. "And if I don't ride away?"

"I'll only make your life hell some of the time."

"I guess that's a better bargain." He lowered his head to kiss her gently. Then, with a groan, he crushed her hard against him. "I don't think I'd've gotten very far, even if you hadn't shot at me."

"No use taking chances. Lucky for you I was trying to shoot over your head."

He only sighed and drew her away. "You owe me a hat, Duchess." Still amazed, he drew it off to poke at the hole. "I guess I'd have to marry any woman who could handle a gun like that."

"Is that a proposal?"

He shrugged and stuck his hat back on his head. "Sounded like it."

She lifted a brow. "And it's the best you can do?"

"I haven't got any five-dollar words." Disgusted, he started back to his horse. Then he stopped and turned back. She was waiting, her arms folded, a half smile on her face. So he swore at her. "There's a preacher comes into town once every few weeks. He can marry us proper enough, with whatever kind of fuss you figure would satisfy you. I'll build you a house, between the mine and the town, with a parlor if that's what you want, and a wood floor, and a real bedroom."

To her it was the most eloquent of proposals. She held out her hands. "We'll need two."

"Two what?"

"Two bedrooms," she said when his hands closed over hers again.

"Listen, Duchess, I've heard they've got some odd ways of doing things back east, but I'm damned if my wife is going to sleep in another room."

"Oh, no." Her smile lit up her face. "I'm going to sleep in the same room, the same bed as you, every night for the rest of my life. But we'll need two bedrooms. At least we will by spring."

"I don't see why—" Then he did, so abruptly, so stunningly, that he could only stare at her. If she had taken the rifle back out and driven it butt first into his gut he would have been less shaken. His fingers went slack on hers, then dropped away. "Are you sure?"

"Yes." She held her breath. "There's going to be a child. Our child."

He wasn't sure he could move, and was less sure he could speak. Slowly, carefully, he framed her face with his hands and kissed her. Then, when emotions swamped him, he simply rested his forehead against hers. "Two bedrooms," he murmured. "To start."

Content, she wrapped her arms around his waist. "Yes. To start."

* * * * *

THE LAW IS A LADY

To all the experts at R&R Lighting Company

Chapter 1

Merle T. Johnson sat on the ripped vinyl seat of a stool in Annie's Cafe, five miles north of Friendly. He lingered over a lukewarm root beer, half listening to the scratchy country number piping out from Annie's portable radio. *"A woman was born to be hurt"* was the lament of Nashville's latest hopeful. Merle didn't know enough about women to disagree.

He was on his way back to Friendly after checking out a complaint on one of the neighboring ranches. Sheep-stealing, he thought as he chugged down more root beer. Might've been exciting if there'd been anything to it. Potts was getting too old to know how many sheep he had in the first place. Sheriff knew there was nothing to it, Merle thought glumly. Sitting in the dingy little cafe with the smell of fried hamburgers and onions clinging to the air, Merle bemoaned the injustice of it.

There was nothing more exciting in Friendly, New Mexico, than hauling in old Silas when he got drunk and disorderly on Saturday nights. Merle T. Johnson had been born too late. If it had been the 1880s instead of the 1980s, he'd have had a chance to face desperados, ride in a posse, face off a gunslinger—the things deputies were supposed to do. And here he was, he told himself fatalistically, nearly twenty-four years old, and the biggest arrest he had made was pulling in the Kramer twins for busting up the local pool hall.

Merle scratched his upper lip where he was trying, without much success, to grow a respectable mustache. The best part of his life was behind him, he decided, and he'd never be more than a deputy in a forgotten little town, chasing imaginary sheep thieves.

If just *once* somebody'd rob the bank. He dreamed over this a minute, picturing himself in a high-speed chase and shootout. That would be something, yessiree. He'd have his picture in the paper, maybe a flesh wound in the shoulder. The idea became more appealing. He could wear a sling for a few days. Now, if the sheriff would only let him carry a gun...

"Merle T., you gonna pay for that drink or sit there dreaming all day?"

Merle snapped back to reality and got hastily to his feet. Annie stood watching him with her hands on her ample hips. She had small, dark eyes, florid skin and an amazing thatch of strawberry-colored hair. Merle was never at his best with women.

"Gotta get back," he muttered, fumbling for his wallet. "Sheriff needs my report."

Annie gave a quick snort and held out her hand, damp palm up. After she snatched the crumpled bill, Merle headed out without asking for his change.

The sun was blinding and brilliant. Merle automatically narrowed his eyes against it. It bounced off the road surface in waves that shimmered almost like liquid. But the day was hot and dusty. On both sides of the ribbon of road stretched nothing but rock and sand and a few tough patches of grass. There was no cloud to break the strong, hard blue of the sky or filter the streaming white light of the sun. He pulled the rim of his hat down over his brow as he headed for his car, wishing he'd had the nerve to ask Annie for his change. His shirt was damp and sticky before he reached for the door handle.

Merle saw the sun radiate off the windshield and chrome of an oncoming car. It was still a mile away, he judged idly as he watched it tool up the long, straight road. He continued to watch its progress with absent-minded interest, digging in his pocket for his keys. As it drew closer his hand remained in his pocket. His eyes grew wide.

That's some car! he thought in stunned admiration.

One of the fancy foreign jobs, all red and flashy. It whizzed by without pausing, and Merle's head whipped around to stare after it. *Oo-wee!* he thought with a grin. *Some* car. Must have been doing seventy easy. Probably has one of those fancy dashboards with— Seventy!

Springing into his car, Merle managed to get the keys out of his pocket and into the ignition. He flipped on his siren and peeled out, spitting gravel and smoking rubber. He was in heaven.

Phil had been driving more than eighty miles nonstop. During the early part of the journey, he'd held an involved conversation on the car phone with his producer in L.A. He was annoyed and tired. The dust-colored scenery and endless flat road only annoyed him further. Thus far, the trip had been a total waste. He'd checked out five different towns in southwest New Mexico, and none of them had suited his needs. If his luck didn't change, they were going to have to use a set after all. It wasn't his style. When Phillip Kincaid directed a film, he was a stickler for authenticity. Now he was looking for a tough, dusty little town that showed wear around the edges. He wanted peeling paint and some grime. He was looking for the kind of place everyone planned to leave and no one much wanted to come back to.

Phil had spent three long hot days looking, and nothing had satisfied him. True, he'd found a couple of sand-colored towns, a little faded, a little worse for wear, but they hadn't had the right feel. As a director— a highly successful director of American films—Phillip Kincaid relied on gut reaction before he settled down to refining angles. He needed a town that gave him a kick in the stomach. And he was running short on time.

Already Huffman, the producer, was getting antsy, pushing to start the studio scenes. Phil was cursing himself again for not producing the film himself when he cruised by Annie's Cafe. He had stalled Huffman for another week, but if he didn't find the right town to represent New Chance, he would have to trust his location manager to find it. Phil scowled down the endless stretch of road. He didn't trust details to anyone but himself. That, and his undeniable talent, were the reasons for his success at the age of thirty-four. He was tough, critical and volatile, but he treated each of his films as though it were a child requiring endless care and patience. He wasn't always so understanding with his actors.

He heard the wail of the siren with mild curiosity. Glancing in the mirror, Phil saw a dirty, dented police car that might have been white at one time. It was bearing down on him enthusiastically. Phil swore, gave momentary consideration to hitting the gas and leaving the annoyance with his dust, then resignedly pulled over. The blast of heat that greeted him when he let down the window did nothing to improve his mood. Filthy place, he thought, cutting the engine. Grimy dust hole. He wished for his own lagoonlike pool and a long, cold drink.

Elated, Merle climbed out of his car, ticket book in hand. Yessiree, he thought again, this was some machine. About the fanciest piece he'd seen outside the TV. Mercedes, he noted, turning the sound of it over in his mind. French, he decided with admiration. Holy cow, he'd stopped himself a French car not two miles out of town. He'd have a story to tell over a beer that night.

The driver disappointed him a bit at first. He didn't look foreign or even rich. Merle's glance passed ignorantly over the gold Swiss watch to take in the T-shirt and jeans. Must be one of those eccentrics, he concluded. Or maybe the car was stolen. Merle's blood began to pound excitedly. He looked at the man's face.

It was lean and faintly aristocratic, with well-defined bones and a long, straight nose. The mouth was unsmiling, even bored. He was clean shaven with the suggestion of creases in his cheeks. His hair seemed a modest brown; it was a bit long and curled over his ears. In the tanned face the eyes were an arresting clear water-blue. They were both bored and annoyed and, if Merle had been able to latch on the word, aloof. He wasn't Merle's image of a desperate foreign-car thief.

"Yes?"

The single frosty syllable brought Merle back to business. "In a hurry?" he asked, adopting what the sheriff would have called his tough-cop stance.

"Yes."

The answer made Merle shift his feet. "License and registration," he said briskly, then leaned closer to the window as Phil reached in the glove compartment. "Glory be, look at the dash! It's got everything and then some. A phone, a phone right there in the car. Those French guys are something."

Phil sent him a mild glance. "German," he corrected, handing Merle the registration.

"German?" Merle frowned doubtfully. "You sure?"

"Yes." Slipping his license out of his wallet, Phil passed it through the open window. The heat was pouring in.

Merle accepted the registration. He was downright sure Mercedes was a French name. "This your car?" he asked suspiciously.

"As you can see by the name on the registration," Phil returned coolly, a sure sign that his temper was frayed around the edges.

Merle was reading the registration at his usual plodding speed. "You streaked by Annie's like a bat out of—" He broke off, remembering that the sheriff didn't hold with swearing on the job. "I stopped you for excessive speed. Clocked you at seventy-two. I bet this baby rides so smooth you never noticed."

"As a matter of fact, I didn't." Perhaps if he hadn't been angry to begin with, perhaps if the heat hadn't been rolling unmercifully into the car, Phil might have played his hand differently. As Merle began to write up the ticket Phil narrowed his eyes. "Just how do I know you clocked me at all?"

"I was just coming out of Annie's when you breezed by," Merle said genially. His forehead creased as he formed the letters. "If I'd waited for my change, I wouldn't have seen you." He grinned, pleased with the hand of fate. "You just sign this," he said as he ripped the ticket from the pad. "You can stop off in town and pay the fine."

Slowly, Phil climbed out of the car. When the sun hit his hair, deep streaks of red shot through it. Merle was reminded of his mother's mahogany server. For a moment they stood eye to eye, both tall men. But one was lanky and tended to slouch, the other lean, muscular and erect.

"No," Phil said flatly.

"No?" Merle blinked against the direct blue gaze. "No what?"

"No, I'm not signing it."

"Not signing?" Merle looked down at the ticket still in his hand. "But you have to."

"No, I don't." Phil felt a trickle of sweat roll down his back. Inexplicably it infuriated him. "I'm not signing, and I'm not paying a penny to some two-bit judge who's feeding his bank account from this speed trap."

"Speed trap!" Merle was more astonished than insulted. "Mister, you were doing better'n seventy, and the road's marked clear: fifty-five. Everybody knows you can't do more than fifty-five."

"Who says I was?"

"I clocked you."

"Your word against mine," Phil returned coolly. "Got a witness?"

Merle's mouth fell open. "Well, no, but…" He pushed back his hat. "Look, I don't need no witness, I'm the deputy. Just sign the ticket."

It was pure perversity. Phil hadn't the least idea how fast he'd been going and didn't particularly care. The road had been long and deserted; his mind had been in L.A. But knowing this wasn't going to make him take the cracked ballpoint the deputy offered him.

"No."

"Look, mister, I already wrote up the ticket." Merle read refusal in Phil's face and set his chin. After all, he was the law. "Then I'm going to have to take you in," he said dangerously. "The sheriff's not going to like it."

Phil gave him a quick smirk and held out his hands, wrists close. Merle stared at them a moment, then looked helplessly from car to car. Beneath the anger, Phil felt a stir of sympathy.

"You'll have to follow me in," Merle told him as he pocketed Phil's license.

"And if I refuse?"

Merle wasn't a complete fool. "Well, then," he said amiably, "I'll have to take you in and leave this fancy car sitting here. It might be all in one piece when the tow truck gets here; then again…"

Phil acknowledged the point with a slight nod, then climbed back into his car. Merle sauntered to his, thinking how fine he was going to look bringing in that fancy red machine.

They drove into Friendly at a sedate pace. Merle nodded occasionally to people who stopped their business to eye the small procession. He stuck his hand out the window to signal a halt, then braked in front of the sheriff's office.

"Okay, inside." Abruptly official, Merle stood straight. "The sheriff'll want to talk to you." But the icy gleam in the man's eye kept Merle from taking his arm. Instead he opened the door and waited for his prisoner to walk through.

Phil glimpsed a small room with two cells, a bulletin board, a couple of spindly chairs and a battered desk. An overhead fan churned the steamy air and whined. On the floor lay a large mound of mud-colored fur that turned out to be a dog. The desk was covered with books and papers and two half-filled cups of coffee. A dark-haired woman bent over all this, scratching industriously on a yellow legal pad. She glanced up as they entered.

Phil forgot his annoyance long enough to cast her in three different films. Her face was classically oval, with a hint of cheekbone under honey-toned skin. Her nose was small and delicate, her mouth just short of wide, with a fullness that was instantly sensual. Her hair was black, left to fall loosely past her shoulders in carelessly sweeping waves. Her brows arched in question. Beneath them her eyes were thickly lashed, darkly green and faintly amused.

"Merle?"

The single syllable was full throated, as lazy and sexy as black silk. Phil knew actresses who would kill for a voice like that one. If she didn't stiffen up in front of a camera, he thought, and if the rest of her went with the face… He let his eyes sweep down. Pinned to her left breast was a small tin badge. Fascinated, Phil stared at it.

"Excess of speed on Seventeen, Sheriff."

"Oh?" With a slight smile on her face, she waited for Phil's eyes to come back to hers. She had recognized the appraisal when he had first walked in, just as she recognized the suspicion now. "Didn't you have a pen, Merle?"

"A pen?" Baffled, he checked his pockets.

"I wouldn't sign the ticket." Phil walked to the desk to get a closer look at her face. "Sheriff," he added. She could be shot from any imaginable angle, he concluded, and still look wonderful. He wanted to hear her speak again.

She met his assessing stare straight on. "I see. What was his speed, Merle?"

"Seventy-two. Tory, you should see his car!" Merle exclaimed, forgetting himself.

"I imagine I will," she murmured. She held out her hand, her eyes still on Phil's. Quickly, Merle gave her the paperwork.

Phil noted that her hands were long, narrow and elegant. The tips were painted in shell pink. What the hell is she doing here? he wondered, more easily visualizing her in Beverly Hills.

"Well, everything seems to be in order, Mr.... Kincaid." Her eyes came back to his. A little mascara, he noticed, a touch of eyeliner. The color's hers. No powder, no lipstick. He wished fleetingly for a camera and a couple of hand-held lights. "The fine's forty dollars," she said lazily. "Cash."

"I'm not paying it."

Her lips pursed briefly, causing him to speculate on their taste. "Or forty days," she said without batting an eye. "I think you'd find it less...inconvenient to pay the fine. Our accommodations won't suit you."

The cool amusement in her tone irritated him. "I'm not paying any fine." Placing his palms on the desk, he leaned toward her, catching the faint drift of a subtle, sophisticated scent. "Do you really expect me to believe you're the sheriff? What kind of scam are you and this character running?"

Merle opened his mouth to speak, glanced at Tory, then shut it again. She rose slowly. Phil found himself surprised that she was tall and as lean as a whippet. A model's body, he thought, long and willowy—the kind that made you wonder what was underneath those clothes. This one made jeans and a plaid shirt look like a million dollars.

"I never argue with beliefs, Mr. Kincaid. You'll have to empty your pockets."

"I will not," he began furiously.

"Resisting arrest." Tory lifted a brow. "We'll have to make it sixty days." Phil said something quick and rude. Instead of being offended, Tory smiled. "Lock him up, Merle."

"Now, just a damn minute—"

"You don't want to make her mad," Merle whispered, urging Phil back toward the cells. "She can be mean as a cat."

"Unless you want us to tow your car…and charge you for that as well," she added, "you'll give Merle your keys." She flicked her eyes over his furious face. "Read him his rights, Merle."

"I know my rights, damn it." Contemptuously he shrugged off Merle's hand. "I want to make a phone call."

"Of course." Tory sent him another charming smile. "As soon as you give Merle your keys."

"Now, look"—Phil glanced down at her badge again—"Sheriff," he added curtly. "You don't expect me to fall for an old game. This one"—he jerked a thumb at Merle—"waits for an out-of-towner to come by, then tries to hustle him out of a quick forty bucks. There's a law against speed traps."

Tory listened with apparent interest. "Are you going to sign the ticket, Mr. Kincaid?"

Phil narrowed his eyes. "No."

"Then you'll be our guest for a while."

"You can't sentence me," Phil began heatedly. "A judge—"

"Justice of the peace," Tory interrupted, then tapped a tinted nail against a small framed certificate. Phil saw the name Victoria L. Ashton.

He gave her a long, dry look. "You?"

"Yes, handy, isn't it?" She cocked her head to the side. "Sixty days, Mr. Kincaid, or two hundred and fifty dollars."

"Two-fifty!"

"Bail's set at five hundred. Would you care to post it?"

"The phone call," he said through clenched teeth.

"The keys," she countered affably.

Swearing under his breath, Phil pulled the keys from his pocket and tossed them to her. Tory caught them neatly. "You're entitled to one local call, Mr. Kincaid."

"It's long distance," he muttered. "I'll use my credit card."

After indicating the phone on her desk, Tory took the keys to Merle. "Two-fifty!" he said in an avid whisper. "Aren't you being a little rough on him?"

Tory gave a quick, unladylike snort. "Mr. Hollywood Kincaid needs a good kick in the ego," she mumbled. "It'll do him a world of good to stew in a cell for a while. Take the car to Bestler's Garage, Merle."

"Me? *Drive* it?" He looked down at the keys in his hand.

"Lock it up and bring back the keys," Tory added. "And don't play with any of the buttons."

"Aw, Tory."

"Aw, Merle," she responded, then sent him on his way with an affectionate look.

Phil waited impatiently as the phone rang. Someone picked up. "Answering for Sherman, Miller and Stein." He swore.

"Where the hell's Lou?" he demanded.

"Mr. Sherman is out of the office until Monday," the

operator told him primly. "Would you care to leave your name?"

"This is Phillip Kincaid. You get Lou now, tell him I'm in—" He turned to cast a dark look at Tory.

"Welcome to Friendly, New Mexico," she said obligingly.

Phil's opinion was a concise four-letter word. "Friendly, New Mexico. In jail, damn it, on some trumped-up charge. Tell him to get his briefcase on a plane, pronto."

"Yes, Mr. Kincaid, I'll try to reach him."

"You reach him," he said tightly and hung up. When he started to dial again, Tory walked over and calmly disconnected him.

"One call," she reminded him.

"I got a damn answering service."

"Tough break." She gave him the dashing smile that both attracted and infuriated him. "Your room's ready, Mr. Kincaid."

Phil hung up the phone to face her squarely. "You're not putting me in that cell."

She looked up with a guileless flutter of lashes. "No?"

"No."

Tory looked confused for a moment. Her sigh was an appealingly feminine sound as she wandered around the desk. "You're making this difficult for me, Mr. Kincaid. You must know I can't manhandle you into a cell. You're bigger than I am."

Her abrupt change of tone caused him to feel more reasonable. "Ms. Ashton…" he began.

"Sheriff Ashton," Tory corrected and drew a .45 out

of the desk drawer. Her smile never wavered as Phil gaped at the large gun in her elegant hand. "Now, unless you want another count of resisting arrest on your record, you'll go quietly into that first cell over there. The linen's just been changed."

Phil wavered between astonishment and amusement. "You don't expect me to believe you'd use that thing."

"I told you I don't argue with beliefs." Though she kept the barrel lowered, Tory quite deliberately cocked the gun.

He studied her for one full minute. Her eyes were too direct and entirely too calm. Phil had no doubt she'd put a hole in him—in some part of his anatomy that she considered unimportant. He had a healthy respect for his body.

"I'll get you for this," he muttered as he headed for the cell.

Her laugh was rich and attractive enough to make him turn in front of the bars. Good God, he thought, he'd like to tangle with her when she didn't have a pistol in her hand. Furious with himself, Phil stalked into the cell.

"Doesn't that line go something like: 'When I break outta this joint, you're gonna get yours'?" Tory pulled the keys from a peg, then locked the cell door with a jingle and snap. Struggling not to smile, Phil paced the cell. "Would you like a harmonica and a tin cup?"

He grinned, but luckily his back was to her. Dropping onto the bunk, he sent her a fulminating glance. "I'll take the tin cup if it has coffee in it."

"Comes with the service, Kincaid. You've got free room and board in Friendly." He watched her walk back to the desk to replace the pistol. Something in the lazy, leggy gait affected his blood pressure pleasantly. "Cream and sugar?" she asked politely.

"Black."

Tory poured the coffee, aware that his eyes were on her. She was partly amused by him, partly intrigued. She knew exactly who he was. Over her basic disdain for what she considered a spoiled, tinsel-town playboy was a trace of respect. He hadn't attempted to influence her with his name or his reputation. He'd relied on his temper. And it was his temper, she knew, that had landed him in the cell in the first place.

Too rich, she decided, too successful, too attractive. And perhaps, she mused as she poured herself a cup, too talented. His movies were undeniably brilliant. She wondered what made him tick. His movies seemed to state one image, the glossies another. With a quiet laugh she thought she might find out for herself while he was her "guest."

"Black," she stated, carrying both cups across the room. "Made to order."

He was watching the way she moved; fluidly, with just a hint of hip. It was those long legs, he decided, and some innate confidence. Under different circumstances he would have considered her quite a woman. At the moment he considered her an outrageous annoyance. Silently he unfolded himself from the bunk and went to accept the coffee she held between the bars. Their fingers brushed briefly.

"You're a beautiful woman, Victoria L. Ashton," he muttered. "And a pain in the neck."

She smiled. "Yes."

That drew a laugh from him. "What the hell are you doing here, playing sheriff?"

"What the hell are you doing here, playing criminal?"

Merle burst in the door, grinning from ear to ear. "Holy cow, Mr. Kincaid, that's *some* car!" He dropped the keys in Tory's hand, then leaned against the bars. "I swear, I could've just sat in it all day. Bestler's eyes just about popped out when I drove it in."

Making a low sound in his throat, Phil turned away to stare through the small barred window at the rear of the cell. He scowled at his view of the town. Look at this place! he thought in frustration. Dusty little nowhere. Looks like all the color was washed away twenty years ago. Baked away, he corrected himself as sweat ran uncomfortably down his back. There seemed to be nothing but brown—dry, sparse mesa in the distance and parched sand. All the buildings, such as they were, were different dull shades of brown, all stripped bare by the unrelenting sun. Damn place still had wooden sidewalks, he mused, sipping at the strong coffee. There wasn't a coat of paint on a storefront that wasn't cracked and peeling. The whole town looked as though it had drawn one long, tired communal breath and settled down to wait until it was all over.

It was a gritty, hopeless-looking place with a sad sort of character under a film of dust and lethargy. People stayed in a town like this when they had no place else to go or nothing to do. Came back when they'd lost hope for anything better. And here he was, stuck in some steamy little cell....

His mind sharpened.

Staring at the tired storefronts and sagging wood, Phil saw it all through the lens of a camera. His fingers wrapped around a window bar as he began to plot out scene after scene. If he hadn't been furious, he'd have seen it from the first moment.

This was Next Chance.

Chapter 2

For the next twenty minutes Tory paid little attention to her prisoner. He seemed content to stare out of the window with the coffee growing cold in his hand. After dispatching Merle, Tory settled down to work.

She was blessed with a sharp, practical and stubborn mind. These traits had made her education extensive. Academically she'd excelled, but she hadn't always endeared herself to her instructors. *Why?* had always been her favorite question. In addition her temperament, which ranged from placid to explosive, had made her a difficult student. Some of her associates called her a tedious annoyance—usually when they were on the opposing side. At twenty-seven Victoria L. Ashton was a very shrewd, very accomplished attorney.

In Albuquerque she kept a small, unpretentious office

in an enormous old house with bad plumbing. She shared it with an accountant, a real-estate broker and a private investigator. For nearly five years she had lived on the third floor in two barnlike rooms while keeping her office below. It was a comfortable arrangement that Tory had had no inclination to alter even when she'd been able to afford to.

Professionally she liked challenges and dealing with finite details. In her personal life she was more lackadaisical. No one would call her lazy, but she saw more virtue in a nap than a brisk jog. Her energies poured out in the office or courtroom—and temporarily in her position as sheriff of Friendly, New Mexico.

She had grown up in Friendly and had been content with its yawning pace. The sense of justice she had inherited from her father had driven her to law school. Still, she had had no desire to join a swank firm on either coast, or in any big city in between. Her independence had caused her to risk starting her own practice. Fat fees were no motivation for Tory. She'd learned early how to stretch a dollar when it suited her—an ability she got from her mother. People, and the way the law could be made to work to their advantage or disadvantage, interested her.

Now Tory settled behind her desk and continued drafting out a partnership agreement for a pair of fledgling songwriters. It wasn't always simple to handle cases long distance, but she'd given her word. Absentmindedly she sipped her coffee. By fall she would be back in Albuquerque, filling her caseload again and trading her badge for a briefcase. In the meantime the weekend was looming. Payday. Tory smiled a little as she wrote. Friendly livened up a bit on Saturday nights. People tended to have an extra beer. And there was a poker game scheduled at Bestler's Garage that she wasn't supposed to know about. Tory knew when it was advantageous to look the other way. Her father would have said people need their little entertainments.

Leaning back to study what she had written, Tory propped one booted foot on the desk and twirled a raven lock around her finger. Abruptly coming out of his reverie, Phil whirled to the door of the cell.

"I have to make a phone call!" His tone was urgent and excited. Everything he had seen from the cell window had convinced him that fate had brought him to Friendly.

Tory finished reading a paragraph, then looked up languidly. "You've had your phone call, Mr. Kincaid. Why don't you relax? Take a tip from Dynamite there," she suggested, wiggling her fingers toward the mound of dog. "Take a nap."

Phil curled his hands around the bars and shook them. "Woman, I have to use the phone. It's important."

"It always is," Tory murmured before she lowered her eyes to the paper again.

Ready to sacrifice principle for expediency, Phil growled at her. "Look, I'll sign the ticket. Just let me out of here."

"You're welcome to sign the ticket," she returned pleasantly, "but it won't get you out. There's also the charge of resisting arrest."

"Of all the phony, trumped-up—"

"I could add creating a public nuisance," she considered, then glanced over the top of her papers with a smile. He was furious. It showed in the rigid stance of his hard body, in the grim mouth and fiery eyes. Tory felt a small twinge in the nether regions of her stomach. Oh, yes, she could clearly see why his name was linked with dozens of attractive women. He was easily the most beautiful male animal she'd ever seen. It was that trace of aristocratic aloofness, she mused, coupled with the really extraordinary physique and explosive temper. He was like some sleek, undomesticated cat.

Their eyes warred with each other for a long, silent moment. His were stony; hers were calm.

"All right," he muttered, "how much?"

Tory lifted a brow. "A bribe, Kincaid?"

He knew his quarry too well by this time. "No. How much is my fine...Sheriff?"

"Two hundred and fifty dollars." She sent her hair over her shoulder with a quick toss of her head. "Or you can post bail for five hundred."

Scowling at her, Phil reached for his wallet. When I get out of here, he thought dangerously, I'm going to make that tasty little morsel pay for this. A glance in his wallet found him more than a hundred dollars short of bond. Phil swore, then looked back at Tory. She still had the gently patient smile on her face. He could cheerfully strangle her. Instead he tried another tack. Charm had always brought him success with women.

"I lost my temper before, Sheriff," he began, sending her the slightly off-center smile for which he was known. "I apologize. I've been on the road for several days and your deputy got under my skin." Tory went on smiling. "If I said anything out of line to you, it was because you just don't fit the image of small-town peace officer." He grinned and became boyishly appealing— Tom Sawyer caught with his hand in the sugar bowl.

Tory lifted one long, slim leg and crossed it over the other on the desk. "A little short, are you, Kincaid?"

Phil clenched his teeth on a furious retort. "I don't like to carry a lot of cash on the road."

"Very wise," she agreed with a nod. "But we don't accept credit cards."

"Damn it, I have to get out of here!"

Tory studied him dispassionately. "I can't buy claustrophobia," she said. "Not when I read you crawled into a two-foot pipe to check camera angles on *Night of Desperation*."

"It's not—" Phil broke off. His eyes narrowed. "You know who I am?"

"Oh, I make it to the movies a couple of times a year," she said blithely.

The narrowed eyes grew hard. "If this is some kind of shakedown—"

Her throaty laughter cut him off. "Your self-importance is showing." His expression grew so incredulous, she laughed again before she rose. "Kincaid, I don't care who you are or what you do for a living, you're a bad-tempered man who refused to accept the law and got obnoxious." She sauntered over to the cell. Again he caught the hint of a subtle perfume that suited French silk, more than faded denim. "I'm obliged to rehabilitate you."

He forgot his anger in simple appreciation of blatant

beauty. "God, you've got a face," he muttered. "I could work a whole damn film around that face."

The words surprised her. Tory was perfectly aware that she was physically attractive. She would have been a fool to think otherwise, and she'd heard men offer countless homages to her looks. This was hardly a homage. But something in his tone, in his eyes, made a tremor skip up her spine. She made no protest when he reached a hand through the bars to touch her hair. He let it fall through his fingers while his eyes stayed on hers.

Tory felt a heat to which she had thought herself immune. It flashed through her as though she had stepped into the sun from out of a cool, dim room. It was the kind of heat that buckled your knees and made you gasp out loud in astonished wonder. She stood straight and absorbed it.

A dangerous man, she concluded, surprised. A very dangerous man. She saw a flicker of desire in his eyes, then a flash of amusement. As she watched, his mouth curved up at the corners.

"Baby," he said, then grinned, "I could make you a star."

The purposely trite words dissolved the tension and made her laugh. "Oh, Mr. Kincaid," she said in a breathy whisper, "can I really have a screen test?" A startled Phil could only watch as she flung herself against the bars of the cell dramatically. "I'll wait for you, Johnny," she said huskily as tears shimmered in her eyes and her soft lips trembled. "No matter how long it takes." Reaching through the bars, she clutched at him. "I'll write you every day," she promised brokenly. "And dream of you every night. Oh, Johnny"—her lashes fluttered down—"kiss me goodbye!"

Fascinated, Phil moved to oblige her, but just before his lips brushed hers, she stepped back, laughing. "How'd I do, Hollywood? Do I get the part?"

Phil studied her in amused annoyance. It was a pity, he thought, that he hadn't at least gotten a taste of that beautiful mouth. "A little overdone," he stated with more asperity than truth. "But not bad for an amateur."

Tory chuckled and leaned companionably against the bars. "You're just mad."

"Mad?" he tossed back in exasperation. "Have you ever spent any time in one of these cages?"

"As a matter of fact I have." She gave him an easy grin. "Under less auspicious circumstances. Relax, Kincaid, your friend will come bail you out."

"The mayor," Phil said on sudden inspiration. "I want to see the mayor. I have a business proposition," he added.

"Oh." Tory mulled this over. "Well, I doubt I can oblige you on a Saturday. The mayor mostly fishes on Saturday. Want to tell me about it?"

"No."

"Okay. By the way, your last film should've taken the Oscar. It was the most beautiful movie I've ever seen."

Her sudden change of attitude disconcerted him. Cautiously, Phil studied her face but saw nothing but simple sincerity. "Thanks."

"You don't look like the type who could make a film with intelligence, integrity and emotion."

With a half laugh he dragged a hand through his hair. "Am I supposed to thank you for that too?"

"Not necessarily. It's just that you really do look like the type who squires all those busty celebrities around. When do you find time to work?"

He shook his head. "I…manage," he said grimly.

"Takes a lot of stamina," Tory agreed.

He grinned. "Which? The work or the busty celebrities?"

"I guess you know the answer to that. By the way," she continued before he could formulate a reasonable response, "don't tell Merle T. you make movies." Tory gave him the swift, dashing grin. "He'll start walking like John Wayne and drive us both crazy."

When he smiled back at her, both of them studied each other in wary silence. There was an attraction on both sides that pleased neither of them.

"Sheriff," Phil said in a friendly tone, "a phone call. Remember the line about the quality of mercy?"

Her lips curved, but before she could agree, the door to the office burst in.

"Sheriff!"

"Right here, Mr. Hollister," she said mildly. Tory glanced from the burly, irate man to the skinny, terrified teenager he pulled in with him. "What's the problem?" Without hurry she crossed back to her desk, stepping over the dog automatically.

"Those punks," he began, puffing with the exertion of running. "I warned you about them!"

"The Kramer twins?" Tory sat on the corner of her desk. Her eyes flickered down to the beefy hand that gripped a skinny arm. "Why don't you sit down, Mr. Hollister. You"—she looked directly at the boy—"it's Tod, isn't it?"

He swallowed rapidly. "Yes, ma'am—Sheriff. Tod Swanson."

"Get Mr. Hollister a glass of water, Tod. Right through there."

"He'll be out the back door before you can spit," Hollister began, then took a plaid handkerchief out of his pocket to wipe at his brow.

"No, he won't," Tory said calmly. She jerked her head at the boy as she pulled up a chair for Hollister. "Sit down, now, you'll make yourself sick."

"Sick!" Hollister dropped into a chair as the boy scrambled off. "I'm already sick. Those—those punks."

"Yes, the Kramer twins."

She waited patiently while he completed a lengthy, sometimes incoherent dissertation on the youth of today. Phil had the opportunity to do what he did best: watch and absorb.

Hollister, he noticed, was a hotheaded old bigot with a trace of fear for the younger generation. He was sweating profusely, dabbing at his brow and the back of his neck with the checkered handkerchief. His shirt was wilted and patched with dark splotches. He was flushed, overweight and tiresome. Tory listened to him with every appearance of respect, but Phil noticed the gentle tap of her forefinger against her knee as she sat on the edge of the desk.

The boy came in with the water, two high spots of color on his cheeks. Phil concluded he'd had a difficult time not slipping out the back door. He judged the boy to be about thirteen and scared right down to the bone. He had a smooth, attractive face, with a mop of dark hair and huge brown eyes that wanted to look everywhere at

once. He was too thin; his jeans and grubby shirt were
nearly in tatters. He handed Tory the water with a hand
that shook. Phil saw that when she took it from him, she
gave his hand a quick, reassuring squeeze. Phillip began
to like her.

"Here." Tory handed Hollister the glass. "Drink this,
then tell me what happened."

Hollister drained the glass in two huge gulps. "Those
punks, messing around out back of my store. I've chased
'em off a dozen times. They come in and steal anything
they can get their hands on. I've told you."

"Yes, Mr. Hollister. What happened this time?"

"Heaved a rock through the window." He reddened
alarmingly again. "This one was with 'em. Didn't run
fast enough."

"I see." She glanced at Tod, whose eyes were glued
to the toes of his sneakers. "Which one threw the rock?"

"Didn't see which one, but I caught this one." Hollister rose, stuffing his damp handkerchief back in his
pocket. "I'm going to press charges."

Phil saw the boy blanch. Though Tory continued to
look at Hollister, she laid a hand on Tod's arm. "Go sit
down in the back room, Tod." She waited until he was
out of earshot. "You did the right thing to bring him in,
Mr. Hollister." She smiled. "And to scare the pants off
him."

"He should be locked up," the man began.

"Oh, that won't get your window fixed," she said
reasonably. "And it would only make the boy look like
a hero to the twins."

"In my day—"

"I guess you and my father never broke a window," she mused, smiling at him with wide eyes. Hollister blustered, then snorted.

"Now, look here, Tory…"

"Let me handle it, Mr. Hollister. This kid must be three years younger than the Kramer twins." She lowered her voice so that Phil strained to hear. "He could have gotten away."

Hollister shifted from foot to foot. "He didn't try," he mumbled. "Just stood there. But my window—"

"How much to replace it?"

He lowered his brows and puffed for a minute. "Twenty-five dollars should cover it."

Tory walked around the desk and opened a drawer. After counting out bills, she handed them over. "You have my word, I'll deal with him—and with the twins."

"Just like your old man," he muttered, then awkwardly patted her head. "I don't want those Kramers hanging around my store."

"I'll see to it."

With a nod he left.

Tory sat on her desk again and frowned at her left boot. She wasn't just like her old man, she thought. He'd always been sure and she was guessing. Phil heard her quiet, troubled sigh and wondered at it.

"Tod," she called, then waited for him to come to her. As he walked in his eyes darted in search of Hollister before they focused, terrified, on Tory. When he stood in front of her, she studied his white, strained face. Her heart melted, but her voice was brisk.

"I won't ask you who threw the rock." Tod opened

his mouth, closed it resolutely and shook his head. "Why didn't you run?"

"I didn't—I couldn't…." He bit his lip. "I guess I was too scared."

"How old are you, Tod?" She wanted to brush at the hair that tumbled over his forehead. Instead she kept her hands loosely folded in her lap.

"Fourteen, Sheriff. Honest." His eyes darted up to hers, then flew away like a small, frightened bird. "Just last month."

"The Kramer twins are sixteen," she pointed out gently. "Don't you have friends your own age?"

He gave a shrug of his shoulders that could have meant anything.

"I'll have to take you home and talk to your father, Tod."

He'd been frightened before, but now he looked up at her with naked terror in his eyes. It wiped the lecture she had intended to give him out of her mind. "Please." It came out in a whisper, as though he could say nothing more. Even the whisper was hopeless.

"Tod, are you afraid of your father?" He swallowed and said nothing. "Does he hurt you?" He moistened his lips as his breath began to shake. "Tod." Tory's voice became very soft. "You can tell me. I'm here to help you."

"He…" Tod choked, then shook his head swiftly. "No, ma'am."

Frustrated, Tory looked at the plea in his eyes. "Well, then, perhaps since this is a first offense, we can keep it between us."

"M-ma'am?"

"Tod Swanson, you were detained for malicious mischief. Do you understand the charge?"

"Yes, Sheriff." His Adam's apple began to tremble.

"You owe the court twenty-five dollars in damages, which you'll work off after school and on weekends at a rate of two dollars an hour. You're sentenced to six months probation, during which time you're to keep away from loose women, hard liquor and the Kramer twins. Once a week you're to file a report with me, as I'll be serving as your probation officer."

Tod stared at her as he tried to take it in. "You're not…you're not going to tell my father?"

Slowly, Tory rose. He was a few inches shorter, so that he looked up at her with his eyes full of confused hope. "No." She placed her hands on his shoulders. "Don't let me down."

His eyes brimmed with tears, which he blinked back furiously. Tory wanted badly to hold him, but knew better. "Be here tomorrow morning. I'll have some work for you."

"Yes, yes, ma'am—Sheriff." He backed away warily, waiting for her to change her mind. "I'll be here, Sheriff." He was fumbling for the doorknob, still watching her. "Thank you." Like a shot, he was out of the office, leaving Tory staring at the closed door.

"Well, Sheriff," Phil said quietly, "you're quite a lady."

Tory whirled to see Phil eyeing her oddly. For the first time she felt the full impact of the clear blue gaze. Disconcerted, she went back to her desk. "Did you enjoy seeing the wheels of justice turn, Kincaid?" she asked.

"As a matter of fact, I did." His tone was grave

enough to cause her to look back at him. "You did the right thing by that boy."

Tory studied him a moment, then let out a long sigh. "Did I? We'll see, won't we? Ever seen an abused kid, Kincaid? I'd bet that fifteen-hundred-dollar watch you're wearing one just walked out of here. There isn't a damn thing I can do about it."

"There are laws," he said, fretting against the bars. Quite suddenly he wanted to touch her.

"And laws," she murmured. When the door swung open, she glanced up. "Merle. Good. Take over here. I have to run out to the Kramer place."

"The twins?"

"Who else?" Tory shot back as she plucked a black flat-brimmed hat from a peg. "I'll grab dinner while I'm out and pick up something for our guest. How do you feel about stew, Kincaid?"

"Steak, medium rare," he tossed back. "Chef's salad, oil and vinegar and a good Bordeaux."

"Don't let him intimidate you, Merle," Tory warned as she headed for the door. "He's a cream puff."

"Sheriff, the phone call!" Phil shouted after her as she started to close the door.

With a heavy sigh Tory stuck her head back in. "Merle T., let the poor guy use the phone. Once," she added firmly, then shut the door.

Ninety minutes later Tory sauntered back in with a wicker hamper over her arm. Phil was sitting on his bunk, smoking quietly. Merle sat at the desk, his feet propped up, his hat over his face. He was snoring gently.

"Is the party over?" Tory asked. Phil shot her a silent

glare. Chuckling, she went to Merle and gave him a jab in the shoulder. He scrambled up like a shot, scraping his boot heels over the desk surface.

"Aw, Tory," he muttered, bending to retrieve his hat from the floor.

"Any trouble with the desperate character?" she wanted to know.

Merle gave her a blank look, then grinned sheepishly. "Come on, Tory."

"Go get something to eat. You can wander down to Hernandez's Bar and the pool hall before you go off duty."

Merle placed his hat back on his head. "Want me to check Bestler's Garage?"

"No," she said, remembering the poker game. Merle would figure it his bound duty to break it up if he happened in on it. "I checked in earlier."

"Well, okay…" He shuffled his feet and cast a sidelong glance at Phil. "One of us should stay here tonight."

"I'm staying." Plucking up the keys, she headed for the cell. "I've got some extra clothes in the back room."

"Yeah, but, Tory…" He wanted to point out that she was a woman, after all, and the prisoner had given her a couple of long looks.

"Yes?" Tory paused in front of Phil's cell.

"Nothin'," he muttered, reminded that Tory could handle herself and always had. He blushed before he headed for the door.

"Wasn't that sweet?" she murmured. "He was worried about my virtue." At Phil's snort of laughter she lifted a wry brow.

"Doesn't he know about the large gun in the desk drawer?"

"Of course he does." Tory unlocked the cell. "I told him if he played with it, I'd break all his fingers. Hungry?"

Phil gave the hamper a dubious smile. "Maybe."

"Oh, come on, cheer up," Tory ordered. "Didn't you get to make your phone call?"

She spoke as though appeasing a little boy. It drew a reluctant grin from Phil. "Yes, I made my phone call." Because the discussion with his producer had gone well, Phil was willing to be marginally friendly. Besides, he was starving. "What's in there?"

"T-bone, medium rare, salad, roasted potato—"

"You're kidding!" He was up and dipping into the basket himself.

"I don't kid a man about food, Kincaid, I'm a humanitarian."

"I'll tell you exactly what I think you are—after I've eaten." Phil pulled foil off a plate and uncovered the steak. The scent went straight to his stomach. Dragging over a shaky wooden chair, he settled down to devour his free meal.

"You didn't specify dessert, so I went for apple pie." Tory drew a thick slice out of the hamper.

"I might just modify my opinion of you," Phil told her over a mouthful of steak.

"Don't do anything hasty," she suggested.

"Tell me something, Sheriff." He swallowed, then indicated the still-sleeping dog with his fork. "Doesn't that thing ever move?"

"Not if he can help it."

"Is it alive?"

"The last time I looked," she muttered. "Sorry about the Bordeaux," she continued. "Against regulations. I got you a Dr Pepper."

"A what?"

Tory pulled out a bottle of soda. "Take it or leave it."

After a moment's consideration Phil held out his hand. "What about the mayor?"

"I left him a message. He'll probably see you tomorrow."

Phil unscrewed the top off the bottle, frowning at her. "You're not actually going to make me sleep in this place."

Cocking her head, Tory met his glance. "You have a strange view of the law, Kincaid. Do you think I should book you a room at the hotel?"

He washed down the steak with the soda, then grimaced. "You're a tough guy, Sheriff."

"Yeah." Grinning, she perched on the edge of the bunk. "How's your dinner?"

"It's good. Want some?"

"No. I've eaten." They studied each other with the same wary speculation. Tory spoke first. "What is Phillip C. Kincaid, boy wonder, doing in Friendly, New Mexico?"

"I was passing through," he said warily. He wasn't going to discuss his plans with her. Something warned him he would meet solid opposition.

"At seventy-two miles per hour," she reminded him.

"Maybe."

With a laugh she leaned back against the brick wall. He watched the way her hair settled lazily over her breasts. A man would be crazy to tangle with that lady, he told himself. Phillip Kincaid was perfectly sane.

"And what is Victoria L. Ashton doing wearing a badge in Friendly, New Mexico?"

She gazed past him for a moment with an odd look in her eyes. "Fulfilling an obligation," she said softly.

"You don't fit the part." Phil contemplated her over another swig from the bottle. "I'm an expert on who fits and who doesn't."

"Why not?" Lifting her knee, Tory laced her fingers around it.

"Your hands are too soft." Thoughtfully, Phil cut another bite of steak. "Not as soft as I expected when I saw that face, but too soft. You don't pamper them, but you don't work with them either."

"A sheriff doesn't work with her hands," Tory pointed out.

"A sheriff doesn't wear perfume that costs a hundred and fifty an ounce that was designed to drive men wild either."

Both brows shot up. Her full bottom lip pushed forward in thought. "Is that what it was designed for?"

"A sheriff," he went on, "doesn't usually look like she just walked off the cover of *Harper's Bazaar,* treat her deputy like he was her kid brother or pay some boy's fine out of her own pocket."

"My, my," Tory said slowly, "you are observant." He shrugged, continuing with his meal. "Well, then, what part would you cast me in?"

"I had several in mind the minute I saw you." Phil shook his head as he finished off his steak. "Now I'm not so sure. You're no fragile desert blossom." When her smile widened, he went on. "You could be if you wanted to, but you don't. You're no glossy sophisticate either. But that's a choice too." Taking the pie, he rose to join her on the bunk. "You know, there are a number of people out in this strange world who would love to have me as a captive audience while they recited their life's story."

"At least three of four," Tory agreed dryly.

"You're rough on my ego, Sheriff." He tasted the pie, approved, then offered her the next bite. Tory opened her mouth, allowing herself to be fed. It was tangy, spicy and still warm.

"What do you want to know?" she asked, then swallowed.

"Why you're tossing men in jail instead of breaking their hearts."

Her laugh was full of appreciation as she leaned her head back against the wall. Still, she wavered a moment. It had been so long, she mused, since she'd been able just to talk to someone—to a man. He was interesting and, she thought, at the moment harmless.

"I grew up here," she said simply.

"But you didn't stay." When she sent him a quizzical look, he fed her another bite of pie. It occurred to him that it had been a long time since he'd been with a woman who didn't want or even expect anything from him. "You've got too much polish, Victoria," he said, finding her name flowed well on his tongue. "You didn't acquire it in Friendly."

"Harvard," she told him, rounding her tones. "Law."

"Ah." Phil sent her an approving nod. "That fits. I can

see you with a leather briefcase and a pin-striped suit. Why aren't you practicing?"

"I am. I have an office in Albuquerque." Her brows drew together. "A pin-striped suit?"

"Gray, very discreet. How can you practice law in Albuquerque and uphold it in Friendly?" He pushed the hair from her shoulder in a casual gesture that neither of them noticed.

"I'm not taking any new cases for a while, so my workload's fairly light." She shrugged it off. "I handle what I can on paper and make a quick trip back when I have to."

"Are you a good lawyer?"

Tory grinned. "I'm a terrific lawyer, Kincaid, but I can't represent you—unethical."

He shoved another bite of pie at her. "So what are you doing back in Friendly?"

"You really are nosy, aren't you?"

"Yes."

She laughed. "My father was sheriff here for years and years." A sadness flickered briefly into her eyes and was controlled. "I suppose in his own quiet way he held the town together—such as it is. When he died, nobody knew just what to do. It sounds strange, but in a town this size, one person can make quite a difference, and he was…a special kind of man."

The wound hasn't healed yet, he thought, watching her steadily. He wondered, but didn't ask, how long ago her father had died.

"Anyway, the mayor asked me to fill in until things settled down again, and since I had to stay around to straighten a few things out anyway, I agreed. Nobody wanted the job except Merle, and he's…" She gave a quick, warm laugh. "Well, he's not ready. I know the law, I know the town. In a few months they'll hold an election. My name won't be on the ballot." She shot him a look. "Did I satisfy your curiosity?"

Under the harsh overhead lights, her skin was flawless, her eyes sharply green. Phil found himself reaching for her hair again. "No," he murmured. Though his eyes never left hers, Tory felt as though he looked at all of her—slowly and with great care. Quite unexpectedly her mouth went dry. She rose.

"It should have," she said lightly as she began to pack up the dirty dishes. "Next time we have dinner, I'll expect your life story." When she felt his hand on her arm, she stopped. Tory glanced down at the fingers curled around her arm, then slowly lifted her eyes to his. "Kincaid," she said softly, "you're in enough trouble."

"I'm already in jail," he pointed out as he turned her to face him.

"The term of your stay can easily be lengthened."

Knowing he should resist and that he couldn't, Phil drew her into his arms. "How much time can I get for making love to the sheriff?"

"What you're going to get is a broken rib if you don't let me go." *Miscalculation,* her mind stated bluntly. This man is never harmless. On the tail of that came the thought of how wonderful it felt to be held against him. His mouth was very close and very tempting. And it simply wasn't possible to forget their positions.

"Tory," he murmured. "I like the way that sounds." Running his fingers up her spine, he caught them in her hair. With her pressed tight against him, he could feel her faint quiver of response. "I think I'm going to have to have you."

A struggle wasn't going to work, she decided, any more than threats. As her own blood began to heat, Tory knew she had to act quickly. Tilting her head back slightly, she lifted a disdainful brow. "Hasn't a woman ever turned you down before, Kincaid?"

She saw his eyes flash in anger, felt the fingers in her hair tighten. Tory forced herself to remain still and relaxed. Excitement shivered through her, and resolutely she ignored it. His thighs were pressed hard against hers; the arms wrapped around her waist were tense with muscle. The firm male feel of him appealed to her, while the temper in his eyes warned her not to miscalculate again. They remained close for one long throbbing moment.

Phil's fingers relaxed before he stepped back to measure her. "There'll be another time," he said quietly. "Another place."

With apparent calm, Tory began gathering the dishes again. Her heart was thudding at the base of her throat. "You'll get the same answer."

"The hell I will."

Annoyed, she turned to see him watching her. With his hands in his pockets he rocked back gently on his heels. His eyes belied the casual stance. "Stick with your bubble-headed blondes," she advised coolly. "They photograph so well, clinging to your arm."

She was angry, he realized suddenly, and much more moved by him than she had pretended. Seeing his advantage, Phil approached her again. "You ever take off that badge, Sheriff?"

Tory kept her eyes level. "Occasionally."

Phil lowered his gaze, letting it linger on the small star. "When?"

Sensing that she was being outmaneuvered, Tory answered cautiously. "That's irrelevant."

When he lifted his eyes back to hers, he was smiling. "It won't be." He touched a finger to her full bottom lip. "I'm going to spend a lot of time tasting that beautiful mouth of yours."

Disturbed, Tory stepped back. "I'm afraid you won't have the opportunity or the time."

"I'm going to find the opportunity and the time to make love with you several times—" He sent her a mocking grin. "—Sheriff."

As he had anticipated, her eyes lit with fury. "You conceited fool," she said in a low voice. "You really think you're irresistible."

"Sure I do." He continued to grin maddeningly. "Don't you?"

"I think you're a spoiled, egotistical ass."

His temper rose, but Phil controlled it. If he lost it, he'd lose his advantage. He stepped closer, keeping a bland smile on his face. "Do you? Is that a legal opinion or a personal one?"

Tory tossed back her head, fuming. "My personal opinion is—"

He cut her off with a hard, bruising kiss.

Taken completely by surprise, Tory didn't struggle. By the time she had gathered her wits, she was too involved to attempt it. His mouth seduced hers expertly, parting her lips so that he could explore deeply and at his leisure. She responded out of pure pleasure. His mouth was hard, then soft—gentle, then demanding. He took her on a brisk roller coaster of sensation. Before she could recover from the first breathtaking plunge, they were climbing again. She held on to him, waiting for the next burst of speed.

He took his tongue lightly over hers, then withdrew it, tempting her to follow. Recklessly, she did, learning the secrets and dark tastes of his mouth. For a moment he allowed her to take the lead; then, cupping the back of her head in his hand, he crushed her lips with one last driving force. He wanted her weak and limp and totally conquered.

When he released her, Tory stood perfectly still, trying to remember what had happened. The confusion in her eyes gave him enormous pleasure. "I plead guilty, Your Honor," he drawled as he dropped back onto the bunk. "And it was worth it."

Hot, raging fury replaced every other emotion. Storming over to him, she grabbed him by the shirt front. Phil didn't resist, but grinned.

"Police brutality," he reminded her. She cursed him fluently, and with such effortless style, he was unable to conceal his admiration. "Did you learn that at Harvard?" he asked when she paused for breath.

Tory released him with a jerk and whirled to scoop up the hamper. The cell door shut behind her with a furious clang. Without pausing, she stormed out of the office.

Still grinning, Phil lay back on the bunk and pulled

out a cigarette. She'd won round one, he told himself. But he'd taken round two. Blowing out a lazy stream of smoke, he began to speculate on the rematch.

Chapter 3

When the alarm shrilled, Tory knocked it off the small table impatiently. It clattered to the floor and continued to shrill. She buried her head under the pillow. She wasn't at her best in the morning. The noisy alarm vibrated against the floor until she reached down in disgust and slammed it off. After a good night's sleep she was inclined to be cranky. After a poor one she was dangerous.

Most of the past night had been spent tossing and turning. The scene with Phil had infuriated her, not only because he had won, but because she had fully enjoyed that one moment of mindless pleasure. Rolling onto her back, Tory kept the pillow over her face to block out the sunlight. The worst part was, she mused, he was going to get away with it. She couldn't in all conscience use the law to punish him for something that had been strictly personal. It had been her own fault for lowering her guard and inviting the consequences. And she had enjoyed talking with him, sparring with someone quick with words. She missed matching wits with a man.

But that was no excuse, she reminded herself. He'd made her forget her duty…and he'd enjoyed it. Disgusted, Tory tossed the pillow aside, then winced at the brilliant sunlight. She'd learned how to evade an advance as a teenager. What had caused her to slip up this time? She didn't want to dwell on it. Grumpily she dragged herself from the cot and prepared to dress.

Every muscle in his body ached. Phil stretched out his legs to their full length and gave a low groan. He was willing to swear Tory had put the lumps in the mattress for his benefit. Cautiously opening one eye, he stared at the man in the next cell. The man slept on, as he had from the moment Tory had dumped him on the bunk the night before. He snored outrageously. When she had dragged him in, Phil had been amused. The man was twice her weight and had been blissfully drunk. He'd called her "good old Tory," and she had cursed him halfheartedly as she had maneuvered him into the cell. Thirty minutes after hearing the steady snoring, Phil had lost his sense of humor.

She hadn't spoken a word to him. With a detached interest Phil had watched her struggle with the drunk. It had pleased him to observe that she was still fuming. She'd been in and out of the office several times before midnight, then had locked up in the same frigid silence. He'd enjoyed that, but then had made a fatal error: When she had gone into the back room to bed, he had tortured himself by watching her shadow play on the wall as she had undressed. That, combined with an impossible mattress and a snoring drunk-and-disorderly, had led to an uneasy night. He hadn't awakened in the best of moods.

Sitting up with a wince, he glared at the unconscious man in the next cell. His wide, flushed face was cherubic, ringed with a curling blond circle of hair. Ruefully, Phil rubbed a hand over his own chin and felt the rough stubble. A fastidious man, he was annoyed at not having a razor, a hot shower or a fresh set of clothes. Rising, he determined to gain access to all three immediately.

"Tory!" His voice was curt, one of a man accustomed to being listened to. He received no response. "Damn it, Tory, get out here!" He rattled the bars, wishing belligerently that he'd kept the tin cup. He could have made enough noise with it to wake even the stuporous man in the next cell. "Tory, get out of that bed and come here." He swore, promising himself he'd never allow anyone to lock him in anything again. "When I get out…" he began.

Tory came shuffling in, carrying a pot of water. "Button up, Kincaid."

"You listen to me," he retorted. "I want a shower and a razor and my clothes. And if—"

"If you don't shut up until I've had my coffee, you're going to take your shower where you stand." She lifted the pot of water meaningfully. "You can get cleaned up as soon as Merle gets in." She went to the coffeepot and began to clatter.

"You're an arrogant wretch when you've got a man caged," he said darkly.

"I'm an arrogant wretch anyway. Do yourself a favor, Kincaid, don't start a fight until I've had two cups. I'm not a nice person in the morning."

"I'm warning you." His voice was as low and dangerous as his mood. "You're going to regret locking me in here."

Turning, she looked at him for the first time that morning. His clothes and hair were disheveled. The clean lines of his aristocratic face were shadowed by the night's growth of beard. Fury was in his stance and in the cool water-blue of his eyes. He looked outrageously attractive.

"I think I'm going to regret letting you out," she muttered before she turned back to the coffee. "Do you want some of this, or are you just going to throw it at me?"

The idea was tempting, but so was the scent of the coffee. "Black," he reminded her shortly.

Tory drained half a cup, ignoring her scalded tongue before she went to Phil. "What do you want for breakfast?" she asked as she passed the cup through the bars.

He scowled at her. "A shower, and a sledgehammer for your friend over there."

Tory cast an eye in the next cell. "Silas'll wake up in an hour, fresh as a daisy." She swallowed more coffee. "Keep you up?"

"Him and the feather bed you provided."

She shrugged. "Crime doesn't pay."

"I'm going to strangle you when I get out of here," he promised over the rim of his cup. "Slowly and with great pleasure."

"That isn't the way to get your shower." She turned

as the door opened and Tod came in. He stood hesi-
tantly at the door, jamming his hands in his pockets.
"Good morning." She smiled and beckoned him in.
"You're early."

"You didn't say what time." He came warily, shifting
his eyes from Phil to Silas and back to Phil again. "You
got prisoners."

"Yes, I do." Catching her tongue between her teeth, she
jerked a thumb at Phil. "This one's a nasty character."

"What's he in for?"

"Insufferable arrogance."

"He didn't kill anybody, did he?"

"Not yet," Phil muttered, then added, unable to resist
the eager gleam in the boy's eyes, "I was framed."

"They all say that, don't they, Sheriff?"

"Absolutely." She lifted a hand to ruffle the boy's
hair. Startled, he jerked and stared at her. Ignoring his
reaction, she left her hand on his shoulder. "Well, I'll put
you to work, then. There's a broom in the back room.
You can start sweeping up. Have you had breakfast?"

"No, but—"

"I'll bring you something when I take care of this
guy. Think you can keep an eye on things for me for a
few minutes?"

His mouth fell open in astonishment. "Yes, ma'am!"

"Okay, you're in charge." She headed for the door,
grabbing her hat on the way. "If Silas wakes up, you can
let him out. The other guy stays where he is. Got it?"

"Sure thing, Sheriff." He sent Phil a cool look. "He
won't pull nothing on me."

Stifling a laugh, Tory walked outside.

Resigned to the wait, Phil leaned against the bars and drank his coffee while the boy went to work with the broom. He worked industriously, casting furtive glances over his shoulder at Phil from time to time. He's a good-looking boy, Phil mused. He brooded over his reaction to Tory's friendly gesture, wondering how he would react to a man.

"Live in town?" Phil ventured.

Tod paused, eyeing him warily. "Outside."

"On a ranch?"

He began to sweep again, but more slowly. "Yeah."

"Got any horses?"

The boy shrugged. "Couple." He was working his way cautiously over to the cell. "You're not from around here," he said.

"No, I'm from California."

"No, kidding?" Impressed, Tod sized him up again. "You don't look like such a bad guy," he decided.

"Thanks." Phil grinned into his cup.

"How come you're in jail, then?"

Phil pondered over the answer and settled for the unvarnished truth. "I lost my temper."

Tod gave a snort of laughter and continued sweeping. "You can't go to jail for that. My pa loses his all the time."

"Sometimes you can." He studied the boy's profile. "Especially if you hurt someone."

The boy passed the broom over the floor without much regard for dust. "Did you?"

"Just myself," Phil admitted ruefully. "I got the sheriff mad at me."

"Zac Kramer said he don't hold with no woman sheriff."

Phil laughed at that, recalling how easily a woman sheriff had gotten him locked in a cell. "Zac Kramer doesn't sound very smart to me."

Tod sent Phil a swift, appealing grin. "I heard she went to their place yesterday. The twins have to wash all Old Man Hollister's windows, inside and out. For free."

Tory breezed back in with two covered plates. "Breakfast," she announced. "He give you any trouble?" she asked Tod as she set a plate on her desk.

"No, ma'am." The scent of food made his mouth water, but he bent back to his task.

"Okay, sit down and eat."

He shot her a doubtful look. "Me?"

"Yes, you." Carrying the other plate, she walked over to get the keys. "When you and Mr. Kincaid have finished, run the dishes back to the hotel." Without waiting for a response, she unlocked Phil's cell. But Phil watched the expression on Tod's face as he started at his breakfast.

"Sheriff," Phil murmured, taking her hand, rather than the plate she held out to him, "you're a very classy lady." Lifting her hand, he kissed her fingers lightly.

Unable to resist, she allowed her hand to rest in his a moment. "Phil," she said on a sigh, "don't be disarming; you'll complicate things."

His brow lifted in surprise as he studied her. "You know," he said slowly, "I think it's already too late."

Tory shook her head, denying it. "Eat your breakfast," she ordered briskly. "Merle will be coming by with your clothes soon."

When she turned to leave, he held her hand another moment. "Tory," he said quietly, "you and I aren't finished yet."

Carefully she took her hand from his. "You and I never started," she corrected, then closed the door of the cell with a resolute clang. As she headed back to the coffeepot she glanced at Tod. The boy was making his way through bacon and eggs without any trouble.

"Aren't you eating?" Phil asked her as he settled down to his own breakfast.

"I'll never understand how anyone can eat at this hour," Tory muttered, fortifying herself on coffee. "Tod, the sheriff's car could use a wash. Can you handle it?"

"Sure thing, Sheriff." He was half out of the chair before Tory put a restraining hand on his shoulder.

"Eat first," she told him with a chuckle. "If you finish up the sweeping and the car, that should do it for today." She sat on the corner of the desk, enjoying his appetite. "Your parents know where you are?" she asked casually.

"I finished my chores before I left," he mumbled with a full mouth.

"Hmmm." She said nothing more, sipping instead at her coffee. When the door opened, she glanced over, expecting to see Merle. Instead she was struck dumb.

"Lou!" Phil was up and holding on to the bars. "It's about time."

"Well, Phil, you look very natural."

Lou Sherman, Tory thought, sincerely awed. One of the top attorneys in the country. She'd followed his cases, studied his style, used his precedents. He looked just as commanding in person as in any newspaper or magazine picture she'd ever seen of him. He was a huge man, six foot four, with a stocky frame and a wild thatch of white hair. His voice had resonated in courtrooms for more than forty years. He was tenacious, flamboyant and feared. For the moment Tory could only stare at the figure striding into her office in a magnificent pearl-gray suit and baby-pink shirt.

Phil called him an uncomplimentary name, which made him laugh loudly. "You'd better have some respect if you want me to get you out of there, son." His eyes slid to Phil's half-eaten breakfast. "Finish eating," he advised, "while I talk to the sheriff." Turning, he gazed solemnly from Tory to Tod. "One of you the sheriff?"

Tory hadn't found her voice yet. Tod jerked his head at her. "She is," he stated with his mouth still full.

Lou let his eyes drift down to her badge. "Well, so she is," he said genially. "Best-looking law person I've seen... No offense," he added with a wide grin.

Remembering herself, Tory rose and extended her hand. "Victoria Ashton, Mr. Sherman. It's a pleasure to meet you."

"My pleasure, Sheriff Ashton," he corrected with a great deal of charm. "Tell me, what's the kid done now?"

"Lou—" Phil began, and got an absent wave of the hand from his attorney.

"Finish your eggs," he ordered. "I gave up a perfectly good golf date to fly over here. Sheriff?" he added with a questioning lift of brow.

"Mr. Kincaid was stopped for speeding on Highway Seventeen," Tory began. "When he refused to sign the ticket, my deputy brought him in." After Lou's heavy sigh she continued. "I'm afraid Mr. Kincaid wasn't cooperative."

"Never is," Lou agreed apologetically.

"Damn it, Lou, would you just get me out of here?"

"All in good time," he promised without looking at him. "Are there any other charges, Sheriff?"

"Resisting arrest," she stated, not quite disguising a grin. "The fine is two hundred and fifty, bail set at five hundred. Mr. Kincaid, when he decided to…cooperate, was a bit short of funds."

Lou rubbed a hand over his chin. The large ruby on his pinky glinted dully. "Wouldn't be the first time," he mused.

Incensed at being ignored and defamed at the same time, Phil interrupted tersely. "She pulled a gun on me."

This information was met with another burst of loud laughter from his attorney. "Damn, I wish I'd been here to see his face."

"It was worth the price of a ticket," Tory admitted.

Phil started to launch into a stream of curses, remembered the boy—who was listening avidly—and ground his teeth instead. "Lou," he said slowly, "are you going to get me out or stand around exchanging small talk all day? I haven't had a shower since yesterday."

"Very fastidious," Lou told Tory. "Gets it from his father. I got him out of a tight squeeze or two as I recall. There was this little town in New Jersey… Ah, well, that's another story. I'd like to consult with my client, Sheriff Ashton."

"Of course." Tory retrieved the keys.

"Ashton," Lou murmured, closing his eyes for a

moment. "Victoria Ashton. There's something about that name." He stroked his chin. "Been sheriff here long?"

Tory shook her head as she started to unlock Phil's cell. "No, actually I'm just filling in for a while."

"She's a lawyer," Phil said disgustedly.

"That's it!" Lou gave her a pleased look. "I knew the name was familiar. The Dunbarton case. You did a remarkable job."

"Thank you."

"Had your troubles with Judge Withers," he recalled, flipping through his memory file. "Contempt of court. What was it you called him?"

"A supercilious humbug," Tory said with a wince.

Lou chuckled delightedly. "Wonderful choice of words."

"It cost me a night in jail," she recalled.

"Still, you won the case."

"Luckily the judge didn't hold a grudge."

"Skill and hard work won you that one," Lou disagreed. "Where did you study?"

"Harvard."

"Look," Phil interrupted testily. "You two can discuss this over drinks later."

"Manners, Phil, you've always had a problem with manners." Lou smiled at Tory again. "Excuse me, Sheriff. Well, Phil, give me one of those corn muffins there and tell me your troubles."

Tory left them in privacy just as Merle walked in, carrying Phil's suitcase. Dynamite wandered in behind him, found his spot on the floor and instantly went to sleep. "Just leave that by the desk," Tory told Merle.

"After Kincaid's taken care of, I'm going out to the house for a while. You won't be able to reach me for two hours."

"Okay." He glanced at the still-snoring Silas. "Should I kick him out?"

"When he wakes up." She looked over at Tod. "Tod's going to wash my car."

Stuffing in the last bite, Tod scrambled up. "I'll do it now." He dashed out the front door.

Tory frowned after him. "Merle, what do you know about Tod's father?"

He shrugged and scratched at his mustache. "Swanson keeps to himself, raises some cattle couple miles north of town. Been in a couple of brawls, but nothing important."

"His mother?"

"Quiet lady. Does some cleaning work over at the hotel now and again. You remember the older brother, don't you? He lit out a couple years ago. Never heard from him since."

Tory absorbed this with a thoughtful nod. "Keep an eye out for the boy when I'm not around, okay?"

"Sure. He in trouble?"

"I'm not certain." She frowned a moment, then her expression relaxed again. "Just keep your eyes open, Merle T.," she said, smiling at him affectionately. "Why don't you go see if the kid's found a bucket? I don't think it would take much persuasion to get him to wash your car too."

Pleased with the notion, Merle strode out again.

"Sheriff"—Tory turned back to the cell as Lou came out—"my client tells me you also serve as justice of the peace?"

"That's right, Mr. Sherman."

"In that case, I'd like to plead temporary insanity on the part of my client."

"You're cute, Lou," Phil muttered from the cell door. "Can I take that shower now?" he demanded, indicating his suitcase.

"In the back," Tory told him. "You need a shave," she added sweetly.

He picked up the case, giving her a long look. "Sheriff, when this is all over, you and I have some personal business."

Tory lifted her half-finished coffee. "Don't cut your throat, Kincaid."

Lou waited until Phil had disappeared into the back room. "He's a good boy," he said with a paternal sigh. Tory burst out laughing.

"Oh, no," she said definitely, "he's not."

"Well, it was worth a try." He shrugged it off and settled his enormous bulk into a chair. "About the charge of resisting arrest," he began. "I'd really hate for it to go on his record. A night in jail was quite a culture shock for our Phillip, Victoria."

"Agreed." She smiled. "I believe that charge could be dropped if Mr. Kincaid pays the speeding fine."

"I've advised him to do so," Lou told her, pulling out a thick cigar. "He doesn't like it, but I'm…" He studied the cigar like a lover. "Persuasive," he decided. He shot her an admiring look. "So are you. What kind of a gun?"

Tory folded her hands primly. "A .45."

Lou laughed heartily as he lit his cigar. "Now, tell me about the Dunbarton case, Victoria."

* * *

The horse kicked up a cloud of brown dust. Responding to Tory's command, he broke into an easy gallop. Air, as dry as the land around them, whipped by them in a warm rush. The hat Tory had worn to shield herself from the sun lay on the back of her neck, forgotten. Her movements were so attuned to the horse, she was barely conscious of his movements beneath her. Tory wanted to think, but first she wanted to clear her mind. Since childhood, riding had been her one sure way of doing so.

Sports had no appeal for her. She saw no sense in hitting or chasing a ball around some court or course. It took too much energy. She might swim a few laps now and again, but found it much more agreeable to float on a raft. Sweating in a gym was laughable. But riding was a different category. Tory didn't consider it exercise or effort. She used it now, as she had over the years, as a way to escape from her thoughts for a short time.

For thirty minutes she rode without any thought of destination. Gradually she slowed the horse to a walk, letting her hands relax on the reins. He would turn, she knew, and head back to the ranch.

Phillip Kincaid. He shot back into her brain. A nuisance, Tory decided. One that should be over. At the moment he should already be back on his way to L.A. Tory dearly hoped so. She didn't like to admit that he had gotten to her. It was unfortunate that despite their clash, despite his undeniable arrogance, she had liked him. He was interesting and funny and sharp. It was difficult to dislike someone who could laugh at himself. There would be no problem if it ended there.

Feeling the insistent beat of the sun on her head, Tory absently replaced her hat. It hadn't ended there because there had been that persistent attraction. That was strictly man to woman, and she hadn't counted on it when she had tossed him in jail. He'd outmaneuvered her once. That was annoying, but the result had been much deeper. When was the last time she had completely forgotten herself in a man's arms? When was the last time she had spent most of the night thinking about a man? Had she ever? Tory let out a deep breath, then frowned at the barren, stone-colored landscape.

No, her reaction had been too strong for comfort— and the fact that she was still thinking about him disturbed her. A woman her age didn't dwell on one kiss that way. Yet, she could still remember exactly how his mouth had molded to hers, how the dark, male taste of him had seeped into her. With no effort at all, she could feel the way his body had fit against hers, strong and hard. It didn't please her.

There were enough problems to be dealt with during her stay in Friendly, Tory reminded herself, without dwelling on a chance encounter with some bad-tempered Hollywood type. She'd promised to ease the town through its transition to a new sheriff; there was the boy, Tod, on her mind. And her mother. Tory closed her eyes for a moment. She had yet to come to terms with her mother.

So many things had been said after her father's death. So many things had been left unsaid. For a woman who was rarely confused, Tory found herself in a turmoil whenever she dealt with her mother. As long as her father had been alive, he'd been the buffer between them. Now, with him gone, they were faced with each other. With a wry laugh Tory decided her mother was just as baffled as she was. The strain between them wasn't lessening, and the distance was growing. With a shake of her head she decided to let it lie. In a few months Tory would be back in Albuquerque and that would be that. She had her life to live, her mother had hers.

The wise thing to do, she mused, was to develop the same attitude toward Phil Kincaid. Their paths weren't likely to cross again. She had purposely absented herself from town for a few hours to avoid him. Tory made a face at the admission. No, she didn't want to see him again. He was trouble. It was entirely too easy for him to be charming when he put his mind to it. And she was wise enough to recognize determination when she saw it. For whatever reason—pique or attraction—he wanted her. He wouldn't be an easy man to handle. Under most circumstances Tory might have enjoyed pitting her will against his, but something warned her not to press her luck.

"The sooner he's back in Tinsel Town, the better," she muttered, then pressed her heels against the horse's sides. They were off at a full gallop.

Phil pulled his car to a halt beside the corral and glanced around. A short distance to the right was a small white-framed house. It was a very simple structure, two stories high, with a wide wooden porch. On the side was a clothesline with a few things baking dry in the sun. There were a few spots of color from flowers in pottery pots on either side of the steps. The grass was short and parched. One of the window screens was torn. In the background he could see a few outbuildings and what appeared to be the beginnings of a vegetable garden. Tory's sheriff's car was parked in front, freshly washed but already coated with a thin film of dust.

Something about the place appealed to him. It was isolated and quiet. Without the car in front, it might fit into any time frame in the past century. There had been some efforts to keep it neat, but it would never be prosperous. He would consider it more a homestead than a ranch. With the right lighting, he mused, it could be very effective. Climbing out of the car, Phil moved to the right to study it from a different angle. When he heard the low drum of hoofs, he turned and watched Tory approach.

He forgot the house immediately and swore at his lack of a camera. She was perfect. Under the merciless sun she rode a palamino the shade of new gold. Nothing could have been a better contrast for a woman of her coloring. With her hat again at her back, her hair flew freely. She sat straight, her movements in perfect timing with the horse's. Phil narrowed his eyes and saw them in slow motion. That was how he would film it—with her hair lifting, holding for a moment before it fell again. The dust would hang in the air behind them. The horse's strong legs would fold and unfold so that the viewer could see each muscle work. This was strength and beauty and a mastery of rider over horse. He wished he could see her hands holding the reins.

He knew the moment she became aware of him. The

rhythm never faltered, but there was a sudden tension in the set of her shoulders. It made him smile. No, we're not through yet, he thought to himself. Not nearly through. Leaning against the corral fence, he waited for her.

Tory brought the palamino to a stop with a quick tug of reins. Remaining in the saddle, she gave Phil a long, silent look. Casually he took sunglasses out of his pocket and slipped them on. The gesture annoyed her. "Kincaid," she said coolly.

"Sheriff," he returned.

"Is there a problem?"

He smiled slowly. "I don't think so."

Tory tossed her hair behind her shoulder, trying to disguise the annoyance she felt at finding him there. "I thought you'd be halfway to L.A. by now."

"Did you?"

With a sound of impatience she dismounted. The saddle creaked with the movement as she brought one slim leg over it, then vaulted lightly to the ground. Keeping the reins in her hand, she studied him a moment. "I assume your fine's been paid. You know the other charges were dropped."

"Yes."

She tilted her head. "Well?"

"Well," he returned amiably, amused at the temper that shot into her eyes. Yes, I'm getting to you, Victoria, he thought, and I haven't even started yet.

Deliberately she turned away to uncinch the saddle. "Has Mr. Sherman gone?"

"No, he's discussing flies and lures with the mayor." Phil grinned. "Lou found a fishing soulmate."

"I see." Tory hefted the saddle from the palamino, then set it on the fence. "Then you discussed your business with the mayor this morning."

"We came to an amicable agreement," Phil replied, watching as she slipped the bit from the horse's mouth. "He'll give you the details."

Without speaking, Tory gave the horse a slap on the flank, sending him inside the corral. The gate gave a long creak as she shut it. She turned then to face Phil directly. "Why should he?"

"You'll want to know the schedule and so forth before the filming starts."

Her brows drew together. "I beg your pardon."

"I came to New Mexico scouting out a location for my new movie. I needed a tired little town in the middle of nowhere."

Tory studied him for a full ten seconds. "And you found it," she said flatly.

"Thanks to you." He smiled, appreciating the irony. "We'll start next month."

Sticking her hands in her back pockets, Tory turned to walk a short distance away. "Wouldn't it be simpler to shoot in a studio or in a lot?"

"No."

At his flat answer she turned back again. "I don't like it."

"I didn't think you would." He moved over to join her. "But you're going to live with it for the better part of the summer."

"You're going to bring your cameras and your people and your confusion into town," she began angrily.

"Friendly runs at its own pace; now you want to bring in a lifestyle most of these people can't even imagine."

"We'll give very sedate orgies, Sheriff," he promised with a grin. He laughed at the fury that leaped to her eyes. "Tory, you're not a fool. We're not coming to party; we're coming to work. Keep an actor out in this sun for ten takes, he's not going to be disturbing the peace at night: He's going to be unconscious." He caught a strand of her hair and twisted it around his finger. "Or do you believe everything you read in *Inside Scoop?*"

She swiped his hand away in an irritated gesture. "I know more about Hollywood than you know about Friendly," she retorted. "I've spent some time in L.A., represented a screenwriter in an assault case. Got him off," she added wryly. "A few years ago I dated an actor, went to a few parties when I was on the coast." She shook her head. "The gossip magazines might exaggerate, Phil, but the values and lifestyle come through loud and clear."

He lifted a brow. "Judgmental, Tory?"

"Maybe," she agreed. "But this is my town. I'm responsible for the people and for the peace. If you go ahead with this, I warn you, one of your people gets out of line, he goes to jail."

His eyes narrowed. "We have our own security."

"Your security answers to me in my town," she tossed back. "Remember it."

"Not going to cooperate, are you?"

"Not any more than I have to."

For a moment they stood measuring each other in silence. Behind them the palamino paced restlessly around the corral. A fleeting, precious breeze came up to stir the heat and dust. "All right," Phil said at length, "let's say you stay out of my way, I'll stay out of yours."

"Perfect," Tory agreed, and started to walk away. Phil caught her arm.

"That's professionally," he added.

As she had in his cell, Tory gave the hand on her arm a long look before she raised her eyes to his. This time Phil smiled.

"You're not wearing your badge now, Tory." Reaching up, he drew off his sunglasses, then hooked them over the corral fence. "And we're not finished."

"Kincaid—"

"Phil," he corrected, drawing her deliberately into his arms. "I thought of you last night when I was lying in that damned cell. I promised myself something."

Tory stiffened. Her palms pressed against his chest, but she didn't struggle. Physically he was stronger, she reasoned. She had to rely on her wits. "Your thoughts and your promises aren't my problem," she replied coolly. "Whether I'm wearing my badge or not, I'm still sheriff, and you're annoying me. I can be mean when I'm annoyed."

"I'll just bet you can be," he murmured. Even had he wanted to, he couldn't prevent his eyes from lingering on her mouth. "I'm going to have you, Victoria," he said softly. "Sooner or later." Slowly he brought his eyes back to hers. "I always keep my promises."

"I believe I have something to say about this one."

His smile was confident. "Say no," he whispered before his mouth touched hers. She started to jerk back, but he was quick. His hand cupped the back of her head and kept her still. His mouth was soft and persuasive. Long before the stiffness left her, he felt the pounding of her heart against his. Patiently he rubbed his lips over hers, teasing, nibbling. Tory let out an unsteady breath as her fingers curled into his shirt.

He smelled of soap, a fragrance that was clean and sharp. Unconsciously she breathed it in as he drew her closer. Her arms had found their way around his neck. Her body was straining against his, no longer stiff but eager. The mindless pleasure was back, and she surrendered to it. She heard his quiet moan before his lips left hers, but before she could protest, he pressed them to her throat. He was murmuring something neither of them understood as his mouth began to explore. The desperation came suddenly, as if it had been waiting to take them both unaware. His mouth was back on hers with a quick savageness that she anticipated.

She felt the scrape of his teeth and answered by nipping into his bottom lip. The hands at her hips dragged her closer, tormenting both of them. Passion flowed between them so acutely that avid, seeking lips weren't enough. He ran his hands up her sides, letting his thumbs find their way between their clinging bodies to stroke her breasts. She responded by diving deep into his mouth and demanding more.

Tory felt everything with impossible clarity: the soft, thin material of her shirt rubbing against the straining points of her breasts as his thumbs pressed against her; the heat of his mouth as it roamed wildly over her face, then back to hers; the vibration of two heartbeats.

He hadn't expected to feel this degree of need. Attraction and challenge, but not pain. It wasn't what he had planned—it wasn't what he wanted, and yet, he couldn't stop. She was filling his mind, crowding his senses. Her hair was too soft, her scent too alluring. And her taste…her taste too exotic. Greedily, he devoured her while her passion drove him further into her.

He knew he had to back away, but he lingered a moment longer. Her body was so sleek and lean, her mouth so incredibly agile. Phil allowed himself to stroke her once more, one last bruising contact of lips before he dragged himself away.

They were both shaken and both equally determined not to admit it. Tory felt her pulse hammering at every point in her body. Because her knees were trembling, she stood very straight. Phil waited a moment, wanting to be certain he could speak. Reaching over, he retrieved his sunglasses and put them back on. They were some defense; a better one was to put some distance between them until he found his control.

"You didn't say no," he commented.

Tory stared at him, warning herself not to think until later. "I didn't say yes," she countered.

He smiled. "Oh, yes," he corrected, "you did. I'll be back," he added before he strode to his car.

Driving away, he glanced in his rearview mirror to see her standing where he had left her. As he punched in his cigarette lighter he saw his hand was shaking. Round three, he thought on a long breath, was a draw.

Chapter 4

Tory stood exactly where she was until even the dust kicked up by Phil's tires had settled. She had thought she knew the meaning of passion, need, excitement. Suddenly the words had taken on a new meaning. For the first time in her life she had been seized by something that her mind couldn't control. The hunger had been so acute, so unexpected. It throbbed through her still, like an ache, as she stared down the long flat road, which was now deserted. How was it possible to need so badly, so quickly? And how was it, she wondered, that a woman who had always handled men with such casual ease could be completely undone by a kiss?

Tory shook her head and made herself turn away from the road Phil had taken. None of it was characteristic. It was almost as if she had been someone else for a moment—someone whose strength and weakness could be drawn out and manipulated. And yet, even now, when she had herself under control, there was something inside her fighting to be recognized. She was going to have to take some time and think about this carefully.

Hoisting the saddle, Tory carried it toward the barn. *I'll be back.* Phil's last words echoed in her ears and sent an odd thrill over her skin. Scowling, Tory pushed open the barn door. It was cooler inside, permeated with the pungent scent of animals and hay. It was a scent of her childhood, one she barely noticed even when returning after months away from it. It never occurred to her to puzzle over why she was as completely at home there as she was in a tense courtroom or at a sophisticated party. After replacing the tack, she paced the concrete floor a moment and began to dissect the problem.

Phil Kincaid was the problem; the offshoots were her strong attraction to him, his effect on her and the fact that he was coming back. The attraction, Tory decided, was unprecedented but not astonishing. He was appealing, intelligent, fun. Even his faults had a certain charm. If they had met under different circumstances, she could imagine them getting to know each other slowly, dating perhaps, enjoying a congenial relationship. Part of the spark, she mused, was due to the way they had met, and the fact that each was determined not to be outdone by the other. That made sense, she concluded, feeling better.

And if that made sense, she went on, it followed that his effect on her was intensified by circumstances. Logic was comfortable, so Tory pursued it. There was something undeniably attractive about a man who wouldn't take no for an answer. It might be annoying, even infuriating, but it was still exciting. Beneath the sheriff's badge and behind the Harvard diploma, Tory was a woman first and last. It didn't hurt when a man knew how to kiss the way Phil Kincaid knew how to kiss, she added wryly. Unable to resist, Tory ran the tip of her tongue over her lips. Oh, yes, she thought with a quick smile, the man was some terrific kisser.

Vaguely annoyed with herself, Tory wandered from the barn. The sun made her wince in defense as she headed for the house. Unconsciously killing time, she poked inside the henhouse. The hens were sleeping in the heat of the afternoon, their heads tucked under their wings. Tory left them alone, knowing her mother had gathered the eggs that morning.

The problem now was that he was coming back. She was going to have to deal with him—and with his own little slice of Hollywood, she added with a frown. At the moment Tory wasn't certain which disturbed her more. Damn, but she wished she'd known of Phil's plans. If she could have gotten to the mayor first… Tory stopped herself with a self-deprecating laugh. She would have changed absolutely nothing. As mayor, Bud Toomey would eat up the prestige of having a major film shot in his town. And as the owner of the one and only hotel, he must have heard the dollars clinking in his cash register.

Who could blame him? Tory asked herself. Her objections were probably more personal than professional in any case. The actor she had dated had been successful and slick, an experienced womanizer and hedonist. She knew too many of her prejudices lay at his feet.

She'd been very young when he'd shown her Holly-wood from his vantage point. But even without that, she reasoned, there was the disruption the filming would bring to Friendly, the effect on the townspeople and the very real possibility of property damage. As sheriff, all of it fell to her jurisdiction.

What would her father have done? she wondered as she stepped into the house. As always, the moment she was inside, memories of him assailed her—his big, booming voice, his laughter, his simple, man-of-the-earth logic. To Tory his presence was an intimate part of everything in the house, down to the hassock where he had habitually rested his feet after a long day.

The house was her mother's doing. There were the clean white walls in the living room, the sofa that had been re-covered again and again—this time it wore a tidy floral print. The rugs were straight and clean, the pictures carefully aligned. Even they had been chosen to blend in rather than to accent. Her mother's collection of cacti sat on the windowsill. The fragrance of a potpourri, her mother's mixture, wafted comfortably in the air. The floors and furniture were painstakingly clean, magazines neatly tucked away. A single geranium stood in a slender vase on a crocheted doily. All her mother's doing; yet, it was her father Tory thought of when she entered her childhood home. It always was.

But her father wouldn't come striding down the steps again. He wouldn't catch her to him for one of his bear hugs and noisy kisses. He'd been too young to die, Tory thought as she gazed around the room as though she were a stranger. Strokes were for old men, feeble men, not strapping men in their prime. There was no justice to it, she thought with the same impotent fury that hit her each time she came back. No justice for a man who had dedicated his life to justice. He should have had more time, might have had more time, if… Her thoughts broke off as she heard the quiet sounds coming from the kitchen.

Tory pushed away the pain. It was difficult enough to see her mother without remembering that last night in the hospital. She gave herself an extra moment to settle before she crossed to the kitchen.

Standing in the doorway, she watched as Helen relined the shelves in the kitchen cabinets. Her mother's consistent tidiness had been a sore point between them since Tory had been a girl. The woman she watched was tiny and blond, a youthful-looking fifty, with ladylike hands and a trim pink housedress. Tory knew the dress had been pressed and lightly starched. Her mother would smell faintly of soap and nothing else. Even physically Tory felt remote from her. Her looks, her temperament, had all come from her father. Tory could see nothing of herself in the woman who patiently lined shelves with dainty striped paper. They'd never been more than careful strangers to each other, more careful as the years passed. Tory kept a room at the hotel rather than at home for the same reason she kept her visits with her mother brief. Invariably their encounters ended badly.

"Mother."

Surprised, Helen turned. She didn't gasp or whirl at the intrusion, but simply faced Tory with one brow slightly lifted. "Tory. I thought I heard a car drive away."

"It was someone else."

"I saw you ride out." Helen straightened the paper meticulously. "There's lemonade in the refrigerator. It's a dry day." Without speaking, Tory fetched two glasses and added ice. "How are you, Tory?"

"Very well." She hated the stiffness but could do nothing about it. So much stood between them. Even as she poured the fresh lemonade from her mother's marigold-trimmed glass pitcher, she could remember the night of her father's death, the ugly words she had spoken, the ugly feelings she had not quite put to rest. They had never understood each other, never been close, but that night had brought a gap between them that neither knew how to bridge. It only seemed to grow wider with time.

Needing to break the silence, Tory spoke as she replaced the pitcher in the refrigerator. "Do you know anything about the Swansons?"

"The Swansons?" The question in Helen's voice was mild. She would never have asked directly. "They've lived outside of town for twenty years. They keep to themselves, though she's come to church a few times. I believe he has a difficult time making his ranch pay. The oldest son was a good-looking boy, about sixteen when he left." Helen replaced her everyday dishes on the shelf in tidy stacks, then closed the cupboard door. "That would have been about four years ago. The younger one seems rather sweet and painfully shy."

"Tod," Tory murmured.

"Yes." Helen read the concern but knew nothing about drawing people out, particularly her daughter. "I heard about Mr. Hollister's window."

Tory lifted her eyes briefly. Her mother's were a calm, deep brown. "The Kramer twins."

A suggestion of a smile flickered on her mother's lips. "Yes, of course."

"Do you know why the older Swanson boy left home?"

Helen picked up the drink Tory had poured her. But she didn't sit. "Rumor is that Mr. Swanson has a temper. Gossip is never reliable," she added before she drank.

"And often based in fact," Tory countered.

They fell into one of the stretches of silence that characteristically occurred during their visits. The refrigerator gave a loud click and began to hum. Helen carefully wiped away the ring of moisture her glass had made on the countertop.

"It seems Friendly is about to be immortalized on film," Tory began. At her mother's puzzled look she continued. "I had Phillip C. Kincaid in a cell overnight. Now it appears he's going to use Friendly as one of the location shoots for his latest film."

"Kincaid," Helen repeated, searching her mind slowly. "Oh, Marshall Kincaid's son."

Tory grinned despite herself. She didn't think Phil would appreciate that sort of recognition; it occurred to her simultaneously that it was a tag he must have fought all of his professional career. "Yes," she agreed thoughtfully. "He's a very successful director," she found herself saying, almost in defense, "with an impressive string of hits. He's been nominated for an Oscar three times."

Though Helen digested this, her thoughts were still on Tory's original statement. "Did you say you had him in jail?"

Tory shook off the mood and smiled a little. "Yes, I did. Traffic violation," she added with a shrug. "It got a little complicated...." Her voice trailed off as she remembered that stunning moment in his cell when his mouth had taken hers. "He's coming back," she murmured.

"To make a film?" Helen prompted, puzzled by her daughter's bemused expression.

"What? Yes," Tory said quickly. "Yes, he's going to do some filming here, I don't have the details yet. It seems he cleared it with the mayor this morning."

But not with you, Helen thought, but didn't say so. "How interesting."

"We'll see," Tory muttered. Suddenly restless, she rose to pace to the sink. The view from the window was simply a long stretch of barren ground that was somehow fascinating. Her father had loved it for what it was—stark and desolate.

Watching her daughter, Helen could remember her husband standing exactly the same way, looking out with exactly the same expression. She felt an intolerable wave of grief and controlled it. "Friendly will be buzzing about this for quite some time," she said briskly.

"It'll buzz all right," Tory muttered. But no one will think of the complications, she added to herself.

"Do you expect trouble?" her mother asked.

"I'll handle it."

"Always so sure of yourself, Tory."

Tory's shoulders stiffened automatically. "Am I, Mother?" Turning, she found her mother's eyes, calm and direct, on her. They had been just that calm, and just that direct, when she had told Tory she had requested her father's regulator be unplugged. Tory had seen no sorrow, no regret or indecision. There had been only the passive face and the matter-of-fact words. For that, more than anything else, Tory had never forgiven her.

As they watched each other in the sun-washed kitchen, each remembered clearly the garishly lit waiting room that smelled of old cigarettes and sweat. Each remembered the monotonous hum of the air conditioner and the click of feet on tile in the corridor outside....

"No!" Tory had whispered the word, then shouted it. "No, you can't! You can't just let him die!"

"He's already gone, Tory," Helen had said flatly. "You have to accept it."

"No!" After weeks of seeing her father lying motionless with a machine pumping oxygen into his body, Tory had been crazy with grief and fear. She had been a long, long way from acceptance. She'd watched her mother sit calmly while she had paced—watched her sip tea while her own stomach had revolted at the thought of food. *Brain-dead.* The phrase had made her violently ill. It was she who had wept uncontrollably at her father's bedside while Helen had stood dry-eyed.

"You don't care," Tory had accused. "It's easier for you this way. You can go back to your precious routine and not be disturbed."

Helen had looked at her daughter's ravaged face and nodded. "It is easier this way."

"I won't let you." Desperate, Tory had pushed her hands through her hair and tried to think. "There are ways to stop you. I'll get a court order, and—"

"It's already done," Helen had told her quietly.

All the color had drained from Tory's face, just as she had felt all the strength drain from her body. Her father was dead. At the flick of a switch he was dead. Her mother had flicked the switch. "You killed him."

Helen hadn't winced or shrunk from the words. "You know better than that, Tory."

"If you'd loved him—if you'd loved him, you couldn't have done this."

"And your kind of love would have him strapped to that machine, helpless and empty."

"Alive!" Tory had tossed back, letting hate wash over the unbearable grief. "Damn you, he was still alive."

"Gone," Helen had countered, never raising her voice. "He'd been gone for days. For weeks, really. It's time you dealt with it."

"It's so easy for you, isn't it?" Tory had forced back the tears because she had wanted—needed—to meet her mother on her own terms. "Nothing—no one—has ever managed to make you *feel*. Not even him."

"There are different kinds of love, Tory," Helen returned stiffly. "You've never understood anything but your own way."

"Love?" Tory had gripped her hands tightly together to keep from striking out. "I've never seen you show anyone love. Now Dad's gone, but you don't cry. You don't mourn. You'll go home and hang out the wash because nothing—by God, nothing—can interfere with your precious routine."

Helen's shoulders had been very straight as she faced her daughter. "I won't apologize for being what I am," she had said. "Any more than I expect you to defend yourself to me. But I do say you loved your father too much, Victoria. For that I'm sorry."

Tory had wrapped her arms around herself tightly, unconsciously rocking. "Oh, you're so cold," she had whispered. "So cold. You have no feelings." She had badly needed comfort then, a word, an arm around her. But Helen was unable to offer, Tory unable to ask. "You did this," she had said in a strained, husky voice. "You took him from me. I'll never forgive you for it."

"No." Helen had nodded slightly. "I don't expect you will. You're always so sure of yourself, Tory."

Now the two women watched each other across a new grave: dry-eyed, expressionless. A man who had been husband and father stood between them still. Words threatened to pour out again—harsh, bitter words. Each swallowed them.

"I have to get back to town," Tory told her. She walked from the room and from the house. After standing in the silence a moment, Helen turned back to her shelves.

The pool was shaped like a crescent and its water was deep, deep blue. There were palm trees swaying gently in the night air. The scent of flowers was strong, almost tropical. It was a cool spot, secluded by trees, banked with blossoming bushes. A narrow terrace outlined the pool with mosaic tile that glimmered in the moonlight. Speakers had been craftily camouflaged so that the strains of Debussy seemed to float out of the air. A tall iced drink laced with Jamaican rum sat on a glass-topped patio table beside a telephone.

Still wet from his swim, Phil lounged on a chaise. Once again he tried to discipline his mind. He'd spent the entire day filming two key scenes in the studio. He'd had a little trouble with Sam Dressler, the leading man. It wasn't surprising. Dressler didn't have a reputation for being congenial or cooperative, just for being good. Phil wasn't looking to make a lifelong friendship, just a film. Still, when the clashes began this early in a production, it wasn't a good omen of things to come. He was going to have to use some strategy in handling Dressler.

At least, Phil mused as he absently picked up his drink, he'd have no trouble with the crew. He'd hand-picked them and had worked with each and every one of them before. Bicks, his cinematographer, was the best in the business—creative enough to be innovative and practical enough not to insist on making a statement with each frame. His assistant director was a workhorse who knew the way Phil's mind worked. Phil knew his crew down to the last gaffer and grip. When they went on location…

Phil's thoughts drifted back to Tory, as they had insisted on doing for days. She was going to be pretty stiff-necked about having her town invaded, he reflected. She'd hang over his shoulder with that tin badge pinned to her shirt. Phil hated to admit that the idea appealed to him. With a little pre-planning, he could find a number of ways to put himself in her path. Oh, yes, he intended to spend quite a bit of time getting under Sheriff Ashton's skin.

Soft, smooth skin, Phil remembered, that smelled faintly of something that a man might find in a harem.

Dark, dusky and titillating. He could picture her in silk, something chic and vivid, with nothing underneath but that long, lean body of hers.

The quick flash of desire annoyed him enough to cause him to toss back half his drink. He intended to get under her skin, but he didn't intend for it to work the other way around. He knew women, how to please them, charm them. He also knew how to avoid the complication of *one* woman. There was safety in numbers; using that maxim, Phil had enjoyed his share of women.

He liked them not only sexually but as companions. A great many of the women whose names he had been romantically linked with were simply friends. The number of women he had been credited with conquering amused him. He could hardly have worked the kind of schedule he imposed on himself if he spent all his time in the bedroom. Still, he had enjoyed perhaps a bit more than his share of romances, always careful to keep the tone light and the rules plain. He intended to do exactly the same thing with Tory.

It might be true that she was on his mind a great deal more often than any other woman in his memory. It might be true that he had been affected more deeply by her than anyone else. But…

Phil frowned over the *but* a moment. But, he reaffirmed, it was just because their meeting had been unique. The memory of his night in the steamy little cell caused him to grimace. He hadn't paid her back for that yet, and he was determined to. He hadn't cared for being under someone else's control. He'd grown used to deference in his life, a respect that had come first through his parents and then through his own talent. He never thought much about money. The fact that he hadn't been able to buy himself out of the cell was infuriating. Though more often than not he did for himself, he was accustomed to servants—perhaps more to having his word obeyed. Tory hadn't done what he ordered, and had done what he asked only when it had suited her.

It didn't matter that Phil was annoyed when people fawned over him or catered to him. That was what he was used to. Instead of fawning, Tory had been lightly disdainful, had tossed out a compliment on his work, then laughed at him. And had made him laugh, he remembered.

He wanted to know more about her. For days he had toyed with the notion of having someone check into Victoria L. Ashton, Attorney. What had stopped him had not been a respect for privacy so much as a desire to make the discoveries himself. Who was a woman who had a face like a madonna, a voice like whiskey and honey and handled a .45? Phil was going to find out if it took all of the dry, dusty summer. He'd find the time, he mused, although the shooting schedule was back-breaking.

Leaning back against the cushion of the chaise, Phil looked up at the sky. He'd refused the invitation to a party on the excuse that he had work and a scene to shoot early in the morning. Now he was thinking of Tory instead of the film, and he no longer had any sense of time. He knew he should work her out of his system so that he could give the film his full attention, without distractions. He knew he wouldn't. Since he'd returned from Friendly, he hadn't had the least inclination to pick up the phone and call any of the women he knew.

He could pacify friends and acquaintances by using the excuse of his work schedule, but he knew. There was only one companion he wanted at the moment, one woman. One lover.

He wanted to kiss her again to be certain he hadn't imagined the emotions he had felt. And the sense of *rightness*. Oddly, he found he didn't want to dilute the sensation with the taste or feel of another woman. It worried him but he brushed it off, telling himself that the obsession would fade once he had Tory where he wanted her. What worried him more was the fact that he wanted to talk to her. Just talk.

Vaguely disturbed, Phil rose. He was tired, that was all. And there was that new script to read before he went to bed. The house was silent when he entered through the glass terrace doors. Even the music had stopped without his noticing. He stepped down into the sunken living room, the glass still in his hand.

The room smelled very faintly of the lemon oil the maid had used that morning. The maroon floor tiles shone. On the deep, plump cushions of the sofa a dozen pillows were tossed with a carelessness that was both inviting and lush. He himself had chosen the tones of blue and green and ivory that dominated the room, as well as the Impressionist painting on the wall, the only artwork in the room. There were mirrors and large expanses of windows that gave the room openness. It held nothing of the opulence of the houses he had grown up in, yet maintained the same ambience of money and success. Phil was easy with it, as he was with his life, himself and his views on his future.

Crossing the room, he walked toward the curving open staircase that led to the second floor. The treads were uncarpeted. His bare feet slapped the wood gently. He was thinking that he had been pleased with the rushes. He and Huffman had watched them together. Now that the filming was progressing, his producer was more amiable. There were fewer mutterings about guarantors and cost overruns. And Huffman had been pleased with the idea of shooting the bulk of the film on location. Financially the deal with Friendly had been advantageous. Nothing put a smile on a producer's face quicker, Phil thought wryly. He went to shower.

The bath was enormous. Even more than the secluded location, it had been Phil's main incentive for buying the house high in the hills. The shower ran along one wall, with the spray shooting from both sides. He switched it on, stripping out of his trunks while the bathroom grew steamy. Even as he stepped inside, he remembered the cramped little stall he had showered in that stifling morning in Friendly.

The soap had still been wet, he recalled, from Tory. It had been a curiously intimate feeling to rub the small cake along his own skin and imagine it sliding over hers. Then he had run out of hot water while he was still covered with lather. He'd cursed her fluently and wanted her outrageously. Standing between the hot crisscrossing sprays, Phil knew he still did. On impulse he reached out and grabbed the phone that hung on the wall beside the shower.

"I want to place a call to Friendly, New Mexico," he told the operator. Ignoring the time, he decided to take a chance. "The sheriff's office." Phil waited while steam rose from the shower. The phone clicked and hummed then rang.

"Sheriff's office."

The sound of her voice made him grin. "Sheriff."

Tory frowned, setting down the coffee that was keeping her awake over the brief she was drafting. "Yes?"

"Phil Kincaid."

There was complete silence as Tory's mouth opened and closed. She felt a thrill she considered ridiculously juvenile and straightened at her desk. "Well," she said lightly, "did you forget your toothbrush?"

"No." He was at a loss for a moment, struggling to formulate a reasonable excuse for the call. He wasn't a love-struck teenager who called his girl just to hear her voice. "The shooting's on schedule," he told her, thinking fast. "We'll be in Friendly next week. I wanted to be certain there were no problems."

Tory glanced over at the cell, remembering how he had looked standing there. "Your location manager has been in touch with me and the mayor," she said, deliberately turning her eyes away from the cell. "You have all the necessary permits. The hotel's booked for you. I had to fight to keep my own room. Several people are making arrangements to rent out rooms in their homes to accommodate you." She didn't have to add that the idea didn't appeal to her. Her tone told him everything. Again he found himself grinning.

"Still afraid we're going to corrupt your town, Sheriff?"

"You and your people will stay in line, Kincaid," she returned, "or you'll have your old room back."

"It's comforting to know you have it waiting for me. Are you?"

"Waiting for you?" She gave a quick snort of laughter. "Just like the Egyptians waited for the next plague."

"Ah, Victoria, you've a unique way of putting things."

Tory frowned, listening to the odd hissing on the line. "What's that noise?"

"Noise?"

"It sounds like water running."

"It is," he told her. "I'm in the shower."

For a full ten seconds Tory said nothing, then she burst out laughing. "Phil, why did you call me from the shower?"

Something about her laughter and the way she said his name had him struggling against a fresh torrent of needs. "Because it reminded me of you."

Tory propped her feet on the desk, forgetting her brief. Something in her was softening. "Oh?" was all she said.

"I remembered running out of hot water halfway through my shower in your guest room." He pushed wet hair out of his eyes. "At the time I wasn't in the mood to lodge a formal complaint."

"I'll take it up with the management." She caught her tongue between her teeth for a moment. "I wouldn't expect deluxe accommodations in the hotel, Kincaid. There's no room service or phones in the bathroom."

"We'll survive."

"That's yet to be seen," she said dryly. "Your group may undergo culture shock when they find themselves without a Jacuzzi."

"You really think we're a soft bunch, don't you?"

Annoyed, Phil switched the phone to his other hand. It nearly slid out of his wet palm. "You may learn a few things about the people in the business this summer, Victoria. I'm going to enjoy teaching you."

"There's nothing I want to learn from you," she said quietly.

"*Want* and *need* are entirely different words," he pointed out. He could almost see the flash of temper leap into her eyes. It gave him a curious pleasure.

"As long as you play by the rules, there won't be any trouble."

"There'll be a time, Tory," he murmured into the receiver, "that you and I will play by my rules. I still have a promise to keep."

Tory pulled her legs from the desk so that her boots hit the floor with a clatter. "Don't forget to wash behind your ears," she ordered, then hung up with a bang.

Chapter 5

Tory was in her office when they arrived. The rumble of cars outside could mean only one thing. She forced herself to complete the form she was filling out before she rose from her desk. Of course she wasn't in any hurry to see him again, but it was her duty to be certain the town remained orderly during the arrival of the people from Hollywood. Still, she hesitated a moment, absently fingering her badge. She hadn't yet resolved how she was going to handle Phil. She knew the law clearly enough, but the law wouldn't help when she had to deal with him without her badge. Tod burst through the door, his eyes wide, his face flushed.

"Tory, they're here! A whole bunch of them in front of the hotel. There're vans and cars and everything!"

Though she felt more like swearing, she had to smile

at him. He only forgot himself and called her Tory when he was desperately excited. And he was such a sweet boy, she mused, so full of dreams. Crossing to him, she dropped an arm over his shoulder. He no longer cringed.

"Let's go see," she said simply.

"Tory—Sheriff," Tod corrected himself, although the words all but tumbled over each other, "do you think that guy'll let me watch him make the movie? You know, the guy you had in jail."

"I know," Tory murmured as they stepped outside. "I imagine so," she answered absentmindedly.

The scene outside was so out of place in Friendly, it almost made Tory laugh. There were several vehicles in front of the hotel, and crowds of people. The mayor stood on the sidewalk, talking to everyone at once. Several of the people from California were looking around the town with expressions of curiosity and as-tonishment. They were being looked over with the same expressions by people from Friendly.

Different planets, Tory mused with a slight smile. Take me to your leader. When she spotted Phil, the smile faded.

He was dressed casually, as he had been on his first visit to town—no different than the members of his crew. And yet, there was a difference. He held the authority; there was no mistaking it. Even while apparently listen-ing to the mayor, he was giving orders. And, Tory added thoughtfully, being obeyed. There seemed to be a certain friendliness between him and his crew, as well as an underlying respect. There was some laughter and a couple of shouts as equipment was unloaded, but the procedure was meticulously orderly. He watched over every detail.

"Wow," Tod said under his breath. "Look at all that stuff. I bet they've got cameras in those boxes. Maybe I'll get a chance to look through one."

"Mmm." Tory saw Phil laugh and heard the sound of it drift to her across the street. Then he saw her.

His smile didn't fade but altered subtly. They assessed each other while his people milled and hers whispered. The assessment became a challenge with no words spoken. She stood very straight, her arm still casually draped around the boy's shoulders. Phil noticed the gesture even as he felt a stir that wasn't wholly pleasant. He ached, he discovered, baffled. Just looking at her made him ache. She looked cool, even remote, but her eyes were directed at his. He could see the small badge pinned to the gentle sweep of her breast. On the dry, sweltering day she was wine, potent and irresistible—and perhaps unwise. One of his crew addressed him twice before Phil heard him.

"What?" His eyes never left Tory's.

"Huffman's on the phone."

"I'll get back to him." Phil started across the street.

When Tory's arm stiffened, Tod glanced up at her in question. He saw that her eyes were fixed on the man walking toward them. He frowned, but when Tory's arm relaxed, so did he.

Phil stopped just short of the sidewalk so that their eyes were at the same level. "Sheriff."

"Kincaid," she said coolly.

Briefly he turned to the boy and smiled. "Hello, Tod. How are you?"

"Fine." The boy stared at him from under a thatch of

tumbled hair. The fact that Phil had spoken to him, and remembered his name, made something move inside Tory. She pushed it away, reminding herself she couldn't afford too many good feelings toward Phil Kincaid. "Can I…" Tod began. He shifted nervously, then drew up his courage. "Do you think I could see some of that stuff?"

A grin flashed on Phil's face. "Sure. Go over and ask for Bicks. Tell him I said to show you a camera."

"Yeah?" Thrilled, he stared at Phil for a moment, then glanced up at Tory in question. When she smiled down at him, Phil watched the boy's heart leap to his eyes.

Uh-oh, he thought, seeing the slight flush creep into the boy's cheeks. Tory gave him a quick squeeze and the color deepened.

"Go ahead," she told him.

Phil watched the boy dash across the street before he turned his gaze back to Tory. "It seems you have another conquest. I have to admire his taste." When she stared at him blankly, he shook his head. "Good God, Tory, the kid's in love with you."

"Don't be ridiculous," she retorted. "He's a child."

"Not quite," he countered. "And certainly old enough to be infatuated with a beautiful woman." He grinned again, seeing her distress as her eyes darted after Tod. "I was a fourteen-year-old boy once myself."

Annoyed that he had pointed out something she'd been oblivious to, Tory glared at him. "But never as innocent as that one."

"No," he agreed easily, and stepped up on the sidewalk. She had to shift the angle of her chin to keep her eyes in line with his. "It's good to see you, Sheriff."

"Is it?" she returned lazily as she studied his face.

"Yes, I wondered if I'd imagined just how beautiful you were."

"You've brought quite a group with you," she commented, ignoring his statement. "There'll be more, I imagine."

"Some. I need some footage of the town, the countryside. The actors will be here in a couple of days."

Nodding, she leaned against a post. "You'll have to store your vehicles at Bestler's. If you have any plans to use a private residence or a store for filming, you'll have to make the arrangements individually. Hernandez's Bar is open until eleven on weeknights, one on Saturday. Consumption of alcohol on the streets is subject to a fifty-dollar fine. You're liable for any damage to private property. Whatever alterations you make for the filming will again have to be cleared individually. Anyone causing a disturbance in the hotel or on the streets after midnight will be fined and sentenced. As this is your show, Kincaid, I'll hold you personally responsible for keeping your people in line."

He listened to her rundown of the rules with the appearance of careful interest. "Have dinner with me."

She very nearly smiled. "Forget it." When she started to walk by him, he took her arm.

"Neither of us is likely to do that, are we?"

Tory didn't shake off his arm. It felt too good to be touched by him again. She did, however, give him a long, lazy look. "Phil, both of us have a job to do. Let's keep it simple."

"By all means." He wondered what would happen if

he kissed her right then and there. It was what he wanted, he discovered, more than anything he had wanted in quite some time. It would also be unwise. "What if we call it a business dinner?"

Tory laughed. "Why don't we call it what it is?"

"Because then you wouldn't come, and I do want to talk to you."

The simplicity of his answer disconcerted her. "About what?"

"Several things." His fingers itched to move to her face, to feel the soft, satiny texture of her skin. He kept them loosely hooked around her arm. "Among them, my show and your town. Wouldn't it simplify matters for both of us if we understood each other and came to a few basic agreements?"

"Maybe."

"Have dinner with me in my room." When her brow arched, he continued lazily. "It's also my office for the time being," he reminded her. "I'd like to clear the air regarding my film. If we're going to argue, Sheriff, let's do it privately."

The *Sheriff* did it. It was both her title and her job. "All right," she agreed. "Seven o'clock."

"Fine." When she started to walk away, he stopped her. "Sheriff," he said with a quick grin, "leave the gun in the desk, okay? It'll kill my appetite."

She gave a snort of laughter. "I can handle you without it, Kincaid."

Tory frowned at the clothes hanging inside her closet. Even while she had been showering, she had considered putting on work clothes—and her badge—for her dinner with Phil. But that would have been petty, and pettiness wasn't her style. She ran a fingertip over an emerald-green silk dress. It was very simply cut, narrow, with a high neck that buttoned to the waist. Serviceable and attractive, she decided, slipping it off the hanger. Laying it across the bed, she shrugged out of her robe.

Outside, the streets were quiet. She hoped they stayed that way, as she'd put Merle in charge for the evening. People would be gathered in their homes, at the drugstore, at the bar, discussing the filming. That had been the main topic of the town for weeks, overriding the heat, the lack of rain and the Kramer twins. Tory smiled as she laced the front of her teddy. Yes, people needed their little entertainments, and this was the biggest thing to happen in Friendly in years. She was going to have to roll with it. To a point.

She slipped the dress over her head, feeling the silk slither on her skin. It had been a long time, she realized, since she had bothered about clothes. In Albuquerque she took a great deal of care about her appearance. A court-room image was as important as an opening statement, particularly in a jury trial. People judged. Still, she was a woman who knew how to incorporate style with comfort.

The dress flattered her figure while giving her complete freedom of movement. Tory looked in the bureau-top mirror to study her appearance. The mirror cut her off at just above the waist. She rose on her toes and turned to the side but was still frustrated with a partial view of herself. Well, she decided, letting her feet go flat again, it would just have to do.

She sprayed on her scent automatically, remembering too late Phil's comment on it. Tory frowned at the delicate bottle as she replaced it on the dresser. She could hardly go and scrub the perfume off now. With a shrug she sat on the bed to put on her shoes. The mattress creaked alarmingly. Handling Phil Kincaid was no problem, she told herself. That was half the reason she had agreed to have dinner with him. It was a matter of principle. She wasn't a woman to be seduced or charmed into submission, particularly by a man of Kincaid's reputation. Spoiled, she thought again, but with a tad too much affection for her liking. He'd grown up privileged, in a world of glitter and glamour. He expected everything to come his way, women included.

Tory had grown up respecting the value of a dollar in a world of ordinary people and day-to-day struggles. She, too, expected everything to come her way—after she'd arranged it. She left the room determined to come out on top in the anticipated encounter. She even began to look forward to it.

Phil's room was right next door. Though she knew he had seen to that small detail himself, Tory planned to make no mention of it. She gave a brisk knock and waited.

When he opened the door, the glib remark Phil had intended to make vanished from his brain. He remembered his own thoughts about seeing her in something silk and vivid and could only stare. *Exquisite.* It was the word that hammered inside his brain, but even that wouldn't come through his lips. He knew at that moment he'd have to have her or go through his life obsessed with the need to.

"Victoria," he managed after a long moment.

Though her pulse had begun to pound at the look in his eyes, at the husky way he had said her name, she gave him a brisk smile. "Phillip," she said very formally. "Shall I come in or eat out here?"

Phil snapped back. Stammering and staring wasn't going to get him very far. He took her hand to draw her inside, then locked the door, uncertain whether he was locking her in or the world out.

Tory glanced around the small, haphazardly furnished room. Phil had already managed to leave his mark on it. The bureau was stacked with papers. There was a note pad, scrawled in from margin to margin, a few stubby pencils and a two-way radio. The shades were drawn and the room was lit with candles. Tory lifted her brows at this, glancing toward the folding card table covered with the hotel's best linen. Two dishes were covered to keep in the heat while a bottle of wine was open. Strolling over, Tory lifted it to study the label.

"Château Haut-Brion Blanc," she murmured with a perfect accent. Still holding the bottle, she sent Phil a look. "You didn't pick this up at Mendleson's Liquors."

"I always take a few...amenities when I go on location."

Tilting her head, Tory set down the bottle. "And the candles?"

"Local drugstore," he told her blandly.

"Wine and candlelight," she mused. "For a business dinner?"

"Humor the director," he suggested, crossing over to pour out two glasses of wine. "We're always setting scenes. It's uncontrollable." Handing her a glass, he touched it with the rim of his own. "Sheriff, to a comfortable relationship."

"Association," she corrected, then drank. "Very nice," she approved. She let her eyes skim over him briefly. He wore casual slacks, impeccably tailored, with an open-collared cream-colored shirt that accented his lean torso. The candlelight picked up the deep tones of red in his hair. "You look more suited to your profession than when I first saw you," she commented.

"And you less to yours," he countered.

"Really?" Turning away, she wandered the tiny room. The small throw rug was worn thin in patches, the headboard of the bed scarred, the nightstand a bit unsteady. "How do you like the accommodations, Kincaid?"

"They'll do."

She laughed into her wine. "Wait until it gets hot."

"Isn't it?"

"Do the immortal words 'You ain't seen nothing yet' mean anything to you?"

He forced himself to keep his eyes from the movements of her body under the silk. "Want to see all the Hollywood riffraff melt away, Tory?"

Turning, she disconcerted him by giving him her dashing smile. "No, I'll wish you luck instead. After all, I invariably admire your finished product."

"If not what goes into making it."

"Perhaps not," she agreed. "What are you feeding me?"

He was silent for a moment, studying the eyes that laughed at him over the rim of a wineglass. "The menu is rather limited."

"Meat loaf?" she asked dubiously, knowing it was the hotel's specialty.

"God forbid. Chicken and dumplings."

Tory walked back to him. "In that case I'll stay." They sat, facing each other across the folding table. "Shall we get business out of the way, Kincaid, or will it interfere with your digestion?"

He laughed, then surprised her by reaching out to take one of her hands in both of his. "You're a hell of a woman, Tory. Why are you afraid to use my first name?"

She faltered a moment, but let her hand lay unresisting in his. *Because it's too personal,* she thought. "Afraid?" she countered.

"Reluctant?" he suggested, allowing his fingertip to trace the back of her hand.

"Immaterial." Gently she removed her hand from his. "I was told you'd be shooting here for about six weeks." She lifted the cover from her plate and set it aside. "Is that firm?"

"According to the guarantors," Phil muttered, taking another sip of wine.

"Guarantors?"

"Tyco, Inc., completion-bond company."

"Oh, yes." Tory toyed with her chicken. "I'd heard that was a new wave in Hollywood. They guarantee that the movie will be completed on time and within budget—or else they pay the overbudget costs. They can fire you, can't they?"

"Me, the producer, the stars, anyone," Phil agreed.

"Practical."

"Stifling," he returned, and stabbed into his chicken.

"From your viewpoint, I imagine," Tory reflected. "Still, as a business, it makes sense. Creative people often have to be shown certain…boundaries. Such as," she continued, "the ones I outlined this morning."

"And boundaries often have to be flexible. Such as," he said with a smile, "some night scenes we'll be shooting: I'm going to need your cooperation. The townspeople are welcome to watch any phase of the shoot, as long as they don't interfere, interrupt or get in the way. Also, some of the equipment being brought in is very expensive and very sensitive. We have security, but as sheriff, you may want to spread the word that it's off limits."

"Your equipment is your responsibility," she reminded him. "But I will issue a statement. Before you shoot your night scenes, you'll have to clear it through my office."

He gave her a long, hard look. "Why?"

"If you're planning on working in the middle of the night in the middle of town, I'll need prior confirmation. In that way I can keep disorder to a minimum."

"There'll be times I'll need the streets blocked off and cleared."

"Send me a memo," she said. "Dates, times. Friendly can't come to a stop to accommodate you."

"It's nearly there in any case."

"We don't have a fast lane." Irresistibly she sent him a grin. "As you discovered."

He gave her a mild glance. "I'd also like to use some of the locals for extras and walk-ons."

Tory rolled her eyes. "God, you are looking for

trouble. Go ahead," she said with a shrug, "send out your casting call, but you'd better use everyone that answers it, one way or another."

As he'd already figured that one out for himself, Phil was unperturbed. "Interested?" he asked casually.

"Hmm?"

"Are you interested?"

Tory laughed as she held out her glass for more wine. "No."

Phil let the bottle hover a moment. "I'm serious, Tory. I'd like to put you on film."

"I haven't got the time or the inclination."

"You've got the looks and, I think, the talent."

She smiled, more amused than flattered. "Phil, I'm a lawyer. That's exactly what I want to be."

"Why?"

He saw immediately that the question had thrown her off balance. She stared at him a moment with the glass to her lips. "Because the law fascinates me," she said after a pause. "Because I respect it. Because I like to think that occasionally I have something to do with the process of justice. I worked hard to get into Harvard, and harder when I got there. It means something to me."

"Yet, you've given it up for six months."

"Not completely." She frowned at the steady flame of the candle. "Regardless, it's necessary. There'll still be cases to try when I go back."

"I'd like to see you in the courtroom," he murmured, watching the quiet light flicker in her eyes. "I bet you're fabulous."

"Outstanding," she agreed, smiling again. "The assistant D.A. hates me." She took another bite of chicken. "What about you? Why directing instead of acting?"

"It never appealed to me." Leaning back, Phil found himself curiously relaxed and stimulated. He felt he could look at her forever. Her fragrance, mixed with the scent of hot wax, was erotic, her voice soothing. "And I suppose I liked the idea of giving orders rather than taking them. With directing you can alter a scene, change a tone, set the pace for an entire story. An actor can only work with one character, no matter how complex it may be."

"You've never directed either of your parents." Tory let the words hang so that he could take them either as a statement or a question. When he smiled, the creases in his cheeks deepened so that she wondered how it would feel to run her fingers along them.

"No." He tipped more wine into his glass. "It might make quite a splash, don't you think? The three of us together on one film. Even though they've been divorced for over twenty-five years, they'd send the glossies into a frenzy."

"You could do two separate films," she pointed out.

"True." He pondered over it a moment. "If the right scripts came along…" Abruptly he shook his head. "I've thought of it, even been approached a couple of times, but I'm not sure it would be a wise move professionally or personally. They're quite a pair," he stated with a grin. "Temperamental, explosive and probably two of the best dramatic actors in the last fifty years. Both of them wring the last drop of blood from a character."

"I've always admired them," Tory agreed. "Especially in the movies they made together. They put a lot of chemistry on the screen."

"And off it," Phil murmured. "It always amazed me that they managed to stay together for almost ten years. Neither of them had that kind of longevity in their other marriages. The problem was that they never stopped competing. It gave them the spark on the screen and a lot of problems at home. It's difficult to live with someone when you're afraid he or she might be just a little better than you are."

"But you're very fond of them, aren't you?" She watched his mobile brow lift in question. "It shows," she told him. "It's rather nice."

"Fond," he agreed. "Maybe a little wary. They're formidable people, together or separately. I grew up listening to lines being cued over breakfast and hearing producers torn to shreds at dinner. My father lived each role. If he was playing a psychotic, I could expect to find a crazed man in the bathroom."

"Obsession," Tory recalled, delighted. "1957."

"Very good," Phil approved. "Are you a fan?"

"Naturally. I got my first kiss watching Marshall Kincaid in *Endless Journey.*" She gave a throaty laugh. "The movie was the more memorable of the two."

"You were in diapers when that movie was made," Phil calculated.

"Ever heard of the late show?"

"Young girls," he stated, "should be in bed at that hour."

Tory suppressed a laugh. Resting her elbows on the table, she set her chin on cupped hands. "And young boys?"

"Would stay out of trouble," he finished.

"The hell they would," Tory countered, chuckling. "As I recall, your…exploits started at a tender age. What was the name of that actress you were involved with when you were sixteen? She was in her twenties as I remember, and—"

"More wine?" Phil interrupted, filling her glass before she could answer.

"Then there was the daughter of that comedian."

"We were like cousins."

"Really?" Tory drew out the word with a doubtful look. "And the dancer…ah, Nicki Clark."

"Great moves," Phil remembered, then grinned at her. "You seem to be more up on my…exploits than I am. Did you spend all your free time at Harvard reading movie magazines?"

"My roommate did," Tory confessed. "She was a drama major. I see her on a commercial now and again. And then I knew someone in the business. Your name's dropped quite a bit at parties."

"The actor you dated."

"Total recall," Tory murmured, a bit uncomfortable. "You amaze me."

"Tool of the trade. What was his name?"

Tory picked up her wine, studying it for a moment. "Chad Billings."

"Billings?" Surprised and not altogether pleased, Phil frowned at her. "A second-rate leech, Tory. I wouldn't think him your style."

"No?" She shot him a direct look. "He was diverting and…educational."

"And married."

"Judgmental, Phil?" she countered, then gave a shrug. "He was in between victims at the time."

"Aptly put," Phil murmured. "If you got your view of the industry through him, I'm surprised you didn't put up roadblocks to keep us out."

"It was a thought," she told him, but smiled again. "I'm not a complete fool, you know."

But Phil continued to frown at her, studying her intensely. He was more upset at thinking of her with Billings than he should have been. "Did he hurt you?" he demanded abruptly.

Surprised, Tory stared at him. "No," she said slowly. "Although I suppose he might have if I'd allowed it. We didn't see each other exclusively or for very long. I was in L.A. on a case at the time."

"Why Albuquerque?" Phil wondered aloud. "Lou was impressed with you, and he's not easily impressed. Why aren't you in some glass and leather office in New York?"

"I hate traffic," Tory sat back now, swirling the wine and relaxing. "And I don't rush."

"L.A.?"

"I don't play tennis."

He laughed, appreciating her more each moment. "I love the way you boil things down, Tory. What do you do when you're not upholding the law?"

"As I please, mostly. Sports and hobbies are too demanding." She tossed back her hair. "I like to sleep."

"You forget, I've seen you ride."

"That's different." The wine had mellowed her mood.

She didn't notice that the candles were growing low and the hour late. "It relaxes me. Clears my head."

"Why do you live in a room in the hotel when you have a house right outside of town?" Her fingers tightened on the stem of the wineglass only slightly: He was an observant man.

"It's simpler."

Leave this one alone for a while, he warned himself. It's a very tender spot.

"And what do you do when you're not making a major statement on film?" she asked, forcing her hand to relax.

Phil accepted her change of subject without question. "Read scripts…watch movies."

"Go to parties," Tory added sagely.

"That too. It's all part of the game."

"Isn't it difficult sometimes, living in a town where so much is pretense? Even considering the business end of your profession, you have to deal with the lunacy, the make-believe, even the desperation. How do you separate the truth from the fantasy?"

"How do you in your profession?" he countered.

Tory thought for a moment, then nodded. "Touché." Rising, she wandered to the window. She pushed aside the shade, surprised to see that the sun had gone down. A few red streaks hovered over the horizon, but in the east the sky was dark. A few early stars were already out. Phil sat where he was, watched her and wanted her.

"There's Merle making his rounds," Tory said with a smile in her voice. "He's got his official expression on. I imagine he's hoping to be discovered. If he can't be a tough lawman from the nineteenth century, he'd settle for playing one." A car pulled into town, stopping in front of the pool hall with a sharp squeal of brakes. "Oh, God, it's the twins." She sighed, watching Merle turn and stride in their direction. "There's been no peace in town since that pair got their licenses. I suppose I'd better go down and see that they stay in line."

"Can't Merle handle a couple of kids?"

Tory's laugh was full of wicked appreciation. "You don't know the Kramers. There's Merle," she went on, "giving them basic lecture number twenty-two."

"Did they wash all of Hollister's windows?" Phil asked as he rose to join her.

Tory turned her head, surprised. "How did you know about that?"

"Tod told me." He peeked through the window, finding he wanted a look at the infamous twins. They seemed harmless enough from a distance, and disconcertingly alike. "Which one's Zac?"

"Ah…on the right, I think. Maybe," she added with a shake of her head. "Why?"

"'Zac Kramer don't hold with no woman sheriff,'" he quoted.

Tory grinned up at him. "Is that so?"

"Just so." Hardly aware he did so, Phil reached for her hair. "Obviously he's not a very perceptive boy."

"Perceptive enough to wash Mr. Hollister's windows," Tory corrected, amused by the memory. "And to call me a foxy chick only under his breath when he thought I couldn't hear. Of course, that could have been Zeke."

"'Foxy chick'?" Phil repeated.

"Yes," Tory returned with mock hauteur. "'A *very* foxy chick.' It was his ultimate compliment."

"Your head's easily turned," he decided. "What if I told you that you had a face that belongs in a Raphael painting?"

Tory's eyes lit with humor. "I'd say you're reaching."

"And hair," he said with a subtle change in his voice. "Hair that reminds me of night…a hot summer night that keeps you awake, and thinking, and wanting." He plunged both hands into it, letting his fingers tangle. The shade snapped back into place, cutting them off from the outside.

"Phil," Tory began, unprepared for the suddenness of desire that rose in both of them.

"And skin," he murmured, not even hearing her, "that makes me think of satin sheets and tastes like something forbidden." He touched his mouth to her cheek, allowing the tip of his tongue to brush over her. "Tory." She felt her name whisper along her skin and thrilled to it. She had her hands curled tightly around his arms, but not in protest. "Do you know how often I've thought of you these past weeks?"

"No." She didn't want to resist. She wanted to feel that wild sweep of pleasure that came from the press of his mouth on hers. "No," she said again, and slid her arms around his neck.

"Too much," he murmured, then swore. "Too damn much." And his mouth took her waiting one.

The passion was immediate, frenetic. It ruled both of them. Each of them sought the mindless excitement they had known briefly weeks before. Tory had thought she had intensified the sensation in her mind as the days had passed. Now she realized she had lessened it. This sort of fervor couldn't be imagined or described. It had to be experienced. Everything inside her seemed to speed up—her blood, her heart, her brain. And all sensation, all emotion, seemed to be centered in her mouth. The taste of him exploded on her tongue, shooting through her until she was so full of him, she could no longer separate herself. With a moan she tilted her head back, inviting him to plunge deeper into her mouth. But he wanted more.

Her hair fell straight behind her, leaving her neck vulnerable. Surrendering to a desperate hunger, he savaged it with kisses. Tory made a sound that was mixed pain and pleasure. Her scent seemed focused there, heated by the pulse at her throat. It drove him nearer the edge. He dragged at the silk-covered buttons, impatient to find the hidden skin, the secret skin that had preyed on his mind. The groan sounded in his throat as he slipped his hand beneath the thin teddy and found her.

She was firm, and slender enough to fit his palm. Her heartbeat pounded against it. Tory turned her head, but only to urge him to give the neglected side of her neck attention. With her hands in his hair she pulled him back to her. His hands searched everywhere with a sort of wild reverence, exploring, lingering, possessing. She could feel his murmurs as his lips played over her skin, although she could barely hear them and understood them not at all. The room seemed to grow closer and hotter, so that she longed to be rid of her clothes and find relief...and delight.

Then he pulled her close so that their bodies pressed urgently. Their mouths met with fiery demand. It seemed the storm had just begun. Again and again they drew from each other until they were both breathless. Though he had fully intended to end the evening with Tory in his bed, Phil hadn't expected to be desperate. He hadn't known that all control could be so easily lost. The warm curves of a woman should bring easy pleasure, not this trembling pain. A kiss was a prelude, not an all-consuming force. He knew only that all of him, much more than his body, was crying out for her. Whatever was happening to him was beyond his power to stop. And she was the only answer he had.

"God, Tory." He took his mouth on a wild journey of her face, then returned to her lips. "Come to bed. For God's sake, come to bed. I want you."

She felt as though she were standing on the edge of a cliff. The plunge had never seemed more tempting— or more dangerous. It would be so easy, so easy, just to lean forward and fly. But the fall… She fought for sanity through a brain clouded with the knowledge of one man. It was much too soon to take the step.

"Phil." Shaken, she drew away from him to lean against the windowsill. "I…no," she managed, lifting both hands to her temples. He drew her back against him.

"Yes," he corrected, then crushed his lips to hers again. Her mouth yielded irresistibly. "You can't pretend you don't want me as much as I want you."

"No." She let her head rest on his shoulder a moment before she pushed out of his arms. "I can't," she agreed in a voice thickened with passion. "But I don't do everything I want. That's one of the basic differences between us."

His eyes flicked briefly down to the unbuttoned dress. "We also seem to have something important in common. This doesn't happen every time—between every man and woman."

"No." Carefully she began to do up her buttons. "It shouldn't have happened between us. I didn't intend it to."

"I did," he admitted. "But not quite this way."

Her eyes lifted to his. She understood perfectly. This had been more intense than either of them had bargained for. "It's going to be a long summer, Phil," she murmured.

"We're going to be together sooner or later, Tory. We both know it." He needed something to balance him. Going to the table, he poured out another glass of wine. He drank, drank again, then looked at her. "I have no intention of backing off."

She nodded, accepting. But she didn't like the way her hands were shaking. "I'm not ready."

"I can be a patient man when necessary." He wanted nothing more than to pull her to the bed and take what they both needed. Instead he took out a cigarette and reminded himself he was a civilized man.

Tory drew herself up straight. "Let's both concentrate on our jobs, shall we?" she said coolly. She wanted to get out, but she didn't want to retreat. "I'll see you around, Kincaid."

"Damn right you will," he murmured as she headed for the door.

She flicked the lock off, then turned to him with a half smile. "Keep out of trouble," she ordered, closing the door behind her.

Chapter 6

Phil sat beside the cameraman on the Tulip crane. "Boom up." At his order the crane operator took them seventeen feet above the town of Friendly. It was just dawn. He'd arranged to have everyone off the streets, although there was a crowd of onlookers behind the crane and equipment. All entrances to town had been blocked off on the off chance that someone might drive through. He wanted desolation and the tired beginning of a new day.

Glancing down, he saw that Bicks was checking the lighting and angles. Brutes, the big spotlights, were set to give daylight balance. He knew, to an inch, where he wanted the shadows to fall. For this shot Phil would act as assistant cameraman, pulling the focus himself.

Phil turned his attention back to the street. He knew

what he wanted, and he wanted to capture it as the sun rose, with as much natural light as possible. He looked through the lens and set the shot himself. The crane was set on tracks. He would have the cameraman begin with a wide shot of the horizon and the rising sun, then dolly back to take in the entire main street of Friendly. No soft focus there, just harsh reality. He wanted to pick up the dust on the storefront windows. Satisfied with what he saw through the camera lens, Phil marked the angle with tape, then nodded to his assistant director.

"Quiet on the set."

"New Chance, scene three, take one."

"Roll it," Phil ordered, then waited. With his eyes narrowed, he could visualize what his cameraman saw through the lens. The light was good. Perfect. They'd have to get it in three takes or less or else they'd have to beef it up with gels and filters. That wasn't what he wanted here. He felt the crane roll backward slowly on cue. A straight shot, no panning right to left. They'd take in the heart of the town in one long shot. Chipped paint, sagging wood, torn screens. Later they'd cut in the scene of the leading man walking in from the train station. He was coming home, Phil mused, because there was no place else to go. And he found it, exactly as he had left it twenty years before.

"Cut." The noise on the ground started immediately. "I want another take. Same speed."

At the back of the crowd Tory watched. She wasn't thrilled with being up at dawn. Both her sense of duty and her curiosity had brought her. Phil had been perfectly clear about anyone peeking through windows during this shot. He wanted emptiness. She told herself she'd come to keep her people out of mischief, but when it was all said and done, she had wanted to see Phil at work.

He was very commanding and totally at ease with it, but, she reasoned as she stuck her hands in her back pockets, it didn't seem so hard. Moving a little to the side, she tried to see the scene she was imagining. The town looked tired, she decided, and a little reluctant to face the new day. Though the horizon was touched with golds and pinks, a gray haze lay over the street and buildings.

It was the first time he had shot anything there. For the past week he had been filming landscapes. Tory had stayed in Friendly, sending Merle out occasionally to check on things. It had kept him happy and had given Tory the distance she wanted. As her deputy came back brimming with reports and enthusiasm, she was kept abreast in any case.

But today the urge to see for herself had been too strong to resist. It had been several days—and several long nights—since their evening together. She had managed to keep herself busier than necessary in order to avoid him. But Tory wasn't a woman to avoid a problem for long. Phil Kincaid was still a problem.

Apparently satisfied, Phil ordered the operator to lower the crane. People buzzed around Tory like bees. A few children complained about being sent off to school. Spotting Tod, Tory smiled and waved him over.

"Isn't it neat?" he demanded the moment he was beside her. "I wanted to go up in it," he continued, indicating the crane, "but Mr. Kincaid said something about insurance. Steve let me see his camera though, even let me take some pictures. It's a thirty-five milli-meter with all kinds of lenses."

"Steve?"

"The guy who was sitting next to Mr. Kincaid. He's the cameraman." Tod glanced over, watching Phil in a discussion with his cameraman and several members of the crew. "Isn't he something?"

"Steve?" Tory repeated, smiling at Tod's pleasure.

"Well, yeah, but I meant Mr. Kincaid." Shaking his head, he let out a long breath. "He's awful smart. You should hear some of the words he uses. And boy, when he says so, everybody jumps."

"Do they?" Tory murmured, frowning over at the man under discussion.

"You bet," Tod confirmed. "And I heard Mr. Bicks say to Steve that he'd rather work with Mr. Kincaid than anybody. He's a tough sonofa—" Catching himself, Tod broke off and flushed. "I mean, he said he was tough, but the best there was."

As she watched, Phil was pointing, using one hand and then the other as he outlined his needs for the next shot. It was very clear that he knew what he wanted and that he'd get it. She could study him now. He was too involved to notice her or the crowd of people who stared and mumbled behind the barrier of equipment.

He wore jeans and a pale blue T-shirt with scuffed sneakers. Hanging from his belt was a case that held sun-glasses and another for a two-way radio. He was very intense, she noted, when working. There was none of the careless humor in his eyes. He talked quickly, punctu-ating the words with hand gestures. Once or twice he interrupted what he was saying to call out another order to the grips who were setting up light stands.

A perfectionist, she concluded, and realized it shouldn't surprise her. His movies projected the intimate care she was now seeing firsthand. A stocky man in a fielder's cap lumbered up to him, talking over an enormous wad of gum.

"That's Mr. Bicks," Tod murmured reverently. "The cinematographer. He's got two Oscars and owns part of a boxer."

Whatever he was saying, Phil listened carefully, then simply shook his head. Bicks argued another moment, shrugged, then gave Phil what appeared to be a solid punch on the shoulder before he walked away. A tough sonofabitch, Tory mused. Apparently so.

Turning to Tod, she mussed his hair absently. "You'd better get to school."

"Aw, but…"

She lifted her brow, effectively cutting off his excuse. "It's nearly time for summer vacation. They'll still be here."

He mumbled a protest, but she caught the look in his eye as he gazed up at her. Uh-oh, she thought, just as Phil had. Why hadn't she seen this coming? She was going to have to be careful to be gentle while pointing the boy in another direction. A teenage crush was nothing to smile at and brush away.

"I'll come by after school," he said, beaming up at her. Before she could respond, he was dashing off, leaving her gnawing on her bottom lip and worrying about him.

"Sheriff."

Tory whirled sharply and found herself facing Phil. He smiled slowly, setting the sunglasses in front of his eyes. It annoyed her that she had to strain to see his expression through the tinted glass. "Kincaid," she responded. "How's it going?"

"Good. Your people are very cooperative."

"And yours," she said. "So far."

He grinned at that. "We're expecting the cast this afternoon. The location manager's cleared it with you about parking the trailers and so forth?"

"She's very efficient," Tory agreed. "Are you getting what you want?"

He took a moment to answer. "With regard to the film, yes, so far." Casually he reached down to run a finger over her badge. "You've been busy the last few days."

"So have you."

"Not that busy. I've left messages for you."

"I know."

"When are you going to see me?"

She lifted both brows. "I'm seeing you right now." He took a step closer and cupped the back of her neck in his hand. "Phil—"

"Soon," he said quietly.

Though she could feel the texture of each of his fingers on the back of her neck, she gave him a cool look. "Kincaid, create your scenes on the other side of the camera. Accosting a peace officer will land you back in that cell. You'll find it difficult to direct from there."

"Oh, I'm going to accost you," he warned under his breath. "With or without that damn badge, Victoria. Think about it."

She didn't step back or remove his hand, although she knew several pair of curious eyes were on them. "I'll give it a few minutes," she promised dryly.

Only the tensing of his fingers on her neck revealed his annoyance. She thought he was about to release her and relaxed. His mouth was on hers so quickly, she could only stand in shock. Before she could think to push him away, he set her free. Her eyes were sharply green and furious when he grinned down at her.

"See you, Sheriff," he said cheerfully, and sauntered back to his crew.

For the better part of the day Tory stayed in her office and fumed. Now and again Phil's voice carried through her open window as he called out instructions. She knew they were doing pans of the town and stayed away from the window. She had work to do, she reminded herself. And in any case she had no interest in the filming. It was understandable that the townspeople would stand around and gawk, but she had better things to do.

I should have hauled him in, she thought, scowling down at her legal pad. I should have hauled him in then and there. And she would have if it wouldn't have given him too much importance. He'd better watch his step, Tory decided. One wrong move and she was going to come down on him hard. She picked up her coffee and gulped it down with a grimace. It was cold. Swearing, she rose to pour a fresh cup.

Through the screen in the window she could see quite a bit of activity and hear a flood of conversation interrupted when the filming was in progress. It was past noon and hot as the devil. Phil had been working straight through for hours. With a grudging respect she admitted that he didn't take his job lightly. Going back to her desk, Tory concentrated on her own.

She hardly noticed that two hours had passed when Merle came bursting into the office. Hot, tired and annoyed with having her concentration broken, she opened her mouth to snap at him, but he exploded with enthusiasm before she had the chance.

"Tory, they're here!"

"Terrific," she mumbled, turning to her notes again. "Who?"

"The actors. Came from the airport in limousines. Long, black limousines. There are a half dozen of those Winnebagos set up outside of town for dressing rooms and stuff. You should see inside them. They've got telephones and TVs and everything."

She lifted her head. "Been busy, Merle T.?" she asked languidly, but he was too excited to notice.

"Sam Dressler," he went on, pacing back and forth with a clatter of boots. "Sam Dressler, right here in Friendly. I guess I've seen every movie he's ever made. He shook my hand," he added, staring down at his own palm, awed. "Thought I was the sheriff." He sent Tory a quick look. "'Course I told him I was the deputy."

"Of course," she agreed, amused now. It was never possible for her to stay annoyed with Merle. "How'd he look?"

"Just like you'd think," he told her with a puzzled shake of his head. "All tanned and tough, with a diamond on his finger fit to blind you. Signed autographs for everybody who wanted one."

Unable to resist, Tory asked, "Did you get one?"

"Sure I did." He grinned and pulled out his ticket book. "It was the only thing I had handy."

"Very resourceful." She glanced at the bold signature Merle held out for her. At the other end of the page were some elegant looping lines. "Marlie Summers," Tory read. She recalled a film from the year before, and the actress's pouting sexuality.

"She's about the prettiest thing I ever saw," Merle murmured.

Coming from anyone else, Tory would have given the remark no notice. In this case, however, her eyes shot up and locked on Merle's. What she saw evoked in her a feeling of distress similar to what she had experienced with Tod. "Really?" she said carefully.

"She's just a little thing," Merle continued, gazing down at the autograph. "All pink and blond. Just like something in a store window. She's got big blue eyes and the longest lashes..." He trailed off, tucking the book back in his pocket.

Growing more disturbed, Tory told herself not to be silly. No Hollywood princess was going to look twice at Merle T. Johnson. "Well," she began casually, "I wonder what her part is."

"She's going to tell me all about it tonight," Merle stated, adjusting the brim of his hat.

"What?" It came out in a quick squeak.

Grinning, Merle gave his hat a final pat, then stroked his struggling mustache. "We've got a date." He strode out jauntily, leaving Tory staring with her mouth open.

"A date?" she asked the empty office. Before she

could react, the phone beside her shrilled. Picking it up, she barked into it, "What is it?"

A bit flustered by the greeting, the mayor stammered. "Tory—Sheriff Ashton, this is Mayor Toomey."

"Yes, Bud." Her tone was still brisk as she stared at the door Merle had shut behind him.

"I'd like you to come over to the office, Sheriff. I have several members of the cast here." His voice rang with importance again. "Mr. Kincaid thought it might be a good idea for you to meet them."

"Members of the cast," she repeated, thinking of Marlie Summers. "I'd love to," she said dangerously, then hung up on the mayor's reply.

Her thoughts were dark as she crossed the street. No Hollywood tootsie was going to break Merle's heart while she was around. She was going to make that clear as soon as possible. She breezed into the hotel, giving several members of Phil's crew a potent stare as they loitered in the lobby. Bicks doffed his fielder's cap and grinned at her.

"Sheriff."

Tory sent him a mild glance and a nod as she sauntered through to the office. Behind her back he rolled his eyes to the ceiling, placing the cap over his heart. A few remarks were made about the advantages of breaking the law in Friendly while Tory disappeared into a side door.

The tiny office was packed, the window air-conditioning unit spitting hopefully. Eyes turned to her. Tory gave the group a brief scan. Marlie was sitting on the arm of Phil's chair, dressed in pink slacks and a frilled halter. Her enviable curves were displayed to perfection. Her hair was tousled appealingly around a piquant face accented with mink lashes and candy-pink lipstick. She looked younger than Tory had expected, almost like a high school girl ready to be taken out for an ice-cream soda. Tory met the baby-blue eyes directly, and with an expression that made Phil grin. He thought mistakenly that she might be a bit jealous.

"Sheriff." The mayor bustled over to her, prepared to act as host. "This is quite an honor for Friendly," he began, in his best politician's voice. "I'm sure you recognize Mr. Dressler."

Tory extended her hand to the man who approached her. "Sheriff." His voice was rich, the cadence mellow as he clasped her hand in both of his. She was a bit surprised to find them callused. "This is unexpected," he murmured while his eyes roamed her face thoroughly. "And delightful."

"Mr. Dressler, I admire your work." The smile was easy because the words were true.

"Sam, please." His brandy voice had only darkened attractively with age, losing none of its resonance. "We get to be a close little family on location shoots. Victoria, isn't it?"

"Yes." She found herself inclined to like him and gave him another smile.

"Bud, here, is making us all quite comfortable," he went on, clapping the mayor on the shoulder. "Will you join us in a drink?"

"Ginger ale's fine, Bud."

"The sheriff's on duty." Hearing Phil's voice, Tory

turned, her head only, and glanced at him. "You'll find she takes her work very seriously." He touched Marlie's creamy bare shoulder. "Victoria Ashton, Marlie Summers."

"Sheriff." Marlie smiled her dazzling smile. The tiniest hint of a dimple peeked at the corner of her mouth. "Phil said you were unusual. It looks like he's right again."

"Really?" Accepting the cold drink Bud handed her, Tory assessed the actress over the rim. Marlie, accustomed to long looks and feminine coolness, met the stare straight on.

"Really," Marlie agreed. "I met your deputy a little while ago."

"So I heard."

So the wind blows in that direction, Marlie mused as she sipped from her own iced sangria. Sensing tension and wanting to keep things smooth, Bud hurried on with the rest of the introductions.

The cast ranged from ingenues to veterans—a girl Tory recognized from a few commercials; an ancient-looking man she remembered from the vague black-and-white movies on late-night television; a glitzy actor in his twenties, suited for heart throbs and posters. Tory managed to be pleasant, stayed long enough to satisfy the mayor, then slipped away. She'd no more than stepped outside when she felt an arm on her shoulder.

"Don't you like parties, Sheriff?"

Taking her time, she turned to face Phil. "Not when I'm on duty." Though she knew he'd worked in the sun all day, he didn't look tired but exhilarated. His shirt was streaked with sweat, his hair curling damply over his ears, but there was no sign of fatigue on his face. It's the pressure that feeds him, she realized. Again she was drawn to him, no less than when they had been alone in his room. "You've put in a long day," she murmured.

He caught her hair in his hand. "So have you. Why don't we go for a drive?"

Tory shook her head. "No, I have things to do." Wanting to steer away from the subject, she turned to what had been uppermost on her mind. "Your Marlie made quite an impression on Merle."

Phil gave a quick laugh. "Marlie usually does."

"Not on Merle," Tory said so seriously that he sobered.

"He's a big boy, Tory."

"A boy," she agreed significantly. "He's never seen anything like your friend in there. I won't let him get hurt."

Phil let out a deep breath. "Your duties as sheriff include advice to the lovelorn? Leave him alone," he ordered before she could retort. "You treat him as though he were a silly puppy who doesn't respond to training."

She took a step back at that. "No, I don't," she disagreed, sincerely shaken by the idea. "He's a sweet boy who—"

"Man," Phil corrected quietly. "He's a man, Tory. Cut the apron strings."

"I don't know what you're talking about," she snapped.

"You damn well do," he corrected. "You can't keep him under your wing the way you do with Tod."

"I've known Merle all my life," she said in a low voice. "Just keep Cotton Candy in line, Kincaid."

"Always so sure of yourself, aren't you?"

Her color drained instantly, alarmingly. For a moment Phil stared at her in speechless wonder. He'd never expected to see that kind of pain in her eyes. Instinctively he reached out for her. "Tory?"

"No." She lifted a hand to ward him off. "Just—leave me alone." Turning away, she walked across the street and climbed into her car. With an oath Phil started to go back into the hotel, then swore again and backtracked. Tory was already on her way north.

Her thoughts were in turmoil as she drove. Too much was happening. She squeezed her eyes shut briefly. Why should that throw her now, she wondered. She'd always been able to take things in stride, handle them at her own pace. Now she had a deep-seated urge just to keep driving, just to keep going. So many people wanted things from her, expected things. Including, she admitted, herself. It was all closing in suddenly. She needed someone to talk to. But the only one who had ever fit that job was gone.

God, she wasn't sure of herself. Why did everyone say so? Sometimes it was so hard to be responsible, to *feel* responsible. Tod, Merle, the mayor, the Kramers, Mr. Hollister. Her mother. She just wanted peace—enough time to work out what was happening in her own life. Her feelings for Phil were closing in on her. Pulling the car to a halt, Tory realized it was those feelings that were causing her—a woman who had always considered herself calm—to be tense. Piled on top of it were problems that had to come first. She'd learned that from her father.

Glancing up, she saw she had driven to the cemetery

without even being aware of it. She let out a long breath, resting her forehead against the steering wheel. It was time she went there, time she came to terms with what she had closed her mind to since that night in the hospital. Climbing out of the car, Tory walked across the dry grass to her father's grave.

Odd that there'd been a breeze here, she mused, looking at the sky, the distant mountains, the long stretches of nothing. She looked at anything but what was at her feet. There should be some shade, she thought, and cupped her elbows in her palms. Someone should plant some trees. I should have brought some flowers, she thought suddenly, then looked down.

WILLIAM H. ASHTON

She hadn't seen the gravestone before—hadn't been back to the cemetery since the day of the funeral. Now a quiet moan slipped through her lips. "Oh, Dad."

It isn't right, she thought with a furious shake of her head. It just isn't right. How can he be down there in the dark when he always loved the sun? "Oh, no," she murmured again. I don't know what to do, she thought silently, pleading with him. I don't know how to deal with it all. I still need you. Pressing a palm on her forehead, she fought back tears.

Phil pulled up behind her car, then got out quietly. She looked very alone and lost standing among the headstones. His first instinct was to go to her, but he suppressed it. This was private for her. Her father, he thought, looking toward the grave at which Tory stared.

He stood by a low wrought-iron gate at the edge of the cemetery and waited.

There was so much she needed to talk about, so much she still needed to say. But there was no more time. He'd been taken too suddenly. Unfair, she thought again on a wave of desolate fury. He had been so young and so good.

"I miss you so much," she whispered. "All those long talks and quiet evenings on the porch. You'd smoke those awful cigars outside so that the smell wouldn't get in the curtains and irritate Mother. I was always so proud of you. This badge doesn't suit me," she continued softly, lifting her hand to it. "It's the law books and the courtroom that I understand. I don't want to make a mistake while I'm wearing it, because it's yours." Her fingers tightened around it. All at once she felt painfully alone, helpless, empty. Even the anger had slipped away unnoticed. And yet the acceptance she tried to feel was blocked behind a grief she refused to release. If she cried, didn't it mean she'd taken the first step away?

Wearily she stared down at the name carved into the granite. "I don't want you to be dead," she whispered. "And I hate it because I can't change it."

When she turned away from the grave, her face was grim. She walked slowly but was halfway across the small cemetery before she saw Phil. Tory stopped and stared at him. Her mind went blank, leaving her with only feelings. He went to her.

For a moment they stood face-to-face. He saw her lips tremble open as if she were about to speak, but she only shook her head helplessly. Without a word he gathered her close. The shock of grief that hit her was stronger than anything that had come before. She trembled first, then clutched at him.

"Oh, Phil, I can't bear it." Burying her face against his shoulder, Tory wept for the first time since her father's death.

In silence he held her, overwhelmed with a tenderness he'd felt for no one before. Her sobbing was raw and passionate. He stroked her hair, offering comfort without words. Her grief poured out in waves that seemed to stagger her and made him hurt for her to a degree that was oddly intimate. He thought he could feel what she felt, and held her tighter, waiting for the first throes to pass.

At length her weeping quieted, lessening to trembles that were somehow more poignant than the passion. She kept her face pressed against his shoulder, relying on his strength when her own evaporated. Light-headed and curiously relieved, she allowed him to lead her to a small stone bench. He kept her close to his side when they sat, his arm protectively around her.

"Can you talk about it?" he asked softly.

Tory let out a long, shuddering sigh. From where they sat she could see the headstone clearly. "I loved him," she murmured. "My mother says too much." Her throat felt dry and abused when she swallowed. "He was everything good. He taught me not just right and wrong but all the shades in between." Closing her eyes, she let her head rest on Phil's shoulder. "He always knew the right thing. It was something innate and effortless. People knew they could depend on him, that he'd make it right. I depended on him, even in college, in Albuquerque—I knew he was there if I needed him."

He kissed her temple in a gesture of simple understanding. "How did he die?"

Feeling a shudder run through her, Phil drew her closer still. "He had a massive stroke. There was no warning. He'd never even been sick that I can remember. When I got here, he was in a coma. Everything…" She faltered, searching for the strength to continue. With his free hand Phil covered hers. "Everything seemed to go wrong at once. His heart just…stopped." She ended in a whisper, lacing her fingers through his. "They put him on a respirator. For weeks there was nothing but that damn machine. Then my mother told them to turn it off."

Phil let the silence grow, following her gaze toward the headstone. "It must have been hard for her."

"No." The word was low and flat. "She never wavered, never cried. My mother's a very decisive woman," she added bitterly. "And she made the decision alone. She told me after it was already done."

"Tory." Phil turned her to face him. She looked pale, bright-eyed and achingly weary. Something seemed to tear inside him. "I can't tell you the right or wrong of it, because there really isn't any. But I do know there comes a time when everyone has to face something that seems impossible to accept."

"If only I could have seen it was done for love and not…expediency." Shutting her eyes, she shook her head. "Hold me again." He drew her gently into his arms. "That last night at the hospital was so ugly between my mother and me. He would have hated that. I couldn't stop it," she said with a sigh. "I still can't."

"Time." He kissed the top of her head. "I know how trite that sounds, but there's nothing else but time."

She remained silent, accepting his comfort, drawing strength from it. If she had been able to think logically, Tory would have found it inconsistent with their relationship thus far that she could share her intimate feelings with him. At the moment she trusted Phil implicitly.

"Once in a while, back there," she murmured, "I panic."

It surprised him enough to draw her back and study her face again. "You?"

"Everyone thinks because I'm Will Ashton's daughter, I'll take care of whatever comes up. There're so many variables to right and wrong."

"You're very good at your job."

"I'm a good lawyer," she began.

"And a good sheriff," he interrupted. Tilting her chin up, he smiled at her. "That's from someone who's been on the wrong side of your bars." Gently he brushed the hair from her cheeks. They were warm and still damp. "And don't expect to hear me say it in public."

Laughing, she pressed her cheek to his. "Phil, you can be a very nice man."

"Surprised?"

"Maybe," she murmured. With a sigh she gave him one last squeeze, then drew away. "I've got work to do."

He stopped her from rising by taking her hands again. "Tory, do you know how little space you give yourself?"

"Yes." She disconcerted him by bringing his hand to her lips. "These six months are for him. It's very important to me."

Standing as she did, Phil cupped her face in his

hands. She seemed to him very fragile, very vulnerable, suddenly. His need to look out for her was strong. "Let me drive you back. We can send someone for your car."

"No, I'm all right. Better." She brushed her lips over his. "I appreciate this. There hasn't been anyone I could talk to."

His eyes became very intense. "Would you come to me if you needed me?"

She didn't answer immediately, knowing the question was more complex than the simple words. "I don't know," she said at length.

Phil let her go, then watched her walk away.

Chapter 7

The camera came in tight on Sam and Marlie. Phil wanted the contrast of youth and age, of dissatisfaction and acceptance. It was a key scene, loaded with tension and restrained sexuality. They were using Hernandez's Bar, where the character Marlie portrayed worked as a waitress. Phil had made almost no alterations in the room. The bar was scarred, the mirror behind it cracked near the bottom. It smelled of sweat and stale liquor. He intended to transmit the scent itself onto film.

The windows were covered with neutral-density paper to block off the stream of the sun. It trapped the stale air in the room. The lights were almost unbearably hot, so that he needed no assistance from makeup to add beads of sweat to Sam's face. It was the sixth take, and the mood was growing edgy.

Sam blew his lines and swore ripely.

"Cut." Struggling with his temper, Phil wiped his forearm over his brow. With some actors a few furious words worked wonders. With Dressler, Phil knew, they would only cause more delays.

"Look, Phil"—Sam tore off the battered Stetson he wore and tossed it aside—"this isn't working."

"I know. Cut the lights," he ordered. "Get Mr. Dressler a beer." He addressed this to the man he had hired to see to Sam's needs on the location shoot. The individual attention had been Phil's way of handling Dressler and thus far had had its benefits. "Sit down for a while, Sam," he suggested. "We'll cool off." He waited until Sam was seated at a rear table with a portable fan and a beer before he plucked a can from the cooler himself.

"Hot work," Marlie commented, leaning against the bar.

Glancing over, Phil noted the line of sweat that ran down the front of her snug blouse. He passed her the can of beer. "You're doing fine."

"It's a hell of a part," she said before she took a deep drink. "I've been waiting for one like this for a long time."

"The next take," Phil began, narrowing his eyes, "when you say the bit about sweat and dust, I want you to grab his shirt and pull him to you."

Marlie thought it over, then set the can on the bar. "Like this?...*There's nothing,*" she spat out, grabbing Phil's damp shirt, "*nothing in this town but sweat and dust.*" She put her other hand to his shirt and pulled him closer. "*Even the dreams have dust on them.*"

"Good."

Marlie flashed a smile before she picked up the beer again. "Better warn Sam," she suggested, offering Phil the can. "He doesn't like improvising."

"Hey, Phil." Phil glanced over to see Steve with his hand on the doorknob. "That kid's outside with the sheriff. Wants to know if they can watch."

Phil took a long, slow drink. "They can sit in the back of the room." His eyes met Tory's as she entered. It had been two days since their meeting in the cemetery. Since then there had been no opportunity—or she'd seen to it that there'd been none—for any private conversation. She met the look, nodded to him, then urged Tod back to a rear table.

"The law of the land," Marlie murmured, causing Phil to look at her in question. "She's quite a woman, isn't she?"

"Yes."

Marlie grinned before she commandeered the beer again. "Merle thinks she's the greatest thing to come along since sliced bread."

Phil pulled out a cigarette. "You're seeing quite a bit of the deputy, aren't you? Doesn't seem your style."

"He's a nice guy," she said simply, then laughed. "His boss would like me run out of town on a rail."

"She's protective."

With an unintelligible murmur that could have meant anything, Marlie ran her fingers through her disordered cap of curls. "At first I thought she had something going with him." In response to Phil's quick laugh she lifted a thin, penciled brow. "Of course, that was before I saw the way you looked at her." It was her turn to laugh when Phil's expression became aloof. "Damn, Phil, you can look like your father sometimes." After handing him the empty can of beer, she turned away. "Makeup!" she demanded.

"Those are 4Ks," Tod was telling Tory, pointing to lights. "They have to put that stuff over the windows so the sun doesn't screw things up. On an inside shoot like this, they have to have something like 175-foot candles."

"You're getting pretty technical, aren't you?"

Tod shifted a bit in his chair, but his eyes were excited when they met Tory's. "Mr. Kincaid had them develop the film I shot in the portable lab. He said it was good. He said there were schools I could go to to learn about cinematography."

She cast a look in Phil's direction, watching him discuss something in undertones with Steve. "You're spending quite a lot of time with him," she commented.

"Well, when he's not busy... He doesn't mind."

"No, I'm sure he doesn't." She gave his hand a squeeze.

Tod returned the pressure boldly. "I'd rather spend time with you," he murmured.

Tory glanced down at their joined hands, wishing she knew how to begin. "Tod..."

"Quiet on the set!"

With a sigh Tory turned her attention to the scene in front of the bar. She'd come because Tod had been so pitifully eager that she share his enthusiasm. And she felt it was good for him to take such an avid interest in the technical aspects of the production. Unobtrusively she had kept her eye on him over the past days, watching him with members of the film crew. Thus far, no one appeared to object to his presence or his questions. In fact, Tory mused, he was becoming a kind of mascot. More and more his conversations were accented with the jargon of the industry. His mind seemed to soak up the terms, and his understanding was almost intuitive. He didn't appear to be interested in the glamorous end of it.

And what was so glamorous about it? she asked herself. The room was airless and steaming. It smelled, none too pleasantly, of old beer. The lights had the already unmerciful temperature rising. The two people in position by the bar were circled by equipment. How could they be so intense with each other, she wondered, when lights and cameras were all but on top of them? Yet, despite herself, Tory became engrossed with the drama of the scene.

Marlie's character was tormenting Sam's, ridiculing him for coming back a loser, taunting him. But somehow a rather abrasive strength came through in her character. She seemed a woman trapped by circumstances who was determined to fight her way out. Somehow she made the differences in their ages inconsequential. As the scene unfolded, an objective viewer would develop a respect for her, perhaps a cautious sympathy. Before long the viewer would be rooting for her. Tory wondered if Dressler realized, for all his reputation and skill, who would be the real star of this scene.

She's very good, Tory admitted silently. Marlie Summers wasn't the pampered, glittery Tinsel Town cutie Tory had been ready to believe her to be. Tory recognized strength when she saw it. Marlie infused both a grit and a vulnerability into the character that was instantly admirable. And the sweat, Tory continued, was her own.

"Cut!" Phil's voice jolted her in her chair. "That's it."

Tory saw Marlie exhale a long breath. She wondered if there was some similarity in finishing a tense scene such as that one and winding up a difficult cross-examination. She decided that the emotion might be very much the same.

"Let's get some reaction shots, Marlie." Painstakingly he arranged for the change in angles and lighting. When the camera was in position, he checked through the lens himself, repositioned Marlie, then checked again. "Roll it…. Cue."

They worked for another thirty minutes, perfecting the shot. It was more than creativity, more than talent. The nuts and bolts end of the filming were tough, technical and wearily repetitious. No one complained, no one questioned, when told to change or to do over. There was an unspoken bond: the film. Perhaps, she reflected, it was because they knew it would outlast all of them. Their small slice of immortality. Tory found herself developing a respect for these people who took such an intense pride in their work.

"Cut. That's a wrap." Tory could almost feel the communal sigh of relief. "Set up for scene fifty-three in…" Phil checked his watch. "Two hours." The moment the lights shut down, the temperature dropped.

"I'm going to see what Mr. Bicks is doing," Tod announced, scrambling up. Tory remained sitting where she was a moment, watching Phil answer questions and give instructions. He never stops, she realized. One might be an actor, another a lighting expert or a cinematographer, but he touches every aspect. Rich and privileged, yes, she reflected, but not afraid of hard work.

"Sheriff."

Tory turned her head to see Marlie standing beside her. "Ms. Summers. You were very impressive."

"Thanks." Without waiting for an invitation, Marlie took a chair. "What I need now is a three-hour shower." She took a long pull from the glass of ice water she held in her hand as the two women studied each other in silence. "You've got an incredible face," Marlie said at length. "If I'd had one like that, I wouldn't have had to fight for a part with some meat on it. Mine's like a sugarplum."

Tory found herself laughing. Leaning back, she hooked her arm over the back of her chair. "Ms. Summers, as sheriff, I should warn you that stealing's a crime. You stole that scene from Sam very smoothly."

Tilting her head, Marlie studied her from a new angle. "You're very sharp."

"On occasion."

"I can see why Merle thinks you hold the answer to the mysteries of the universe."

Tory sent her a long, cool look. "Merle is a very naive, very vulnerable young man."

"Yes." Marlie set down her glass. "I like him." They gave each other another measuring look. "Look, let me ask you something, from one attractive woman to another. Did you ever find it pleasant to be with a man who liked to talk to you, to listen to you?"

"Yes, of course." Tory frowned. "Perhaps it's that I can't imagine what Merle would say to interest you."

Marlie gave a quick laugh, then cupped her chin on her palm. "You're too used to him. I've been scrambling my way up the ladder since I was eighteen. There's nothing I want more than to be on top. Along the way, I've met a lot of men. Merle's different."

"If he falls in love with you, he'll be hurt," Tory pointed out. "I've looked out for him on and off since we were kids."

Marlie paused a moment. Idly she drew patterns through the condensation on the outside of her water glass. "He's not going to fall in love with me," she said slowly. "Not really. We're just giving each other a bit of the other's world for a few weeks. When it's over, we'll both have something nice to remember." She glanced over her shoulder and spotted Phil. "We all need someone now and again, don't we, Sheriff?"

Tory followed the direction of Marlie's gaze. At that moment Phil's eyes lifted to hers. "Yes," she murmured, watching him steadily. "I suppose we do."

"I'm going to get that shower now." Marlie rose. "He's a good man," she added. Tory looked back at her, knowing who she referred to now.

"Yes, I think you're right." Deep in thought, Tory sat a moment longer. Then, standing, she glanced around for Tod.

"Tory." Phil laid a hand on her arm. "How are you?"

"Fine." She smiled, letting him know she hadn't forgotten the last time they had been together. "You're tougher than I thought, Kincaid, working in this oven all day."

He grinned. "That, assuredly, is a compliment."

"Don't let it go to your head. You're sweating like a pig."

"Really," he said dryly. "I hadn't noticed."

She spotted a towel hung over the back of a chair and plucked it up. "You know," she said as she wiped off his face, "I imagined directors would do more delegating than you do."

"My film," he said simply, stirred by the way she brushed the cloth over his face. "Tory." He captured her free hand. "I want to see you—alone."

She dropped the towel back on the table. "Your film," she reminded him. "And there's something I have to do." Her eyes darted past him, again in search of Tod.

"Tonight," he insisted. He'd gone beyond the point of patience. "Take the evening off, Tory."

She brought her eyes back to his. She'd gone beyond the point of excuses. "If I can," she agreed. "There's a place I know," she added with a slow smile. "South of town, about a mile. We used it as a swimming hole when I was a kid. You can't miss it; it's the only water around."

"Sunset?" He would have lifted her hand to his lips, but she drew it away.

"I can't promise." Before he could say anything else, she stepped past him, then called for Tod.

Even as she drew the boy back outside, he was expounding. "Tory, it's great, isn't it? About the greatest thing to happen in town in forever! If I could, I'd go with them when they leave." He sent her a look from under his tumbled hair. "Wouldn't you like to go, Tory?"

"To Hollywood?" she replied lightly. "Oh, I don't think it's my style. Besides, I'll be going back to Albuquerque soon."

"I want to come with you," he blurted out.

They were just outside her office door. Tory turned

and looked down at him. Unable to resist, she placed her hand on his cheek. "Tod," she said softly.

"I love you, Tory," he began quickly. "I could—"

"Tod, come inside." For days she had been working out what she would say to him and how to say it. Now, as they walked together into her office, she felt completely inadequate. Carefully she sat on the edge of her desk and faced him. "Tod—" She broke off and shook her head. "Oh, I wish I were smarter."

"You're the smartest person I know," he said swiftly. "And so beautiful, and I love you, Tory, more than anything."

Her heart reached out for him even as she took his hands. "I love you, too, Tod." As he started to speak she shook her head again. "But there are different kinds of love, different ways of feeling."

"I only know how I feel about you." His eyes were very intense and just above hers as she sat on the desk. Phil had been right, she realized. He wasn't quite a child.

"Tod, I know this won't be easy for you to understand. Sometimes people aren't right for each other."

"Just because I'm younger," he began heatedly.

"That's part of it," Tory agreed, keeping her voice quiet. "It's hard to accept, when you feel like a man, that you're still a boy. There's so much you have to experience yet, and to learn."

"But when I do…" he began.

"When you do," she interrupted, "you won't feel the same way about me."

"Yes, I will!" he insisted. He surprised both of them

by grabbing her arms. "It won't change because I don't want it to. And I'll wait if I have to. I love you, Tory."

"I know you do. I know it's very real." She lifted her hands to cover his. "Age doesn't mean anything to the heart, Tod. You're very special to me, a very important part of my life."

"But you don't love me." The words trembled out with anger and frustration.

"Not in the way you mean." She kept her hands firm on his when he would have jerked away.

"You think it's funny."

"No," she said sharply, rising. "No, I think it's lovely. And I wish things could be different because I know the kind of man you'll be. It hurts—for me too."

He was breathing quickly, struggling with tears and a sharp sense of betrayal. "You don't understand," he accused, pulling away from her. "You don't care."

"I do. Tod, please—"

"No." He stopped her with one ravaged look. "You don't." With a dignity that tore at Tory's heart, he walked out of the office.

She leaned back against the desk, overcome by a sense of failure.

The sun was just setting when Tory dropped down on the short, prickly grass by the water. Pulling her knees to her chest, she watched the flaming globe sink toward the horizon. There was an intensity of color against the darkening blue of the sky. Nothing soft or mellow. It was a vivid and demanding prelude to night.

Tory watched the sky with mixed emotions. The day

as a whole was the kind she would have liked to wrap up and ship off to oblivion. The situation with Tod had left her emotionally wrung out and edgy. As a result she had handled a couple of routine calls with less finesse than was her habit. She'd even managed to snarl at Merle before she had gone off duty. Glancing down at the badge on her breast, she considered tossing it into the water.

A beautiful mess you've made of things, Sheriff, she told herself. Ah, the hell with it, she decided, resting her chin on her knees. She was taking the night off. Tomorrow she would straighten everything out, one disaster at a time.

The trouble was, she thought with a half smile, she'd forgotten the art of relaxation over the past few weeks. It was time to reacquaint herself with laziness. Lying back, Tory shut her eyes and went instantly to sleep.

Drifting slowly awake with the feather-light touch of fingers on her cheek. Tory gave a sleepy sigh and debated whether she should open her eyes. There was another touch—a tracing of her lips this time. Enjoying the sensation, she made a quiet sound of pleasure and let her lashes flutter up.

The light was dim, deep, deep dusk. Her eyes focused gradually on the sky above her. No clouds, no stars, just a mellow expanse of blue. Taking a deep breath, she lifted her arms to stretch. Her hand was captured and kissed. Tory turned her head and saw Phil sitting beside her.

"Hello."

"Watching you wake up is enough to drive a man crazy," he murmured, keeping her hand in his. "You're sexier sleeping than most women are wide awake."

She gave a lazy laugh. "Sleeping's always been one of my best things. Have you been here long?"

"Not long. The filming ran a bit over schedule." He flexed his back muscles, then smiled down at her. "How was your day?"

"Rotten." Tory blew out a breath and struggled to sit up. "I talked with Tod this afternoon. I didn't handle it well. Damn." Tory rested her forehead on her knees again. "I didn't want to hurt that boy."

"Tory"—Phil stroked a hand down her hair—"there was no way he wouldn't be hurt some. Kids are resilient; he'll bounce back."

"I know." She turned her head to look at him, keeping her cheeks on her knees. "But he's so fragile. Love's fragile, isn't it? So easily shattered. I suppose it's best that he hate me for a while."

"He won't." Phil disagreed. "You mean too much to him. After a while his feelings will slip into perspective. I imagine he'll always think of you as his first real love."

"It makes me feel very special, but I don't think I made him believe that. Anyway," she continued, "after I'd made a mess out of that, I snarled at one of the town fathers, bit off the head of a rancher and took a few swipes at Merle." She swore with the expertise he had admired before. "Sitting here, I knew I was in danger of having a major pity party, so I went to sleep instead."

"Wise choice. I came near to choking my overseer."

"Overseer? Oh, the guarantor." Tory laughed, shaking back her hair. "So we both had a lovely day."

"Let's drink to it." Phil picked up a bottle of champagne from beside him.

"Well, how about that." Tory glanced at the label and pursed her lips. "You always go first-class, Kincaid."

"Absolutely," he agreed, opening the bottle with a pop and fizz. He poured the brimming wine into a glass. Tory took it, watching the bubbles explode as he filled his own. "To the end of the day."

"To the end of the day!" she agreed, clinking her glass against his. The ice-cold champagne ran excitedly over her tongue. "Nice," she murmured, shutting her eyes and savoring. "Very nice."

They drank in companionable silence as the darkness deepened. Overhead a few stars flickered hesitantly while the moon started its slow rise. The night was as hot and dry as the afternoon and completely still. There wasn't even a whisper of breeze to ripple the water. Phil leaned back on an elbow, studying Tory's profile.

"What are you thinking?"

"That I'm glad I took the night off." Smiling, she turned her head so she faced him fully. The pale light of the moon fell over her features, accenting them.

"Good God, Tory," he breathed. "I've got to get that face on film."

She threw back her head and laughed with a freedom she hadn't felt in days. "So take a home movie, Kincaid."

"Would you let me?" he countered immediately.

She merely filled both glasses again. "You're obsessed," she told him.

"More than's comfortable, yes," he murmured. He sipped, enjoying the taste, but thinking of her. "I wasn't sure you'd come."

"Neither was I." She studied the wine in her glass

with apparent concentration. "Another glass of this and I might admit I enjoy being with you."

"We've half a bottle left."

Tory lifted one shoulder in a shrug before she drank again. "One step at a time," she told him. "But then," she murmured, "I suppose we've come a few steps already, haven't we?"

"A few." His fingers ran over the back of her hand. "Does it worry you?"

She gave a quick, rueful laugh. "More than's comfortable, yes."

Sitting up, he draped a casual arm around her shoulders. "I like the night best. I have the chance to think." He sensed her complete relaxation, feeling a pleasant stir as she let her head rest on his shoulder. "During the day, with all the pressure, the demands, when I think, I think on my feet."

"That's funny." She lifted a hand across her body to lace her fingers with his. "In Albuquerque I did some of my best planning in bed the night before a court date. It's easier to let things come and go in your head at night." Tilting her face, Tory brushed his lips with hers. "I do enjoy being with you."

He returned the kiss, but with equal lightness. "I didn't need the champagne?"

"Well…it didn't hurt." When he chuckled, she settled her head in the crook of his shoulder again. It felt right there, as if it belonged. "I've always loved this spot," Tory said quietly. "Water's precious around here, and this has always been like a little mirage. It's not very big, but it's pretty deep in places. The townspeople enjoy calling it a lake." She laughed suddenly. "When we were kids, we'd troop out here sometimes on an unbearably hot day. We'd strip and jump in. Of course, it was frowned on when we were teenagers, but we still managed."

"Our decadent youth."

"Good, clean fun, Kincaid," she disagreed.

"Oh, yeah? Why don't you show me?"

Tory turned to him with a half smile. When he only lifted a brow in challenge, she grinned. A small pulse of excitement beat deep inside her. "You're on." Pushing him away, she tugged off her shoes. "The name of the game is to get in first."

As he stripped off his shirt it occurred to him that he'd never seen her move quickly before. He was still pulling off his shoes when she was naked and racing for the water. The moonlight danced over her skin, over the hair that streamed behind her back, causing him to stop and stare after her. She was even more exquisite than he had imagined. Then she was splashing up to her waist and diving under. Shaking himself out of the trance, Phil stripped and followed her.

The water was beautifully cool. It shocked his heated skin on contact, then caressed it. Phil gave a moan of pure pleasure as he sank to his shoulders. The small swimming hole in the middle of nowhere gave him just as much relief as his custom-made pool. More, he realized, glancing around for Tory. She surfaced, face lifted, hair slicked back. The moonlight caught the glisten of water on her face. A naiad, he thought. She opened her eyes. They glimmered green, like a cat's.

"You're slow, Kincaid."

He struggled against an almost painful flood of desire. This wasn't the moment to rush. They both knew this was their time, and there were hours yet to fill. "I've never seen you move fast before," he commented, treading water.

"I save it up." The bottom was just below her toes. Tory kicked lazily to keep afloat. "Conserving energy is one of my personal campaigns."

"I guess that means you don't want to race."

She gave him a long look. "You've got to be kidding."

"Guess you wouldn't be too hard to beat," he considered. "Skinny," he added.

"I am not." Tory put the heel of her hand into the water, sending a spray into his face.

"Couple of months in a good gym might build you up a bit." He smiled, calmly wiping the water from his eyes.

"I'm built up just fine," she returned. "Is this amateur psychology, Kincaid?"

"Did it work?" he countered.

In answer she twisted and struck out, kicking up a curtain of water into his face as she headed for the far side of the pool. Phil grinned, observing that she could move like lightning when she put her mind to it, then started after her.

She beat him by two full strokes, then waited, laughing, while she shook back her hair. "Better keep up your membership to that gym, Kincaid."

"You cheated," he pointed out.

"I won. That's what counts."

He lifted a brow, amused and intrigued that she wasn't even winded. Apparently her statement about strong energy was perfectly true. "And that from an officer of the law."

"I'm not wearing my badge."

"I noticed."

Tory laughed again, moving out in a gentle side-stroke toward the middle of the pool. "I guess you're in pretty good shape…for a Hollywood director."

"Is that so?" He swam alongside of her, matching her languid movements.

"You don't have a paunch—yet," she added, grinning. Gently but firmly, Phil pushed her head under. "So you want to play dirty," she murmured when she surfaced. In a quick move she had his legs scissored between hers, then gave his chest a firm shove. Off guard, Phil went over backward and submerged. He came up, giving his head a toss to free his eyes of dripping hair. Tory was already a few yards away, treading water and chuckling.

"Basic Self-Defense 101," she informed him. "Though you have to make allowances for buoyancy in the water."

This time Phil put more effort into his strokes. Before Tory had reached the other side, he had a firm grip on her ankle. With a tug he took her under the water and back to him. Sputtering, she found herself caught in his arms.

"Want to try a few free throws?" he invited.

A cautious woman, Tory measured her opponent and the odds. "I'll pass. Water isn't my element."

Her arms were trapped between their bodies, but when she tried to free them, he only brought her closer. His smile faded into a look of understanding. She felt her heart begin a slow, dull thud.

He took her mouth with infinite care, wanting to savor the moment. Her lips were wet and cool. With no hesitation her tongue sought his. The kiss deepened slowly, luxuriously while he supported her, keeping her feet just above the sandy bottom. The feeling of weightlessness aroused her and she allowed herself to float, holding on to him as though he were an anchor. Their lips warmed from an intimate heat before they began to search for new tastes.

Without hurry they roamed each other's faces, running moist kisses over moist skin. With quiet whispers the water lapped around them as they shifted and searched.

Finding her arms free at last, Tory wrapped them about his neck, pressing her body against his. She heard Phil suck in his breath at the contact, felt the shudder race through him before his mouth crushed down on hers. The time had passed for slow loving. Passion too long suppressed exploded as mouth sought eager mouth. Keeping one arm firm at her waist, he began to explore her as he had longed to do. His fingers slid over her wet skin.

Tory moved against him, weakening them both so that they submerged, locked together. Streaming wet, they surfaced with their lips still fused, then gasped for air. Her hands ran over him, drawing him closer, then away, to seek more of him. Unable to bear the hunger, she thrust her fingers into his hair and pulled his lips back to hers. With a sudden violence he bent her back until her hair streamed behind her on the surface of the water. His mouth rushed over her face, refusing her efforts to halt it with hers while he found her breast with his palm.

The throaty moan that wrenched from her evoked a

new wave of passion. Phil lifted her so he could draw her hot, wet nipple into his mouth. His tongue tormented them both until her hands fell into the pool in a submission he hadn't expected. Drunk on power, he took his mouth over her trembling skin, down to where the water separated him from her. Frustrated with the barrier, he let his mouth race up again to her breast until Tory clutched at his shoulders, shuddering.

Her head fell back as he lowered her so that her neck was vulnerable and glistening in the moonlight. He kissed it hungrily, hearing her cry with anguished delight.

Cool, cool water, but she was so hot that his legs nearly buckled at the feel of her. Tory was beyond all but dark, vivid sensations. To her the water felt steamy, heated by her own body. Her breathing seemed to echo in the empty night, then shudder back to her. She would have shouted for him to take her, but his name would only come as a gasp through her lips. She couldn't bear it; the need was unreasonable. With a strength conceived in passion she locked her legs tightly around his waist and lowered herself to him.

They swayed for a moment, equally stunned. Then he gripped her legs, letting her take him on a wild, impossible journey. There was a rushing, like the sound of the wind inside her head. Trembling, they slid down into the water.

With some vague recollection of where they were, Phil caught Tory against him again. "We'd better get out of here," he managed. "We'll drown."

Tory let her head fall on his shoulder. "I don't mind."

With a low, shaky laugh, Phil lifted her into his arms and carried her from the pond.

Chapter 8

He laid her down, then dropped on his back on the grass beside her. For some time the only sound in the night was their mixed breathing. The stars were brilliant now, the moon nearly full. Both of them stared up.

"You were saying something," Phil began in a voice that still wasn't steady, "about water not being your element."

Tory gave a choke of laughter that turned into a bubble, then a burst of pure appreciation. "I guess I could be wrong."

Phil closed his eyes, the better to enjoy the heavy weakness that flowed through his system.

Tory sighed and stretched. "That was wonderful."

He drew her closer against his side. "Cold?"

"No."

"This grass—"

"Terrible, isn't it?" With another laugh Tory twisted so that she lay over his chest. Her wet skin slid over his. Lazily he ran a hand down the length of her back as she smiled back at him. Her hair was slicked close to her head, her skin as pale and exquisite as marble in the moonlight. A few small drops of water clung to her lashes.

"You're beautiful when you're wet," he told her, drawing her down for a slow, lingering kiss.

"So are you." When he grinned, she ran both thumbs from his jaw to his cheekbones. "I like your face," she decided, tilting her head as she studied it. "That aristocratic bone structure you get from your father. It's no wonder he was so effective playing those swashbuckling roles early in his career." She narrowed her eyes as if seeking a different perspective. "Of course," she continued thoughtfully, "I rather like it when yours takes on that aloof expression."

"Aloof?" He shifted a bit as the grass scratched his bare skin.

"You do it very well. Your eyes have a terrific way of saying 'I beg your pardon' and meaning 'Go to hell.' I've noticed it, especially when you talk to that short man with the little glasses."

"Tremaine," Phil muttered. "Associate producer and general pain in the neck."

Tory chuckled and kissed his chin. "Don't like anyone else's hands on your movie, do you?"

"I'm very selfish with what belongs to me." He took her mouth again with more fervor than he had intended. As the kiss lengthened and deepened he gave a quick sound of pleasure and pressed her closer. When their lips parted, their eyes met. Both of them knew they were heading for dangerous ground. Both of them treaded carefully. Tory lowered her head to his chest, trying to think logically.

"I suppose we knew this was going to happen sooner or later."

"I suppose we did."

She caught her bottom lip between her teeth a moment. "The important thing is not to let it get complicated."

"No." He frowned up at the stars. "We both want to avoid complications."

"In a few weeks we'll both be leaving town." They were unaware that they had tightened their holds on the other. "I have to pick up my case load again."

"I have to finish the studio scenes," he murmured.

"It's a good thing we understand each other right from the beginning." She closed her eyes, drawing in his scent as though she were afraid she might forget it. "We can be together like this, knowing no one will be hurt when it's over."

"Yeah."

They lay in silence, dealing with a mutual and unstated sense of depression and loss. We're adults, Tory thought, struggling against the mood. Attracted to each other. It isn't any more than that. Can't be any more than that. But she wasn't as sure of herself as she wanted to be.

"Well," she said brightly, lifting her head again. "So tell me how the filming's going? That scene today seemed to click perfectly."

Phil forced himself to match her mood, ignoring the

doubts forming in his own head. "You came in on the last take," he said dryly. "It was like pulling teeth."

Tory reached across him for the bottle of champagne. The glass was covered with beads of sweat. "It looked to me like Marlie Summers came out on top," she commented as she poured.

"She's very good."

Resting her arm on his chest, Tory drank. The wine still fizzled cold. "Yes, I thought so, too, but I wish she'd steer away from Merle."

"Worried about his virtue, Tory?" he asked dryly.

She shot him an annoyed look. "He's going to get hurt."

"Why?" he countered. "Because a beautiful woman's interested enough to spend some time with him? Now, look," he continued before she could retort, "you have your own view of him; it's possible someone else might have another."

Frowning, she drank again. "How's he going to feel when she leaves?"

"That's something he'll have to deal with," Phil said quietly. "He already knows she's going to."

Again their eyes met in quick, almost frightened recognition. Tory looked away to study the remaining wine in her glass. It was different, she told herself. She and Phil both had certain priorities. When they parted, it would be without regret or pain. It had to be.

"It might not be easy to accept," she murmured, wanting to believe she still spoke of Merle.

"On either side," he replied after a long pause.

Tory turned her head to find his eyes on hers, light and clear and very intense. The ground was getting shaky again. "I suppose it'll work out for the best…for everyone." Determined to lighten the mood, she smiled down at him. "You know, the whole town's excited about those scenes you're shooting with them as extras. The Kramer twins haven't gotten out of line for an entire week."

"One of them asked me if he could have a close-up."

"Which one?"

"Who the hell can tell?" Phil demanded. "This one tried to hustle a date with Marlie."

Tory laughed, pressing the back of her wrist to her mouth to hold in a swallow of champagne. "Had to be Zac. He's impossible. Are you going to give him his close-up?"

"I'll give him a swift kick in the pants if he messes around the crane again," Phil returned.

"Uh-oh, I didn't hear about that."

Phil shrugged. "It didn't seem necessary to call the law on him."

"Tempting as it might be," she returned. "I wouldn't have thrown him in the penitentiary. Handling the Kramers has become an art."

"I had one of my security guards put the fear of God into him," Phil told her easily. "It seemed to do the trick."

"Listen, Phil, if any of my people need restraining, I expect to be informed."

With a sigh, he plucked the glass from her hand, tossed it aside, then rolled on top of her. "You've got the night off, Sheriff. We're not going to talk about it."

"Really." Her arms were already linked around his neck. "Just what are we going to talk about, then?"

"Not a damn thing," he muttered and pressed his mouth to hers.

Her response was a muffled sound of agreement. He could taste the champagne on her tongue and lingered over it. The heat of the night had already dried their skin, but he ran his hands through the cool dampness of her hair. He could feel her nipples harden against the pressure of his chest. This time, he thought, there would be no desperation. He could enjoy her slowly—the long, lean lines of her body, the silken texture of her skin, the varied, heady tastes of her.

From the wine-flavored lips he took an unhurried journey to the warmer taste of her throat. But his hands were already roaming demandingly. Tory moved under him with uncontrollable urgency as his thumb found the peak of her breast, intensifying her pleasure. To his amazement Phil found he could have taken her immediately. He banked the need. There was still so much of her to learn of, so much to experience. Allowing the tip of his tongue to skim along her skin, he moved down to her breast.

Tory arched, pressing him down. His slow, teasing kisses made her moan in delighted frustration. Beneath the swell of her breast, his mouth lingered to send shivers and more shivers of pleasure through her. His tongue flicked lazily over her nipple, then retreated to soft flesh. She moaned his name, urging him back. He circled slowly, mouth on one breast, palm on the other, thrilling to her mindless murmurs and convulsive movements beneath him. Taking exquisite care, he captured a straining peak between his teeth. Leaving it moist and wanting, he journeyed to her other breast to savor, to linger, then to devour.

His hands had moved lower, so that desire throbbed over her at so many points, she was delirious for fulfillment. Anxious to discover all she could about his body, Tory ran her fingertips over the taut muscles of his shoulders, down the strong back. Through a haze of sensation she felt him shudder at her touch. With delicious slowness she skimmed her fingers up his rib cage. She heard him groan before his teeth nipped into her tender flesh. Open and hungry, his mouth came swiftly back to hers.

When she reached for him, he drew in a sharp breath at the contact. Burying his face in her neck, Phil felt himself drowning in pleasure. The need grew huge, but again he refused it.

"Not yet," he murmured to himself and to her. "Not yet."

He passed down the valley between her breasts, wallowing in the hot scent that clung to her skin. Her stomach quivered under his lips. Tory no longer felt the rough carpet of grass under her back, only Phil's seeking mouth and caressing hands. His mouth slipped lower and she moaned, arching—willing, wanting. His tongue was quick and greedy, shooting pleasure from the core of her out even to her fingertips. Her body was heavy with it, her head light. He brought her to a shuddering crest, but relentlessly allowed no time for recovery. His fingers sought her even as his mouth found fresh delight in the taste of her thigh.

She shook her head, unable to believe she could be

so helpless. Her fingers clutched at the dry grass while her lips responded to the dizzying pace he set. Her skin was damp again, quivering in the hot night air. Again and again he drove her up, never letting her settle, never allowing her complete release.

"Phil," she moaned between harsh, shallow breaths. "I need..."

He'd driven himself to the verge of madness. His body throbbed in one solid ache for her. Wildly he took his mouth on a frantic journey up her body. "What?" he demanded. "What do you need?"

"You," she breathed, no longer aware of words or meanings. "You."

With a groan of triumph he thrust into her, catapulting them both closer to what they insisted on denying.

She'd warned him about the heat. Still, Phil found himself cursing the unrelenting sun as he set up for another outdoor shot. The grips had set up stands with butterflies—long black pieces of cloth—to give shade between takes. The cameraman stood under a huge orange and white umbrella and sweated profusely. The actors at least could spend a few moments in the shade provided while Phil worked almost exclusively in the streaming sun, checking angles, lighting, shadows. Reflectors were used to bounce the sunlight and carbon arcs balanced the back lighting. A gaffer, stripped to the waist, adjusted a final piece of blue gel over a bulb. The harsh, glaring day was precisely what Phil wanted, but it didn't make the work any more pleasant.

Forcing down more salt tablets, he ordered the next

take. Oddly, Dressler seemed to have adjusted to the heat more easily than the younger members of the cast and crew. Or, Phil mused as he watched him come slowly down the street with the fledgling actor who played his alter ego, he's determined not to be outdone. As time went on, he became more competitive—and the more competitive he became, particularly with Marlie, the more Phil was able to draw out of him.

Yeah, Phil thought as Dressler turned to the younger actor with a look of world-weariness. He ran through his dialogue slowly, keeping the pace just short of dragging. He was a man giving advice reluctantly, without any confidence that it was viable or would be listened to in any case. He talked almost to himself. For a moment Phil forgot his own discomfort in simple admiration for a pro who had found the heart of his character. He was growing old and didn't give a damn—wanted to be left alone, but had no hope that his wishes would be respected. Once he had found his moment of glory, then had lost it. He saw himself in the younger man and felt a bitter pity. Ultimately he turned and walked slowly away. The camera stayed on him for a silent thirty seconds.

"Cut. Perfect," Phil announced in a rare show of unconditional approval. "Lunch," he said dropping a hand on the younger actor's shoulder. "Get out of the sun for a while; I'll need you for reaction shots in thirty minutes." He walked over to meet Sam. "That was a hell of a job."

Grinning, Sam swiped at his brow. "Somebody's got to show these kids how it's done. That love scene with Marlie's going to be interesting," he added a bit ruefully. "I keep remembering she's my daughter's age."

"That should keep you in character."

Sam laughed, running his fingers through his thick salt-and-pepper hair. "Well, the girl's a pro," he said after a moment. "This movie's going to shoot her into the fast lane quick." He sent Phil a long, steady look. "And you and I," he added, "are going to win each other an Oscar." When Phil only lifted a brow, Sam slapped him on the back. "Don't give me that look, boy," he said, amused. "You're talking to one who's been passed over a few times himself. You can be lofty and say awards don't mean a damn…but they do." Again his eyes met Phil's. "I want this one just as much as you do." He ran a hand over his stomach. "Now I'm going to get myself a beer and put my feet up."

He sauntered off, leaving Phil looking after him. He didn't want to admit, even to himself, that he desired his profession's ultimate accolade. In a few short words Dressler had boiled it all down. Yes, he wanted to direct outstanding films—critically and financially successful, lasting, important. But he wanted that little gold statue. With a wry grin Phil swiped at his brow with his forearm. It seemed that the need to win, and to be acknowledged, didn't fade with years. Dressler had been in the business longer than Phil had been alive; yet, he was still waiting for the pot at the end of the rainbow. Phil adjusted his sunglasses, admitting he wasn't willing to wait thirty-five years.

"Hey, Phil." Bicks lumbered over to him, mopping his face. "Look, you've got to do something about that woman."

Phil pulled out a cigarette. "Which?"

"That sheriff." Bicks popped another piece of gum

into his mouth. "Great looker," he added. "Got a way of walking that makes a man home right in on her…" He trailed off, observing the look in Phil's eyes. "Just an observation," he muttered.

"What do you expect me to do about the way Sheriff Ashton walks, Bicks?"

Catching the amusement in Phil's tone, Bicks grinned. "Nothing, please. A man's got to have something pleasant to look at in this place. But damn it, Phil, she gave me a ticket and slapped a two-hundred-and-fifty-dollar fine on me."

Phil pushed his glasses up on his head with a weary sigh. He'd wanted to catch a quick shower before resuming the shoot. "What for?"

"Littering."

"Littering?" Phil repeated over a snort of laughter.

"Two hundred and fifty bucks for dropping gum wrappers in the street," Bicks returned, not seeing the humor. "Wouldn't listen to reason either. I'd have picked 'em up and apologized. Two hundred and fifty bucks for a gum wrapper, Phil. Jeez."

"All right, all right, I'll talk to her." After checking his watch, Phil started up the street. "Set up for the next scene in twenty minutes."

Tory sat with her feet propped up on the desk as she struggled to decipher Merle's report on a feud between two neighboring ranches. It seemed that a dispute over a line of fence was becoming more heated. It was going to require her attention. So was the letter she had just received from one of her clients in Albuquerque. When Phil walked in, she glanced up from the scrawled pad and smiled.

"You look hot," she commented.

"Am hot," he countered, giving the squeaking fan above their heads a glance. "Why don't you get that thing fixed?"

"And spoil the atmosphere?"

Phil stepped over the sleeping dog, taking a seat on the corner of her desk. "We're going to be shooting one of the scenes with the townspeople milling around later. Are you going to watch?"

"Sure."

"Want to do a cameo?" he asked with a grin.

"No, thanks."

Leaning over, he pressed his lips to hers. "Dinner in my room tonight?"

Tory smiled. "You still have those candles?"

"All you want," he agreed.

"You talked me into it," she murmured, drawing his face back for a second kiss.

"Tory, if I brought a camera out to your ranch one day, would you let me film you riding that palomino?"

"Phil, for heaven's sake—"

"Home movies?" he interrupted, twirling her hair around his finger.

She gave a capitulating sigh. "If it's important to you."

"It is." He straightened, checked his watch, then pulled out a cigarette. "Listen, Tory, Bicks tells me you fined him for littering."

"That's right." The phone rang, and Phil waited while she took the call. After a moment he realized her tone was slightly different. With interest he listened to the legal jargon roll off her tongue. It must be Albuquerque, he realized. He watched her carefully, discovering this was a part of her life he knew nothing of. She'd be tough in court, he mused. There was an intensity under that languid exterior that slipped out at unexpected moments. And what did she do after a day in court or a day in the office?

There'd be men, he thought, instantly disliking the image. A woman like Tory would only spend evenings alone, nights alone, if she chose to. He looked away, taking a deep drag on his cigarette. He couldn't start thinking along those lines, he reminded himself. They were both free agents. That was the first rule.

"Phil?"

He turned back to see that she had replaced the receiver. "What?"

"You were saying?"

"Ah…" He struggled to remember the point of his visit. "Bicks," he continued.

"Yes, what about him?"

"A two-hundred-and-fifty-dollar fine for littering," Phil stated, not quite erasing the frown that had formed between his brows.

"Yes, that's the amount of the fine."

"Tory, be reasonable."

Her brow lifted. "Reasonable, Kincaid?"

Her use of his surname told him what level they were dealing on. "It's certainly extreme for a gum wrapper."

"We don't vary the fine according to the style of trash," she replied with an easy shrug. "A tin of caviar would have cost him the same amount."

Goaded, Phil rose. "Listen, Sheriff—"

"And while we're on the subject," she interrupted,

"you can tell your people that if they don't start picking up after themselves more carefully, they're all going to be slapped with fines." She gave him a mild smile. "Let's keep Friendly clean, Kincaid."

He took a slow drag. "You're not going to hassle my people."

"You're not going to litter my town."

He swore, coming around the desk when the door opened. Pleased to see Tod, Tory swung her legs to the floor and started to stand. It was then that she saw the dull bruise on the side of his face. Fury swept through her so quickly, she was forced to clench her hands into fists to control it. Slowly she walked to him and took his face in her hands.

"How did you get this?"

He shrugged, avoiding her eyes. "It's nothing."

Fighting for calm. Tory lifted his hands, examining the knuckles carefully. There was no sign that he'd been fighting. "Your father?"

He shook his head briskly. "I came to do the sweeping up," he told her, and tried to move away.

Tory took him firmly by the shoulders. "Tod, look at me."

Reluctantly he lifted his eyes. "I've still got five dollars to work off," he said tightly.

"Did your father put this bruise on your face?" she demanded. When he started to drop his eyes again, she gave him a quick shake. "You answer me."

"He was just mad because—" He broke off, observing the rage that lit her face. Instinctively he cringed away from it. Tory set him aside and started for the door.

"Where are you going?" Moving quickly, Phil was at the door with her, his hand over hers on the knob.

"To see Swanson."

"No!" They both turned to see Tod standing rigid in the center of the room. "No, you can't. He won't like it. He'll get awful mad at you."

"I'm going to talk to your father, Tod," Tory said in a careful voice, "to explain to him why it's wrong for him to hurt you this way."

"Only when he loses his temper." Tod dashed across the room to grab her free hand. "He's not a bad man. I don't want you to put him in jail."

Though her anger was lethal, Tory gave Tod's hand a reassuring squeeze. "I'm just going to talk to him, Tod."

"He'll be crazy mad if you do, Tory. I don't want him to hurt you either."

"He won't, don't worry." She smiled, seeing by the expression in Tod's eyes that she'd already been forgiven. "Go get the broom now. I'll be back soon."

"Tory, please..."

"Go on," she said firmly.

Phil waited until the boy had disappeared into the back room. "You're not going."

Tory sent him a long look, then pulled open the door. Phil spun her around as she stepped outside. "I said you're not going."

"You're interfering with the law, Kincaid."

"The hell with that!" Infuriated, Phil pushed her back against the wall. "You're crazy if you think I'm going to let you go out there."

"You don't *let* me do anything," she reminded him.

"I'm sworn to protect the people under my jurisdiction. Tod Swanson is one of my people."

"A man who punches a kid isn't going to hesitate to take a swing at you just because you've got that little piece of tin on your shirt."

Because her anger was racing, Tory forced herself to speak calmly. "What do you suggest I do? Ignore what I just saw?"

Frustrated by the image of Tod's thin face, Phil swore. "I'll go."

"You have no right." She met his eyes squarely. "You're not the law, and what's more, you're an outsider."

"Send Merle."

"Don't you hold with no woman sheriff, Kincaid?"

"Damn it, Tory." He shook her, half in fear, half in frustration. "This isn't a joke."

"No, it's not," she said seriously. "It's my job. Now, let go of me, Phil."

Furious, Phil complied, then watched her stride to her car. "Tory," he called after her, "if he puts a hand on you, I'll kill him."

She slipped into the car, driving off without looking back.

Tory took the short drive slowly, wanting to get her emotions under control before she confronted Swanson. She had to be objective, she thought, as her knuckles whitened on the steering wheel. But first she had to be calm. It wasn't possible to do what she needed to do in anger, or to let Phil's feelings upset her. To live up to the badge on her shirt, she had to set all that aside.

She wasn't physically afraid, not because she was foolishly brave, but because when she saw a blatant injustice, Tory forgot everything but the necessity of making it right. As she took the left fork toward the Swanson ranch, however, she had her first stirring of self-doubt.

What if she mishandled the situation? she thought in sudden panic. What if her meeting with Swanson only made more trouble for the boy? The memory of Tod's terrified face brought on a quick queasiness that she fought down. No, she wasn't going to mishandle it, she told herself firmly as the house came into view. She was going to confront Swanson and at the very least set the wheels in motion for making things right. Tory's belief that all things could be set right with patience, through the law, had been indoctrinated in childhood. She knew and accepted no other way.

She pulled up behind Swanson's battered pickup, then climbed out of the sheriff's car. Instantly a dog who had been sleeping on the porch sent out angry, warning barks. Tory eyed him a moment, wary, then saw that he came no farther than the edge of the sagging porch. He looked as old and unkempt as the house itself.

Taking a quick look around, Tory felt a stir of pity for Tod. This was borderline poverty. She, too, had grown up where a tightened belt was often a rule, but between her mother's penchant for neatness and the hard work of both her parents, their small ranch had always had a homey charm. This place, on the other hand, looked desolate and hopeless. The grass grew wild, long overdue for trimming. There were no brightening spots of color from flowers or potted plants. The house itself was frame, the paint faded down to the wood in places. There was no chair on the porch, no sign that anyone had the time or inclination to sit and appreciate the view.

No one came to the door in response to the dog's barking. Tory debated calling out from where she stood or taking a chance with the mangy mutt. A shout came from the rear of the house with a curse and an order to shut up. The dog obeyed, satisfying himself with low growls as Tory headed in the direction of the voice.

She spotted Swanson working on the fence of an empty corral. The back of his shirt was wet with sweat, while his hat was pulled low to shade his face. He was a short, stocky man with the strong shoulders of a laborer. Thinking of Tod's build, Tory decided he had inherited it, and perhaps his temperament, from his mother.

"Mr. Swanson?"

His head jerked up. He had been replacing a board on the fence; the hand that swung the hammer paused on the downswing. Seeing his face, Tory decided he had the rough, lined face of a man constantly fighting the odds of the elements. He narrowed his eyes; they passed briefly over her badge.

"Sheriff," he said briefly, then gave the nail a final whack. He cared little for women who interfered in a man's work.

"I'd like to talk to you, Mr. Swanson."

"Yeah?" He pulled another nail out of an old coffee can. "What about?"

"Tod." Tory waited until he had hammered the nail into the warped board.

"That boy in trouble?"

"Apparently," she said mildly. She told herself to overlook his rudeness as he turned his back to take out another nail.

"I handle my own," he said briefly. "What's he done?"

"He hasn't done anything, Mr. Swanson."

"Either he's in trouble or he's not." Swanson placed another nail in position and beat it into the wood. The sound echoed in the still air. From somewhere to the right, Tory heard the lazy moo of a cow. "I ain't got time for conversation, Sheriff."

"He's in trouble, Mr. Swanson," she returned levelly. "And you'll talk to me here or in my office."

The tone had him taking another look and measuring her again. "What do you want?"

"I want to talk to you about the bruise on your son's face." She glanced down at the meaty hands, noting that the knuckles around the hammer whitened.

"You've got no business with my boy."

"Tod's a minor," she countered. "He's very much my business."

"I'm his father."

"And as such, you are not entitled to physically or emotionally abuse your child."

"I don't know what the hell you're talking about." The color in his sun-reddened face deepened angrily. Tory's eyes remained calm and direct.

"I'm well aware that you've beaten the boy before," she said coolly. "There are very strict laws to protect a child against this kind of treatment. If they're unknown to you, you might want to consult an attorney."

"I don't need no damn lawyer," he began, gesturing at Tory with the hammer as his voice rose.

"You will if you point that thing at me again," she told him quietly. "Attempted assault on a peace officer is a very serious crime."

Swanson looked down at the hammer, then dropped it disgustedly to the ground. "I don't assault women," he muttered.

"Just children?"

He sent her a furious glance from eyes that watered against the sun. "I got a right to discipline my own. I got a ranch to run here." A gesture with his muscular arm took in his pitiful plot of land. "Every time I turn around, that boy's off somewheres."

"Your reasons don't concern me. The results do."

With rage burning on his face, he took a step toward her. Tory held her ground. "You just get back in your car and get out. I don't need nobody coming out here telling me how to raise my boy."

Tory kept her eyes on his, although she was well aware his hands had clenched into fists. "I can start proceedings to make Tod a ward of the court."

"You can't take my boy from me."

Tory lifted a brow. "Can't I?"

"I got rights," he blustered.

"So does Tod."

He swallowed, then turned back to pick up his hammer and nails. "You ain't taking my boy."

Something in his eyes before he had turned made Tory pause. Justice, she reminded herself, was individual. "He wouldn't want me to," she said in a quieter tone. "He told me you were a good man and asked me not to put you in jail. You bruise his face, but he doesn't stop loving you."

She watched Swanson's back muscles tighten. Abruptly he flung the hammer and the can away. Nails scattered in the wild grass. "I didn't mean to hit him like that," he said with a wrench in his voice that kept Tory silent. "Damn boy should've fixed this fence like I told him." He ran his hands over his face. "I didn't mean to hit him like that. Look at this place," he muttered, gripping the top rail of the fence. "Takes every minute just to keep it up and scrape by, never amount to anything. But it's all I got. All I hear from Tod is how he wants to go off to school, how he wants this and that, just like—"

"His brother?" Tory ventured.

Swanson turned his head slowly, and his face was set. "I ain't going to talk about that."

"Mr. Swanson, I know something about what it takes to keep up a place like this. But your frustrations and your anger are no excuse for misusing your boy."

He turned away again, the muscles in his jaw tightening. "He's gotta learn."

"And your way of teaching him is to use your fists?"

"I tell you I didn't mean to hit him." Furious, he whirled back to her. "I don't mean to take a fist to him the way my father done to me. I know it ain't right, but when he pushes me—" He broke off again, angry with himself for telling his business to an outsider. "I ain't going to hit him anymore," he muttered.

"But you've told yourself that before, haven't you?"

Tory countered. "And meant it, I'm sure." She took a deep breath, as he only stared at her. "Mr. Swanson, you're not the only parent who has a problem with control. There are groups and organizations designed to help you and your family."

"I'm not talking to any psychiatrists and do-gooders."

"There are ordinary people, exactly like yourself, who talk and help each other."

"I ain't telling strangers my business. I can handle my own."

"No, Mr. Swanson, you can't." For a moment Tory wished helplessly that there was an easy answer. "You don't have too many choices. You can drive Tod away, like you did your first boy." Tory stood firm as he whirled like a bull. "Or," she continued calmly, "you can seek help, the kind of help that will justify your son's love for you. Perhaps your first decision is what comes first, your pride or your boy."

Swanson stared out over the empty corral. "It would kill his mother if he took off too."

"I have a number you can call, Mr. Swanson. Someone who'll talk to you, who'll listen. I'll give it to Tod."

His only acknowledgment was a shrug. She waited a moment, praying her judgment was right. "I don't like ultimatums," she continued. "But I'll expect to see Tod daily. If he doesn't come to town, I'll come here. Mr. Swanson, if there's a mark on that boy, I'll slap a warrant on you and take Tod into custody."

He twisted his head to look at her again. Slowly, measuringly, he nodded. "You've got a lot of your father in you, Sheriff."

Automatically Tory's hand rose to her badge. She smiled for the first time. "Thanks." Turning, she walked away. Not until she was out of sight did she allow herself the luxury of wiping her sweaty palms on the thighs of her jeans.

Chapter 9

Tory was stopped at the edge of town by a barricade. Killing the engine, she stepped out of the car as one of Phil's security men approached her.

"Sorry, Sheriff, you can't use the main street. They're filming."

With a shrug Tory leaned back on the hood of her car. "It's all right. I'll wait."

The anger that had driven her out to the Swanson ranch was gone. Now Tory appreciated the time to rest and think. From her vantage point she could see the film crew and the townspeople who were making their debut as extras. She watched Hollister walk across the street in back of two actors exchanging lines in the scene. It made Tory smile, thinking how Hollister would brag about this moment of glory for years to come. There were a dozen people she knew, milling on the streets or waiting for their opportunity to mill. Phil cut the filming, running through take after take. Even with the distance Tory could sense he was frustrated. She frowned, wondering if their next encounter would turn into a battle. She couldn't back down, knowing that she had done the right thing—essentially the only thing.

Their time together was to be very brief, she mused. She didn't want it plagued by arguments and tension. But until he accepted the demands and responsibilities of her job, tension was inevitable. It had already become very important to Tory that the weeks ahead be unmarred. Perhaps, she admitted thoughtfully, too important. It was becoming more difficult for her to be perfectly logical when she thought of Phil. And since the night before, the future had become blurred and distant. There seemed to be only the overwhelming present.

She couldn't afford that, Tory reminded herself. That wasn't what either one of them had bargained for. She shifted her shoulders as her shirt grew hot and damp against her back. There was the summer, and just the summer, before they both went their separate ways. It was, of course, what each of them wanted.

"Sheriff…ah, Sheriff Ashton?"

Disoriented, Tory shook her head and stared at the man beside her. "What—? Yes?"

The security guard held out a chilled can of soda. "Thought you could use this."

"Oh, yeah, thanks." She pulled the tab, letting the air out in a hiss. "Do you think they'll be much longer?"

"Nah." He lifted his own can to drink half of it down

without a breath. "They've been working on this one scene over an hour now."

Gratefully, Tory let the icy drink slide down her dry throat. "Tell me, Mr.—"

"Benson, Chuck Benson, ma'am."

"Mr. Benson," Tory continued, giving him an easy smile. "Have you had any trouble with any of the townspeople?"

"Nothing to speak of," he said as he settled beside her against the hood. "Couple of kids—those twins."

"Oh, yes," Tory murmured knowingly.

"Only tried to con me into letting them on the crane." He gave an indulgent laugh, rubbing the cold can over his forehead to cool it. "I've got a couple teenagers of my own," he explained.

"I'm sure you handled them, Mr. Benson." Tory flashed him a dashing smile that lifted his blood pressure a few degrees. "Still, I'd appreciate hearing about it if anyone in town gets out of line—particularly the Kramer twins."

Benson chuckled. "I guess those two keep you busy."

"Sometimes they're a full-time job all by themselves." Tory rested a foot on the bumper and settled herself more comfortably. "So tell me, how old are your kids?"

By the time Phil had finished shooting the scene, he'd had his fill of amateurs for the day. He'd managed, with a good deal of self-control, to hold on to his patience and speak to each one of his extras before he dismissed them. He wanted to shoot one more scene before they wrapped up for the day, so he issued instructions immediately. It would take an hour to set up, and with luck they'd have the film in the can before they lost the light.

The beeper at his hip sounded, distracting him. Impatiently, Phil drew out the walkie-talkie. "Yeah, Kincaid."

"Benson. I've got the sheriff here. All right to let her through now?"

Automatically, Phil looked toward the edge of town. He spotted Tory leaning lazily against the hood, drinking from a can. He felt twin surges of relief and annoyance. "Let her in," he ordered briefly, then shoved the radio back in place. Now that he knew she was perfectly safe, Phil had a perverse desire to strangle her. He waited until she had parked in front of the sheriff's office and walked up the street to meet her. Before he was halfway there, Tod burst out of the door.

"Sheriff!" He teetered at the edge of the sidewalk, as if unsure of whether to advance any farther.

Tory stepped up and ran a fingertip down the bruise on his cheek. "Everything's fine, Tod."

"You didn't…" He moistened his lips. "You didn't arrest him?"

She rested her arms on his shoulders. "No." Tory felt his shuddering sigh.

"He didn't get mad at you or…" He trailed off again and looked at her helplessly.

"No, we just talked. He knows he's wrong to hurt you, Tod. He wants to stop."

"I was scared when you went, but Mr. Kincaid said you knew what you were doing and that everything would be all right."

"Did he?" Tory turned her head as Phil stepped beside her. The look held a long and not quite comfortable moment. "Well, he was right." Turning back to Tod, she gave his shoulders a quick squeeze. "Come inside a minute. There's a number I want you to give to your father. Want a cup of coffee, Kincaid?"

"All right."

Together, they walked into Tory's office. She went directly to her desk, pulling out a smart leather-bound address book that looked absurdly out of place. After flipping through it, she wrote a name and phone number on a pad, then ripped off the sheet. "This number is for your whole family," she said as she handed Tod the paper. "Go home and talk to your father, Tod. He needs to understand that you love him."

He folded the sheet before slipping it into his back pocket. Shifting from foot to foot, he stared down at the cluttered surface of her desk. "Thanks. Ah…I'm sorry about the things I said before." Coloring a bit, he glanced at Phil. "You know," he murmured, lowering his gaze to the desk again.

"Don't be sorry, Tod." She laid a hand over his until he met her eyes. "Okay?" she said, and smiled.

"Yeah, okay." He blushed again, but drew up his courage. Giving Tory a swift kiss on the cheek, he darted for the door.

With a low laugh she touched the spot where his lips had brushed. "I swear," she murmured, "if he were fifteen years older…" Phil grabbed both her arms.

"Are you really all right?"

"Don't I look all right?" she countered.

"Damn it, Tory!"

"Phil." Taking his face in her hands, she gave him a hard, brief kiss. "You had no reason to worry. Didn't you tell Tod that I knew what I was doing?"

"The kid was terrified." And so was I, he thought as he pulled her into his arms. "What happened out there?" he demanded.

"We talked," Tory said simply. "He's a very troubled man. I wanted to hate him and couldn't. I'm counting on him calling that number."

"What would you have done if he'd gotten violent?"

"I would have handled it," she told him, drawing away a bit. "It's my job."

"You can't—"

"Phil"—Tory cut him off quickly and firmly—"I don't tell you how to set a scene; don't tell me how to run my town."

"It's not the same thing and you know it." He gave her an angry shake. "Nobody takes a swing at me when I do a retake."

"How about a frustrated actor?"

His eyes darkened. "Tory, you can't make a joke out of this."

"Better a joke than an argument," she countered. "I don't want to fight with you. Phil, don't focus on something like this. It isn't good for us."

He bit off a furious retort, then strode away to stare out the window. Nothing seemed as simple as it had been since the first time he'd walked into that cramped little room. "It's hard," he murmured. "I care."

Tory stared at his back while a range of emotions swept

through her. Her heart wasn't listening to the strict common sense she had imposed on it. No longer sure what she wanted, she suppressed the urge to go to him and be held again. "I know," she said at length. "I care too."

He turned slowly. They looked at each other as they had once before, when there were bars between them— a bit warily. For a long moment there was only the sound of the whining fan and the mumble of conversation outside. "I have to get back," he told her, carefully slipping his hands in his pockets. The need to touch her was too strong. "Dinner?"

"Sure." She smiled, but found it wasn't as easy to tilt her lips up as it should have been. "It'll have to be a little later—around eight?"

"That's fine. I'll see you then."

"Okay." She waited until the door had closed behind him before she sat at her desk. Her legs were weak. Leaning her head on her hand, she let out a long breath.

Oh, boy, she thought. Oh, boy. The ground was a lot shakier than she had anticipated. But she couldn't be falling in love with him, she reassured herself. Not that. Everything was intensified because of the emotional whirlwind of the past couple of days. She wasn't ready for the commitments and obligations of being in love, and that was all there was to it. Rising, she plugged in the coffeepot. She'd feel more like herself if she had a cup of coffee and got down to work.

Phil spent more time than he should have in the shower. It had been a very long, very rough twelve-hour day. He was accustomed to impossible hours and impossible demands in his job. Characteristically he took them in stride. Not this time.

The hot water and steam weren't drawing out the tension in his body. It had been there from the moment when Tory had driven off to the Swanson ranch, then had inexplicably increased during their brief conversation in her office. Because he was a man who always dealt well with tension, he was annoyed that he wasn't doing so this time.

He shut his eyes, letting the water flood over his head. She'd been perfectly right, he mused, about his having no say in her work. For that matter he had no say in any aspect of her life. There were no strings on their relationship. And he didn't want them any more than Tory did. He'd never had this problem in a relationship before. Problem? he mused, pushing wet hair out of his eyes. A perspective problem, he decided. What was necessary was to put his relationship with Tory back in perspective.

And who better to do that than a director? he thought wryly, then switched off the shower with a jerk of the wrist. He was simply letting too much emotion leak into the scene. Take two, he decided, grabbing a towel. Somehow he'd forgotten a very few basic, very vital rules. Keep it simple, keep it light, he reminded himself. Certainly someone with his background and experience was too smart to look for complications. What was between him and Tory was completely elemental and without strain, because they both wanted to keep it that way.

That was one of the things that had attracted him to her in the first place, Phil remembered. Hooking a towel loosely around his waist, he grabbed another to rub his hair dry. She wasn't a woman who expected a commitment, who looked for a permanent bond like love or marriage. Those were two things they were both definitely too smart to get mixed up with. In the steam-hazed mirror Phil caught the flicker of doubt in his own eyes.

Oh, no, he told himself, absolutely not. He wasn't in love with her. It was out of the question. He cared, naturally: She was a very special woman—strong, beautiful, intelligent, independent. And she had a great deal of simple sweetness that surfaced unexpectedly. It was that one quality that kept a man constantly off-balance. So he cared about her, Phil mused, letting the second towel fall to the floor. He could even admit that he felt closer to her than to many people he'd known for years. There was nothing unusual about that. They had something in common that clicked—an odd sort of friendship, he decided. That was safe enough. It was only because he'd been worried about her that he'd allowed things to get out of proportion for a time.

But he was frowning abstractedly at his reflection when he heard the knock on the door.

"Who is it?"

"Room service."

The frown turned into a grin instantly as he recognized Tory's voice.

"Well, hi." Tory gave him a look that was both encompassing and lazy when he opened the door. "You're a little late for your reservation, Kincaid."

He stepped aside to allow her to enter with a large tray. "I lost track of time in the shower. Is that our dinner?"

"Bud phoned me." Tory set the tray on the card table

they'd used before. "He said you'd ordered dinner for eight but didn't answer your phone. Since I was starving, I decided to expedite matters." Slipping her arms around his waist, she ran her hands up his warm, damp back. "Ummm, you're tense," she murmured, enjoying the way his hair curled chaotically around his face. "Rough day?"

"And then some," he agreed before he kissed her.

He smelled clean—of soap and shampoo—yet, Tory found the scent as arousing as the darker musky fragrance she associated with him. Her hunger for food faded as quickly as her hunger for him rose. Pressing closer, she demanded more. His arms tightened; his muscles grew taut. He was losing himself in her again, and found no power to control it.

"You really are tense," Tory said against his mouth. "Lie down."

He gave a half chuckle, nibbling on her bottom lip. "You work fast."

"I'll rub your back," she informed him as she drew away. "You can tell me all the frustrating things those nasty actors did today while you were striving to be brilliant."

"Let me show you how we deal with smart alecks on the coast," Phil suggested.

"On the bed, Kincaid."

"Well…" He grinned. "If you insist."

"On your stomach," she stated when he started to pull her with him.

Deciding that being pampered might have its advantages, he complied. "I've got a bottle of wine in the cooler." He sighed as he stretched out full length. "It's a hell of a place to keep a fifty-year-old Burgundy."

"Don't be a snob," Tory warned, sitting beside him. "You must have worked ten or twelve hours today," she began. "Did you get much accomplished?"

"Not as much as we should have." He gave a quiet groan of pleasure as she began to knead the muscles in his shoulders. "That's wonderful."

"The guys in the massage parlor always asked for Tory." His head came up. "What?"

"Just wanted to see if you were paying attention. Down, Kincaid." She chuckled softly, working down his arms. "Were there technical problems or temperament ones?"

"Both," he answered, settling again. He found closing his eyes was a sensuous luxury. "Had some damaged dichroics. With luck the new ones'll get here tomorrow. Most of the foul-ups came during the crowd scene. Your people like to grin into the camera," he said dryly. "I expected one of them to wave any minute."

"That's show biz," Tory concluded as she shifted to her knees. She hiked her dress up a bit for more freedom. Opening his eyes, Phil was treated to a view of thigh. "I wouldn't be surprised if the town council elected to build a theater in Friendly just to show your movie. Think of the boon to the industry."

"Merle walked across the street like he's sat on a horse for three weeks." Because her fingers were working miracles over his back muscles, Phil shut his eyes again.

"Merle's still seeing Marlie Summers."

"Tory."

"Just making conversation," she said lightly, but dug a bit harder than necessary into his shoulder blades.

"Ouch!"

"Toughen up, Kincaid." With a laugh she placed a loud, smacking kiss in the center of his back. "You're not behind schedule, are you?"

"No. With all the hazards of shooting on location, we're doing very well. Another four weeks should wrap it up."

They were both silent for a moment, unexpectedly depressed. "Well, then," Tory said briskly, "you shouldn't have to worry about the guarantor."

"He'll be hanging over my shoulder until the film's in the can," Phil muttered. "There's a spot just to the right…oh, yeah," he murmured as her fingers zeroed in on it.

"Too bad you don't have any of those nifty oils and lotions," she commented. In a fluid movement Tory straddled him, the better to apply pressure. "You're a disappointment, Kincaid. I'd have thought all you Hollywood types would carry a supply of that kind of thing."

"Mmmm." He would have retorted in kind, but his mind was beginning to float. Her fingers were cool and sure as they pressed on the small of his back just above the line of the towel. Her legs, clad in thin stockings, brushed his sides, arousing him with each time she flexed. The scent of her shampoo tickled his nostrils as she leaned up to knead his shoulders again. Though the sheet was warm—almost too warm—beneath him, he couldn't summon the energy to move. As the sun was setting, the light shifted, dimming. The room was filled with a golden haze that suited his mood. He could hear the rumble of a car on the street below, then only the sound of Tory's light, even breathing above him. His muscles were relaxed and limber, but he didn't consider telling her to stop. He'd forgotten completely about the dinner growing cold on the table behind them.

Tory continued to run her hands along his back, thinking him asleep. He had a beautiful body, she mused, hard and tanned and disciplined. The muscles in his back were supple and strong. For a moment she simply enjoyed exploring him. When she shifted lower, the skirt of her dress rode up high on her thighs. With a little sound of annoyance she unzipped the dress and pulled it over her head. She could move with more freedom in her sheer teddy.

His waist was trim. She allowed her hands to slide over it, approving its firmness. Before their lovemaking had been so urgent, and she had been completely under his command. Now she enjoyed learning the lines and planes of his body. Down the narrow hips, over the brief swatch of towel, to his thighs. There were muscles there, too, she discovered, hardened by hours of standing, tennis, swimming. The light mat of hair over his skin made her feel intensely feminine. She massaged his calves, then couldn't resist the urge to place a light kiss on the back of his knee. Phil's blood began to heat in a body too drugged with pleasure to move. It gave her a curiously warm feeling to rub his feet.

He worked much harder than she'd initially given him credit for, she mused as she roamed slowly back up his legs. He spent hours in the sun, on his feet, going over and over the same shot until he'd reached the perfection he strove for. And she had come to know that the film was never far from his thoughts, even during his free hours. Phillip Kincaid, she thought with a gentle smile, was a very impressive man—with much more depth than the glossy playboy the press loved to tattle on. He'd earned her respect during the time he'd been in Friendly, and she was growing uncomfortably certain he'd earned something more complex. She wouldn't think of it now. Perhaps she would have no choice but to think of it after he'd gone. But for now, he was here. That was enough.

With a sigh she bent low over his back to lay her cheek on his shoulder. The need for him had crept into her while she was unaware. Her pulse was pounding, and a thick warmth, like heated honey, seemed to flow through her veins.

"Phil." She moved her mouth to his ear. Her tongue traced it, slipping inside to arouse him to wakefulness. She heard his quiet groan as her heart began to beat jerkily. With her teeth she pulled and tugged on the lobe, then moved to experiment with the sensitive area just below. "I want you," she murmured. Quickly she began to take her lips over him with the same thorough care as her fingers.

He seemed so pliant as she roamed over him that when a strong arm reached out to pull her down, it took her breath away. Before she could recover it, his mouth was on hers. His lips were soft and warm, but the kiss was bruisingly potent. His tongue went deep to make an avid search of moist recesses as his weight pressed her into the mattress. He took a quick, hungry journey across her face before he looked down at her. There was nothing sleepy in his expression. The look alone had her breath trembling.

"My turn," he whispered.

With nimble fingers he loosened the range of tiny buttons down the front of her teddy. His lips followed, to send a trail of fire along the newly exposed skin. The plunge of the V stopped just below her navel. He lingered there, savoring the soft, honey-hued flesh. Tory felt herself swept through a hurricane of sensation to the heavy, waiting air of the storm's eye. Phil's hands cupped her upper thighs, his thumbs pressing insistently where the thin silk rose high. Expertly he unhooked her stockings, drawing them off slowly, his mouth hurrying to taste. Tory moaned, bending her leg to help him as torment and pleasure tangled.

For one heady moment his tongue lingered at the top of her thigh. With his tongue he gently slipped beneath the silk, making her arch in anticipation. His breath shot through the material into the core of her. But he left her moist and aching to come greedily back to her mouth. Tory met the kiss ardently, dragging him closer. She felt his body pound and pulse against hers with a need no greater than her own. He found her full bottom lip irresistible and nibbled and sucked gently. Tory knew a passion so concentrated and volatile, she struggled under him to find the ultimate release.

"Here," he whispered, moving down to the spot on her neck that always drew him. "You taste like no one else," he murmured. Her flavor seemed to tremble on the tip of his tongue. With a groan he let his voracious appetite take over.

Her breasts were hard, waiting for him. Slowly he moistened the tips with his tongue, listening to her shuddering breathing as he journeyed from one to the other—teasing, circling, nibbling, until her movements beneath him were abandoned and desperate. Passion built to a delicious peak until he drew her, hot and moist, into his mouth to suckle ravenously. She wasn't aware when he slipped the teddy down her shoulders, down her body, until she was naked to the waist. The last lights of the sun poured into the room like a dark red mist. It gave her skin an exotic cast that aroused him further. He drew the silk lower and still lower, until it was lost in the tangle of sheets.

Desperate, Tory reached for him. She heard Phil's sharp intake of breath as she touched him, felt the sudden, convulsive shudder. She wanted him now with an intensity too strong to deny.

"More," he breathed, but was unable to resist as she drew him closer.

"Now," she murmured, arching her hips to receive him.

Exhausted, they lay in silence as the first fingers of moonlight flickered into the room. He knew he should move—his full weight pushed Tory deep into the mattress. But they felt so right, flesh to flesh, his mouth nestled comfortably against her breast. Her fingers were in his hair, tangling and stroking with a sleepy gentleness. Time crept by easily—seconds to minutes without words or the need for them. He could hear her heartbeat gradually slow and level. Lazily he flicked his tongue over a still-erect nipple and felt it harden even more.

"Phil," she moaned in weak protest.

He laughed quietly, enormously pleased that he could move her so effortlessly. "Tired?" he asked, nibbling a moment longer.

"Yes." She gave a low groan as he began to toy with her other breast. "Phil, I can't."

Ignoring her, he brought his mouth to hers for long, slow kisses while his hands continued to stroke. He had intended only to kiss her before taking his weight from her. Her lips were unbearably soft and giving. Her breath shuddered into him, rebuilding his passion with dizzying speed. Tory told herself it wasn't possible as sleepy desire became a torrent of fresh need.

Phil found new delight in the lines of her body, in the heady, just-loved flavor of her skin. A softly glowing spark rekindled a flame. "I want a retake," he murmured.

He took her swiftly, leaving them both staggered and damp and clinging in a room speckled with moonlight.

"How do you feel?" Phil murmured later. She was close to his side, one arm flung over his chest.

"Astonished."

He laughed, kissing her temple. "So do I. I guess our dinner got cold."

"Mmm. What was it?"

"I don't remember."

Tory yawned and snuggled against him. "That's always better cold anyway." She knew with very little effort she could sleep for a week.

"Not hungry?"

She considered a moment. "Is it something you have to chew?"

He grinned into the darkness. "Probably."

"Uh-uh." She arched like a contented cat when he ran a hand down her back. "Do you have to get up early?"

"Six."

Groaning, she shut her eyes firmly. "You're ruining your mystique," she told him. "Hollywood Casanovas don't get up at six."

He gave a snort of laughter. "They do if they've got a film to direct."

"I suppose when you leave, you'll still have a lot of work to do before the film's finished."

His frown mirrored hers, although neither was aware of it. "There's still a lot to be shot in the studio, then the editing...I wish there was more time."

She knew what he meant, and schooled her voice carefully. "We both knew. I'll only be in town a few weeks longer than you," she added. "I've got a lot of work to catch up on in Albuquerque."

"It's lucky we're both comfortable with the way things are." Phil stared up at the ceiling while his fingers continued to tangle in her hair. "If we'd fallen in love, it would be an impossible situation."

"Yes," Tory murmured, opening her eyes to the darkness. "Neither of us has the time for impossible situations."

Chapter 10

Tory pulled up in front of the ranch house. Her mother's geraniums were doing beautifully. White and pink plants had been systematically placed between the more common red. The result was an organized, well tended blanket of color. Tory noted that the tear in the window screen had been mended. As always, a few articles of clothing hung on the line at the side of the house. She dreaded going in.

It was an obligation she never shirked but never did easily. At least once a week she drove out to spend a strained half hour with her mother. Only twice since the film crew had come to Friendly had her mother made the trip into town. Both times she had dropped into Tory's office, but the visits had been brief and uncomfortable for both women. Time was not bridging the gap, only widening it.

Normally, Tory confined her trips to the ranch to Sunday afternoons. This time, however, she had driven out a day early in order to placate Phil. The thought caused her to smile. He'd finally pressured her into agreeing to his "home movies." When he had wound up the morning's shoot in town, he would bring out one of the backup video cameras. Though she could hardly see why it was so vital to him to put her on film, Tory decided it wouldn't do any harm. And, she thought wryly, he wasn't going to stop bringing it up until she agreed. So let him have his fun, she concluded as she slipped from the car. She'd enjoy the ride.

From the corral the palomino whinnied fussily. He pawed the ground and pranced as Tory watched him. He knew, seeing Tory, that there was a carrot or apple in it for him, as well as a bracing ride. They were both aware that he could jump the fence easily if he grew impatient enough. As he reared, showing off for her, Tory laughed.

"Simmer down, Justice. You're going to be in the movies." She hesitated a moment. It would be so easy to go to the horse, pamper him a bit in return for his unflagging affection. There were no complications or undercurrents there. Her eyes drifted back to the house. With a sigh she started up the walk.

Upon entering, Tory caught the faint whiff of bee's wax and lemon and knew her mother had recently polished the floors. She remembered the electric buffer her father had brought home one day. Helen had been as thrilled as if he'd brought her diamonds. The windows glittered in the sun without a streak or speck.

How does she do it? Tory wondered, gazing around the spick-and-span room. How does she stand spending each and every day chasing dust? Could it really be all she wants out of life?

As far back as she could remember, she could recall her mother wanting nothing more than to change slip-covers or curtains. It was difficult for a woman who always looked for angles and alternatives to understand such placid acceptance. Perhaps it would have been easier if the daughter had understood the mother, or the mother the daughter. With a frustrated shake of her head she wandered to the kitchen, expecting to find Helen fussing at the stove.

The room was empty. The appliances winked, white and gleaming, in the strong sunlight. The scent of fresh-baked bread hovered enticingly in the air. Whom did she bake it for? Tory demanded of herself, angry without knowing why. There was no one there to appreciate it now—no one to break off a hunk and grin as he was scolded. Damn it, didn't she know that everything was different now? Whirling away, Tory strode out of the room.

The house was too quiet, she realized. Helen was certainly there. The tired little compact was in its habitual place at the side of the house. It occurred to Tory that her mother might be in one of the outbuildings. But then, why hadn't she come out when she heard the car drive up? Vaguely disturbed, Tory glanced up the stairs. She opened her mouth to call, then stopped. Something impelled her to move quietly up the steps.

At the landing she paused, catching some faint sound coming from the end of the hall. Still moving softly,

Tory walked down to the doorway of her parents' bedroom. The door was only half closed. Pushing it open, Tory stepped inside.

Helen sat on the bed in a crisp yellow housedress. Her blond hair was caught back in a matching kerchief. Held tight in her hands was one of Tory's father's work shirts. It was a faded blue, frayed at the cuffs. Tory remembered it as his favorite, one that Helen had claimed was fit only for a dust rag. Now she clutched it to her breast, rocking gently and weeping with such quiet despair that Tory could only stare.

She'd never seen her mother cry. It had been her father whose eyes had misted during her high school and college graduations. It had been he who had wept with her when the dog she had raised from a puppy had died. Her mother had faced joy and sadness with equal restraint. But there was no restraint in the woman Tory saw now. This was a woman in the depths of grief, blind and deaf to all but her own mourning.

All anger, all resentment, all sense of distance, vanished in one illuminating moment. Tory felt her heart fill with sympathy, her throat burn from her own grief.

"Mother."

Helen's head jerked up. Her eyes were glazed and confused as they focused on Tory. She shook her head as if in denial, then struggled to choke back the sobs.

"No, don't." Tory rushed to her, gathering her close. "Don't shut me out."

Helen went rigid in an attempt at composure, but Tory only held her tighter. Abruptly, Helen collapsed, dropping her head on her daughter's shoulder and weeping without restraint. "Oh, Tory, Tory, why couldn't it have been me?" With the shirt caught between them, Helen accepted the comfort of her daughter's strong arms. "Not Will, never Will. It should have been me."

"No, don't say that." Hot tears coursed down her face. "You mustn't think that way. Dad wouldn't want you to."

"All those weeks, those horrible weeks, in the hospital I prayed and prayed for a miracle." She gripped Tory tighter, as if she needed something solid to hang on to. "They said no hope. No hope. Oh, God, I wanted to scream. He couldn't die without me…not without me. That last night in the hospital before…I went into his room. I begged him to show them they were wrong, to come back. He was gone." She moaned and would have slid down if Tory hadn't held her close. "He'd already left me. I couldn't leave him lying there with that machine. I couldn't do that, not to Will. Not to my Will."

"Oh, Mother." They rocked together, heads on each other's shoulders. "I'm so sorry. I didn't know—I didn't think…I'm so sorry."

Helen breathed a long, shuddering sigh as her sobs quieted. "I didn't know how to tell you or how to explain. I'm not good at letting my feelings out. I knew how much you loved your father," she continued. "But I was too angry to reach out. I suppose I wanted you to lash out at me. It made it easier to be strong, even though I knew I hurt you more."

"That doesn't matter now."

"Tory—"

"No, it doesn't." Tory drew her mother back, looking

into her tear-ravaged eyes. "Neither of us tried to understand the other that night. We were both wrong. I think we've both paid for it enough now."

"I loved him so much." Helen swallowed the tremor in her voice and stared down at the crumpled shirt still in her hand. "It doesn't seem possible that he won't walk through the door again."

"I know. Every time I come in the house, I still look for him."

"You're so like him." Hesitantly, Helen reached up to touch her cheek. "There's been times it's been hard for me even to look at you. You were always his more than mine when you were growing up. My fault," she added before Tory could speak. "I was always a little awed by you."

"Awed?" Tory managed to smile.

"You were so smart, so quick, so demanding. I always wondered how much I had to do with the forming of you. Tory"—she took her hands, staring down at them a moment—"I never tried very hard to get close to you. It's not my way."

"I know."

"It didn't mean that I didn't love you."

She squeezed Helen's hands. "I know that too. But it was always him we looked at first."

"Yes." Helen ran a palm over the crumpled shirt. "I thought I was coping very well," she said softly. "I was going to clean out the closet. I found this, and… He loved it so. You can still see the little holes where he'd pin his badge."

"Mother, it's time you got out of the house a bit,

starting seeing people again." When Helen started to shake her head, Tory gripped her hands tighter. "Living again."

Helen glanced around the tidy room with a baffled smile. "This is all I know how to do. All these years…"

"When I go back to Albuquerque, why don't you come stay with me awhile? You've never been over."

"Oh, Tory, I don't know."

"Think about it," she suggested, not wanting to push. "You might enjoy watching your daughter rip a witness apart in cross-examination."

Helen laughed, brushing the lingering tears briskly away. "I might at that. Would you be offended if I said sometimes I worry about you being alone—not having someone like your father to come home to?"

"No." The sudden flash of loneliness disturbed her far more than the words. "Everyone needs something different."

"Everyone needs someone, Tory," Helen corrected gently. "Even you."

Tory's eyes locked on her mother's a moment, then dropped away. "Yes, I know. But sometimes the some-one—" She broke off, distressed by the way her thoughts had centered on Phil. "There's time for that," she said briskly. "I still have a lot of obligations, a lot of things I want to do, before I commit myself…to anyone."

There was enough anxiety in Tory's voice to tell Helen that "anyone" had a name. Feeling it was too soon to offer advice, she merely patted Tory's hand. "Don't wait too long," she said simply. "Life has a habit of moving quickly." Rising, she went to the closet again. The need to be busy was too ingrained to allow her to sit for long. "I didn't expect you today. Are you going to ride?"

"Yes." Tory pressed a hand down on her father's shirt before she stood. "Actually I'm humoring the director of the film being shot in town." Wandering to the window, she looked down to see Justice pacing the corral restlessly. "He has this obsession with getting me on film. I flatly refused to be an extra in his production, but I finally agreed to let him shoot some while I rode Justice."

"He must be very persuasive," Helen commented.

Tory gave a quick laugh. "Oh, he's that all right."

"That's Marshall Kincaid's son," Helen stated, remembering. "Does he favor his father?"

With a smile Tory thought that her mother would be more interested in the actor than the director. "Yes, actually he does. The same rather aristocratic bone structure and cool blue eyes." Tory saw the car kicking up dust on the road leading to the ranch. "He's coming now, if you'd like to meet him."

"Oh, I…" Helen pressed her fingers under her eyes. "I don't think I'm really presentable right now, Tory."

"All right," she said as she started toward the door. In the doorway she hesitated a moment. "Will you be all right now?"

"Yes, yes, I'm fine. Tory…" She crossed the room to give her daughter's cheek a brief kiss. Tory's eyes widened in surprise at the uncharacteristic gesture. "I'm glad we talked. Really very glad."

Phil again stopped his car beside the corral. The horse pranced over to hang his head over the fence, waiting for attention. Leaving the camera in the backseat, Phil walked over to pat the strong golden neck. He found the palomino avidly nuzzling at his pockets.

"Hey!" With a half laugh he stepped out of range.

"He's looking for this." Holding a carrot in her hand, Tory came down the steps.

"Your friend should be arrested for pickpocketing," Phil commented as Tory drew closer. His smile of greeting faded instantly. "Tory…" He took her shoulders, studying her face. "You've been crying," he said in an odd voice.

"I'm fine." Turning, she held out the carrot, letting the horse pluck in from her hand.

"What's wrong?" he insisted, pulling her back to him again. "What happened?"

"It was my mother."

"Is she ill?" he demanded quickly.

"No." Touched by the concern in his voice, Tory smiled. "We talked," she told him, then let out a long sigh. "We really talked, probably for the first time in twenty-seven years."

There was something fragile in the look as she lifted her eyes to his. He felt much as he had the day in the cemetery—protective and strong. Wordlessly he drew her into the circle of his arms. "Are you okay?"

"Yes, I'm fine." She closed her eyes as her head rested against his shoulder. "Really fine. It's going to be so much easier now."

"I'm glad." Tilting her face to his, he kissed her softly. "If you don't feel like doing this today—"

"No you don't, Kincaid," she said with a quick grin.

"You claimed you were going to immortalize me, so get on with it."

"Go fix your face first, then." He pinched her chin. "I'll set things up."

She turned away to comply, but called back over her shoulder. "There's not going to be any of that 'Take two' business. You'll have to get it right the first time."

He enjoyed her hoot of laughter before he reached into the car for the camera and recorder.

Later, Tory scowled at the apparatus. "You said film," she reminded him. "You didn't say anything about sound."

"It's tape," he corrected, expertly framing her. "Just saddle the horse."

"You're arrogant as hell when you play movies, Kincaid." Without fuss Tory slipped the bit into the palomino's mouth. Her movements were competent as she hefted the saddle onto the horse's back. She was a natural, he decided. No nerves, no exaggerated gestures for the benefit of the camera. He wanted her to talk again. Slowly he circled around for a new angle. "Going to have dinner with me tonight?"

"I don't know." Tory considered as she tightened the cinches. "That cold steak you fed me last night wasn't very appetizing."

"Tonight I'll order cold cuts and beer," he suggested. "That way it won't matter when we get to it."

Tory sent him a grin over her shoulder. "It's a deal."

"You're a cheap date, Sheriff."

"Uh-uh," she disagreed, turning to him while she wrapped a companionable arm around the horse's neck. "I'm expecting another bottle of that French champagne very soon. Why don't you let me play with the camera now and you can stand next to the horse?"

"Mount up."

Tory lifted a brow. "You're one tough cookie, Kincaid." Grasping the saddle horn, Tory swung into the saddle in one lazy movement. "And now?"

"Head out, the direction you took the first time I saw you ride. Not too far," he added. "When you come back, keep it at a gallop. Don't pay any attention to the camera. Just ride."

"You're the boss," she said agreeably. "For the moment." With a kick of her heels Tory sent the palomino west at a run.

She felt the exhilaration instantly. The horse wanted speed, so Tory let him have his head as the hot air whipped at her face and hair. As before, she headed toward the mountains. There was no need to escape this time, but only a pleasure in moving fast. The power and strength below her tested her skill.

Zooming in on her, Phil thought she rode with understated flair. No flash, just confidence. Her body hardly seemed to move as the horse pounded up dust. It almost seemed as though the horse led her, but something in the way she sat, in the way her face was lifted, showed her complete control.

When she turned, the horse danced in place a moment, still anxious to run. He tossed his head, lifting his front feet off the ground in challenge. Over the still, silent air, Phil heard Tory laugh. The sound of it sent shivers down his spine.

Magnificent, he thought, zooming in on her as close

as the lens would allow. She was absolutely magnificent. She wasn't looking toward him. Obviously she had no thoughts about the camera focused on her. Her face was lifted to the sun and the sky as she controlled the feisty horse with apparent ease. When she headed back, she started at a loping gallop that built in speed.

The palomino's legs gathered and stretched, sending up a plume of dirt in their wake. Behind them was a barren land of little more than rock and earth with the mountains harsh in the distance. She was Eve, Phil thought. The only woman. And if this Eve's paradise was hard and desolate, she ruled it in her own style.

Once, as if remembering he was there, Tory looked over, full into the camera. With her face nearly filling the lens, she smiled. Phil felt l is palms go damp. If a man had a woman like that, he realized abruptly, he'd need nothing and no one else. The only woman, he thought again, then shook his head as if to clear it.

With a quick command and a tug on the reins, Tory brought the horse to a stop. Automatically she leaned forward to pat his neck. "Well, Hollywood?" she said lazily.

Knowing he wasn't yet in complete control, Phil kept the camera trained on her. "Is that the best you can do?"

She tossed her hair behind her head. "What did you have in mind?"

"No fancy tricks?" he asked, moving around the horse to vary the angle.

Tory looked down on him with tolerant amusement. "If you want to see someone stand on one foot in the saddle, go to the circus."

"We could set up a couple of small jumps—if you can handle it."

As she ruffled the palomino's blond mane, she gave a snort of laughter. "I thought you wanted me to ride, not win a blue ribbon." Grinning, she turned the horse around. "But okay," she said obligingly. At an easy lope she went for the corral fence. The horse took the four feet in a long, powerful glide. "Will that do?" she asked as she doubled back and rode past.

"Again," Phil demanded, going down on one knee. With a shrug Tory took the horse over the fence again. Lowering his camera for the first time, Phil shaded his eyes and looked up at her. "If he can do that, how do you keep him in?"

"He knows a good thing when he's got it," Tory stated, letting the palomino prance a bit while she rubbed his neck. "He's just showing off for the camera. Is that a wrap, Kincaid?"

Lifting the camera again, he aimed it at her. "Is that all you can do?"

"Well…" Tory considered a moment, then sent him a slow smile. "How about this?" Keeping one hand loosely on the reins, she started to unbutton her blouse.

"I like it."

After three buttons she paused, catching her tongue between her teeth. "I don't want you to lose your G rating," she decided. Swinging a leg over the saddle, she slid to the ground.

"This is a private film," he reminded her. "The censors'll never see it."

She laughed, but shook her head. "Fade out," she suggested, loosening the horse's girth. "Put your toy away, Kincaid," she told him as he circled around the horse, still taping.

"Look at me a minute." With a half smile Tory complied. "God, that face," he muttered. "One way or the other, I'm going to get it on the screen."

"Forget it." Tory lifted the saddle to balance it on the fence. "Unless you start videotaping court cases."

"I can be persistent."

"I can be stubborn," she countered. At her command the palomino trotted back into the corral.

After loading the equipment back in the car, Phil turned to gather Tory in his arms. Without a word their mouths met in long, mutual pleasure. "If there was a way," he murmured as he buried his face in her hair, "to have a few days away from here, alone…"

Tory shut her eyes, feeling the stir…and the ache. "Obligations, Phil," she said quietly. "We both have a job to do."

He wanted to say the hell with it, but knew he couldn't. Along with the obligations was the agreement they had made at the outset. "If I called you in Albuquerque, would you see me?"

She hesitated. It was something she wanted and feared. "Yes." She realized abruptly that she was suffering. For a moment she stood still, absorbing the unexpected sensation. "Phil, kiss me again."

She found his mouth quickly to let the heat and pleasure of the kiss dull the pain. There were still a few precious weeks left, she told herself as she wrapped her arms tighter around him. There was still time before…

with a moan she pressed urgently against him, willing her mind to go blank. There was a sigh, then a tremble, before she rested her head against his shoulder. "I have to put the tack away," she murmured. It was tempting to stay just as she was, held close, with her blood just beginning to swim. Taking a long breath, she drew away from him and smiled. "Why don't you be macho and carry the saddle?"

"Directors don't haul equipment," he told her as he tried to pull her back to him.

"Heave it up, Kincaid." Tory swung the reins over her shoulder. "You've got some great muscles."

"Yeah?" Grinning, he lifted the saddle and followed her toward the barn. Bicks was right, Phil mused, watching her walk. She had a way of moving that drove men mad.

The barn door creaked in protest when Tory pulled it open. "Over here." She moved across the concrete floor to hang the reins on a peg.

Phil set down the saddle, then turned. The place was large, high-ceilinged and refreshingly cool. "No animals?" he asked, wandering to an empty stall.

"My mother keeps a few head of cattle," Tory explained as she joined him. "They're grazing. We had more horses, but she doesn't ride much." Tory lifted a shoulder. "Justice has the place mostly to himself."

"I've never been in a barn."

"A deprived child."

He sent her a mild glance over his shoulder as he roamed. "I don't think I expected it to be so clean."

Tory's laugh echoed. "My mother has a vendetta

against dirt," she told him. Oddly, she felt amusement now rather than resentment. It was a clean feeling. "I think she'd have put curtains on the windows in the loft if my father had let her."

Phil found the ladder and tested its sturdiness. "What's up there?"

"Hay," Tory said dryly. "Ever seen hay?"

"Don't be smug," he warned before he started to climb. Finding his fascination rather sweet, Tory exerted the energy to go up with him. "The view's incredible." Standing beside the side opening, he could see for miles. The town of Friendly looked almost neat and tidy with the distance.

"I used to come up here a lot." Tucking her hands in her back pockets, Tory looked over his shoulder.

"What did you do?"

"Watch the world go by," she said, nodding toward Friendly. "Or sleep."

He laughed, turning back to her. "You're the only person I know who can turn sleeping into an art."

"I've dedicated quite a bit of my life to it." She took his hand to draw him away.

Instead he pulled her into a dim corner. "There's something I've always wanted to do in a hayloft."

With a laugh Tory stepped away. "Phil, my mother's in the house."

"She's not here," he pointed out. He hooked a hand in the low V where she had loosened her blouse. A hard tug had her stumbling against him.

"Phil—"

"It must have been carrying that saddle," he mused,

giving her a gentle push that had her falling backward into a pile of hay.

"Now, wait a minute…" she began, and struggled up on her elbows.

"And the primitive surroundings," he added as he pressed her body back with his own. "If I were directing this scene, it would start like this." He took her mouth in a hot, urgent kiss that turned her protest into a moan. "The lighting would be set so that it seemed one shaft of sunlight was slanting down across here." With a fingertip he traced from her right ear, across her throat, to the hollow between her breasts. "Everything else would be a dull gold, like your skin."

She had her hands pressed against his shoulders, holding him off, although her heart was beating thickly. "Phil, this isn't the time."

He placed two light kisses at either corner of her mouth. He found it curiously exciting to have to persuade her. Light as a breeze, his hand slipped under her blouse until his fingers found her breast. The peak was already taut. At his touch her eyes lost focus and darkened. The hands at his shoulders lost their resistance and clutched at him. "You're so sensitive," he murmured, watching the change in her face. "It drives me crazy to know when I touch you like this your bones turn to water and you're completely mine."

Letting his fingers fondle and stroke, he lowered his mouth to nibble gently at her yielding lips. *Strong, self-sufficient, decisive.* Those were words he would have used to describe her. Yet, he knew, when they were together like this, he had the power to mold her. Even now, as she lifted them to his face to urge him closer, he felt the weakness come over him in thick waves. It was both frightening and irresistible.

She could have asked anything of him, and he would have been unable to deny her. Even his thoughts could no longer be considered his own when she was so intimately entwined in them. The fingers that loosened the rest of her buttons weren't steady. He should have been used to her by now, he told himself as he sought the tender skin of her neck almost savagely. It shouldn't be so intense every time he began to make love to her. Each time he told himself the desperation would fade; yet, it only returned—doubled, tripled, until he was completely lost in her.

There was only her now, over the clean, country smell of hay. Her subtly alluring fragrance was a contrast too exciting to bear. She was murmuring to him as she drew his shirt over his head. The sound of her voice seemed to pulse through his system. The sun shot through the window to beat on his bare back, but he only felt the cool stroking of her fingers as she urged him down until they were flesh to flesh.

His mouth devoured hers as he tugged the jeans over her hips. Greedily he moved to her throat, her shoulders, her breasts, ravenous for each separate taste. His mouth ranged over her, his tongue moistening, savoring, as her skin heated. She was naked but for the brief swatch riding low on her hips. He hooked his fingers beneath it, tormenting them both by lowering it fraction by fraction while his lips followed the progress.

The pleasure grew unmanageable. He began the

wild journey back up her body, his fingers fumbling with the snap of his jeans until Tory's brushed them impatiently away.

She undressed him swiftly, while her own mouth streaked over his skin. The sudden change from pliancy to command left him stunned. Then she was on top of him, straddling him while her lips and teeth performed dark magic at the pulse in his throat. Beyond reason, he grasped her hips, lifting her. Tory gave a quick cry as they joined. In delight her head flung back as she let this new exhilaration rule her. Her skin was shiny with dampness when she crested. Delirious, she started to slide toward him, but he rolled her over, crushing her beneath him as he took her to a second peak, higher than the first.

As they lay, damp flesh to damp flesh, their breaths shuddering, she knew a contentment so fulfilling, it brought the sting of tears to her eyes. Hurriedly blinking them away, Tory kissed the curve of his shoulder.

"I guess there's more to do in a hayloft than sleep."

Phil chuckled. Rolling onto his back, he drew her against his side to steal a few more moments alone with her.

Chapter 11

One of the final scenes to be filmed was a tense night sequence outside Hernandez's Bar. Phil had opted to shoot at night with a low light level rather than film during the day with filters. It would give the actors more of a sense of the ambience and keep the gritty realism in the finished product. It was a scene fraught with emotion that would lose everything if overplayed. From the beginning nothing seemed to go right.

Twice the sound equipment broke down, causing lengthy delays. A seasoned supporting actress blew her lines repeatedly and strode off the set, cursing herself. A defective bulb exploded, scattering shards of glass that had to be painstakingly picked up. For the first time since the shooting began, Phil had to deal with a keyed-up, uncooperative Marlie.

"Okay," he said, taking her by the arm to draw her away. "What the hell's wrong with you?"

"I can't get it right," she said furiously. With her hands on her hips she strode a few paces away and kicked at the dirt. "Damn it, Phil, it just doesn't *feel* right."

"Look, we've been at this over two hours. Everybody's a little fed up." His own patience was hanging on by a thread. In two days at the most, he'd have no choice but to head back to California. He should have been pleased that the bulk of the filming was done—that the rushes were excellent. Instead he was tense, irritable and looking for someone to vent his temper on. "Just pull yourself together," he told Marlie curtly. "And get it done."

"Now, just a damn minute!" Firing up instantly, Marlie let her own frustration pour out in temper. "I've put up with your countless retakes, with that stinking, sweaty bar and this godforsaken town because this script is gold. I've let you work me like a horse because I need you. This part is my ticket into the big leagues and I know it right down to the gut."

"You want the ticket," Phil tossed back, "you pay the price."

"I've paid my dues," she told him furiously. A couple of heads turned idly in their direction, but no one ventured over. "I don't have to take your lousy temper on the set because you've got personal problems."

He measured her with narrowed eyes. "You have to take exactly what I give you."

"I'll tell you something, Kincaid"—she poked a small finger into his chest—"I don't have to take anything, because I'm every bit as important to this movie

as you are, and we both know it. It doesn't mean a damn
who's getting top billing. Kate Lohman's the key to this
picture, and I'm Kate Lohman. Don't you forget it, and
don't throw your weight around with me."

When she turned to stride off, Phil grabbed her arm,
jerking her back. His eyes had iced. The fingers on her arm
were hard. Looking down at her set face, he felt temper
fade into admiration. "Damn you, Marlie," he said quietly,
"you know how to stay in character, don't you?"

"I know this one inside out," she returned. The stiffness went out of her stance.

"Okay, what doesn't feel right?"

The corners of her mouth curved up. "I wanted to
work with you," she began, "because you're the best out
there these days. I didn't expect to like you. All right,"
she continued, abruptly professional, "when Sam
follows me out of the bar, grabs me, finally losing
control, he's furious. Everything he's held in comes
pouring out. His dialogue's hard."

"You haven't been off his back since he came into
town," Phil reminded her, running over the scene in his
mind. "Now he's had enough. After the scene he's going
to take you back to your room and make love. You win."

"Do I?" Marlie countered. "My character is a tough
lady. She's got reason to be; she's got enough vul-
nerabilities to keep the audience from despising her,
but she's no pushover."

"So?"

"So he comes after me, he calls me a tramp—a cold,
money-grabbing whore, among other things—and my
response is to take it—damp-eyed and shocked."

Phil considered, a small smile growing. "What would you do?"

"I'd punch the jerk in the mouth."

His laugh echoed down the street. "Yeah, I guess you would at that."

"Tears, maybe," Marlie went on, tasting victory, "but anger too. She's becoming very close to what he's accusing her of. And she hates it—and him, for making it matter."

Phil nodded, his mind already plotting the changes and the angles. Frowning, he called Sam over and outlined the change.

"Can you pull this off without busting my caps?" Sam demanded of Marlie.

She grinned. "Maybe."

"After she hits you," Phil interrupted, "I want dead silence for a good ten seconds. You wipe your mouth with the back of your hand, slow, but don't break the eye contact. Let's set it up from where Marlie walks out of the bar. Bicks!" He left the actors to give his cinematographer a rundown.

"*Quiet.... Places.... Roll....*" Standing by the cameraman's shoulder, Phil watched the scene unfold. The adrenaline was pumping now. He could see it in Marlie's eyes, in the set of her body, as she burst out the door of the bar onto the sidewalk. When Sam grabbed her, instead of merely being whirled around, she turned on him. The mood seemed to fire into him as well, as his lines became harsher, more emotional. Before there had been nothing in the scene but the man's anger; now there was the woman's too. Now the underlying sexuality was there. When she hit him, it seemed everyone on the set held their breath. The gesture was completely unexpected and, Phil mused as the silence trembled, completely in character. He could almost feel Sam's desire to strike her back, and his inability to do so. She challenged him to, while her throat moved gently with a nervous swallow. He wiped his mouth, never taking his eyes from hers.

"Cut!" Phil swore jubilantly as he walked over and grabbed Marlie by the shoulders. He kissed her, hard. "Fantastic," he said, then kissed her again. "Fantastic." Looking up, he grinned at Sam.

"Don't try that on me," Sam warned, nursing his lower lip. "She packs a hell of a punch." He gave her a rueful glance. "Ever heard about pulling right before you make contact?" he asked. "Show biz, you know."

"I got carried away."

"I nearly slugged you."

"I know." Laughing, she pushed her hair back with both hands.

"Okay, let's take it from there." Phil moved back to the cameraman. "Places."

"Can't we take it from right before the punch?" Marlie asked with a grin for Sam. "It would sort of give me a roll into the rest of the scene."

"Stand-in!" Sam called.

In her office Tory read over with care a long, detailed letter from an opposing attorney. The tone was very clear through the legal terms and flowery style. The case was going through litigation, she thought with a frown. It might take two months or more, she mused, but this suit wasn't going to be settled out of court. Though normally she would have wanted to come to terms without a trial, she began to feel a tiny flutter of excitement. She'd been away from her own work for too long. She would be back in Albuquerque in a month. Tory discovered she wanted—needed—something complicated and time-consuming on her return.

Adjustments, she decided as she tried to concentrate on the words in the letter. There were going to be adjustments to be made when she left Friendly this time. When she left Phil. No, she corrected, catching the bridge of her nose between her thumb and forefinger. He was leaving first—tomorrow, the day after. It was uncomfortably easy to see the hole that was already taking shape in her life. Tory reminded herself that she wasn't allowed to think of it. The rules had been made plain at the outset—by both of them. If things had begun to change for her, she simply had to backpedal a bit and reaffirm her priorities. *Her* work, *her* career, *her* life. At that moment the singular possessive pronoun never sounded more empty. Shaking her head, Tory began to read the letter from the beginning a second time.

Merle paced the office, casting quick glances at Tory from time to time. He'd made arrangements for Marlie to meet him there after her work was finished. What he hadn't expected was for Tory to be glued to her desk all evening. No expert with subtleties, Merle had no idea how to move his boss along and have the office to himself. He peeked out the window, noting that the floodlights up the street were being shut off. Shuffling his feet and clearing his throat, he turned back to Tory.

"Guess you must be getting tired," he ventured.

"Hmmm."

"Things are pretty quiet tonight," he tried again, fussing with the buttons on his shirt.

"Um-hmm." Tory began to make notations on her yellow pad.

Merle lifted his eyes to the ceiling. Maybe the direct approach would do it, he decided. "Why don't you knock off and go home."

Tory continued to write. "Trying to get rid of me, Merle T.?"

"Well, no, ah…" He looked down at the dusty tips of his shoes. Women never got any easier to handle.

"Got a date?" she asked mildly as she continued to draft out her answer to the letter.

"Sort of…well, yeah," he said with more confidence.

"Go ahead, then."

"But—" He broke off, stuffing his hands in his pockets.

Tory looked up and studied him. The mustache, she noted, had grown in respectability. It wasn't exactly a prizewinner, but it added maturity to a face she'd always thought resembled a teddy bear's. He still slouched, and even as she studied him, color seeped into his cheeks. But he didn't look away as he once would have done. His eyes stayed on hers so that she could easily read both frustration and embarrassment. The old affection stirred in her.

"Marlie?" she asked gently.

"Yeah." He straightened his shoulders a bit.

"How are you going to feel when she leaves?"

With a shrug Merle glanced toward the window again. "I guess I'll miss her. She's a terrific lady."

The tone caused Tory to give his profile a puzzled look. There was no misery in it, just casual acceptance. With a light laugh she stared back at her notes. Odd, she thought, it seemed their reactions had gotten reversed somewhere along the line. "You don't have to stay, Merle," she said lightly. "If you'd planned to have a late supper or—"

"We did," he interrupted. "Here."

Tory looked up again. "Oh, I see." She couldn't quite control the smile. "Looks like I'm in the way."

Uncomfortable, he shuffled again. "Aw, Tory."

"It's okay." Rising, she exaggerated her accommodating tone. "I know when I'm not wanted. I'll just go back to my room and work on this all by myself."

Merle struggled with loyalty and selfishness while Tory gathered her papers. "You could have supper with us," he suggested gallantly.

Letting the papers drop, Tory skirted the desk. With her hands on his shoulders, she kissed both of his cheeks. "Merle T.," she said softly, "you're a jewel."

Pleased, he grinned as the door opened behind them. "Just like I told you, Phil," Marlie stated as they entered. "Beautiful woman can't keep away from him. You'll have to stand in line, Sheriff," she continued, walking over to hook her arm through Merle's. "I've got first dibs tonight."

"Why don't I get her out of your way?" Phil suggested. "It's the least I can do after that last scene."

"The man is totally unselfish," Marlie confided to Tory. "No sacrifice is too great for his people."

With a snort Tory turned back to her desk. "I might let him buy me a drink," she considered while slipping her papers into a small leather case. When he sat on the corner of her desk, she cast him a look. "And dinner," she added.

"I might be able to come up with some cold cuts," he murmured.

Tory's low, appreciative laugh was interrupted by the phone. "Sheriff's office." Her sigh was automatic as she listened to the excited voice on the other end. "Yes, Mr. Potts." Merle groaned, but she ignored him. "I see. What kind of noise?" Tory waited while the old man jabbered in her ear. "Are your doors and windows locked? No, Mr. Potts, I don't want you going outside with your shotgun. Yes, I realize a man has to protect his property." A sarcastic sound from Merle earned him a mild glare. "Let me handle it. I'll be there in ten minutes. No, I'll be quiet, just sit tight."

"Sheep thieves," Merle muttered as Tory hung up.

"Burglars," she corrected, opening the top drawer of her desk.

"Just what do you think you're going to do with that?" Phil demanded as he saw Tory pull out the gun.

"Absolutely nothing, I hope." Coolly she began to load it.

"Then why are you—? Wait a minute," he interrupted himself, rising. "Do you mean that damn thing wasn't loaded?"

"Of course not." Tory slipped in the last bullet. "Nobody with sense keeps a loaded gun in an unlocked drawer."

"You got me into that cell with an empty gun?"

She sent him a lazy smile as she strapped on a holster. "You were so cute, Kincaid."

Ignoring amusement, he took a step toward her. "What would you have done if I hadn't backed down?"

"The odds were in my favor," she reminded him. "But I'd have thought of something. Merle, keep an eye on things until I get back."

"Wasting your time."

"Just part of the job."

"If you're wasting your time," Phil began as he stopped her at the door, "why are you taking that gun?"

"It looks so impressive," Tory told him as she walked outside.

"Tory, you're not going out to some sheep ranch with a gun at your hip like some modern-day Belle Starr."

"She was on the wrong side," she reminded him.

"Tory, I mean it!" Infuriated, Phil stepped in front of the car to block her way.

"Look, I said I'd be there in ten minutes; I'm going to have to drive like a maniac as it is."

He didn't budge. "What if there is someone out there?"

"That's exactly why I'm going."

When she reached for the door handle, he put his hand firmly over hers. "I'm going with you."

"Phil, I don't have time."

"I'm going."

Narrowing her eyes, she studied his face. There was no arguing with that expression, she concluded. "Okay, you're temporarily deputized. Get in and do what you're told."

Phil lifted a brow at her tone. The thought of her

going out to some secluded ranch with only a gun for company had him swallowing his pride. He slid across to the passenger seat. "Don't I get a badge?" he asked as Tory started the engine.

"Use your imagination," she advised.

Tory's speed was sedate until they reached the town limits. Once the buildings were left behind, Phil watched the climbing speedometer with growing trepidation. Her hands were relaxed and competent on the wheel. The open window caused her hair to fly wildly, but her expression was calm.

She doesn't think there's anything to this, he decided as he watched the scenery whiz by. But if she did, his thoughts continued, she'd be doing exactly the same thing. The knowledge gave him a small thrill of fear. The neat black holster at her side hid an ugly, very real weapon. She had no business chasing burglars or carrying guns. She had no business taking the remotest chance with her own well-being. He cursed the phone call that had made it all too clear just how potentially dangerous her position in Friendly was. It had been simpler to think of her as a kind of figurehead, a referee for small-town squabbles. The late-night call and the gun changed everything.

"What will you do if you have to use that thing?" he demanded suddenly.

Without turning, Tory knew where his thoughts centered. "I'll deal with that when the time comes."

"When's your term up here?"

Tory took her eyes from the road for a brief two seconds. Phil was looking straight ahead. "Three weeks."

"You're better off in Albuquerque," he muttered.

Safer was the word heard but not said. Tory recalled the time a client had nearly strangled her in his cell before the guards had pulled him off. She decided it was best unmentioned. Hardly slackening the car's speed, she took a right turn onto a narrow, rut-filled dirt road. Phil swore as the jolting threw him against the door.

"You should have strapped in," she told him carelessly.

His response was rude and brief.

The tiny ranch house had every light blazing. Tory pulled up in front of it with a quick squeal of brakes.

"Think you missed any?" Phil asked her mildly as he rubbed the shoulder that had collided with the door.

"I'll catch them on the way back." Before he could retort, Tory was out of the car and striding up the porch steps. She knocked briskly, calling out to identify herself. When Phil joined her on the porch, the door opened a crack. "Mr. Potts," she began.

"Who's he?" the old man demanded through the crack in the door.

"New deputy," Tory said glibly. "We'll check the grounds and the outside of the house now."

Potts opened the door a bit more, revealing an ancient, craggy face and a shiny black shotgun. "I heard them in the bushes."

"We'll take care of it, Mr. Potts." She put her hands on the butt of his gun. "Why don't you let me have this for now?"

Unwilling, Potts held firm. "I gotta have protection."

"Yes, but they're not in the house," she reminded him gently. "I could really use this out here."

He hesitated, then slackened his grip. "Both barrels,"

he told her, then slammed the door. Tory heard the triple locks click into place.

"That is not your average jolly old man," Phil commented.

Tory took the two shells out of the shotgun. "Alone too long," she said simply. "Let's take a look around."

"Go get 'em, big guy."

Tory barely controlled a laugh. "Just keep out of the way, Kincaid."

Whether she considered it a false alarm or not, Phil noted that Tory was very thorough. With the empty shotgun in one hand and a flashlight in the other, she checked every door and window on the dilapidated ranch house. Watching her, he walked into a pile of empty paint cans, sending them clattering. When he swore, Tory turned her head to look at him.

"You move like a cat, Kincaid," she said admiringly.

"The man's got junk piled everywhere," he retorted. "A burglar doesn't have a chance."

Tory smothered a chuckle and moved on. They circled the house, making their way through Potts's obstacle course of old car parts, warped lumber and rusted tools. Satisfied that no one had attempted to break into the house for at least twenty-five years, Tory widened her circle to check the ground.

"Waste of time," Phil muttered, echoing Merle.

"Then let's waste it properly." Tory shone her light on the uneven grass as they continued to walk. Resigned, Phil kept to her side. There were better ways, he was thinking, to spend a warm summer night. And the moon was full. Pure white, he observed as he gazed up at it. Cool and full and promising. He wanted to make love to her under it, in the still, hot air with nothing and no one around for miles. The desire came suddenly, intensely, washing over him with a wave of possession that left him baffled.

"Tory," he murmured, placing a hand on her shoulder.

"Ssh!"

The order was sharp. He felt her stiffen under his hand. Her eyes were trained on a dry, dying bush directly in front of them. Even as he opened his mouth to say something impatient, Phil saw the movement. His fingers tightened on Tory's shoulder as he automatically stepped forward. The protective gesture was instinctive, and so natural neither of them noticed it. He never thought: This is my woman, and I'll do anything to keep her from harm; he simply reacted. With his body as a shield for hers, they watched the bush in silence.

There was a slight sound, hardly a whisper on the air, but Tory felt the back of her neck prickle. The dry leaves of the bush cracked quietly with some movement. She reached in her pocket for the two shells, then reloaded the shotgun. The moonlight bounced off the oiled metal. Her hands were rock steady. Phil was poised, ready to lunge as Tory aimed the gun at the moon and fired both barrels. The sound split the silence like an axe.

With a terrified bleat, the sheep that had been grazing lazily behind the bush scrambled for safety. Without a word Phil and Tory watched the dirty white blob run wildly into the night.

"Another desperate criminal on the run from the law," Tory said dryly.

Phil burst into relieved laughter. He felt each separate muscle in his body relax. "I'd say 'on the lamb.'"

"I was hoping you wouldn't." Because the hand holding the gun was shaking, Tory lowered it to her side. She swallowed; her throat was dry. "Well, let's go tell Potts his home and hearth are safe. Then we can go have that drink."

Phil laid his hands on her shoulders, looking down on her face in the moonlight. "Are you all right?"

"Sure."

"You're trembling."

"That's you," she countered, smiling at him.

Phil slid his hand down to her wrist to feel the race of her pulse. "Scared the hell out of you," he said softly.

Tory's eyes didn't waver. "Yeah." She was able to smile again, this time with more feeling. "How about you?"

"Me too." Laughing, he gave her a light kiss. "I'm not going to need that badge after all." And I'm not going to feel safe, he added silently, until you take yours off for the last time.

"Oh, I don't know, Kincaid." Tory led the way back with the beam of her flashlight. "First night on the job and you flushed out a sheep."

"Just give the crazy old man his gun and let's get out of here."

It took ten minutes of Tory's diplomacy to convince Potts that everything was under control. Mollified more by the fact that Tory had used his gun than the information that his intruder was one of his own flock, he locked himself in again. After contacting Merle on the radio, she headed back to town at an easy speed.

"I guess I could consider this a fitting climax to my

sojourn to Friendly," Phil commented. "Danger and excitement on the last night in town."

Tory's fingers tightened on the wheel, but she managed to keep the speed steady. "You're leaving tomorrow."

He listened for regret in the statement but heard none. Striving to match her tone, he continued to stare out the window. "We finished up tonight, a day ahead of schedule. I'll head out with the film crew tomorrow. I want to be there when Huffman sees the film."

"Of course." The pain rammed into her, dazzlingly physical. It took concentrated control to keep from moaning with it. "You've still quite a lot of work to do before it's finished, I suppose."

"The studio scenes," he agreed, struggling to ignore twin feelings of panic and desolation. "The editing, the mixing... I guess your schedule's going to be pretty tight when you get back to Albuquerque."

"It looks that way." Tory stared at the beams of the headlights. A long straight road, no curves, no hills. No end. She bit the inside of her lip hard before she trusted herself to continue. "I'm thinking about hiring a new law clerk."

"That's probably a good idea." He told himself that the crawling emptiness in his stomach was due to a lack of food. "I don't imagine your case load's going to get any smaller."

"No, it should take me six months of concentrated work to get it under control again. You'll probably start on a new film the minute this one's finished."

"It's being cast now," he murmured. "I'm going to produce it, too."

Tory smiled. "No guarantors?"

Phil answered the smile. "We'll see."

They drove for another half mile in silence. Slowing down, Tory pulled off onto a small dirt road and stopped. Phil took a quick glance around at nothing in particular, then turned to her. "What are we doing?"

"Parking." She scooted from under the steering wheel, winding her arms around his neck.

"Isn't there some legality about using an official car for illicit purposes?" His mouth was already seeking hers, craving.

"I'll pay the fine in the morning." She silenced his chuckle with a deep, desperate kiss.

As if by mutual consent, they went slowly. All pleasure, all desire, was concentrated in tastes. Lips, teeth and tongues brought shuddering arousal, urging them to hurry. But they would satisfy needs with mouths only first. Her lips were silkily yielding even as they met and increased his demand. Wild, crazy desires whipped through him, but her mouth held him prisoner. He touched her nowhere else. This taste—spiced honey, this texture—heated satin—would live with him always.

Tory let her lips roam his face. She knew each crease, each angle, each slope, more intimately than she knew her own features. With her eyes closed she could see him perfectly, and knew she had only to close her eyes again, in a year, in ten years, to have the same vivid picture. The skin on his neck was damp, making the flavor intensify as her tongue glided over it. Without thinking, she ran her fingers down his shirt, nimbly loosening buttons. When his chest was vulnerable, she spread both palms over it to feel his quick shudder. Then she brought her mouth, lazily, invitingly, back to his.

Her fingertips sent a path of ice, a path of fire, over his naked skin. Her mouth was drawing him in until his head swam. His labored breathing whispered on the night air. Wanting her closer, he shifted, cursed the cramped confines of the car, then dragged her across his lap. Lifting her to him, he buried his face against the side of her neck. He fed there, starving for her until she moaned and brought his hand to rest on her breast. With torturous slowness he undid the series of buttons, allowing his fingertips to trail along her skin as it was painstakingly exposed. He let the tips of his fingers bring her to desperation.

The insistent brush of his thumb over the point of her breast released a shaft of exquisite pain so sharp, she cried out with it, dragging him closer. Open and hungry, her mouth fixed on his while she fretted to touch more of him. Their position made it impossible, but her body was his. He ran his hands over it, feeling her skin jump as he roamed to the waistband of her jeans. Loosening them, he slid his hand down to warm, moist secrets. His mouth crushed hers as he drank in her moan.

Tory struggled, maddened by the restrictions, wild with desire, as his fingers aroused her beyond belief. He kept her trapped against him, knowing once she touched him that his control would shatter. This night, he thought, this final night, would last until there was no tomorrow.

When she crested, he rose with her, half delirious. No woman was so soft, no woman was so responsive. His heart pounded, one separate pain after another, as he drove her up again.

Her struggles ceased. Compliance replaced them. Tory lay shuddering in a cocoon of unrivaled sensations. She was his. Though her mind was unaware of the total gift of self, her body knew. She'd been his, perhaps from the first, perhaps only for that moment, but there would never be any turning back. Love swamped her; desire sated her. There was nothing left but the need to possess, to be possessed, by one man. In that instant she conceded her privacy.

The change in her had something racing through him. Phil couldn't question, couldn't analyze. He knew only that they must come together now—now, while there was something magic shimmering. It had nothing to do with the moonlight beaming into the car or the eerie silence surrounding them. It concerned only them and the secret that had grown despite protests. He didn't think, he didn't deny. With a sudden madness he tugged on her clothes and his own. Speed was foremost in his mind. He had to hurry before whatever trembled in the tiny confines was lost. Then her body was beneath his, fused to his, eager, asking.

He took her on the seat of the car like a passionate teenager. He felt like a man who had been given something precious, and as yet unrecognizable.

Chapter 12

A long sleepy time. Moonlight on the back of closed lids…night air over naked skin. The deep, deep silence of solitude by the whispering breathing of intimacy.

Tory floated in that luxurious plane between sleep and wakefulness—on her side, on the narrow front seat, with her body fitted closely against Phil's. Their legs were tangled, their arms around each other, as much for support as need. With his mouth near her ear, his warm breath skipped along her skin.

There were two marginally comfortable beds back at the hotel. They could have chosen either of them for their last night together, but they had stayed where they were, on a rough vinyl seat, on a dark road, as the night grew older. There they were alone completely. Morning still seemed very far away.

A hawk cried out as it drove toward earth. Some small animal screamed in the brush. Tory's lids fluttered up to find Phil's eyes open and on hers. In the moonlight his irises were very pale. Needing no words, perhaps wanting none, Tory lifted her mouth to his. They made love again, quietly, slowly, with more tenderness than either was accustomed to.

So they dozed again, unwilling to admit that the night was slipping away from them. When Tory awoke, there was a faint lessening in the darkness—not light, but the texture that meant morning was close.

A few more hours, she thought, gazing at the sky through the far window as she lay beside him. When the sun came up, it would be over. Now his body was warm against hers. He slept lightly, she knew. She had only to shift or murmur his name and he would awaken. She remained still. For a few more precious moments she wanted the simple unity that came from having him sleep at her side. There would be no stopping the sun from rising in the east—or stopping her lover from going west. It was up to her to accept the second as easily as she accepted the first. Closing her eyes, she willed herself to be strong. Phil stirred, dreaming.

He walked through his house in the hills, purposely, from room to room, looking, searching, for what was vague to him; but time after time he turned away, frustrated. Room after room after room. Everything was familiar: the colors, the furniture, even small personal objects that identified his home, his belongings. Something was missing. Stolen, lost? The house echoed emptily around him as he continued to search for something vital and unknown. The emotions of the man in the dream communicated themselves to the man dreaming. He felt the helplessness, the anger and the panic.

Hearing him murmur her name, Tory shifted yet closer. Phil shot awake, disoriented. The dream slipped into some corner of his mind that he couldn't reach.

"It's nearly morning," she said quietly.

A bit dazed, struggling to remember what he had dreamed that had left him feeling so empty, Phil looked at the sky. It was lightening. The first pale pinks bloomed at the horizon. For a moment they watched in silence as the day crept closer, stealing their night.

"Make love to me again," Tory whispered. "Once more, before morning."

He could see the quiet need in her eyes, the dark smudges beneath that told of patchy sleep, the soft glow that spoke clearly of a night of loving. He held the picture in his mind a moment, wanting to be certain he wouldn't lose it when time had dimmed other memories. He lowered his mouth to hers in bittersweet goodbye.

The sky paled to blue. The horizon erupted with color. The gold grew molten and scarlet bled into it as dawn came up. They loved intensely one final time. As morning came they lost themselves in each other, pretending it was still night. Where he touched, she trembled. Where she kissed, his skin hummed until they could no longer deny the need. The sun had full claim when they came together, so that the light streamed without mercy. Saying little, they dressed, then drove back to town.

* * *

When Tory stopped in front of the hotel, she felt she was in complete control again. No regrets, she reminded herself, as she turned off the ignition. We've just come to the fork in the road. We knew it was there when we started. Turning, she smiled at Phil.

"We're liable to be a bit stiff today."

Grinning, he leaned over and kissed her chin. "It was worth it."

"Remember that when you're moaning for a hot bath on your way back to L.A." Tory slid from the car. When she stepped up on the sidewalk, Phil took her hand. The contact threatened her control before she snapped it back into place.

"I'm going to be thinking of you," he murmured as they stepped into the tiny lobby.

"You'll be busy." She let her hand slide on the banister as they mounted the stairs.

"Not that busy." Phil turned her to him when they reached the top landing. "Not that busy, Tory," he said again.

Her courtroom experience came to her aid. Trembling inside, Tory managed an easy smile. "I'm glad. I'll think of you too." *Too often, too much. Too painful.*

"If I call you—"

"I'm in the book," she interrupted. Play it light, she ordered herself. The way it was supposed to be, before… "Keep out of trouble, Kincaid," she told him as she slipped her room key into its lock.

"Tory."

He stepped closer, but she barred the way into the room.

"I'll say goodbye now." With another smile she rested a hand on his cheek. "It'll be simpler, and I think I'd better catch a couple hours' sleep before I go into the office."

Phil took a long, thorough study of her face. Her eyes were direct, her smile easy. Apparently there was nothing left to say. "If that's what you want."

Tory nodded, not fully trusting herself. "Be happy, Phil," she managed before she disappeared into her room. Very carefully Tory turned the lock before she walked to the bed. Lying down, she curled into a ball and wept, and wept, and wept.

It was past noon when Tory awoke. Her head was pounding. Dragging herself to the bathroom, she studied herself objectively in the mirror over the sink. Terrible, she decided without emotion. The headache had taken the color from her cheeks, and her eyes were swollen and red from tears. Dispassionately, Tory ran the water until it was icy cold, then splashed her face with it. When her skin was numb, she stripped and stepped under the shower.

She decided against aspirin. The pills would dull the pain, and the pain made it difficult to think. Thinking was the last thing she felt she needed to do at the moment. Phil was gone, back to his own life. She would go on with hers. The fact that she had fallen in love with him over her own better judgment was simply her hard luck. In a few days she would be able to cope with it easily enough. Like hell you will, she berated herself as she dried her skin with a rough towel. You fell hard, and some bruises take years to heal…if ever.

Wasn't it ironic, she mused as she went back into the

bedroom to dress. Victoria L. Ashton, Attorney at Law, dedicated to straightening out other people's lives, had just made a beautiful mess of her own. And yet, there hadn't been any options. A deal was a deal.

Phil, she said silently, I've decided to change our contract. Circumstances have altered, and I'm in love with you. I propose we include certain things like commitment and reciprocal affection into our arrangement, with options for additions such as marriage and children, should both parties find it agreeable.

She gave a short laugh and pulled on a fresh shirt. Of course, she could merely have clung to him, tearfully begging him not to leave her. What man wouldn't love to find himself confronted with a hysterical woman who won't let go?

Better this way, she reminded herself, tugging on jeans. Much better to have a clean, civilized break. Aloud, she said something potent about being civilized as she pinned on her badge. The one thing she had firmly decided during her crying jag was that it was time for her to leave Friendly. Merle could handle the responsibilities of the office for the next few weeks without too much trouble. She had come to terms with her father's death, with her mother. She felt confident that she'd helped in Tod's family situation. Merle had grown up a bit. All in all, Tory felt she wasn't needed any longer. In Albuquerque she could put her own life in motion again. She needed that if she wasn't going to spend three weeks wallowing in self-pity and despair. At least, she decided, it was something she could start on. Naturally she would have to talk to the mayor and officially resign. There would be a visit to her mother. If she spent a day briefing Merle, she should be able to leave before the end of the week.

Her own rooms, Tory thought, trying to work up some excitement. The work she was trained for—a meaty court case that would take weeks of preparation and a furnace of energy. She felt suddenly that she had a surplus of it and nowhere to go. Back in the bath, she applied a careful layer of makeup to disguise the effects of tears, then brushed her hair dry. The first step was the mayor. There was no point putting it off.

It took thirty minutes for Tory to convince the mayor she was serious and another fifteen to assure him that Merle was capable of handling the job of acting sheriff until the election.

"You know, Tory," Bud said when he saw her mind was made up, "we're going to be sorry to lose you. I guess we all kept hoping you'd change your mind and run. You've been a good sheriff, I guess you come by it naturally."

"I appreciate that—really." Touched, Tory took the hand he offered her. "Pat Rowe and Nick Merriweather are both fair men. Whoever wins, the town's in good hands. In a few years Merle will make you a fine sheriff."

"If you ever change your mind..." Bud trailed off wanting to leave the door open.

"Thanks, but my niche in the law isn't in enforcement. I have to get back to my practice."

"I know, I know." He sighed, capitulating. "You've done more than we had a right to expect."

"I did what I wanted to do," she corrected.

"I guess things will be quiet for a while, especially with the movie people gone." He gave a regretful glance toward the window. Excitement, he mused, wasn't meant for Friendly. "Come by and see me before you leave town."

Outside, the first thing Tory noticed was the absence of the movie crew. There were no vans, no sets, no lights or packets of people. Friendly had settled back into its yawning pace as though there had never been a ripple. Someone had written some graffiti in the dust on the window of the post office. A car puttered into town and stopped in front of the hardware store. Tory started to cross the street, but stopped in the center when she was hailed. Shielding her eyes, she watched Tod race toward her.

"Sheriff, I've been looking for you."

"Is something wrong?"

"No." He grinned the quick-spreading grin that transformed his thin face. "It's real good, I wanted you to know. My dad…well, we've been talking, you know, and we even drove out to see those people you told us about."

"How'd it go?"

"We're going to go back—my mom too."

"I'm happy for you." Tory brushed her knuckles over his cheek. "It's going to take time, Tod. You'll all have to work together."

"I know, but…" He looked up at her, his eyes wide and thrilled. "He really loves me. I never thought he did. And my mom, she wondered if you could come out to the house sometime. She wants to thank you."

"There isn't any need for that."

"She wants to."

"I'll try." Tory hesitated, finding that this goodbye would be more difficult than most. "I'm going away in a couple of days."

His elated expression faded. "For good?"

"My mother lives here," she reminded him. "My father's buried here. I'll come back from time to time."

"But not to stay."

"No," Tory said softly. "Not to stay."

Tod lowered his gaze to the ground. "I knew you'd leave. I guess I was pretty stupid that day in your office when I…" He trailed off with a shrug and continued to stare at the ground.

"I didn't think you were stupid. It meant a lot to me." Tory put out a hand to lift his face. "*Means* a lot to me."

Tod moistened his lips. "I guess I still love you—if you don't mind."

"Oh." Tory felt the tears spring to her eyes and pulled him into her arms. "I'm going to miss you like crazy. Would you think I was stupid if I said I wish I were a fourteen-year-old girl?"

Grinning, he drew away. Nothing she could have said could have pleased him more. "I guess if you were I could kiss you goodbye."

With a laugh Tory brushed a light kiss on his lips. "Go on, get out of here," she ordered unsteadily. "Nothing undermines the confidence of a town more than having its sheriff crying in the middle of the street."

Feeling incredibly mature, Tod dashed away. Turning, he ran backward for a moment. "Will you write sometime?"

"Yes, yes, I'll write." Tory watched him streak off

at top speed. Her smile lost some of its sparkle. She was losing, she discovered, quite a bit in one day. Briskly shaking off the mood, she turned in the direction of her office. She was still a yard away when Merle strolled out.

"Hey," he said foolishly, glancing from her, then back at the door he'd just closed.

"Hey yourself," she returned. "You just got yourself a promotion, Merle T."

"Tory, there's— Huh?"

"Incredibly articulate," she replied with a fresh smile. "I'm resigning. You'll be acting sheriff until the election."

"Resigning?" He gave her a completely baffled look. "But you—" He broke off, shaking his head at the door again. "How come?"

"I need to get back to my practice. Anyway"—she stepped up on the sidewalk—"it shouldn't take long for me to fill you in on the procedure. You already know just about everything. Come on inside and we'll get started."

"Tory." In an uncharacteristic gesture he took her arm and stopped her. Shrewdly direct, his eyes locked on hers. "Are you upset about something?"

Merle was definitely growing up, Tory concluded. "I just saw Tod." It was part of the truth, and all she would discuss. "That kid gets to me."

His answer was a slow nod, but he didn't release her arm. "I guess you know the movie people left late this morning."

"Yes, I know." Hearing her own clipped response, Tory took a mental step back. "I don't suppose it was easy for you to say goodbye to Marlie," she said more gently.

"I'll miss her some," he admitted, still watching Tory critically. "We had fun together."

His words were so calm that Tory tilted her head as she studied him. "I was afraid you'd fallen in love with her."

"In love with her?" He let out a hoot of laughter. "Shoot, I ain't ready for that. No way."

"Sometimes being ready doesn't make any difference," Tory muttered. "Well," she said more briskly, "since you're not crying in your beer, why don't we go over some things? I'd like to be in Albuquerque before the end of the week."

"Ah…yeah, sure." Merle glanced around the empty street. "I gotta talk to somebody first over at, um…the hotel," he announced. "Be right back."

Tory shot him an exasperated glance as he loped across the street. "Well," she murmured, "some things never change." Deciding she could spend the time packing her books and papers, Tory walked into the office.

Seated at her desk, casually examining the .45, was Phil Kincaid. She stopped dead, gaping at him. "Sheriff," he said mildly, giving the barrel an idle spin.

"Phil." She found her voice, barely. "What are you doing here?"

He didn't rise, but propped his feet up on the desk instead. "I forgot something. Did you know you didn't unload this thing last night?"

She didn't even glance at the gun, but stood rooted to the spot. "I thought you'd left hours ago."

"Did you?" He gave her a long, steady look. The cold water and makeup had helped, but he knew her face intimately. "I did," he agreed after a moment. "I came back."

"Oh." So now she would have to deal with the goodbye a second time. Tory ignored the ache in her stomach and smiled. "What did you forget?"

"I owe you something," he said softly. The gesture with the gun was very subtle, but clear enough.

Only partially amused, Tory lifted a brow. "Let's call it even," she suggested. Wanting to busy her hands, she went to the shelf near the desk to draw out her books.

"No," he said mildly. "I don't think so. Turn around, Sheriff."

Annoyance was the least painful of her emotions, so Tory let it out. "Look, Phil—"

"In the cell," he interrupted. "I can recommend the first one."

"You're out of your mind." With a thud she dropped the books. "If that thing's loaded, you could hurt someone."

"I have some things to say to you," he continued calmly. "In there." Again he gestured toward the cell.

Her hands went to her hips. "All right, Kincaid, I'm still sheriff here. The penalty for armed assault on a peace officer—"

"Shut up and get in," Phil ordered.

"You can take that gun," Tory began dangerously, "and—"

Her suggestion was cut off when Phil grabbed her arm and hauled her into a cell. Stepping in with her, he pulled the door shut with a shattering clang.

"You *idiot!*" Impotently, Tory gave the locked door a furious jerk. "Now just how the hell are we supposed to get out?"

Phil settled comfortably on the bunk, propped on

one elbow, with the gun lowered toward the floor. It was just as empty as it had been when Tory had bluffed him. "I haven't anyplace better to go."

Fists on hips, Tory whirled. "Just what is this all about, Kincaid?" she demanded. "You're supposed to be halfway to L.A.; instead you're propped up at my desk. Instead of a reasonable explanation, you throw that gun around like some two-bit hood—"

"I thought I did it with such finesse," he complained, frowning at the object under discussion. "Of course, I'd rather have a piece with a bit more style." He grinned up at her. "Pearl handle, maybe."

"Do you have to behave like such a fool?"

"I suppose."

"When this is over, you're going to find yourself locked up for months. Years, if I can manage it," she added, turning to tug uselessly on the bars again.

"That won't work," he told her amiably. "I shook them like crazy a few months ago."

Ignoring him, Tory stalked to the window. Not a soul on the street. She debated swallowing her pride and calling out. It would look terrific, she thought grimly, to have the sheriff shouting to be let out of one of her own cells. If she waited for Merle, at least she could make him swear to secrecy.

"All right, Kincaid," she said between her teeth. "Let's have it. Why are you here and why the devil are we locked in the cell?"

He glanced down at the gun again, then set it on the edge of the bunk. Automatically, Tory judged the distance. "Because"—and his voice had altered enough to lure her eyes to his—"I found myself in an impossible situation."

At those words Tory felt her heart come to a stop, then begin again at a furious rate. Cautiously she warned herself not to read anything into the statement. True, she remembered his use of the phrase when talking about love, but it didn't follow that he meant the same thing now.

"Oh?" she managed, and praised herself for a brilliant response.

"*'Oh?'*" Phil pushed himself off the bunk in a quick move. "Is that all you can say? I got twenty miles out of town," he went on in sudden fury. "I told myself that was it. You wanted—I wanted—a simple transient relationship. No complications. We'd enjoyed each other— it was over."

Tory swallowed. "Yes, we'd agreed—"

"The hell with what we agreed." Phil grabbed her shoulders, shaking her until her mouth dropped open in shock. "It got complicated. It got very, very complicated." Releasing her abruptly, he began to pace the cell he had locked them both into.

"Twenty miles out of town," he repeated, "and I couldn't make it. Even last night I told myself it was all for the best. You'd go your way, I'd go mine. We'd both have some great memories." He turned to her then; although his voice lowered, it was no calmer. "Damn it, Tory, I want more than memories of you. I need more. You didn't want this to happen, I know that." Agitated, he ran a hand through his hair, while she said nothing. "I didn't want it, either, or thought I didn't. I'm not sure anymore. It might have been the first minute I walked in here, or that day at the cemetery. It might have been that night at the lake or a hundred other times. I don't know when it happened, why it happened." He shook his head as though it was a problem he'd struggled with and ultimately given up on. "I only know I love you. And God knows I can't leave you. I tried—I can't."

With a shuddering sigh Tory walked back to the bars and rested her head against them. The headache she had awoken with was now a whirling dizziness. A minute, she told herself. I just need a minute to take it in.

"I know you've got a life in Albuquerque," Phil continued, fighting against the fluttering panic in his stomach. "I know you've got a career that's important to you. It isn't something I'm asking you to choose between. There are ways to balance things if people want to badly enough. I broke the rules; I'm willing to make the adjustments."

"Adjustments…" Tory managed before she turned back to him.

"I can live in Albuquerque," he told her as he crossed the cell. "That won't stop me from making movies."

"The studio—"

"I'll buy a plane and commute," he said quickly. "It's been done before."

"A plane." With a little laugh she walked away, dragging a hand through her hair. "A plane."

"Yes, damn it, a plane." Her reaction was nothing that he had expected. The panic grew. "You didn't want me to go," he began in defense, in fury. "You've been crying. I can tell."

A bit steadier, Tory faced him again. "Yes, I cried.

No, I didn't want you to go. Still, I thought it was best for both of us."

"Why?"

"It wouldn't be easy, juggling two careers and one relationship."

"Marriage," he corrected firmly. "Marriage, Tory. The whole ball of wax. Kids, too. I want you to have my children." He saw the change in her eyes—shock, fear? Unable to identify it, Phil went to her again. "I said I love you." Again he took her by the shoulders. This time he didn't shake her but held her almost tentatively. "I have to know what you feel for me."

She spent a moment simply looking into his eyes. Loved her? Yes, she realized with something like a jolt. She could see it. It was real. And more, he was hurting because he wasn't sure. Doubts melted away. "I've been in an impossible situation, I think, from the first moment Merle hauled you in here."

She felt his fingers tense, then relax again. "Are you sure?" he asked, fighting the need to drag her against him.

"That I'm in love with you?" For the first time a ghost of a smile hovered around her mouth. "Sure enough that I nearly died when I thought you were leaving me. Sure enough that I was going to let you go because I'm just as stupid as you are."

His hands dove into her hair. "Stupid?" he repeated, drawing her closer.

"'He needs his own life. We agreed not to complicate things. He'd hate it if I begged him to stay.'" She smiled more fully. "Sound familiar?"

"With a slight change in the personal pronoun." Phil

pulled her close just to hold her. *Mine,* they thought simultaneously, then clung. "Ah, Tory, last night was so wonderful—and so terrible."

"I know, thinking it was the last time." She drew back only enough so their mouths could meet. "I've been giving some thought to it for a while," she murmured, then lost the trend of thought as they kissed again.

"To what?"

"To…oh, to moving to the coast."

Framing her face with his hands, Phil tilted it to his. "You don't have to do that. I told you, I can—"

"Buy a plane," she finished on a laugh. "And I'm sure you can. But I have given some thought lately to moving on. Why not California?"

"We'll work that out."

"Eventually," she agreed, drawing his mouth back to hers.

"Tory." He held her off a moment, his eyes serious again. "Are you going to marry me?"

She considered a moment, letting her fingers twine in his hair. "It might be wise," she decided, "since we're going to have those kids."

"When?"

"It takes nine months," she reminded him.

"Marriage," he corrected, nipping her bottom lip.

"Well, after you've served your sentence…about three months."

"Sentence?"

"Illegal use of a handgun, accosting a peace officer, improper use of a correctional facility…" She shrugged, giving him her dashing grin. "Time off for good behavior, you should be out in no time. Remember, I'm still sheriff here, Kincaid."

"The hell you are." Pulling the badge from her blouse, he tossed it through the bars of the window. "Besides, you'll never make it stick."

* * * * *

Don't miss the sizzling new Lone Star Sisters series by *New York Times* bestselling author

SUSAN MALLERY

Sibling rivalry takes on a whole new meaning as the high-society Titan sisters vie for their tyrant father's business and respect...and fall unexpectedly in love with three sexy men along the way!

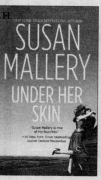
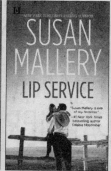
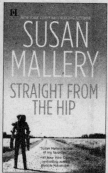

Available wherever books are sold!

And don't miss the final Lone Star Sisters tale, HOT ON HER HEELS, coming this winter!

HQN™

We *are* romance™

www.HQNBooks.com

PHSM-T2009

HQN™

We *are* romance™

Trouble and temptation clash in a Texas border town as an undercover agent falls hard for the woman he's sworn to protect.

Fiercely independent Gloryanne Barnes refuses to be deterred from providing immigrant farmers with sustaining work, despite the desire her new farmhand Rodrigo evokes, and despite the danger about to shatter all their lives....

Fearless

Don't miss this riveting new novel, available in stores May 2009!

www.HQNBooks.com

PHDP369

HQN™

We *are* romance™

For business...or pleasure?

#1 *New York Times* bestselling author

LISA JACKSON

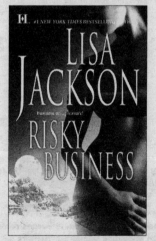

Two classic tales of passionate suspense
in an incredible new volume.

Risky Business

Pick up a copy today wherever books are sold!

www.HQNBooks.com

PHLJ373

REQUEST YOUR FREE BOOKS!

2 FREE NOVELS PLUS 2 FREE GIFTS!

Silhouette® Romantic
SUSPENSE

Sparked by Danger, Fueled by Passion!

YES! Please send me 2 FREE Silhouette® Romantic Suspense novels and my 2 FREE gifts (gifts are worth about $10). After receiving them, if I don't wish to receive any more books, I can return the shipping statement marked "cancel." If I don't cancel, I will receive 4 brand-new novels every month and be billed just $4.24 per book in the U.S. or $4.99 per book in Canada. That's a savings of at least 15% off the cover price! It's quite a bargain! Shipping and handling is just 50¢ per book*. I understand that accepting the 2 free books and gifts places me under no obligation to buy anything. I can always return a shipment and cancel at any time. Even if I never buy another book from Silhouette, the two free books and gifts are mine to keep forever.

240 SDN EYL4 340 SDN EYMC

Name	(PLEASE PRINT)	
Address		Apt. #
City	State/Prov.	Zip/Postal Code
Signature (if under 18, a parent or guardian must sign)		

Mail to the **Silhouette Reader Service:**
IN U.S.A.: P.O. Box 1867, Buffalo, NY 14240-1867
IN CANADA: P.O. Box 609, Fort Erie, Ontario L2A 5X3

Not valid to current subscribers of Silhouette Romantic Suspense books.

Want to try two free books from another line?
Call 1-800-873-8635 or visit www.morefreebooks.com.

* Terms and prices subject to change without notice. Prices do not include applicable taxes. Sales tax applicable in N.Y. Canadian residents will be charged applicable provincial taxes and GST. Offer not valid in Quebec. This offer is limited to one order per household. All orders subject to approval. Credit or debit balances in a customer's account(s) may be offset by any other outstanding balance owed by or to the customer. Please allow 4 to 6 weeks for delivery. Offer available while quantities last.

Your Privacy: Silhouette is committed to protecting your privacy. Our Privacy Policy is available online at www.eHarlequin.com or upon request from the Reader Service. From time to time we make our lists of customers available to reputable third parties who may have a product or service of interest to you. If you would prefer we not share your name and address, please check here. ☐

SR

HQN™

We *are* romance™

One mischievous girl on a mission...

From acclaimed author

GEORGETTE HEYER

Resigned to remarry after the death of his true love
many years ago, wealthy, handsome Sir Gareth solicits
the hand of Lady Hester Theale—a woman he respects
and admires. But when fate has him encounter the saucy,
unchaperoned young lady known as "Amanda Smith,"
Sir Gareth will never be the same again....

Sprig Muslin

Available now wherever books are sold!

www.HQNBooks.com

PHGH386

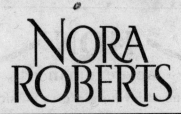

NORA ROBERTS

28575	THE MacKADE BROTHERS: RAFE AND JARED	__ $7.99 U.S.	__ $8.99 CAN.
28574	CHARMED & ENCHANTED	__ $7.99 U.S.	__ $7.99 CAN.
28573	LOVE BY DESIGN	__ $7.99 U.S.	__ $7.99 CAN.
28571	FIRST IMPRESSIONS	__ $7.99 U.S.	__ $7.99 CAN.
28569	THE MacGREGOR GROOMS	__ $7.99 U.S.	__ $7.99 CAN.
28568	WAITING FOR NICK & CONSIDERING KATE	__ $7.99 U.S.	__ $7.99 CAN.
28566	MYSTERIOUS	__ $7.99 U.S.	__ $9.50 CAN.
28565	TREASURES	__ $7.99 U.S.	__ $9.50 CAN.
28562	STARS	__ $7.99 U.S.	__ $9.50 CAN.
28561	THE GIFT	__ $7.99 U.S.	__ $9.50 CAN.
28560	THE MacGREGOR BRIDES	__ $7.99 U.S.	__ $9.50 CAN.
28559	THE MacGREGORS: ROBERT & CYBIL	__ $7.99 U.S.	__ $9.50 CAN.
28545	THE MacGREGORS: DANIEL & IAN	__ $7.99 U.S.	__ $9.50 CAN.
28541	IRISH DREAMS	__ $7.99 U.S.	__ $9.50 CAN.

(limited quantities available)

TOTAL AMOUNT	$	_____
POSTAGE & HANDLING	$	_____
($1.00 FOR 1 BOOK, 50¢ for each additional)		
APPLICABLE TAXES*	$	_____
TOTAL PAYABLE	$	_____

(check or money order—please do not send cash)

To order, complete this form and send it, along with a check or money order for the total above, payable to Harlequin Books, to: **In the U.S.** 3010 Walden Avenue, P.O. Box 9077, Buffalo, NY 14269-9077 **In Canada:** P.O. Box 636, Fort Erie, Ontario, L2A 5X3.

Name: _____
Address: _____ City: _____
State/Prov.: _____ Zip/Postal Code: _____
Account Number (if applicable): _____

075 CSAS

*New York residents remit applicable sales taxes.
*Canadian residents remit applicable GST and provincial taxes.

Silhouette®
Where love comes alive™

Visit Silhouette Books at www.eHarlequin.com

PSNR0509